NIGHT CHILLS

"As frightening as *PSYCHO* . . . will keep readers turning the pages."

—*Minneapolis Tribune*

"A master of sheer fright!"

—*Florida Times-Union*

Don't Miss These Other Hair-Raising Thrillers by Dean R. Koontz . . .

WATCHERS

"Thoroughly frightening and entertaining . . . His best story yet!"

—*Publishers Weekly*

"The suspense holds to the end!"

—*New York Times*

"A breakthrough for Koontz . . . imaginative and unusual."

—*Kirkus*

"Unrelentingly suspenseful . . . first class entertainment!"

—*Cleveland Plain Dealer*

Continued . . .

TWILIGHT EYES

"A spine-chilling adventure . . . will keep you turning pages to the very end."

—*Rave Reviews*

"Chilling . . . superbly scary."

—*Los Angeles Times*

"Terrific scares and action, filled out with rich, fertile prose."

—*Fangoria*

"An entertaining writer . . . a sure-fire plot!"

—*Edward Bryant*

STRANGERS

"A unique spellbinder that captures the reader on the first page. Exciting, enjoyable, and an intensely satisfying read."

—*Mary Higgins Clark*

"The best novel he has written."

—*Stephen King*

"You'll be reading . . . well into morning!"

—*New York Times*

"Gripping!"

—United Press International

DARKFALL

"A fast-paced tale . . . one of the scariest chase scenes ever!"

—*Houston Post*

"Swift, entertaining . . . a classic race to the rescue."

—*Publishers Weekly*

Berkley Books by Dean R. Koontz

DARKFALL
THE FACE OF FEAR
NIGHT CHILLS
PHANTOMS
SHATTERED
STRANGERS
TWILIGHT EYES
THE VISION
WATCHERS
WHISPERS

DEAN R. KOONTZ

Night Chills

BERKLEY BOOKS, NEW YORK

For Gerda

This Berkley book contains the complete
text of the original hardcover edition.
It has been completely reset in a typeface
designed for easy reading and was printed
from new film.

NIGHT CHILLS

A Berkley Book / published by arrangement with
the author

PRINTING HISTORY
Atheneum edition published 1976
W. H. Allen & Co. edition published 1977
Berkley edition / March 1983

ISBN: 0-425-09864-8

A BERKLEY BOOK ® TM 757,375
Berkley Books are published by The Berkley Publishing Group,
200 Madison Avenue, New York, NY 10016.
The name "Berkley" and the "B" logo
are trademarks belonging to Berkley Publishing Corporation.

PRINTED IN THE UNITED STATES OF AMERICA

22   21   20   19

Author's Introduction

BY THE TIME they have finished this book, many readers will
be uneasy, frightened, perhaps even horrified. Once enter-
tained, however, they will be tempted to dismiss *Night Chills*
as quickly as they might a novel about demonic possession or
reincarnation. Although this story is intended primarily to be
a "good read," I cannot stress strongly enough that the basic
subject matter is more than merely a fantasy of mine; it is a
reality and already a major influence on all our lives.

Subliminal and subaudial advertising, carefully planned
manipulation of our subconscious minds, became a serious
threat to individual privacy and freedom at least as long ago
as 1957. In that year Mr. James Vicary gave a public demon-
stration of the tachistoscope, a machine for flashing messages
on a motion picture screen so fast that they can be read only
by the subconscious mind. As discussed in chapter two of this
book, the tachistoscope has been replaced, for the most part,
by more sophisticated—and shocking—devices and processes. The science of behavior modification, as achieved

through the use of subliminal advertising, is coming into a Golden Age of technological breakthroughs and advancements in theory.

Particularly sensitive readers will be dismayed to learn that even such details as the infinity transmitter (chapter ten) are not figments of the author's imagination. Robert Farr, the noted electronic security expert, discusses wiretapping with infinity transmitters in his *The Electronic Criminals*, as noted in the reference list at the end of this novel.

The drug that plays a central role in *Night Chills* is a novelist's device. It does not exist. It is the only piece of the scientific background that I have allowed myself to create from whole cloth. Countless behavioral researchers have conceived of it. Therefore, when I say that it does not exist, perhaps I should add one cautionary word—*yet*.

Those who are studying and shaping the future of subliminal advertising will say that they have no intention of creating a society of obedient robots, that such a goal would be in violation of their personal moral codes. However, as have thousands of other scientists in this century of change, they will surely learn that their concepts of right and wrong will not restrict the ways in which more ruthless men will use their discoveries.

D.R.K.

Contents

THE BEGINNING

Holbrook lowered the tailgate. A light winked on inside the Rover. He threw aside a tarpaulin, revealing two pairs of rubber hip boots, two flashlights, and other equipment.

Rossner was shorter, slimmer, and quicker than Holbrook. He got his boots on first. Then he dragged the last two pieces of their gear from the car.

The main component of each device was a pressurized tank much like an aqualung cylinder, complete with shoulder straps and chest belt. A hose led from the tank to a stainless-steel, pin-spray nozzle.

They helped each other into the straps, made certain their shoulder holsters were accessible, and paced a bit to get accustomed to the weight on their backs.

At 3:10 Rossner took a compass from his pocket, studied it in his flashlight beam, put it away, and moved off into the forest.

Holbrook followed, surprisingly quiet for such a large man.

The land rose rather steeply. They had to stop twice in the next half hour to rest.

At 3:40 they came within sight of the Big Union sawmill. Three hundred yards to their right, a complex of two- and three-story clapboard and cinder-block buildings rose out of the trees. Lights glowed at all the windows, and arc lamps bathed the fenced storage yard in fuzzy purplish-white light. Within the huge main building, giant saws stuttered and whined continuously. Logs and cut planks toppled from conveyor belts and boomed when they landed in metal bins.

Rossner and Holbrook circled around the mill to avoid being seen. They reached the top of the ridge at four o'clock.

They had no difficulty locating the man-made lake. One end of it shimmered in the wan moonlight, and the other end was shadowed by a higher ridge that rose behind it. It was a neat oval, three hundred yards long and two hundred yards wide, fed by a gushing spring. It served as the reservoir for both the Big Union mill and the small town of Black River that lay three miles away in the valley.

They followed the six-foot-high fence until they came to the main gate. The fence was there to keep out animals, and the gate was not even locked. They went inside.

At the shadowed end of the reservoir, Rossner entered the water and walked out ten feet before it rose nearly to the tops of his hip boots. The walls of the lake slanted sharply, and the depth at the center was sixty feet.

He unraveled the hose from a storage reel on the side of the tank, grasped the steel tube at the end of it, and thumbed a button. A colorless, odorless chemical exploded from the nozzle. He thrust the end of the tube underwater and moved it back and forth, fanning the fluid as widely as possible.

In twenty minutes his tank was empty. He wound the hose around the reel and looked toward the far end of the lake. Holbrook had finished emptying his tank and was climbing out onto the concrete apron.

They met at the gate. "Okay?" Rossner asked.

"Perfect."

By 5:10 they were back at the Land Rover. They got shovels from the back of the car and dug two shallow holes in the rich black earth. They buried the empty tanks, boots, holsters, and guns.

For two hours Holbrook drove along a series of rugged dirt trails, crossed St. John River on a timber ridge, picked up a graveled lane, and finally connected with a paved road at half past eight.

From there Rossner took the wheel. They didn't say more than a dozen words to each other.

At twelve thirty Holbrook got out at the Starlite Motel on Route 15 where he had a room. He closed the car door without saying good-by, went inside, locked the motel door, and sat by the telephone.

Rossner had the Rover's tank filled at a Sunoco station and picked up Interstate 95 south to Waterville and past Augusta. From there he took the Maine Turnpike to Portland, where he stopped at a service area and parked near a row of telephone booths.

The afternoon sun made mirrors of the restaurant windows and flashed off the parked cars. Shimmering waves of hot air rose from the pavement.

He looked at his watch. 3:35.

He leaned back and closed his eyes. He appeared to be napping, but every five minutes he glanced at his watch. At 3:55 he got out of the car and went to the last booth in the row.

At four o'clock the phone rang.

"Rossner."

The voice at the other end of the line was cold and sharp: "I am the key, Mr. Rossner."

"I am the lock," Rossner said dully.

"How did it go?"

"As scheduled."

"You missed the three-thirty call."

"Only by five minutes."

The man at the other end hesitated. Then: "Leave the turnpike at the next exit. Turn right on the state route. Put the Rover up to at least one hundred miles an hour. Two miles along, the road takes a sudden turn, hard to the right; it's banked by a fieldstone wall. Do not apply your brakes when you reach the curve. Do not turn with the road. Drive straight into that wall at a hundred miles an hour."

Rossner stared through the glass wall of the booth. A young woman was crossing from the restaurant toward a little red sports car. She was wearing tight white shorts with dark stitching. She had nice legs.

"Glenn?"

"Yes, sir."

"Do you understand me?"

"Yes."

"Repeat what I've said."

Rossner went through it, almost word for word.

"Very good, Glenn. Now go do it."

"Yes, sir."

Rossner returned to the Land Rover and drove back onto the busy turnpike.

Holbrook sat quietly, patiently in the unlighted motel room. He switched on the television set, but he didn't watch it. He got up once to use the bathroom and to get a drink of water, but that was the only break in his vigil.

At 4:10 the telephone rang.

He picked it up. "Holbrook."

"I am the key, Mr. Holbrook."

"I am the lock."

The man on the other end of the line spoke for half a minute. "Now repeat what I've said."

Holbrook repeated it.

"Excellent. Now do it."

He hung up, went into the bathroom, and began to draw a tub full of warm water.

When he turned right onto the state route, Glenn Rossner pressed the accelerator all the way to the floor. The engine roared. The car's frame began to shimmy. Trees and houses and other cars flashed past, mere blurs of color. The steering wheel jumped and vibrated in his hands.

For the first mile and a half, he didn't look away from the road for even a second. When he saw the curve ahead, he glanced at the speedometer and saw that he was doing slightly better than a hundred miles per hour.

He whimpered, but he didn't hear himself. The only things he could hear were the tortured noises produced by the car. At the last moment he gritted his teeth and shuddered.

The Land Rover hit the four-foot-high stone wall so hard that the engine was jammed back into Rossner's lap. The car plowed part of the way through the wall. Stones shot up and rained back down. The Rover tipped onto its crushed front end, rolled over on its roof, slid across the ruined wall, and burst into flames.

Holbrook undressed and climbed into the tub. He settled down in the water and picked up the single-edge razor blade that lay on the porcelain rim. He held the blade by the blunt end, firmly between the thumb and first finger of his right hand, then slashed open the veins in his left wrist.

He tried to cut his right wrist. His left hand could not hold the blade. It slipped from his fingers.

He plucked it out of the darkening water, held it in his right hand once more, and cut across the bridge of his left foot.

Then he leaned back and closed his eyes.

Slowly, he drifted down a lightless tunnel of the mind, into ever deepening darkness, getting dizzy and weak, feeling surprisingly little pain. In thirty minutes he was comatose. In forty minutes he was dead.

Sunday, August 7, 1977

AFTER WORKING ALL WEEK on the midnight shift, Buddy Pellineri was unable to change his sleeping habits for the weekend. At four o'clock Sunday morning, he was in the kitchen of his tiny, two-room apartment. The radio, his most prized possession, was turned down low: music from an all-night Canadian station. He was sitting at the table, next to the window, staring fixedly at the shadows on the far side of the street. He had seen a cat running along the walk over there, and the hairs had stood up on the back of his neck.

There were two things that Buddy Pellineri hated and feared more than all else in life: cats and ridicule.

For twenty-five years he had lived with his mother, and for twenty years she had kept a cat in the house, first Caesar and then Caesar the Second. She had never realized that the cats were quicker and far more cunning than her son and, therefore, a bane to him. Ceasar—first or second; it made no difference—liked to lie quietly atop bookshelves and cupboards and highboys, until Buddy walked past. Then he leaped on

Buddy's back. The cat never scratched him badly; for the most part it was concerned with getting a good grip on his shirt so that he could not shake it loose. Every time, as if following a script, Buddy would panic and run in circles or dart from room to room in search of his mother, with Caesar spitting in his ear. He never suffered much pain from the game; it was the suddenness of the attack, the surprise of it that terrified him. His mother said Caesar was only being playful. At times he confronted the cat to prove he was unafraid. He approached it as it sunned on a window sill and tried to stare it down. But he was always the first to look away. He couldn't understand *people* all that well, and the alien gaze of the cat made him feel especially stupid and inferior.

He was able to deal with ridicule more easily than he could deal with cats, if only because it never came as a surprise. When he was a boy, other children had teased him mercilessly. He had learned to be prepared for it, learned how to endure it. Buddy was bright enough to know that he was different from others. If his intelligence quotient had been several points lower, he wouldn't have known enough to be ashamed of himself, which was what people expected of him. If his I.Q. had been a few points higher, he would have been able to cope, at least to some extent, with both cats and cruel people. Because he fell in between, his life was lived as an apology for his stunted intellect—a curse he bore as a result of a malfunctioning hospital incubator where he had been placed after being born five weeks prematurely.

His father had died in a mill accident when Buddy was five, and the first Caesar had entered the house two weeks later. If his father hadn't died, perhaps there would have been no cats. And Buddy liked to think that, with his father alive, no one would dare ridicule him.

Ever since his mother had succumbed to cancer ten years ago, when he was twenty-five, Buddy had worked as an assistant night watchman at the Big Union Supply Company mill. If he suspected that certain people at Big Union felt responsible for him and that his job was make-work, he had never admitted it, not even to himself. He was on duty from midnight to eight, five nights a week, patrolling the storage yards, looking for smoke, sparks, and flames. He was proud of his position. In the last ten years he had come to enjoy a

measure of self-respect that would have been inconceivable
before he had been hired.

Yet there were times when he felt like a child again, humil-
iated by other children, the brunt of a joke he could not understand. His boss at the mill, Ed McGrady, the chief
watchman on the graveyard shift, was a pleasant man. He
was incapable of hurting anyone. However, he smiled when
others did the teasing. Ed always told them to stop, always
rescued his friend Buddy—but always got a laugh from it.

That was why Buddy hadn't told anyone what he had seen
Saturday morning, nearly twenty-four hours ago. He didn't
want them to laugh.

Around that time he left the storage yard and walked well
off into the trees to relieve himself. He avoided the lavatory
whenever he could because it was there the other men teased
him the most and showed the least mercy. At a quarter to
five, he was standing by a big pine tree, shrouded in darkness, taking a pee, when he saw two men coming down from
the reservoir. They carried hooded flashlights that cast narrow
yellow beams. In the backwash of the lights, as the men
passed within five yards of him, Buddy saw they were wearing rubber hip boots, as if they had been fishing. They
couldn't fish in the reservoir, could they? There were no fish
up there. Another thing . . . each man wore a tank on his
back, like skin divers wore on television. And they were carrying guns in shoulder holsters. They looked so out of place
in the woods, so strange.

They frightened him. He sensed they were killers. Like on
the television. If they knew they had been seen, they would
kill him and bury him out here. He was sure of it. But then
Buddy always expected the worst; life had taught him to think
that way.

He stood perfectly still, watched them until they were out
of sight, and ran back to the storage yard. But he quickly
realized he couldn't tell anyone what he had seen. They
wouldn't believe him. And by God, if he was going to be
ridiculed for telling what was only the truth, then he would
keep it secret!

Just the same he wished he could tell *someone*, if not the
watchmen at the mill. He thought and thought about it but
still could not make sense of those skin divers or whatever
they were. In fact, the more he thought about it, the more

bizarre it seemed. He was frightened by what he could not understand. He was certain that if he told someone, it could be explained to him. Then he wouldn't be afraid. But if they laughed . . . Well, he didn't understand their laughter either, and that was even more frightening than the mystery men in the woods.

On the far side of Main Street, the cat scampered from the heavy purple shadows and ran east toward Edison's General Store, startling Buddy out of his reverie. He pressed against the windowpane and watched the cat until it turned the corner. Afraid that it would try to sneak back and climb up to his third-floor rooms, he kept a watch on the place where it had vanished. For the moment he had forgotten the men in the woods because his fear of cats was far greater than his fear of guns and strangers.

Part One

CONSPIRACY

1.

Saturday, August 13, 1977

WHEN HE DROVE AROUND THE CURVE, into the small valley, Paul Annendale felt a change come over him. After five hours behind the wheel yesterday and five more today, he was weary and tense—but suddenly his neck stopped aching and his shoulders unknotted. He felt at peace, as if nothing could go wrong in this place, as if he were Hugh Conway in *Lost Horizon* and had just entered Shangri-La.

Of course, Black River was not Shangri-La, not by any stretch of the imagination. It existed and maintained its population of four hundred solely as an adjunct of the mill. For a company town it *was* quite clean and attractive. The main street was lined with tall oak and birch trees. The houses were New England colonials, white frame and brick saltboxes. Paul supposed he responded to it so positively because he had no bad memories to associate with it, only good ones; and that could not be said of many places in a man's life.

"There's Edison's store! There's Edison's!" Mark Annendale leaned over from the back seat, pointing through the windshield.

Smiling, Paul said, "Thank you, Coonskin Pete, scout of the north."

Rya was as excited as her brother, for Sam Edison was like a grandfather to them. But she was more dignified than Mark. At eleven she yearned for the womanhood that was still years ahead of her. She sat up straight in her safety harness beside Paul on the front seat. She said, "Mark, sometimes I think you're five years old instead of nine."

"Oh, yeah? Well, sometimes I think you're *sixty* instead of eleven!"

"Touché," Paul said.

Mark grinned. Usually, he was no match for his sister. This sort of quick response was not his style.

Paul glanced sideways at Rya and saw that she was blushing. He winked to let her know that he wasn't laughing *at* her.

Smiling, sure of herself again, she settled back in her seat. She could have topped Mark's line with a better one and left him mumbling. But she was capable of generosity, not a particularly common quality in children her age.

The instant the station wagon stopped at the curb, Mark was out on the pavement. He bounded up the three concrete steps, raced across the wide roofed veranda, and disappeared into the store. The screen door slammed shut behind him just as Paul switched off the engine.

Rya was determined not to make a spectacle of herself, as Mark had done. She took her time getting out of the car, stretched and yawned, smoothed the knees of her jeans, straightened the collar of her dark blue blouse, patted her long brown hair, closed the car door, and went up the steps. By the time she reached the porch, however, she too had begun to run.

Edison's General Store was an entire shopping center in three thousand square feet. There was one room, a hundred feet long and thirty feet wide, with an ancient pegged pine floor. The east end of the store was a grocery. The west end held dry goods and sundries as well as a gleaming, modern drug counter.

As his father had been before him, Sam Edison was the town's only licensed pharmacist.

In the center of the room, three tables and twelve oak

chairs were grouped in front of a wood-burning country stove. Ordinarily, you could find elderly men playing cards at one of those tables, but at the moment the chairs were empty. Edison's store was not just a grocery and pharmacy; it was also Black River's community center.

Paul opened the heavy lid on the soda cooler and plucked a bottle of Pepsi from the icy water. He sat down at one of the tables.

Rya and Mark were standing at an old-fashioned glass-fronted candy counter, giggling at one of Sam's jokes. He gave them sweets and sent them to the paperback and comic book racks to choose presents for themselves; then he came over and sat with his back to the cold stove.

They shook hands across the table.

At a glance, Paul thought, Sam looked hard and mean. He was very solidly built, five eight, one hundred sixty pounds, broad in the chest and shoulders. His short-sleeved shirt revealed powerful forearms and biceps. His face was tanned and creased, and his eyes were like chips of gray slate. Even with his thick white hair and beard, he looked more dangerous than grandfatherly, and he could have passed as a decade younger than his fifty-five years.

But that forbidding exterior was misleading. He was a warm and gentle man, a push-over for children. Most likely, he gave away more candy than he sold. Paul had never seen him angry, had never heard him raise his voice.

"When did you get in town?"

"This is our first stop."

"You didn't say in your letter how long you'd be staying this year. Four weeks?"

"Six, I think."

"Wonderful!" His gray eyes glittered merrily; but in that very craggy face, the expression might have appeared to be malice to anyone who didn't know him well. "You're staying the night with us, as planned? You aren't going up into the mountains today?"

Paul shook his head: no. "Tomorrow will be soon enough. We've been on the road since nine this morning. I don't have strength to pitch camp this afternoon."

"You're looking good, though."

"I'm *feeling* good now that I'm in Black River."

"Needed this vacation, did you?"

"God, yes." Paul drank some of the Pepsi. "I'm sick to death of hypertense poodles and Siamese cats with ring-worms."

Sam smiled. "I've told you a hundred times. Haven't I? You can't expect to be an honest veterinarian when you set up shop in the suburbs of Boston. Down there you're a nurse-maid for neurotic house pets—and their neurotic owners. Get out into the country, Paul."

"You mean I ought to involve myself with cows calving and mares foaling?"

"Exactly."

Paul sighed. "Maybe I will one day."

"You should get those kids out of the suburbs, out where the air is clean and the water drinkable."

"Maybe I will." He looked toward the rear of the store, toward a curtained doorway. "Is Jenny here?"

"I spent all morning filling prescriptions, and now she's out delivering them. I think I've sold more drugs in the past four days than I usually sell in four weeks."

"Epidemic?"

"Yeah. Flu, grippe, whatever you want to call it."

"What does Doc Troutman call it?"

Sam shrugged. "He's not really sure. Some new breed of flu, he thinks."

"What's he prescribing?"

"A general purpose antibiotic. Tetracycline."

"That's not particularly strong."

"Yes, but this flu isn't all that devastating."

"Is the tetracycline helping?"

"It's too soon to tell."

Paul glanced at Rya and Mark.

"They're safer here than anywhere else in town," Sam said. "Jenny and I are about the only people in Black River who haven't come down with it."

"If I get up there in the mountains and find I've got two sick kids on my hands, what should I expect? Nausea? Fever?"

"None of that. Just night chills."

Paul tilted his head quizzically.

"Damned scary, as I understand it." Sam's eyebrows drew together in one bushy white bar. "You wake up in the middle of the night, as if you've jùst had a terrible dream. You shake so hard you can't hold on to anything. You can barely walk. Your heart is racing. You're pouring sweat—and I mean sweating pints—like you've got awfully high blood pressure. It lasts as much as an hour, then it goes away as if it never was. Leaves you weak most of the next day."

Frowning, Paul said, "Doesn't sound like flu."

"Doesn't sound like much of anything. But it scares hell out of people. Some of them got sick Tuesday night, and most of the others joined in on Wednesday. Every night they wake up shaking, and every day they're weak, a bit tired. Damned few people around here have had a good night's sleep this week."

"Has Doc Troutman gotten a second opinion on any of these cases?"

"Nearest other doctor is sixty miles away," Sam said. "He did call the State Health Authority yesterday afternoon, asked for one of their field men to come up and have a look. But they can't send anyone until Monday. I guess they can't get very excited about an epidemic of night chills."

"The chills could be the tip of an iceberg."

"Could be. But you know bureaucrats." When he saw Paul glance at Rya and Mark again, Sam said, "Look, don't worry about it. We'll keep the kids away from everyone who's sick."

"I was supposed to take Jenny up the street to Ultman's Cafe. We were going to have a nice quiet dinner together."

"If you catch the flu from a waitress or another customer, you'll pass it on to the kids. Skip the cafe. Have dinner here. You know I'm the best cook in Black River."

Paul hesitated.

Laughing softly, stroking his beard with one hand, Sam said, "We'll have an early dinner. Six o'clock. That'll give you and Jenny plenty of time together. You can go for a ride later. Or I'll keep myself and the kids out of the den if you'd rather just stay home."

Paul smiled. "What's on the menu?"

"Manicotti."

"Who needs Ultman's Cafe?"

Sam nodded agreement. "Only the Ultmans."

Rya and Mark hurried over to get Sam's approval of the

2.

Thirty-one Months Earlier:
Friday, January 10, 1975

OGDEN SALSBURY ARRIVED ten minutes early for his three o'clock appointment. That was characteristic of him.

H. Leonard Dawson, president and principal stockholder of Futurex International, did not at once welcome Salsbury into his office. In fact Dawson kept him waiting until three fifteen. *That* was characteristic of *him*. He never allowed his associates to forget that his time was inestimably more valuable than theirs.

When Dawson's secretary finally ushered Salsbury into the great man's chambers, it was as if she were showing him to the altar in a hushed cathedral. Her attitude was reverent. The outer office had Muzak, but the inner office had pure silence. The room was sparsely furnished: a deep blue carpet, two somber oil paintings on the white walls, two chairs on this side of the desk, one chair on the other side of it, a coffee table, rich blue velvet drapes drawn back from seven hundred square feet of lightly tinted glass that overlooked midtown Manhattan. The secretary bowed out almost like an altar boy retreating from the sanctuary.

"How are you, Ogden?" He reached out to shake hands.

"Fine. Just fine—Leonard."

Dawson's hand was hard and dry; Salsbury's was damp.

"How's Miriam?" He noticed Salsbury's hesitation. "Not ill?"

"We were divorced," Salsbury said.

"I'm sorry to hear that."

Was there a trace of disapproval in Dawson's voice? Salsbury wondered. And why the hell should I care if there is?

"When did you split up?" Dawson asked.

"Twenty-five years ago—Leonard." Salsbury felt as if he ought to use the other man's last name rather than his first, but he was determined not to be intimidated by Dawson as he had been when they were both young men.

"It *has* been a long time since we've talked," Dawson said. "That's a shame. We had so many great times together."

They had been fraternity brothers at Harvard and casual friends for a few years after they left the university. Salsbury could not remember a single "great" time they might have shared. Indeed, he had always thought of the name. H. Leonard Dawson as a synonym for both prudery and boredom.

"Have you remarried?" Dawson asked.

"No."

Dawson frowned. "Marriage is essential to an ordered life. It gives a man stability."

"You're right," Salsbury said, although he didn't believe it. "I've been the worse for bachelorhood."

Dawson had always made him uneasy. Today was no exception.

He felt ill at east partly because they were so different from each other. Dawson was six feet two, broad in the shoulders, narrow at the hips, athletic. Salsbury was five feet nine, slope-shouldered, and twenty pounds overweight. Dawson had thick graying hair, a deep tan, clear black eyes, and matinee-idol features; whereas Salsbury was pale with receding hair and myopic brown eyes that required thick glasses. They were both fifty-four. Of the two, Dawson had weathered the years far better.

Then again, Salsbury thought, he *began* with better looks than I did. With better looks, more advantages, more money . . .

If Dawson radiated authority, Salsbury radiated servility. In the laboratory on his own familiar turf, Ogden was as impressive as Dawson. They were not in the laboratory now, however, and he felt out of place, out of his class, inferior.

"How is Mrs. Dawson?"

The other man smiled broadly. "Wonderful! Just wonderful. I've made thousands of good decisions in my life, Ogden. But she was the best of them." His voice grew deeper and more solemn; it was almost theatrical in effect. "She's a good, God-fearing, church-loving woman."

You're still a Bible thumper, Salsbury thought. He suspected that this might help him achieve what he had come here to do.

They stared at each other, unable to think of any more small talk.

"Sit down," Dawson said. He went behind the desk while Salsbury settled in front of it. The four feet of polished oak between them further established Dawson's dominance.

Sitting stiffly, briefcase on his knees, Salsbury looked like the corporate equivalent of a lap dog. He knew he should relax, that it was dangerous to let Dawson see how easily he could be intimidated. Nevertheless, knowing this, he could only pretend relaxation by folding his hands atop his briefcase.

"This letter . . ." Dawson looked at the paper on his blotter.

Salsbury had written the letter, and he knew it by heart.

Dear Leonard:

Since we left Harvard, you've made more money than I have. However, I haven't wasted my life. After decades of study and experimentation, I have nearly perfected a process that is priceless. The proceeds in a single year could exceed your accumulated wealth. I am entirely serious.

Could I have an appointment at your convenience? You won't regret having given it to me.

Make the appointment for "Robert Stanley," a subterfuge to keep my name out of your date book. As you can see from the letterhead on this stationery, I direct operations at the main biochem research laboratory for Creative Development Associates, a subsidiary of Futurex International. If you know the nature of CDA's business, you will understand the need for circumspection.

As ever,

Ogden Salsbury

He had expected to get a quick response with that letter, and his expectations had been met. At Harvard, Leonard had been guided by two shining principles: money and God. Salsbury had supposed, and rightly, that Dawson hadn't changed. The letter was mailed on Tuesday. Late Wednesday, Dawson's secretary called to make the appointment.

"I don't ordinarily sign for registered letters," Dawson said sternly. "I accepted it only because your name was on it. After I read it I very nearly threw it in the trash."

Salsbury winced.

"Had it been from anyone else, I *would* have thrown it away. But at Harvard you were no braggart. Have you overstated your case?"

"No."

"You've discovered something you think is worth millions?"

"Yes. And more." His mouth was dry.

Dawson took a manila folder from the center desk drawer. "Creative Development Associates. We bought that company seven years ago. You were with it when we made the acquisition."

"Yes, sir. Leonard."

As if he had not noticed Salsbury's slip of the tongue, Dawson said, "CDA produces computer programs for universities and government bureaus involved in sociological and psychological studies." He didn't bother to page through the report. He seemed to have memorized it. "CDA also does research for government and industry. It operates seven laboratories that are examining the biological, chemical, and biochemical causes of certain sociological and psychological phenomena. You're in charge of the Brockert Institute in Connecticut." He frowned. "The entire Connecticut facility is devoted to top secret work for the Defense Department." His black eyes were exceptionally sharp and clear. "So secret, in fact, that even I couldn't find out what you're doing up there. Just that it's in the general field of behavior modification.''

Clearing his throat nervously, Salsbury wondered if Dawson was broadminded enough to grasp the value of what he was about to be told. "Are you familiar with the term 'subliminal perception'?''

"It has to do with the subconscious mind.''

"That's right—as far as it goes. I'm afraid I'm going to sound rather pedantic, but a lecture is in order.''

Dawson leaned back as Salsbury leaned forward. "By all means.''

Extracting two eight-by-ten photographs from the brief-case, Salsbury said, "Do you see any difference between photo A and photo B?''

Dawson examined them closely. They were black and white studies of Salsbury's face. "They're identical.''

"On the surface, yes. They're prints of the same photograph.''

"What's the point?''

"I'll explain later. Hold on to them for now.''

Dawson stared suspiciously at the pictures. Was this some sort of game? He didn't like games. They were a waste of time. While you were playing a game, you could just as easily be earning money.

"The human mind," Salsbury said, "has two primary monitors for data input: the conscious and the subconscious.''

"My church recognizes the subconscious," Dawson said affably. "Not all churches will admit it exists.''

Unable to see the point of that, Salsbury ignored it. "These monitors observe and store two different sets of data. In a manner of speaking, the conscious mind is aware only of what happens in its direct line of sight, while the subconscious has peripheral vision. These two halves of the mind operate independently of each other, and often in opposition to each other—''

"Only in the abnormal mind," Dawson said.

"No, no. In everyone's mind. Yours and mine included.''

Disturbed that anyone should think his mind performed in any state other than perfect harmony with itself, Dawson started to speak.

"For example," Salsbury said quickly, "a man is sitting at a bar. A beautiful woman takes the stool next to his. With conscious intent he tries to seduce her. At the same time, however, without being consciously aware of it, he may be terrified of sexual involvement. He may be afraid of rejection, failure, or impotency. With his conscious mind he performs as society expects him to perform in the company of a sexy woman. But his subconscious works effectively against his conscious. Therefore, he alienates the woman. He talks too loudly and brashly. Although he's ordinarily an interesting fellow, he bores her with stock market reports. He spills his drink on her. That behavior is the product of his subconscious fear. His outer mind says 'Go' even as his inner mind shouts 'Stop.'''

Dawson's expression was sour. He didn't appreciate the nature of the example. Nevertheless, he said, "Go on."

"The subconscious is the dominant mind. The conscious sleeps, but the subconscious never does. The conscious has no access to the data in the subconscious, but the subconscious knows everything that transpires in the conscious mind. The conscious is essentially nothing more than a computer, while the subconscious is the computer programmer.

"The data stored in the different halves of the mind are collected in the same way: through the five known senses. But the subconscious sees, hears, smells, tastes, and feels far more than does the outer mind. It apprehends everything that passes too quickly or too subtly to impress the conscious mind. For our purposes, in fact, that is the definition of 'subliminal': anything that happens too quickly or too subtly to make an impression on the conscious mind. More than ninety percent of the stimuli that we observe through our five senses is subliminal input."

"Ninety percent?" Dawson said. "You mean I see, feel, smell, taste, and hear ten times more than I think I do? An example?"

Salsbury had one ready. "The human eye fixates on objects at least one hundred thousand times a day. A fixation lasts from a fraction of a second to a third of a minute. However, if you tried to list the hundred thousand things you had looked at today, you wouldn't be able to recall more than a few hundred of them. The rest of those stimuli were observed by and stored in the subconscious—as were the additional two million stimuli reported to the brain by the other four senses."

Closing his eyes as if to block out all of those sights he wasn't aware of seeing, Dawson said, "You've made three points." He ticked them off on his manicured fingers. "One, the subconscious is the dominant half of the mind. Two, we don't know what our subconscious minds have observed and remembered. We can't recall that data at will. Three, subliminal perception is nothing strange or occult; it is an integral part of our lives."

"Perhaps the *major* part of our lives."

"And you've discovered a commercial use for subliminal perception."

Salsbury's hands were shaking. He was close to the core of his proposition, and he didn't know whether Dawson would be fascinated or outraged by it. "For two decades, advertisers of consumer products have been able to reach the subconscious minds of potential customers by the use of subliminal perception. The ad agencies refer to these techniques by several other names. Subliminal reception. Threshold regulation. Unconscious perception. Subception. Are you aware of this? Have you heard of it?"

Still enviably relaxed, Dawson said, "There were several experiments conducted in movie theaters—fifteen—maybe twenty years ago. I remember reading about them in the newspapers."

Salsbury nodded rapidly. "Yes. The first was in 1957."

"During an ordinary showing of some film, a special message was superimposed on the screen. 'You are thirsty,' or something of that sort. It was flashed off and on so fast that no one realized it was there. After it had been flashed—what, a thousand times?—nearly everyone in the theater went to the lobby and bought soft drinks."

In those first crude experiments, which were carefully regulated by motivation researchers, subliminal messages had been delivered to the audience with a tachistoscope, a machine patented by a New Orleans company, Precon Process and Equipment Corporation, in October of 1962. The tachistoscope was a standard film projector with a high-speed shutter. It could flash a message twelve times a minute at $1/3000$ of a second. The image appeared on the screen for too short a time to be perceived by the conscious mind, but the subconscious was fully aware of it. During a six-week test of the tachistoscope, forty-five thousand theater-goers were subjected to two messages: "Drink Coca-Cola" and "Hungry? Eat Popcorn." The results of these experiments left no doubt about the effectiveness of subliminal advertisement. Popcorn sales rose sixty percent, and Coca-Cola sales rose nearly twenty percent.

The subliminals apparently had influenced people to buy these products even though they were not hungry or thirsty.

"You see," Salsbury said, "the subconscious mind believes everything it is told. Even though it constructs behavioral sets based on the information it receives, and although those sets guide the conscious mind—it can't distinguish between truth and falsehood! The behavior that it programs into the conscious mind is often based on misconceptions."

"But if that were correct, we'd all behave irrationally."

"And we all do," Salsbury said, "in one way or another. Don't forget, the subconscious doesn't *always* construct programs based on wrong-headed ideas. Just sometimes. This explains why intelligent men, paragons of reason in most things, harbor at least a few irrational attitudes." Like your religious fanaticism, he thought. He said: "Racial and religious bigotry, for instance. Xenophobia, claustrophobia, acrophobia . . . If a man can be made to analyze one of these fears on a conscious level, he'll reject it. But the conscious resists analysis. Meanwhile, the inner half of the mind continues to misguide the outer half."

"These messages on the movie screen—the conscious mind wasn't aware of them; therefore, it couldn't reject them."

Salsbury sighed. "Yes. That's the essence of it. The subconscious saw the messages and caused the outer mind to act on them."

Dawson was growing more interested by the minute. "But why did the subliminals sell more popcorn than soda?"

"The first messasge—'Drink Coca-Cola'—was a declarative sentence," Salsbury said, "a direct order. Sometimes the subconscious obeys an order that's delivered subliminally— and sometimes it doesn't."

"Why is that?"

Salsbury shrugged. "We don't know. But you see, the second subliminal was not entirely a direct order. It was more sophisticated. It began with a question: 'Hungry?' The question was designed to cause anxiety in the subconscious. It helped to generate a need. It established a 'motivational equation.' The need, the anxiety, is on the left side of the equals sign. To fill the right side, to balance the equation, the subconscious programs the conscious to buy the popcorn. One side cancels out the other. The buying of the popcorn cancels out the anxiety.''

"The method is similar to posthypnotic suggestion. But I've heard that a man can't be hypnotized and made to do something he finds morally unacceptable. In other words, if he isn't a killer by nature, he can't be made to kill while under hypnosis.''

"That's not true,'' Salsbury said. "Anyone can be made to do anything under hypnosis. The inner mind can be manipulated so easily . . . For example, if I hypnotized you and told you to kill your wife, you wouldn't obey me.''

"Of course I wouldn't!'' Dawson said indignantly.

"You love your wife.''

"I certainly do!''

"You have no reason to kill her.''

"None whatsoever.''

Judging by Dawson's emphatic denials, Salsbury thought the man's subconscious must be brimming with repressed hostility toward his God-fearing, church-loving wife. He didn't dare say as much. Dawson would have denied it—and might have tossed him out of the office. "However, if I hypnotized you and told you that your wife was having an affair with your best friend and that she was plotting to kill you in order to inherit your estate, you would believe me and—''

"I would not. Julia would be incapable of such a thing.''

Salsbury nodded patiently. "Your conscious mind would reject my story. It can reason. But after I'd hypnotized you, I'd be speaking to your subconscious—which can't distinguish between lies and truth.''

"Ah. I see.''

"Your subconscious won't act on a direct order to kill because a direct order doesn't establish a motivational equation. But it *will* believe my warning that she intends to kill you. And so believing, it will construct a new behavioral set based on the lies—and it will program your conscious mind for murder. Picture the equation, Leonard. On the left of the equals sign there is anxiety generated by the 'knowledge' that your wife intends to do away with you. On the right side, to balance the equation, to banish the anxiety, you need the death of your wife. If your subconscious was convinced that she was going to kill you in your sleep tonight, it would cause you to murder her before you ever went to bed.''

"Why wouldn't I just go to the police?"

Smiling, more sure of himself than he had been when he entered the office, Salsbury said, "The hypnotist could guard against that by telling your subconscious that your wife would make it look like an accident, that she was so clever the police would never prove anything against her.''

Raising one hand, Dawson waved at the air as if he were shooing away flies. "This is all very interesting,'' he said in a slightly bored tone of voice. "But it seems academic to me.''

Ogden's self-confidence was fragile. He began to tremble again. "Academic?''

"Subliminal advertising has been outlawed. There was quite a to-do at the time.''

"Oh, yes,'' Salsbury said, relieved. "There were hundreds of newspaper and magazine editorials. *Newsday* called it the most alarming invention since the atomic bomb. *The Saturday Review* said that the subconsious mind was the most delicate apparatus in the universe and that it must never be sullied or twisted to boost the sales of popcorn or anything else.

"In the late 1950s, when the experiments with the tachisto-scope were publicized, nearly everyone agreed that subliminal advertising was an invasion of privacy. Congressman James Wright of Texas sponsored a bill to outlaw any device, film, photograph, or recording 'designed to advertise a product or indoctrinate the public by means of making an impression on the subconscious mind.' Other congressmen and senators drafted legislation to deal with the menace, but none of the bills got out of committee. No law was passed restricting or forbidding subliminal advertising.''

Dawson raised his eyebrows. "Do politicians use it?''

"Most of them don't understand the potential. And the advertising agencies would just as soon keep them ignorant. Every major agency in the U.S. has a staff of media and behavioral scientists to develop subliminals for magazine and television ads. Virtually every consumer item produced by Futurex and its subsidiaries is sold with subliminal advertising.''

"I don't believe it," Dawson said. "I would know about it."

"Not unless you wanted to know and made an effort to learn. Thirty years ago, when you were starting out, this sort of thing didn't exist. By the time it came into use, you were no longer closely tied to the sales end of your businesses. You were more concerned with stock issues, mergers—wheeling and dealing. In a conglomerate of this size, the president can't possibly pass approval on every ad for every product of every subsidiary."

Leaning forward in his chair, a look of distaste on his handsome face, Dawson said, "But I find it rather—repulsive."

"If you accept the fact that a man's mind can be programmed without his knowledge, you're rejecting the notion that every man is at all times captain of his fate.. It scares hell out of people.

"For two decades Americans have refused to face the unpleasant truth about subliminal advertising. Opinion polls indicate that, of those who have heard of subliminal advertising, ninety percent are certain it has been outlawed. They have no facts to support this opinion, but they don't want to believe anything else. Furthermore, between fifty and seventy percent of those polled say they don't believe subliminals work. They are so revolted by the thought of being controlled and manipulated that they reject the possibility out of hand. Rather than educate themselves about the actuality of subliminal advertising, rather than rise up and rage against it, they dismiss it as a fantasy, as science fiction."

Dawson shifted uneasily in his chair. Finally, he got up, went to the huge windows and stared out at Manhattan.

Snow had begun to fall. There was very little light in the sky. Wind, like the voice of the city, moaned on the far side of the glass.

Turning back to Salsbury, Dawson said, "One of our subsidiaries is an ad agency. Woolring and Messner. You mean every time they make a television commercial, they build into it a series of subliminally flashed messages with a tachistoscope?"

"The advertiser has to request subliminals," Salsbury said. "The service costs extra. But to answer your question—no, the tachistoscope is out of date.

"The science of subliminal behavior modification developed so rapidly that the tachistoscope was obsolete soon after it was patented. By the mid-1960s, most subliminals in television commercials were implanted with rheostatic photography. Everyone has seen a rheostatic control for a lamp or overhead light: by turning it, one can make the light dimmer or brighter. The same principle can be used in motion picture photography. First, the commercial is shot and edited to sixty seconds in the conventional manner. This is the half of the advertisement that registers with the conscious mind. Another minute of film, containing the subliminal message, is shot with minimal light intensity, with the rheostat turned all the way down. The resultant image is too dim to register with the conscious mind. When it is projected on a screen, the screen appears to be blank. However, the subconscious sees and absorbs it. These two films are projected simultaneously and printed on a third length of film. It is this composite version that is used on television. While the audience watches the commercial, the subconscious mind watches—and obeys, to one degree or another—the subliminal directive.

"And that's only the basic technique," Salsbury said. "The refinements are even more clever."

Dawson paced. He wasn't nervous. He was just—excited.

He's beginning to see the value, Salsbury thought happily.

"I see how subliminals could be hidden in a piece of film that's full of motion, light and shadow," Dawson said. "But magazine ads? That's a static medium. One image, no movement. How could a subliminal be concealed on one page?"

Pointing to the photographs he had given Dawson earlier, Salsbury said, "For that picture I kept my face expressionless. Two copies were made from the same negative. Copy A was printed over a vague image of the word 'anger.' And B was printed over the word 'joy.'"

Comparing the photos, Dawson said, "I don't see either word."

"I'd be displeased if you did. They aren't meant to be seen."

"What was the purpose?"

"One hundred students at Columbia were given photo A and asked to identify the emotion expressed by the face. Ten students had no opinion. Eight said 'displeasure' and eighty-two said 'anger.' A different group studied photo B. Eight expressed no opinion. Twenty-one said 'happiness' and seventy-one said 'joy.'"

"I see," Dawson said thoughtfully.

Salsbury said, "But that's as crude as the tachistoscope. Let me show you some sophisticated subliminal ads." He plucked a sheet of paper from his briefcase. It was a page from *Time* magazine. He put the page on Dawson's blotter.

"It's an ad for Gilbey's Gin," Dawson said.

At a glance it was a simple liquor advertisement. A five-word headline stood at the top of the page: BREAK OUT THE FROSTY BOTTLE. The only other copy was toward the lower right-hand corner: AND KEEP YOUR TONICS DRY! The accompanying illustration held three items. The most prominent of these was a bottle of gin which glistened with water droplets and frost. The cap of the bottle lay at the bottom of the page. Beside the bottle was a tall glass filled with ice cubes, a lime slice, a swizzle stick and, presumably, gin. The background was green, cool, pleasant.

The message intended for the conscious mind was clear: This gin is refreshing and offers an escape from everyday cares.

What the page had to say to the subconscious mind was far more interesting. Salsbury explained that most of the subliminal content was buried beneath the threshold of conscious recognition, but that some of it could be seen and analyzed, although only with an open mind and perseverance. The subliminal that the conscious could most easily comprehend was hidden in the ice cubes. There were four ice cubes stacked one atop the other. The second cube from the top and the lime slice formed a vague letter S which the conscious mind could see when prompted. The third cube held a very evident letter E in the area of light and shadow that comprised the cube itself. The fourth chunk of ice contained the subtle but unmistakable outline of the letter X: S-E-X.

Salsbury had come around behind Dawson's desk and had carefully traced these three letters with his forefinger. "Do you see it?"

Scowling, Dawson said, "I saw the E immediately and the other two without much trouble. But I'm finding it hard to believe they were put there on purpose. It could be an accident of shading."

"Ice cubes usually don't photograph well," Salsbury said.

"When you see them in an advertisement, they've nearly always been drawn by an artist. In fact, this entire ad has been painted over a photograph. But there's more than the word in the ice."

Squinting at the page, Dawson said, "What else?"

"The bottle and glass are on a reflective surface." Salsbury circled that area of the reflection that dealt with the bottle and the cap. "Without stretching your imagination too far, can you see that the reflection of the bottle is divided in two, forming what might be taken to be a pair of legs? Do you see, also, that the reflected bottle cap resembles a penis thrusting out from between those legs?"

Dawson bristled. 'I can see it," he said coldly.

Too interested in his own lecture to notice Dawson's uneasiness, Salsbury said, "Of course, the melting ice on the bottle cap could be semen. That image was never meant to be entirely subliminal. The conscious mind might recognize the intent here. But it would not recognize the reflection in that table unless it was *guided* to the recognition." He pointed to another spot on the page. "Would it be going too far to say these shadows between the reflections of the bottle and the glass form vaginal lips? And that this drop of water on the table is positioned on the shadows precisely where the clitoris would be on a vagina?"

When he perceived the subliminal sex organ, its lips parted, Dawson blushed. "I see it. Or I think I do."

Salsbury reached in his briefcase. "I've got other examples."

One of them was a two-page subscription solicitation that had appeared shortly before Christmas several years before, in *Playboy*. On the right-hand page, Playmate Liv Lindeland, a busty blonde, knelt on a white carpet. On the lefthand page stood an enormous walnut wreath. She was tying a red bow to the top of the wreath.

In one test, Salsbury explained, a hundred subjects spent an hour studying two hundred advertisements, including this one. When the hour ended they were asked to list the first ten of those items that they could remember. Eighty-five percent listed the *Playboy* ad. In describing it, all but two subjects mentioned the wreath. Only five of them mentioned the girl. When questioned further, they had trouble recalling if she was a blonde, brunette, or redhead. They remembered that her breasts were uncovered, but they couldn't say for sure whether she was wearing a hat or was clothed from the waist down. (She had no hat and was nude.) None of them had trouble describing the wreath, for it was there that the subconscious had been riveted.

"Do you see why?" Salsbury asked. "There's not a walnut in that 'walnut' wreath. It's composed of objects that resemble the heads of penises and vaginal slits."

Unable to speak, Dawson leafed through the other advertisements without asking Salsbury to explain them. Finally he said, "Camel cigarettes, Seagram's, Sprite, Bacardi Rum . . . Some of the most prominent companies in the country are using subliminals to sell their products."

"Why shouldn't they? It's legal. If the competition uses them, what choice does even the most morally uplifted company really have? Everyone has to stay competitive. In short, there are no individual villains. The whole system is the villain."

Dawson returned to his executive chair, his face a book of his thoughts. One could read there that he disliked any talk against "the system" and that he was nonetheless shocked by what he had been shown. He was also trying to see how he could make a profit from it. He operated with the conviction that God wanted him to to sit in an executive chair at the pinnacle of a billion-dollar corporation; and he was certain that the Lord would help him to see that, although subliminal advertising had a cheap and possibly immoral side to it, there was also an aspect of it that could aid him in his divine mission. As he saw it, his mission was to pile up profits for the Lord; when he and Julia were dead, the Dawson holdings would belong to the church.

Salsbury returned to his seat in front of the desk. The litter of magazine pages on the blotter and bare oak seemed like a collection of pornography. He felt as if he had been trying to titillate Dawson. Irrationally, he was embarrassed.

"You've shown me that a great deal of creative effort and money goes into subliminal commercials and ads," Dawson said. "Evidently, there's a generally held theory that subconscious sexual stimulation sells goods. But does it? Enough to be worth the expense?"

"Unquestionably! Psychological studies have proved that most Americans react to sexual stimuli with subconscious anxiety and tension. So if the subliminal half of a television commercial for XYZ soda shows a couple having intercourse, the viewer's subconscious starts bubbling with anxiety—and that establishes a motivational equation. On the left side of the equals sign, there's anxiety and tension. To complete the equation and cancel out these bad feelings, the viewer buys the product, a bottle or a case of XYZ. The equation is finished, the blackboard wiped clean.''

Dawson was surprised. ''Then he doesn't buy the product because he believes it will give him a better sex life?''

''Just the opposite,''. Salsbury said. ''He buys it to escape from sex. The ad fills him with desire on a subconscious level, and by buying that product he is able to satisfy the desire without risking rejection, impotence, humiliation, or some other unsatisfactory experience with a woman. Or if the viewer is a woman, she buys the product to satisfy desire and thus avoids an unhappy affair with a man. For both men and women, the desire is well relieved if the product has an oral aspect. Like food or soda.''

''Or cigarettes,'' Dawson said. ''Could that explain why so many people have trouble giving up cigarettes?''

''Nicotine *is* addictive,'' Salsbury said. ''But there's no question that subliminals in cigarette ads reinforce the habit in most people.''

Scratching his square chin, Dawson said, ''If these are so effective, why don't I smoke? I've seen the ads before.''

''The science hasn't been perfected yet,'' Salsbury said. ''If you think smoking is a disgusting habit, if you've decided never to smoke, subliminals can't change your mind. On the other hand, if you're young, just entering the cigarette market, and have no real opinions about the habit, subliminals can influence you to pick it up. Or if you were once a heavy smoker but kicked the habit, subliminals can persuade you to resume smoking. Subliminals also affect people who have no strong brand preferences. For example, if you don't drink gin or don't like to drink at all, subliminals in the Gilbey's ad won't make you run out to the liquor store. If you *do* drink, and if you do like gin, and if you don't care which brand of gin you drink, these ads could establish a brand preference for you. They work, Leonard. Subliminals sell hundreds of millions of dollars' worth of goods every year, a substantial percentage of which the public might never buy if it were not subliminally manipulated.''

Dawson said, "You've been working on subliminal perception up there in Connecticut for the last ten years?"

"Yes."

"Perfecting the science?"

"That's correct."

"The Pentagon sees a weapon in it?"

"Definitely. Don't you see it?"

Quietly, reverently, Dawson said, "If you've perfected the science . . . you're talking about total mind control. Not just behavior modification, but absolute, ironlike *control*."

For a moment neither of them could speak.

"Whatever you've discovered," Dawson said, "you apparently want to keep it from the Defense Department. They might call that treason."

"I don't care what they call it," Salsbury said sharply. "With your money and my knowledge, we don't need the Defense Department—or anyone else. We're more powerful than all the world's governments combined."

Dawson couldn't conceal his excitement. "What is it? What have you got?"

Salsbury went to the windows and watched the snow spiraling down on the city. He felt as if he had taken hold of a live wire. A current buzzed through him. Shaking with it, almost able to imagine that the snowflakes were sparks exploding from him, feeling himself to be at the vortex of a God-like power, he told Dawson what he had found and what role Dawson could play in his scenario of conquest.

Half an hour later, when Ogden finished, Dawson—who had never before been humble anywhere but in church—said, "Dear God." He stared at Salsbury as a devout Catholic might have gazed upon the vision at Fatima. "Ogden, the two of us are going to—inherit the earth?" His face was suddenly split by an utterly humorless smile.

3.

Saturday, August 13, 1977

IN ONE OF THE THIRD-FLOOR GUEST BEDROOMS of the Edison
house, Paul Annendale arranged his shaving gear on top of
the dresser. From left to right: a can of foam, a mug containing a lather brush, a straight razor in a plastic safety case,
a dispenser full of razor blades, a styptic pencil, a bottle of
skin conditioner, and a bottle of after-shave lotion. Those
seven items had been arranged in such an orderly fashion that
they looked as if they belonged in one of those animated car-
toons in which everyday items come to life and march around
like soldiers.

He turned from the dresser and went to one of the two large
windows. In the distance the mountains rose above the valley
walls, majestic and green, mottled by purple shadows from a
few passing clouds. The nearer ridges—decorated with stands
of pines, scattered elms, and meadows—sloped gently toward
the town. On the far side of Main Street, birch trees rustled in
the breeze. Men in short-sleeved shirts and women in crisp
summer dresses strolled along the sidewalk. The veranda roof

and the sign for Edison's store were directly below the window.

As his gaze moved back and back from the distant mountains, Paul became aware of his own reflection in the window glass. At five ten and one hundred fifty pounds, he was neither tall nor short, heavy nor thin. In some ways he looked older than thirty-eight, and in other ways he looked younger. His crinkly, almost frizzy light brown hair was worn full on the sides but not long. It was a hair style more suited to a younger man, but it looked good on him. His eyes were so blue that they might have been chips of mirrors reflecting the sky above. The expression of pain and loss lying beneath the surface brightness of those eyes belonged to a much older man. His features were narrow, somewhat aristocratic; but a deep tan softened the sharp angles of his face and saved him from a haughty look. He appeared to be a man who would feel at ease both in an elegant drawing room and in a waterfront bar.

He was wearing a blue workshirt, blue jeans, and black square-toed boots; however, he did not seem to be casually dressed. Indeed, in spite of the jeans, there was an air of formality about his outfit. He wore those clothes better than most men wore tuxedos. The sleeves of his shirt had been carefully pressed and creased. His open collar stood up straight and stiff, as if it had been starched. The silvery buckle on his belt had been carefully polished. Like his shirt, his jeans seemed to have been tailored. His low-heeled boots shone almost like patent leather.

He had always been compulsively neat. He couldn't remember a time when his friends hadn't kidded him about it. As a child he had kept his toy box in better order than his mother had kept the china closet.

Three and a half years ago, after Annie died and left him with the children, his need for order and neatness had become almost neurotic. On a Wednesday afternoon, ten months after the funeral, when he caught himself rearranging the contents of a cabinet in his veterinary clinic for the seventh time in two hours, he realized that his compulsion for neatness could become a refuge from life and especially from grief. Alone in the clinic, standing before an array of instruments—forceps, syringes, scalpels—he cried for the first time since he learned Annie was dead. Under the misguided belief that he had to hide his grief from the children in order to provide them with an example of strength, he had never given vent to the powerful emotions that the loss of his wife had engendered. Now he cried, shook, and raged at the cruelty of it. He rarely used foul language, but now he strung together all the vile words and phrases that he knew, cursing God and the universe and life—and himself. After that, his compulsive neatness ceased to be a neurosis and became, again, just another facet of his character, which frustrated some people and charmed others.

Someone knocked on the bedroom door.

He turned away from the window. "Come in."

Rya opened the door. "It's seven o'clock, Daddy. Suppertime."

In faded jeans and a short-sleeved white sweater, with her dark hair falling past her shoulders, she looked startlingly like her mother. She tilted her head to one side, just as Annie use to do, as if trying to guess what he was thinking.

"Is Mark ready?"

"Oh," she said, "he was ready an hour ago. He's in the kitchen, getting in Sam's way."

"Then we'd better get down there. Knowing Mark's appetite, I'd say he has half the food eaten already."

As he came toward her, she stepped back a pace. "You look absolutely marvelous, Daddy."

He smiled at her and lightly pinched her cheek. If she had been complimenting Mark, she would have said that he looked "super," but she wanted him to know that she was judging him by grown-up standards, and she had used grown-up language. "You really think so?" he asked.

"Jenny won't be able to resist you," she said.

He made a face at her.

"It's true," Rya said.

"What makes you think I care whether or not Jenny can resist me?"

Her expression said he should stop treating her as a child. "When Jenny came down to Boston in March, you were altogether different."

"Different from what?"

"Different from the way you usually are. For two whole weeks," she said, "when you came home from the clinic, you didn't once grump about sick poodles and Siamese cats."

"Well, that's because the only patients I had for those two weeks were elephants and giraffes."

"Oh, daddy."

"And a pregnant kangaroo."

Rya sat on the bed. "Are you going to ask her to marry you?"

"The kangaroo?"

She grinned, partly at the joke and partly at the way he was trying to evade the question. "I'm not sure I'd like a kangaroo for a mother," she said. "But if the baby is yours, you're going to have to marry her if you want to do the right thing."

"I swear it's not mine," he said. "I'm not romantically inclined toward kangaroos."

"Toward Jenny?" she asked.

"Whether or not I'm attracted to her, the important question is whether Jenny likes me."

"You don't know?" Rya asked. "Well . . . I'll find out for you."

Teasing her, he said, "How will you do that?"

"Ask her."

"And make me look like Miles Standish?"

"Oh, no," she said. "I'll be subtle about it." She got up from the bed and went to the door. "Mark must have eaten three-fourths of the food by now."

"Rya?"

She looked back at him.

"Do you like Jenny?"

She grinned. "Oh, very much."

For seven years, since Mark was two and Rya four, the Annendales had been taking their summer vacation in the mountains above Black River. Paul wanted to communicate to his children his own love of wild places and wild things. During these four- and six-week vacations, he educated them in the ways of nature so that they might know the satisfaction of being in harmony with it. This was a joyous education, and they looked forward to each outing.

The year that Annie died, he almost canceled the trip. At first it had seemed to him that going without her would only make their loss more evident. Rya had convinced him otherwise. "It's like Mommy is still in this house," Rya had said. "When I go from one room to another, I expect to find her there, all pale and drawn like she was near the end. If we go camping up beyond Black River, I guess maybe I'll expect to see her in the woods too, but at least I won't expect to see her pale and drawn. When we went to Black River, she was so pretty and healthy. And she was always so happy when we were out in the forest." Because of Rya, they took their vacation as usual that year, and it proved to be the best thing they could have done.

The first year that he and Annie took the children to Black River, they bought their dry goods and supplies at Edison's General Store. Mark and Rya had fallen in love with Sam Edison the day they met him. Annie and Paul came under his spell nearly as quickly. By the end of their four-week vacation, they had come down from the mountain twice to have dinner at Edison's, and when they left for home they had promised to keep in touch with an occasional letter. The following year, Sam told them that they were not to go up into the mountains to set up camp after the long tiring drive from Boston. Instead, he insisted they spend the night at his place and get a fresh start in the morning. That first-night stop-over had become their yearly routine. By now Sam was like a grandfather to Rya and Mark. For the past two years, Paul had brought the children north to spend Christmas week at Edison's.

Paul had met Jenny Edison just last year. Of course, Sam had mentioned his daughter many times. She had gone to Columbia and majored in music. In her senior year she married a musician and moved to California where he was playing in a band. But after more than seven years, the marriage had turned sour, and she had come home to get her wits about her and to decide what she wanted to do next. As proud a father as he had been, Sam had never shown pictures of her. That was not his style. On his first day in Black River last year, walking into Edison's where she was waiting on children at the candy counter—and catching sight of her— Paul had for a moment been unable to get his breath.

It happened that quickly between them. Not love at first sight. Something more fundamental than love. Something more basic that had to come first, before love could develop. Instinctively, intuitively, even though he had been certain there could be no one after Annie, he had known that she was right for him. Jenny felt the attraction too, powerfully, immediately—but almost unwillingly.

If he had told all of this to Rya, she would have said, "So why aren't you married?" If life were only that simple . . .

* * *

After dinner, while Sam and the children washed the dishes, Paul and Jenny retired to the den. They propped their feet up on an antique woodcarver's bench, and he put his arm around her shoulder. Their conversation had been free and easy at the table, but now it was stilted. She was hard and angular under his arm, tense. Twice, he leaned over and kissed her gently on the corner of the mouth, but she remained stiff and cool. He decided that she was inhibited by the possibility that Rya or Mark or her father might walk into the room at any moment, and he suggested they take a drive.

"I don't know . . ."

He stood up. "Come on. Some fresh night air will be good for you."

Outside, the night was chilly. As they got in the car, she said, "We almost need the heater."

"Not at all," he said. "Just snuggle up and share body heat." He grinned at her. "Where to?"

"I know a quiet little bar in Bexford."

"I thought we were staying out of public places?"

"They don't have the flu in Bexford," she said.

"They don't? It's only thirty miles down the road."

She shrugged. "That's just one of the curiosities of this plague."

He put the car in gear and drove out into the street. "So be it. A quiet little bar in Bexford."

She found an all-night Canadian radio station playing American swing music from the 1940s. "No more talk for a while," she said. She sat close to him with her head against his shoulder.

The drive from Black River to Bexford was a pleasant one. The narrow black-top road rose and fell and twisted gracefully through the lightless, leafy countryside. For miles at a time, trees arched across the roadway, forming a tunnel of cool night air. After a while, in spite of the Benny Goodman music, Paul felt that they were the only two people in the world—and that was a surprisingly agreeable thought.

She was even lovelier than the mountain night, and as mysterious in her silence as some of the deep, unsettled northern hollows through which they passed. For such a slender woman, she had great presence. She took up very little space on the seat, and yet she seemed to dominate the car and overwhelm him. Her eyes, so large and dark, were closed, yet he felt as if she were watching him. Her face—too beautiful to appear in *Vogue;* she would have made the other models in the magazine look like horses—was in repose. Her full lips were slightly parted as she sang softly with the music; and this bit of animation, this parting of the lips had more sensual impact than a heavy-eyed, full-faced leer from Elizabeth Taylor. As she leaned against him, her dark hair fanned across his shoulder, and her scent—clean and soapy—rose to him.

In Bexford, he parked across the street from the tavern.

She switched off the radio and kissed him once, quickly, as a sister might. "You're a nice man."

"What did I do?"

"I didn't want to talk, and you didn't make me."

"It wasn't any hardship," he said. "You and me . . . we communicate with silence as well as with words. Hadn't you noticed?"

She smiled. "I've noticed."

"But maybe you don't put enough value on that. Not as much as you should."

"I put a great deal of value on it," she said.

"Jenny, what we have is—"

She put one hand on his lips. "I didn't mean for the conversation to take such a serious turn," she said.

"But I think we should talk seriously. We're long overdue for that."

"No," she said. "I don't want to talk about us, not seriously. And because you're such a nice man, you're going to do what I want." She kissed him again, opened her door, and got out of the car.

The tavern was a warm, cozy place. There was a rustic bar along the left-hand wall, about fifteen tables in the center of the room, and a row of maroon leatherette booths along the right wall. The shelves behind the bar were lit with soft blue bulbs. Each of the tables in the center of the room held a tall candle in a red glass lantern, and an imitation stained-glass Tiffany lamp hung over each of the booths. The jukebox was playing a soulful country ballad by Charlie Rich. The bartender, a heavyset man with a walrus mustache, joked continuously with the customers. Without trying for it, without being aware of it, he sounded like W. C. Fields. There were four men at the bar, half a dozen couples at the tables, and other couples in the booths. The last booth was open, and they took it.

When they had ordered and received their drinks from a perky red-headed waitress—Scotch for him and a dry vodka martini for her—Paul said, "Why don't you come up and spend a few days with us at camp? We have an extra sleeping bag."

"I'd like that," she said.

"When?"

"Maybe next week."

"I'll tell the kids. Once they're expecting you, you won't be able to back out of it."

She laughed. "Those two are something else," she said.

"How true."

"Do you know what Rya said to me when she was helping me pour the coffee after dinner?" Jenny took a sip of her drink. "She asked if I had divorced my first husband because he was a lousy lover."

"Oh, no! She didn't really."

"Oh, yes, she did."

"I know that girl's only eleven. But sometimes I wonder . . ."

"Reincarnation?" Jenny asked.

"Maybe that's it. She's only eleven years old in *this* life, but maybe she lived to be seventy in another life. What did you say to her when she asked?"

Jenny shook her head as if she were amazed at her gullibility. Her black hair swung away from her face. "Well, when she saw that I was about to tell her it was none of her business whether or not my first husband was a lousy lover, she told me I mustn't be cross with her. She said she wasn't just being nosy. She said she was just a growing girl, a bit mature for her age, who had a perfectly understandable curiosity about adults, love and marriage. Then she really began to con me."

Paul grimaced. "I can tell you the line she used: Poor little orphan girl. Confused by her own pubescence. Bewildered by a new set of emotions and body chemistry."

"So she's used it on you."

"Many times."

"And you fell for it?"

"Everyone falls for it."

"I sure did. I felt so sorry for her. She had a hundred questions—"

"All of them intimate," Paul said.

"—and I answered all of them. And then I found out the whole conversation was meant to lead up to one line. After she had learned more about my husband than she could ever want to know, she told me that she and her mother had had long talks a year or so before Annie died, and that her mother told her you were just a fantastic lover."

Paul groaned.

"I said to her, 'Rya, I believe you're trying to sell your father to me.' She got indignant and said that was a terrible thing to think. I said, 'Well, I can't believe that your mother ever said anything of the sort to you. How old would you have been then? Six?' And she said, 'Six, that's right. But even when I was six, I was very mature for my age.'"

When he was done laughing, Paul said, "Well, you can't blame her. She's only playing the matchmaker because she likes you. So does Mark." He leaned toward her and lowered his voice slightly. "So do I."

She looked down at her drink. "Read any good books lately?"

He stirred his Scotch and sighed. "Since I'm such a nice man, I'm supposed to let you change the subject that easily."

"That's right."

Jenny Leigh Edison distrusted romance and feared marriage. Her ex-husband, whose name she had gladly surrendered, was one of those men who despise education, work, and sacrifice, but who nonetheless think they deserve fame and fortune. Because, year after year, he achieved neither goal, he needed some excuse for failure. She made a good one. He said he hadn't been able to put together a successful band because of her. He hadn't been able to get a recording contract with a major company because of her. She was holding him back, he said. She was getting in his way, he said. After seven years of supporting him by playing cocktail-bar piano, she suggested that they would both be happier if the marriage were dissolved. At first, he accused her of deserting him. "Love and romance aren't enough to make a marriage work," she had once told Paul. "You need something else. Maybe it's respect. Until I do know what it is, I'm in no hurry to get back to the altar."

Like the nice man that he was, he had changed the subject at her request. They were talking about music when Bob and Emma Thorp came over to the booth and said hello.

Bob Thorp was chief of the four-man police force in Black River. Ordinarily, a town so small would have boasted no more than a single constable. But in Black River, more than a constable was needed to maintain order when the logging camp men came into town for some relaxation; therefore, Big Union Supply Company paid for the four-man force. Bob was a six-foot-two, two-hundred-pound ex-MP with martial arts training. With his square face, deep-set eyes, and low forehead, he looked both dangerous and dim-witted. He could be dangerous, but he was not stupid. He wrote an amusing column for Black River's weekly newspaper, and the quality of thought and language in those pieces would have been a credit to any big city newspaper's editorial page. This combination of brute strength and unexpected intelligence made Bob a match even for lumbermen much bigger than he was.

At thirty-five Emma Thorp was still the prettiest woman in Black River. She was a green-eyed blonde with a spectacular figure, a combination of beauty and sex appeal that had gotten her into the finals of the Miss U.S.A. Contest ten years ago. That achievement made her Black River's only genuine celebrity. Her son, Jeremy, was the same age as Mark. Jeremy stayed at the Annendale camp for a few days every year. Mark valued him as a playmate—but valued him more because his mother was Emma. Mark was deeply in puppy love with Emma and mooned around her every chance he got.

"Are you here on vacation?" Bob asked.

"Just got in this afternoon."

Jenny said, "We'd ask you to sit down, but Paul's trying to keep an arm's length from everyone who has the flu. If he picked it up, he'd just pass it on to the kids."

"It's nothing serious," Bob said. "Not the flu, really. Just night chills."

"Maybe you can live with them," Emma said. "But I think they're pretty serious. I haven't had a good sleep all week. They aren't just night chills. I tried to take a nap this afternoon, and I woke up shaking and sweating."

Paul said, "You both *look* very good."

"I tell you," Bob said, "it's nothing serious. Night chills. My grandmother used to complain of them."

"Your grandmother complained of everything," Emma

said. "Night chills, rheumatiz, the ague, hot flashes . . ."

Paul hesitated, smiled, and said, "Oh hell, sit down. Let me buy you a drink."

Glancing at his watch, Bob said, "Thanks, but we really can't. They have a poker game in the back room here every Saturday night. Emma and I usually play. They're expecting us."

"You play, Emma?" Jenny asked.

"Better than Bob does," Emma said. "Last time, he lost fifteen dollars, and I won thirty-two."

Bob grinned at his wife and said, "Tell the truth now. It's not so much skill. It's just that when you're playing, most of the men don't spend enough time looking at their cards."

Emma touched the low-cut neckline of her sweater. "Well, bluffing is an important part of good poker playing. If the damn fools can be bluffed by some cleavage, then they just don't play as well as I do."

On the way home, ten miles out of Bexford, Paul started to turn off the blacktop road onto a scenic overlook that was a favorite lovers' lane.

"Please, don't stop," Jenny said.

"Why not?"

"I want you."

He put the car in park, half on the road, half off. "And that's a reason *not* to stop?"

She avoided looking at him. "I want you, but you aren't the kind of man that can be satisfied with just the sex. You want something more from me. It's got to be a deeper commitment with you—love, emotion, caring. I'm not up to that part of it."

Cupping her chin in his hand, he gently turned her face to him. "When you were down to Boston in March, you were very changeable. One moment you thought we could make it together, and the next moment you thought we couldn't. But then, the last few days, just before you went home, you seemed to have made up your mind. You said that we were right for each other, that you just needed a little more time." He had proposed to her last Christmas. Ever since, in bed and out, he had been trying to convince her that they were two halves of an organism, that neither of them could be whole without the other. In March, he thought he had made some headway. "Now," he said, "you've cahnged your mind again."

She took his hand from her chin, and kissed the palm. "I've got to be *sure*."

"I'm not like your husband," he said.

"I know you're not. You're a—"

"Very nice man?" he asked.

"I need more time."

"How much more?"

"I don't know."

He studied her for a moment, then put the car in gear and drove back onto the blacktop. He switched on the radio.

A few minutes later she said, "Are you angry?"

"No. Just disappointed."

"You're too positive about us," she said. "You should be more careful. You should have some doubts like I do."

"I have no doubts," he said. "We're right for each other."

"But you *should* have doubts," she said. "For instance, doesn't it seem odd to you that I'm such a physical match for your first wife, for Annie? She was the same build as I am, the same size. She had the same color hair, the same eyes. I've seen those photographs of her."

He was a little upset by that. "Do you think I've fallen for you only because you remind me of her?"

"You loved her a great deal."

"That has nothing to do with us. I just like sexy, dark women." He smiled, trying to make a joke of it—both to convince her and to stop himself from wondering if she was at least partly right.

She said, "Maybe."

"Dammit, there's no maybe about it. I love you because you're you, not because you're like anyone else."

They rode in silence.

The eyes of several deer glittered in the brush at the side of the road. When the car passed, the herd moved. Paul caught a glimpse of them in the rearview mirror—graceful, ghostly figures—as they crossed the pavement.

At last Jenny said, "You're so sure we're meant for each other. Maybe we are—under the right circumstances. But Paul, all we've ever shared is good times. We've never known adversity together. We've never shared a painful experience. Marriage is full of big and little crises. My husband and I were fairly good together too, until the crises came. Then we were at each other's throats. I just can't . . . I *won't* gamble my future on a relationship that has never been tested with hard times.''

"Should I start praying for sickness, financial ruin, and bad luck?"

She sighed and leaned against him. ''You make me sound foolish.''

''I don't mean to.''

''I know.''

Back in Black River, they shared one kiss and went to separate rooms to lie awake most of the night.

4.

Twenty-eight Months Earlier: Saturday, April 12, 1975

THE HELICOPTER—A PLUSH, luxuriously appointed Bell JetRanger II—chopped up the dry Nevada air and flung it down at the Las Vegas Strip. The pilot gingerly approached the landing pad on the roof of the Fortunata Hotel, hovered over the red target circle for a moment, then put down with consummate skill.

As the rotors stopped churning overhead, Ogden Salsbury slid open his door and stepped out onto the hotel roof. For a few seconds he was disoriented. The cabin of the JetRanger had been air-conditioned. Out here, the air was like a parching gust from a furnace. A Frank Sinatra album was playing on a stereo, blasting forth from speakers mounted on six-foot-high poles. Sunlight reflected from the rippling water in the roof-top pool, and Salsbury was partially blinded in spite of his sunglasses. Somehow, he had expected the roof to bobble and sway under him as the helicopter had done; and when it did not, he staggered slightly.

The swimming pool and the glass-walled recreation room beside it were adjuncts to the enormous thirtieth-floor presidential suite of the Fortunata Hotel. This afternoon there were only two people using it: a pair of voluptuous young women in skimpy white string bikinis. They were sitting on the edge of the pool, near the deep end, dangling their legs in the water. A squat, powerfully built man in gray slacks and a short-sleeved white silk shirt was hunkered down beside them, talking to them. All three had the perfect nonchalance that, Ogden thought, came only with power or money. They appeared not even to have noticed the arrival of the helicopter.

Salsbury crossed the roof to them. "General Klinger?"

The squat man looked up at him.

The girls didn't seem to know that he existed. The blonde had begun to lather the brunette with tanning lotion. Her hands lingered on the other girl's calves and knees, then inched lovingly along her taut brown thighs. Obviously, they were more than just good friends.

"My name's Salsbury."

Klinger stood up. He didn't offer to shake hands. "I've got one suitcase. Be with you in a minute." He walked back toward the glass-walled recreation room.

Salsbury stared at the girls. They had the longest, loveliest legs he had ever seen. He cleared his throat and said, "I'll bet you're in show business."

Neither of them looked at him. The blonde squeezed lotion into her left hand and massaged the swelling tops of the brunette's large breasts. Her fingers trailed under the bikini bra, flicked across the hidden nipples.

Salsbury felt like a fool—as he always had around beautiful women. He was certain that they were making fun of him. *You stinking bitches!* he thought viciously. *Some day I'll have any of you I want. Some day I'll tell you what I want, and you'll do it, and you'll love it because I'll tell you to love it.*

Klinger returned, carrying one large suitcase. He had put on a two-hundred-dollar, blue-and-gray-plaid sportcoat.

Looks like a gorilla dressed up for a circus act, Salsbury thought.

In the passengers' compartment of the helicopter, as they lifted away from the roof, Klinger pressed his face to the window and watched the girls dwindle into sexless specks. Then he sighed and sat back and said, "Your boss knows how to arrange a man's vacation."

Salsbury blinked in confusion. "My boss?"

Glancing at him, Klinger said, "Dawson." He took a packet of cheroots from an inside coat pocket. He fished one out and lit it for himself without offering one to Salsbury. "What did you think of Crystal and Daisy?"

Salsbury took off his sunglasses. "What?"

"Crystal and Daisy. The girls at the pool."

"Nice. Very nice."

Pausing for a long drag of his cheroot, Klinger blew out smoke and said, "You wouldn't believe what those girls can do."

"I thought they were dancers," Salsbury said.

Klinger looked at him disbelievingly, and then threw back his head and laughed. "Oh, they are! They dance their little asses off every night on the Fortunata's main showroom. But they've also been performing in the penthouse suite. And let me tell you, dancing is the least of their talents."

Salsbury was perspiring even though the cabin of the JetRanger was cool. *Women* . . . He feared them—and wanted them desperately. To Dawson, mind control meant unlimited wealth, a financial stranglehold on the entire world. To Klinger it might mean unrestricted power, the satisfaction of unquestioned command. But to Salsbury, it meant having sex as often as he wanted it, in as many ways as he wanted it, with any woman he desired.

Blowing smoke at the cabin ceiling, Klinger said, "I'll bet you'd like having those two in your bed, shoving it in them, one after the other. Would you like that?"

"Who wouldn't?"

"They're hard on a man," Klinger said, chuckling. "Takes a man with real stamina to keep them happy. You think you could handle both Crystal *and* Daisy?"

"I could give it a good try."

Klinger laughed loudly.

Salsbury hated him for that.

This crude bastard was nothing more than an influence peddler, Ogden thought. He could be bought—and his price was cheap. In one way or another, he helped Futurex International in its competitive bidding for Pentagon contracts. In return, he took free vacations in Las Vegas, and some sort of stipend was paid into a Swiss bank account. There was only one element of this arrangement that Salsbury was unable to reconcile with Leonard Dawson's personal philosophy. He said to Klinger: "Does Leonard pay for the girls too?"

"Well, *I* don't. I've never had to *pay* for it." He stared hard at Salsbury, until he was convinced that the scientist believed him. "The hotel picks up the tab. That's one of Futurex's subsidiaries. But both Leonard and I pretend he doesn't know about the girls. Whenever he asks me how I enjoyed a vacation, he acts as if all I've done is sit around the pool, by myself, reading the latest books." He was amused. He sucked on his cheroot. "Leonard is a Puritan, but he knows better than to let his personal feelings interfere with business." He shook his head. "Your boss is some man."

"He's not my boss," Salsbury said.

Klinger didn't seem to have heard him.

"Leonard and I are partners," Salsbury said.

Klinger looked him up and down. "Partners."

"That's right."

Their eyes met.

Reluctantly, after a few seconds, Salsbury looked away.

"Partners," Klinger said. He didn't believe it.

We *are* partners, Salsbury thought. Dawson may own this helicopter, the Fortunata Hotel, Crystal, Daisy, and you. But he doesn't own me, and he never will. Never.

At the Las Vegas airport, the helicopter put down thirty yards from a dazzling, white Grumman Gulf Stream jet. Red letters on the fuselage spelled FUTUREX INTERNATIONAL.

Fifteen minutes later they were airborne, on their way to an exclusive landing strip near Lake Tahoe.

Klinger unbuckled his seat belt and said, "I understand you're to give me a briefing."

"That's right. We've got two hours for it." He put his briefcase on his lap. "Have you ever heard of subliminal—"

"Before we get going, I'd like a Scotch on the rocks."

"I believe there's a bar aboard."

"Fine. Just fine."

"It's back there." Salsbury gestured over his shoulder.

Klinger said, "Make mine four ounces of Scotch and four ice cubes in an eight-ounce glass."

At first Salsbury gazed at him uncomprehendingly. Then he

got it: generals didn't mix their own drinks. Don't let him intimidate you, he thought. Against his will, however, he found himself getting up and moving toward the back of the plane. It was as if he were not in control of his body. When he returned with the drink, Klinger didn't even thank him.

"You say you're one of Leonard's partners?"

Salsbury realized that, by acting more like a waiter than like a host, he had only reinforced the general's conviction that the word "partner" did not fit him. The bastard had been testing him.

He began to wonder if Dawson and Klinger were too much for him. Was he a bantam in a ring with heavyweights? He might be setting himself up for a knockout punch.

He quickly dismissed that thought. Without Dawson and the general, he could not keep his discoveries from the government, which had financed them and owned them and would be jealous of them if it knew that they existed. He had no choice but to associate with these people; and he knew he would have to be cautious, suspicious, and watchful. But a man *could* safely make his bed with the devil so long as he slept with a loaded gun under his pillow.

Couldn't he?

Pine House, the twenty-five-room Dawson mansion that overlooked Lake Tahoe, Nevada, had won two design awards for its architect and been featured in *House Beautiful*. It stood at the water's edge on a five-acre estate, with a backdrop of more than one hundred towering pine trees; and it seemed to rise naturally from the landscape rather than intrude upon it, even though its lines were quite modern. The first level was large, circular, of stone and without windows. The second story—a circle the same size but not concentric to the first level—was a step up from the ground floor. Lakeside, at the back of the house, the second story overhung the first, sheltering a small boat dock; and here there was a twelve-foot-long window that provided a magnificent view of the water and the distant pine-covered slopes. The dome-shaped, black slate roof was crowned with a slender, needlelike eight-foot spire.

When he first saw the place, Salsbury thought that it was a cousin to those futuristic churches that had been rising in wealthy and progressive parishes over the last ten or fifteen years. Without a thought for tact, he had said as much—and Leonard had taken the comment as a compliment. Having been refamiliarized with his host's eccentricities during their weekly meetings over the past three months, Ogden was fairly certain that the house was *supposed* to resemble a church, that Dawson meant for it to be a temple, a holy monument to wealth and power.

Pine House had cost nearly as much as a church: one and a half million dollars, including the price of the land. Nevertheless, it was only one of five houses and three large apartments that Dawson and his wife maintained in the United States, Jamaica, England, and Europe.

After dinner the three men reclined in easy chairs in the living room, a few feet from the picture window. Tahoe, one of the highest and deepest lakes in the world, shimmered with light and shadow as the last rays of the sun, already gone behind the mountains, drained from the sky. In the morning the water had a clear, greenish cast. By afternoon it was a pure, crystalline blue. Now, soon to be as black as a vast spill of oil, it was like purple velvet folded against the shoreline. For five or ten minutes they enjoyed the view, speaking only to remark on the meal they had just finished and on the brandy they were sipping.

At last Dawson turned to the general and said, "Ernst, what do you think of subliminal advertising?"

The general had anticipated this abrupt shift from relaxation to business. "Fascinating stuff."

"You have no doubts?"

"That it exists? None whatsoever. Your man here has the proof. But he didn't explain what subliminal advertising has to do with me."

Sipping brandy, savoring it, Dawson nodded toward Salsbury.

Putting down his own drink, angry with Klinger for referring to him as Dawson's man and angry with Dawson for not correcting the general, reminding himself not to address Klinger by his military title, Ogden said, "Ernst, we never met until this morning. I've never told you where I work— but I'm sure you know."

"The Brockert Institute," Klinger said without hesitation.

General Ernst Klinger supervised a division of the Pentagon's vitally important Department of Security for Weapons

Research. His authority within the department extended to the states of Ohio, West Virginia, Virginia, Maryland, Delaware, Pennsylvania, New Jersey, New York, Connecticut, Massachusetts, Rhode Island, Vermont, New Hampshire, and Maine. It was his responsibility to choose, oversee the installation of, and regularly inspect the traditional and electronic systems that protected all laboratories, factories, and test sites where weapons research was conducted within those fourteen states. Several laboratories belonging to Creative Development Associates, including the Brockert facility in Connecticut, came under his jurisdiction; and Salsbury would have been surprised if the general had *not* known the name of the scientist in charge of the work at Brockert.

"Do you know what sort of research we're conducting up there?" Salsbury asked.

"I'm responsible for the security, not the research," Klinger said. "I only know what I need to know. Like the backgrounds of the people who work there, the layout of the buildings, and the nature of the surrounding countryside. I *don't* need to know about your work."

"It has to do with subliminals."

Stiffening as if he had sensed stealthy movement behind him, some of the brandy-inspired color seeping from his face, Klinger said, "I believe you've signed a secrecy pledge like everyone else at Brockert."

"Yes, I have."

"You just now violated it."

"I am aware of that."

"Are you aware of the penalty?"

"Yes. But I'll never suffer it."

"You're sure of yourself, aren't you?"

"Damned sure," Salsbury said.

"It makes no difference, you know, that I'm a general in the United States Army or that Leonard is a loyal and trusted citizen. You've still broken the pledge. Maybe they can't put you away for treason when you've only talked to the likes of us—but they *can* at least give you eighteen months for declassifying information without the authority to do so."

Salsbury glanced at Dawson.

Leaning forward in his chair, Dawson patted the general's knee. "Let Ogden finish."

Klinger said, "This could be a setup."

"A what?"

"A setup. A trap."

"To get you?" Dawson asked.

"Could be."

"Why would I want to set you up?" Dawson asked. He seemed genuinely hurt by the suggestion.

In spite of the fact, Salsbury thought, that he has probably set up and destroyed hundreds of men over the last thirty years.

Klinger seemed to be thinking the same thing, although he shrugged and pretended that he had no answer to Dawson's question.

"That's not the way I operate," Dawson said, either unable or unwilling to conceal his bruised pride. "You know me better than that. My whole career, my whole *life*, is based on Christian principles."

"I don't know anyone well enough to risk a charge of treason," the general said gruffly.

Feigning exasperation—it was a bit too obvious to be real—Dawson said, "Old friend, we've made a great deal of money together. But all of it amounts to pocket change when compared to the money we can make if we cooperate with Ogden. There is literally unlimited wealth here—for all of us." He watched the general for a moment, and when he could get no reaction he said, "Ernst, I have never misled you. Never. Not once."

Unconvinced, Klinger said, "All you ever did before was pay me for advice—"

"For your influence."

"For my advice," Klinger insisted. "And even if I did sell my influence—which I didn't—that's a long way from treason."

They stared at each other.

Salsbury felt as if he were not in the room with them, as if he were watching them from the eyepiece of a mile-long telescope.

With less of an edge to his voice than there had been a minute ago, Klinger finally said, "Leonard, I suppose you realize that I could be setting *you* up."

"Of course."

"I could agree to hear your man out, listen to everything he has to say—only to get evidence against you and him."

"String us along."

"Give you enough rope to hang yourselves," Klinger said. "I only warn you because you're a friend. I like you. I don't want to see you in trouble."

Dawson settled back in his chair. "Well, I've an offer to make you, and I need your cooperation. So I'll just have to take that risk, won't I?"

"That's your choice."

Smiling, apparently pleased with the general, Dawson raised his brandy glass and silently proposed a toast.

Grinning broadly, Klinger raised his own glass.

What in the hell is going on here? Salsbury wondered.

When he had sniffed and sipped his brandy, Dawson looked at Salsbury for the first time in several minutes and said, "You may proceed, Ogden."

Suddenly, Salsbury grasped the underlying purpose of the conversation to which he had just listened. In the unlikely event that Dawson actually *was* setting a trap for an old friend, on the off chance that the meeting was being taped, Klinger had deftly provided himself with at least *some* protection against successful prosecution. He was now on record as having warned Dawson about the consequences of his actions. In court or before a military review board, the general could argue that he had only been playing along with them in order to collect evidence against them; and even if no one believed him, he more than likely would manage to retain both his freedom and his rank.

Ogden got up, leaving his brandy glass behind him, went to the window and stood with his back to the darkening lake. He was too nervous to sit still while he talked. Indeed, for a few seconds he was too nervous to speak at all.

Like a pair of lizards perched half in warm sunlight and half in chilly shadows, waiting for the light balance to change enough to warrant movement, Dawson and Klinger watched him. They were sitting in identical high-backed black leather easy chairs with burnished silvery buttons and studs. A small round cocktail table with a dark oak top stood between them. The only light in the richly furnished room came from two floor lamps that flanked the fireplace, twenty feet away. The right side of each man's face was softened and somewhat concealed by shadows, while the left side was starkly detailed by amber light; and their eyes blinked with saurian patience.

Whether or not the scheme was a success, Salsbury thought, both Dawson and Klinger would come through it unscathed. They both wore effective armor: Dawson his wealth; Klinger his ruthlessness, cleverness, and experience.

However, Salsbury didn't possess any armor of his own. He hadn't even realized—as Klinger had when he protected himself with that spiel about secrecy pledges and treason— that he might need it. He had assumed that his discovery would generate enough money and power to satisfy all three of them, but he had just begun to understand that greed could not be sated as easily as a hearty appetite or a demanding thirst. If he had any defensive weapon at all, it was his intelligence, his lightning-quick mind; but his intellect had been directed for so long into narrow channels of specialized scientific inquiry that it now served him far less well in the common matters of life than it did in the laboratory.

Be cautious, suspicious, and watchful, he reminded himself for the second time that day. With men as aggressive as these, caution was a damned thin armor, but it was the only one he had.

He said, "For ten years the Brockert Institute has been fully devoted to a Pentagon study of subliminal advertising. We haven't been interested in the technical, theoretical, or sociological aspects of it; that work is being done elsewhere. We've been concerned solely with the biological mechanisms of subliminal perception. From the start we have been trying to develop a drug that will 'prime' the brain for subception, a drug that will make a man obey without question every subliminal directive that's given to him." Scientists at another CDA laboratory in northern California were trying to engineer a viral or bacterial agent for the same purpose. But they were on the wrong track. He knew that for a fact because *he* was on the right one. "Currently, it's possible to use subliminals to influence people who have no unshakable opinions about a particular subject or product. But the Pentagon wants to be able to use subliminal messages to alter the fundamental attitudes of people who *do* have very strong, stubbornly held opinions."

"Mind control," Klinger said matter-of-factly.

Dawson took another sip from his brandy glass.

"If such a drug can be synthesized," Salsbury said, "it will change the course of history. That's no exaggeration. For one thing, there will never again be war, not in the traditional sense. We will simply contaminate our enemies' water supplies with the drug, then inundate them, through their own media—television, radio, motion pictures, newspapers, and magazines—with a continuing series of carefully structured subliminals that will convince them to see things our way. Gradually, subtly, we can transform our enemies into our allies—and let them think that the transformation was their own idea.''

They were silent for perhaps a minute, thinking about it.

Klinger lit a cheroot. Then he said, ''There would also be a number of domestic uses for a drug like that.''

''Of course,'' Salsbury said.

''At long last,'' Dawson said almost wistfully, ''we could achieve national unity, put an end to all the bickering and protest and disagreement that's holding back this great country.''

Ogden turned away from them and stared through the window. Night had fully claimed the lake. He could hear the water lapping at the boat dock pilings a few feet below him, just beyond the glass. He listened and allowed the rhythmic sound to calm him. He was certain now that Klinger would cooperate, and he saw the incredible future that lay before him, and he was so excited by the vision that he did not trust himself to speak.

To his back Klinger said, ''You're primarily the director of research at Brockert. But apparently you're not just a desk man.''

''There are certain lines of study I've reserved for myself,'' Salsbury admitted.

''And you've discovered a drug that works, a drug that primes the brain for subception.''

''Three months ago,'' Ogden said to the glass.

''Who knows about it?''

''The three of us.''

''No one at Brockert?''

''No one.''

''Even if you have, as you say, reserved some lines of study for yourself, you must have a lab assistant.''

''He's not all that bright,'' Salsbury said. ''That's why I chose him. Six years ago.''

Klinger said, ''You were thinking about taking the discovery for yourself all that long ago?''

''Yes.''

"You've doctored your daily work record? The forms that go to Washington at the end of every week?"

"I only had to falsify them for a few days. As soon as I saw what I had come upon, I stopped working on it at once and changed the entire direction of my research."

"And your assistant didn't figure the switch?"

"He thought I'd given up on that avenue of research and was ready to try another. I told you, he's not terribly clever."

Dawson said, "Ogden hasn't perfected this drug of his, Ernst. There's still a great deal of work to be done."

"How much work?" the general asked.

Turning from the window, Salsbury said, "I'm not absolutely certain. Perhaps as little as six months—or as much as a year and a half."

"He can't work on it at Brockert," Dawson said. "He couldn't possibly get away with falsifying his records for such a length of time. Therefore, I'm putting together a completely equipped laboratory for him in my house in Greenwich, forty minutes from the Brockert Institute."

Raising his eyebrows, Klinger said, "You've got a house so big you can turn it into a lab?"

"Ogden doesn't need a great deal of room, really. A thousand square feet. Eleven hundred at the outside. And most of that will be taken up with computers. Hideously expensive computers, I might add. I'm backing Ogden with nearly two million of my own money, Ernst. That's an indication of the tremendous faith I have in him."

"You really think he can develop, test, and perfect this drug in a jerry-built lab?"

"Two million is hardly jerry-built," Dawson said. "And don't forget that billions of dollars' worth of preliminary research has already been paid for by the government. I'm financing just the final stage."

"How can you possibly maintain secrecy?"

"There are thousands of uses for the computer system. We won't be incriminating ourselves just by purchasing it. Furthermore, we'll arrange for it through one of Futurex's subsidiaries. There won't be any record that it was sold to us. There won't be any questions asked," Dawson said.

"You'll need lab technicians, assistants, clerks—"

"No," Dawson said. "So long as Ogden has the computer—and a complete data file of his past research—he can handle everything himself. For ten years he's had a full lab staff to do the drudgery; but most of that kind of work is behind him now.''

''If he quits at Brockert,'' Klinger said, ''there will be an exhaustive security investigation. They'll want to know why he quit—and they'll find out.''

They were talking about Salsbury as if he were somewhere else and unable to hear them, and he didn't like that. He moved away from the window, took two steps toward the general and said, ''I'm not leaving my position at Brockert. I'll report for work as usual, five days a week, from nine to four. While I'm there I'll labor diligently on a useless research project.''

''When will you find time to work at this lab Leonard's setting up for you?''

''In the evenings,'' Salsbury said. ''And on weekends. Besides that, I've accumulated a lot of sick leave and vacation time. I'll take most of it—but I'll spread it out evenly over the next year or so.''

Klinger stood up and went to the elegant copper and glass bar cart that a servant had left a few feet from the easy chairs. His thick and hairy arms made the crystal decanters look more delicate than they actually were. As he poured another double shot of brandy for himself, he said, ''And what role do you see me playing in all of this?''

Salsbury said, ''Leonard can get the computer system I need. But he *can't* provide me with a magnetic tape file of all the research I've done for CDA *or* a set of master program tapes designed for my research. I'll need both of those before Leonard's computers are worth a penny to me. Now, given three or four weeks, I could make duplicates of those tapes at Brockert without much risk of being caught. But once I've got eighty or niney cumbersome mag tapes and five-hundred-yard print-outs, how do I get them out of Brockert? There's just no way. Security procedures, entering and leaving, are tight, too tight for my purpose. Unless . . .''

''I see,'' Klinger said. He returned to his chair and sipped at his brandy.

Sliding forward to the edge of his seat, Dawson said, ''Ernst, you're the ultimate authority for security at Brockert. You know more about that system than anyone else. If there's a weak spot in their security, you're the man to find it—or make it.''

Studying Salsbury as if he were assessing the danger and

questioning the wisdom of being associated with someone of such obviously inferior character, Klinger said, "I'm supposed to let you smuggle out nearly one hundred magnetic tapes full of top-secret data and sophisticated computer programs?"

Ogden nodded slowly.

"Can you do it?" Dawson asked.

"Probably."

"That's all you can say?"

"There's a better than even chance it can be done."

"That's not sufficient, Ernst."

"All *right*," Klinger said, slightly exasperated. "I can do it. I can find a way."

Smiling, Dawson said, "I knew you could."

"But if I *did* find a way and was caught either during or after the operation—I'd be dumped into Leavenworth and left to rot. Earlier, when I used the word 'treason,' I wasn't tossing it around lightly."

"I didn't suppose you were," Dawson said. "But you wouldn't be required ever to see these mag tapes, let alone touch them. That would be a risk that only Ogden would have to take. They could convict you of nothing more serious than negligence for permitting or overlooking the gap in security."

"Even so, I'd be forced into early retirement or drummed out of the service with only a partial pension."

Amazed, Dawson shook his head and said, "I'm offering him one-third of a partnership that will earn millions, and Ernst is worrying about a government pension."

Salsbury was perspiring heavily. The back of his shirt was soaked and felt like a cold compress against his skin. To Klinger he said, "You've told us that you can do it. But the big question is whether you *will* do it."

Klinger stared into his brandy glass for a while, then finally looked up at Salsbury and said, "Once you've perfected the drug—what's our first step?"

Getting to his feet, Dawson said, "We'll establish a front corporation in Liechtenstein."

"Why there?"

Liechtenstein did not require that a corporation list its true owners. Dawson could hire lawyers in Vaduz and appoint them as corporate officers—and they could not be forced by law to reveal the identities of their clients.

"Furthermore," Dawson said, "I will acquire for each of us a set of forged papers, complete with passports, so that we can travel and do business under assumed names. If the lawyers in Vaduz are forced by extralegal means to reveal the names of their clients, they *still* won't endanger us because they won't know our real names."

Dawson's caution was not excessive. The corporation would quite rapidly become an incredibly successful venture, so successful that a great many powerful people in both business and government would eventually be prying at it quietly, trying to find out who lay behind the phony officers in Vaduz. With Salsbury's drug and extensive programs of carefully structured subliminals, the three of them could establish a hundred different businesses and literally *demand* that customers, associates, and even rivals produce a substantial profit for them. Every dollar they earned would *seem* to be spotlessly clean, produced by a legitimate form of commerce. But, of course, a great many people would feel that it was not at all legitimate to manipulate the competition and the buying public by means of a powerful new drug. In the event that the corporation got caught using the drug—stolen, as it was, from a U.S. weapons research project—what had once appeared to be excessive caution might well prove no more than adequate.

"And once we've got the corporation?" Klinger asked.

Money and business arrangements were Dawson's vocation and his avocation. He began to declaim almost in the manner of a Baptist preacher, full of vigor and fierce intent, thoroughly enjoying himself. "The corporation will purchase a walled estate somewhere in Germany or France. At least one hundred acres. On the surface it will appear to be an executive retreat. But in reality it will be used for the indoctrination of mercenary soldiers."

"Mercenaries?" Klinger's hard, broad face expressed the institutional soldier's disdain for the free-lancer.

The corporation, Dawson explained, would hire perhaps a dozen of the very best mercenaries available, men who had fought in Asia and Africa. They would be brought to the company estate, ostensibly to be briefed on their assignments and to meet their superiors. The water supply and all bottled beverages on the estate would be used as media for the drug. Twenty-four hours after the mercenaries had taken their first

few drinks, when they were primed for total subliminal brain-
washing, they would be shown four hours of films on each of
three successive days—travelogues, industrial studies, and
technical documentaries detailing the use of a variety of
weapons and electronic devices—which would be presented
as essential background material for their assignments. Un-
knowingly, of course, they would be watching twelve hours
of sophisticated subliminals telling them to obey without
question any order prefaced by a certain code phrase; and
when those three days had passed, all twelve men would
cease to be merely hired hands and would become something
quite like programmed robots.

Outwardly, they would not appear to have changed. They
would look and behave as they always had done. Nevertheless, they would obey any order to lie, steal, or kill *anyone*,
obey without hesitation, so long as that order was preceded
by the proper code phrase.

"As mercenary soldiers, they would be professional killers
to begin with," Klinger said.

"That's true," Dawson said. "But the glory lies in their
unconditional, unquestioning obedience. As hired mercenaries, they would be able to reject any order or assignment
that they didn't like. But as our programmed staff, they will
do precisely what they are told to do."

"There are other advantages, too," Salsbury said, not unaware that Dawson, now that he was in a proselytizing mood,
resented being nudged from the pulpit. "For one thing, you
can order a man to kill and then to erase all memory of the
murder from both his conscious and subconscious mind. He
would never be able to testify against the corporation or
against us; and he would pass any polygraph examination."

Klinger's Neanderthal face brightened a bit. He appreciated
the importance of what Salsbury had said. "Even if they used
pentothal or hypnotic regression—he *still* couldn't remember?"

" "Sodium pentothal is much overrated as a truth
serum," Salsbury said. "As for the other . . . Well, they
could put him in a trance and regress him to the time of the
murder. But he would only draw a blank. Once he has been
told to erase the event from his mind, it is beyond his recall
just as surely as obsolete data is beyond the recall of a computer that has had its memory banks wiped clean."

Having finished his second brandy, Klinger returned to the bar cart. This time he filled a twelve-ounce tumbler with ice and Seven-Up.

Salsbury thought, He's right about that: any man who doesn't keep a clear head here, tonight, is plainly suicidal.

To Dawson, Klinger said, "Once we've got these twelve 'robots' what do we do with them?"

Because he had spent the last three months thinking about that while he and Salsbury worked out the details of their approach to the general, Dawson had a quick answer. "We can do anything we want with them. Anything at all. But as a first step—I thought we might use them to introduce the drug into the water supplies of every major city in Kuwait. Then we could saturate that country with a multimedia subliminal campaign specially structured for the Arab psyche, and within a month we could quietly seize control without anyone, even the government of Kuwait, knowing what we've done."

"Take over an entire country *as a first step?*" Klinger asked incredulously.

Preaching again, striding back and forth between Salsbury and the general, gesturing expansively, Dawson said, "The population of Kuwait is less than eight hundred thousand. The greatest part of that is concentrated in a few urban areas, chiefly in Hawalli and the capital city. Furthermore, *all* of the members of the government and virtually all of the wealthy reside in those metropolitan centers. The handful of super-rich families who own desert enclaves get their water by truck from the cities. In short, we could take control of everyone of influence within the country—giving us a behind-the-scenes managerial dictatorship over the Kuwait oil reserves, which compose twenty percent of the entire world supply. That done, Kuwait would become our base of operations, from which we could subvert Saudi Arabia, Iraq, Yemen, and every other oil-exporting nation in the Mideast."

"We could smash the OPEC cartel," Klinger said thoughtfully.

"Or strengthen it," Dawson said. "Or alternately weaken and strengthen it in order to cause major fluctuations in the value of oil stocks. Indeed, we could affect the entire stock market. And because we'd know about each fluctuation well in advance, we could take rare advantage of it. Within a year of assuming control of a half-dozen Mideastern countries, we should be able to siphon one and a half billion dollars into the corporation in Liechtenstein. Thereafter, it will be a matter of no more than five or six years until *everything,* quite literally *everything,* is ours."

"It sounds—crazy, mad," Klinger said.

Dawson frowned. "Mad?"

"Incredible, unbelievable, impossible," the general said, clarifying his first statement when he saw that it disturbed Dawson.

"There was a time when heavier-than-air flight seemed impossible," Salsbury said. "The nuclear bomb seemed incredible to many people even after it was dropped on Japan. And in 1961, when Kennedy launched the Apollo Space Program, very few Americans believed that a man would ever walk on the moon."

They stared at one another.

The silence in the room was so perfect that each tiny wave breaking against the boat dock, although it was little more than a gentle ripple and was muffled by the window, sounded like an ocean turf. At least it did to Salsbury; it reverberated within his nearly fevered mind.

Finally Dawson said, "Ernst? Will you help us get those magnetic tapes?"

Klinger looked at Dawson for a long moment, then at Salsbury. A shudder—either of fear or pleasure; Ogden could not be certain which—passed through him. He said, "I'll help."

Ogden sighed.

"Champagne?" Dawson asked. "It's a bit crude after brandy. But I believe that we should raise a toast to one another and to the project."

Fifteen minutes later, after a servant had brought a chilled bottle of Moët et Chandon and he had uncorked it, after the three of them had toasted success, Klinger smiled at Dawson and said, "What if I'd been terrified of this drug? What if I'd thought your offer was more than I could handle?"

"I know you well, Ernst," Dawson said. "Perhaps better than you think I do. I'd be surprised if there was anything that you couldn't handle."

"But suppose I'd balked, for whatever reason. Suppose I hadn't wanted to come in with you."

Dawson rolled some champagne over his tongue, swallowed, inhaled through his mouth to savor the aftertaste, and said, "Then you wouldn't have left this estate alive, Ernst. I'm afraid you'd have had an accident."

"Which you arranged for a week ago."

"Nearly that."

"I knew you wouldn't disappoint me."

"You came with a gun?" Dawson asked.

"A thirty-two automatic."

"It doesn't show."

"It's taped to the small of my back."

"You've practiced drawing it?"

"I can have it in my hand in less than five seconds."

Dawson nodded approval. "And you would have used me as a shield to get off the estate."

"I would have tried."

They both laughed and regarded each other with something very near to affection. They were delighted with themselves.

Jesus Christ! Salsbury thought. He nervously sipped his champagne.

5.

Friday, August 19, 1977

PAUL AND MARK SAT cross-legged, side by side on the dew-damp mountain grass. They were as still as stones. Even Mark, who loathed inactivity and to whom patience was an irritant rather than a virtue, did no more than blink his eyes.

Around them lay a breath-taking panorama of virtually unspoiled land. On three sides of their clearing, a dense, purple-green, almost primeval forest rose like walls. To their right the clearing opened at the head of a narrow valley; and the town of Black River, two miles away, shimmered like a patch of opalescent fungus on the emerald quilt of the wild land. The only other scar of civilization was the Big Union mill, which was barely visible, three miles on the other side of Black River. Even so, from this distance the huge buildings did not resemble millworks so much as they did the ramparts, gates, and towers of castles. The planned forests that supplied Big Union, and which were less attractive than the natural woods, were out of sight beyond the next mountain. Blue sky and fast-moving white clouds overhung what could have passed for a scene of Eden in a biblical film.

Paul and Mark were not interested in the scenery. Their attention was fixed on a small, red-brown squirrel.

For the past five days they had been putting out food for the squirrel—dry roasted peanuts and sectioned apples—hoping to make friends with it and gradually to domesticate it. Day by day it crept closer to the food, and yesterday it took a few bites before succumbing to fear and scampering away.

Now, as they watched, it came forth from the perimeter of the woods, three or four quick yet cautious steps at a time, pausing again and again to study the man and boy. When it finally reached the food, it picked up a piece of the apple in its tiny forepaws and, sitting back on its haunches, began to eat.

When the animal finished the first slice and picked up another, Mark said, "He won't take his eyes off us. Not even for a second."

As the boy spoke the squirrel became suddenly as still as they were. It cocked its head and fixed them with one large brown eye.

Paul had said they could whisper, breaking their rule of silence, if the squirrel had gained courage since yesterday and managed to stay at the food for more than a few seconds. If they were to domesticate it, the animal would have to become accustomed to their voices.

"Please don't be scared," Mark said softly. Paul had promised that, if the squirrel *could* be tamed, Mark would be allowed to take it home and make a pet of it. "Please, don't run away."

Not yet prepared to trust them, it dropped the slice of apple, turned, bounded into the forest, and scrambled to the upper branches of a maple tree.

Mark jumped up. "Ah, heck! We wouldn't have hurt you, you dumb squirrel!" Disappointment lined his face.

"Stay calm. He'll be back again tomorrow," Paul said. He stood and stretched his stiff muscles.

"He'll *never* trust us."

"Yes, he will. Little by little."

"We'll never tame him."

"Little by little," Paul said. "He can't be converted in one week. You've got to be patient."

"I'm not very good at being patient."

"I know. But you'll learn."

"Little by little?"

"That's right," Paul said. He bent over, picked up the apple slices and peanuts, and dropped them into a plastic bag.

"Hey," Mark said, "maybe he's mad at us because we always take the food when we leave."

Paul laughed. "Maybe so. But if he got in the habit of sneaking back and eating after we've gone, he wouldn't have any reason to come out while we're here."

As they started back toward camp, which lay at the far end of the two-hundred-yard-long mountain meadow, Paul gradually became aware again of the beautiful day as if it were a mosaic for all the senses, falling into place around him, piece by piece. The warm summer breeze. White daisies gleaming in the grass, and here and there a buttercup. The odor of grass and earth and wild flowers. The constant rustle of leaves and the gentle soughing of the breeze in the pine boughs. The trilling of birds. The solemn shadows of the forest. High above, a hawk wheeled into sight, the last piece of the mosaic; its shrill cry seemed filled with pride, as if it knew that it had capped the scene, as if it thought it had pulled down the sky with its wings.

The time had come for their weekly trip into town to replenish their supply of perishable goods—but for a moment he didn't want to leave the mountain. Even Black River—small, nearly isolated from the modern world, singularly peaceful—would seem raucous when compared to the serenity of the forest.

But of course Black River offered more than fresh eggs, milk, butter, and other groceries: Jenny was there.

As they drew near the camp, Mark ran ahead. He pushed aside a pair of yellow canvas flaps and peered into the large tent that they had erected in the shadow of several eight-foot hemlocks and firs. A second later he turned away from the tent, cupped his hands around his mouth, and shouted, "Rya! Hey, Rya!"

"Here," she said, coming out from behind the tent.

For an instant Paul couldn't believe what he saw: a small young squirrel perched on her right arm, its claws hooked through the sleeve of her corduroy jacket. It was chewing on a piece of apple, and she was petting it gently.

"How did you do it?" he asked.

"Chocolate."

"Chocolate?"

She grinned. "I started out trying to lure it with the same bait you and Mark have been using. But then I figured that a squirrel can probably get nuts and apples on his own. But he can't get chocolate. I figured the smell would be irresistible— and it was! He was eating out of my hand by Wednesday, but I didn't want you to know about him until I was sure he'd gotten over the worst of his fear of humans."

"He's not eating chocolate now."

"Too much of it wouldn't be good for him."

The squirrel raised its head and looked quizzically at Paul. Then it continued gnawing on the piece of apple in its forepaws.

"Do you like him, Mark?" Rya asked. As she spoke her grin melted into a frown.

Paul saw why: the boy was close to tears. He wanted a squirrel of his own—but he knew they couldn't take *two* of the animals home with them. His lower lip quivered; however, he was determined not to cry.

Rya recovered quickly. Smiling, she said, "Well, Mark? Do you like him? I'll be upset if you don't. I went to an awful lot of trouble to get him for you."

You little sweetheart, Paul thought.

Blinking back tears, Mark said, "For me?"

"Of course," she said.

"You mean you're giving him to me?"

She feigned surprise. "Who else?"

"I thought he was yours."

"Now what would I want with a pet squirrel?" she asked. "He'll be a good pet for a boy. But he would be all wrong for a girl." She put the animal on the ground and hunkered down beside it. Fishing a piece of candy from a pocket, she said, "Come on. You've got to feed him some chocolate if you really want to make friends with him."

The squirrel plucked the candy from Mark's hand and nibbled it with obvious pleasure. The boy was also in ecstasy as he gently stroked its flanks and long tail. When the chocolate was gone, the animal sniffed first at Mark and then at Rya; and when it realized there would be no more treats today, it slipped out from between them and dashed toward the trees.

"Hey!" Mark said. He ran after it until he saw that it was much faster than he.

"Don't worry," Rya said. "He'll come back tomorrow, so

long as we have some chocolate for him.''

"If we tame him," Mark said, "can I take him into town next week?"

"We'll see," Paul said. He looked at his watch. "If we're going to spend *today* in town, we'd better get moving."

The station wagon was parked half a mile away, at the end of a weed-choked dirt lane that was used by hunters in late autumn and early winter.

True to form, Mark shouted, "Last one to the car's a dope!" He ran ahead along the path that snaked down through the woods, and in a few seconds he was out of sight.

Rya walked at Paul's side.

"That was a very nice thing you did," he said.

She pretended not to know what he meant. "Getting the squirrel for Mark? It was fun."

"You didn't get it for Mark."

"Sure I did. Who else would I get it for?"

"Yourself," Paul said. "But when you saw how much it meant to him to have a squirrel of his own, you gave it up."

She grimaced. "You must think I'm a saint or something! If I'd really wanted that squirrel, I wouldn't have given him away. Not in a million years."

"You're not a good liar," he said affectionately.

Exasperated, she said, "Fathers!" Hoping he wouldn't notice her embarrassment, she ran ahead, shouting to Mark, and was soon out of sight beyond a dense patch of mountain laurel.

"Children!" he said aloud. But there was no exasperation in his voice, only love.

Since Annie's death he had spent more time with the children than he might have done if she had lived—partly because there was something of her in Mark and Rya, and he felt that he was keeping in touch with her through them. He had learned that each of them was quite different from the other, each with his unique outlook and abilities, and he cherished their individuality. Rya would always know more about life, people, and the rules of the game than Mark would. Curious, probing, patient, seeking knowledge, she would enjoy life from an intellectual vantage point. She would know that especially intense passion—sexual, emotional, mental—which none but the very bright ever experience. On the other hand, although Mark would face life with far less understanding than Rya, he was not to be pitied. Not for a moment!

Brimming with enthusiasm, quick to laugh, overwhelmingly optimistic, he would live every one of his days with gusto. If he was denied complex pleasures and satisfactions—well, to compensate for that, he would ever be in tune with the simple joys of life in which Rya, while understanding them, would never be able to indulge herself fully without some self-consciousness. Paul knew that, in days to come, each of his children would bring him a special kind of happiness and pride—unless death took them from him.

As if he had walked into an invisible barrier, he stopped in the middle of the trail and swayed slightly from side to side.

That last thought had taken him completely by surprise. When he lost Annie, he had thought for a time that he had lost all that was worth having. Her death made him painfully aware that everything—even deeply felt, strong personal relationships that nothing in life could twist or destroy—was temporary, pawned to the grave. For the past three and a half years, in the back of his mind, a small voice had been telling him to be prepared for death, to expect it, and not to let the loss of Mark or Rya or anyone else, if it came, shatter him as Annie's death had nearly done. But until now the voice had been almost subconscious, an urgent counsel of which he was only vaguely aware. This was the first time that he had let it pop loose from the subconscious. As it rose to the surface, it startled him. A shiver passed through him from head to foot. He had an eerie sense of precognition. Then it was gone as quickly as it had come.

An animal moved in the underbrush.

Overhead, above the canopy of trees, a hawk screamed.

Suddenly the summer forest seemed much too dark, too dense, too wild: sinister.

You're being foolish, he thought. You're no fortune teller. You're no clairvoyant.

Nevertheless, he hurried along the winding path, anxious to catch up with Mark and Rya.

At 11:15 that morning, Dr. Walter Troutman was at the big mahogany desk in his surgery. He was eating an early lunch—two roast beef sandwiches, an orange, a banana, an apple, a cup of butterscotch pudding, and several glasses of iced tea—and reading a medical journal.

As the only physician in Black River, he felt that he had two primary responsibilities to the people in the area. The first was to be certain that, in the event of a catastrophe at the mill or some other medical crisis, he would never find himself undernourished and in want of energy to fulfill his duties. The second was to be aware of all developments in medical techniques and theory, so that the people who came to him would receive the most modern treatment available. Scores of satisfied patients—and the reverence and affection with which the whole town regarded him—testified to his success in meeting his second responsibility. As for the first, he stood five eleven and weighed two hundred and seventy pounds.

When an overweight patient, in the middle of one of the doctor's lectures, had the temerity to mention Troutman's own excess poundage, he was always countered with the same joke. "Obese? Me?" Troutman would ask, clearly astonished. "This isn't fat I'm carrying. It's stored energy, ready to be tapped if there's ever a catastrophe up at the mill." Then he would continue his lecture.

In truth, of course, he was an almost compulsive eater and had been all of his life. By the time he was thirty, he had given up dieting and psychotherapy as truly lost causes. The same year, having been guaranteed a handsome stipend by the Big Union Supply Company, he had come to Black River where the people were so pleased to have a doctor of their own that they didn't care if he was fat, thin, white, black, or green. For twenty years now, he had been accommodating his compulsion, stuffing himself with cakes and cookies and pies and five square meals a day; and in sum he felt that his life held more enjoyment than that of any other man he knew.

As he was about to enjoy it even more, as he was picking up the second roast beef sandwich, the telephone rang. He considered not answering it. But he was the kind of doctor who went out on house calls at any hour of the day or night. Even lunch had to be put aside if a patient needed help. He picked up the receiver. "Hello?"

"Dr. Troutman?"

"Yes."

The voice on the other end of the line was cold and sharp. "I am the key, Dr. Troutman."

"I am the lock," Troutman said without hesitation.

"Are you alone in the house?"

"Yes."

"Where is your nurse, Miss MacDonald?"

"I don't know. At home, I suppose."

"When will she be coming to work?"

"Half an hour before the office opens."

"And the office opens at one thirty?"

"That's correct," Troutman said.

"Are you expecting anyone else before one o'clock?"

"No. No one."

The stranger was silent for a moment.

Troutman listened to his desk clock ticking. He glanced at the food laid out on a linen napkin in front of him, picked a sliver of roast beef from the sandwich, and ate it quickly like a fish taking a fly.

When the man on the other end of the line had decided on his approach, he said, "I'm going to ask you a number of important questions, Doctor. You will give me complete answers to the best of your ability."

"Yes, of course."

"Have you recently had an epidemic of any sort in Black River?"

"Yes, we have."

"Of what?"

"Night chills."

"Explain what you mean by that term, Doctor."

"Severe chills, cold sweats, nausea but without vomiting—and the resultant insomnia."

"When were the first cases reported to you?"

"Wednesday, the tenth of this month. Nine days ago."

"Did any of your patients mention nightmares?"

"Every one of them said he'd been awakened by a terrible dream."

"Could any of them remember what it was?"

"No. None of them."

"What treatment did you provide?"

"I gave placebos to the first few. But when I suffered the chills myself on Wednesday night, and when there were scores of new cases on Thursday, I began to prescribe a low-grade antibiotic."

"That had no effect, of course."

"None whatsoever."

"Did you refer any patients to another physician?"

"No. The nearest other doctor is sixty miles away—and he's in his late seventies. However, I did request an investigation by the State Health Authority."

The stranger was silent for a moment. Then: "You did that

merely because there was an epidemic of rather mild influenza?''

"It was mild," Troutman said, "but decidedly unusual. No fever. No swelling of the glands. And yet, for as mild as it was, it spread throughout the town and the mill within twenty-four hours. Everyone had it. Of course I wondered if it might not be influenza at all but some sort of poisoning."

"Poisoning?"

"Yes. Of a common food or water supply."

"When did you contact the Health Authority?"

"Friday the twelfth, late in the afternoon."

"And they sent a man?"

"Not until Monday."

"Was there still an epidemic at that time?"

"No," Troutman said. "Everyone in town had the chills, the cold sweats, and the nausea again Saturday night. But *no one* was ill Sunday night. Whatever it was, it disappeared even more suddenly than it came."

"Did the State Health Authority still run an investigation?"

Intently studying the food on the napkin, Troutman shifted in his chair and said, "Oh, yes. Dr. Evans, one of their junior field men, spent all of Monday and most of Tuesday interviewing people and taking tests."

"Tests? You mean of food and water?"

"Yes. Blood and urine samples too."

"Did he take water samples from the reservoir?"

"Yes. He filled at least twenty vials and bottles."

"Has he filed his report yet?"

Troutman licked his lips and said, "Yes. He called me last evening to give me the results of the tests."

"I suppose he found nothing?"

"That's correct. All the tests were negative."

"Does he have any theories?" the stranger asked, a vague trace of anxiety in his voice.

That bothered Troutman. The key should not be anxious. The key had all the answers. "He believes that we've experienced a rare case of mass psychological illness."

"An epidemic of formulated hysteria?"

"Yes. Exactly."

"Then he's making no recommendations?"

"None that I know of."

"He has terminated the investigation?"

"That's what he told me."

The stranger sighed softly. "Doctor, earlier you told me that *everyone* in town and at the mill had experienced the night chills. Were you speaking figuratively or literally?"

"Figuratively," Troutman said. "There were exceptions. Perhaps twenty children, all under eight years of age. And two adults. Sam Edison and his daughter, Jenny.

"The people who run the general store?"

"That's correct."

"They didn't suffer from the chills at all?"

"Not at all."

"Are they connected to the town's water supply?"

"Everyone in town is."

"All right. What about the lumbermen who work in the planned forests beyond the mill? Some of them virtually live out there. Were they all affected?"

"Yes. That was something Dr. Evans wanted to know too," Troutman said. "He interviewed all of them."

The stranger said, "I've no more questions, Dr. Troutman, but I do have some orders for you. When you hang up your receiver, you will instantly wipe all memory of our conversation from your mind. Do you understand?"

"Yes. Perfectly."

"You'll forget every word we've exchanged. You'll erase this memory from both your conscious and subconscious, so that it can never be recalled no matter how much you might wish to recall it. Understood?"

Troutman nodded somberly. "Yes."

"When you hang up your receiver, you will remember only that the phone rang—and that it was a wrong number. Is that clear?"

"A wrong number. Yes, that's clear."

"Very well. Hang up, Doctor."

Carelessness, Troutman thought, a bit irritably, as he put down the receiver. If people paid attention to what they were doing, they wouldn't dial so many wrong numbers or make one-tenth of the other mistakes that peppered their lives. How many patients, badly cut or burned, had he treated who had been injured only because they were inattentive, careless? Scores. Hundreds. Thousands! Sometimes, when he opened the door of his waiting room and peered inside, he had the feeling that he had just pulled a pan from the oven and was staring not at people but at a row of wall-eyed trout with gaping mouths. And now, tying up a doctor's line with a wrong number, even for half a minute or so—well, that could be damned serious.

He shook his head, dismayed by the ineptitude and inefficiency of his fellow citizens.

Then he grabbed the roast beef sandwich and took an enormous bite from it.

At 11:45 Paul Annendale stepped into Sam Edison's study on the second floor of the house, just above the general store. "Squire Edison, I wish to arrange to take your daughter to lunch."

Sam was standing in front of a bookcase. A large volume lay open in his left hand, and he was paging through it with his right. "Sit down, vassal," he said without looking up. "The squire will be with you in just a minute."

If Sam had chosen to refer to this place as his library rather than his study, he would have been justified. Two lushly cushioned, somewhat tattered armchairs and two matching footstools stood in the center of the room, facing the only window. Two yellow-shaded floor lamps, one behind each chair, provided adequate but restful light, and a small rectangular table lay between the chairs. A pipe was turned upside down in a large ash tray on the table, and the air was redolent with the cherry scent of Sam's tobacco. The room was only twelve feet by fifteen feet; but two entire walls, from floor to ceiling, were lined with thousands of books and hundreds of issues of various psychology journals.

Paul sat down and put his feet up on a stool.

He didn't know the title of the volume that the other man was looking through, but he did know that ninety percent of these books dealt with Hitler, Nazism, and anything else that was even remotely related to that philosophical-political nightmare. Sam's interest in the subject had been unwavering for thirty-two years.

In April of 1945, as a member of an American intelligence unit, Sam went into Berlin less than twenty-four hours behind the first Allied troops. He was shocked by the extent of the destruction. In addition to the ruin caused by Allied bombers, mortars, and tank fire, there was damage directly attributable to the Führer's scorch-the-earth policy. In the final days of the war, the madman had decreed that the victors must be allowed to seize nothing of value, that Germany must be transformed into a barren plain of rubble, that not even one house could be left standing to come under foreign domination. Of course, most Germans were not prepared to take this final step into oblivion—although many of them were. It seemed to Sam that the Germans he saw in the devastated streets were survivors not merely of the war but also of the frenzied suicide of an entire nation.

On May 8, 1945, he was transferred to an intelligence unit that was collecting data on the Nazi death camps. As the full story of the holocaust became known, as it was discovered that millions of men and women and children had passed through the gas chambers and that hundreds of thousands of others had been shot in the back and buried in trenches, Sam Edison, a young man from the backwoods of Maine, found nothing within his experience to explain such mind-numbing horror. Why had so many once-rational, basically good people committed themselves to fulfilling the evil fantasies of an obvious lunatic and a handful of subordinate madmen? Why had one of the most professional armies in the world disgraced itself by fighting to protect the SS murderers? Why had millions of people gone with so little protest to the concentration camps and gas chambers? What did Adolf Hitler know about the psychology of the masses that had helped him to achieve such absolute power? The ruin of the German cities and the death camp data raised all of these questions but provided answers to none of them.

He was sent back to the States and mustered out of the service in October of 1945, and as soon as he was home he began to buy books about Hitler, the Nazis, and the war. He read everything of value that he could find. Bits and pieces of explanations, theories and arguments seemed valid to him. But the complete answer that he sought eluded him; therefore, he extended his area of study and began collecting books on totalitarianism, militarism, war games, battle strategy, German history, German philosophy, bigotry, racism, paranoia, mob psychology, behavior modification, and mind control. His undiminishable fascination with Hitler did not have its roots in morbid curiosity, but came instead from a fearful certainty that the German people were not at all unique and that his own neighbors in Maine, given the right set of circumstances, would be capable of the same atrocities.

Sam suddenly closed the book through which he'd been paging for the past few minutes and returned it to the shelf. "Dammit, I know they're here somewhere."

From his armchair Paul said, "What are you looking for?"

His head tilted slightly to the right, Sam continued to read the titles on the bindings. "We've got a sociologist doing research in town. I know I've got several of his articles in my collection, but I'll be damned if I can find them."

"Sociologist? What sort of research?"

"I don't know exactly. He came into the store early this morning. Had dozens of questions to ask. Said he was a sociologist, come all the way up from Washington, and was making a study of Black River. Said he'd rented a room at Pauline Vicker's place and would be here for three weeks or so. According to him, Black River's pretty special."

"In what way?"

"For one thing, it's a prosperous company town in an age when company towns have supposedly fallen into decay or vanished altogether. And because we're geographically isolated, it'll be easier for him to analyze the effects of television on our social patterns. Oh, he had at least half a dozen good reasons why we're ripe material for sociological research, but I don't think he got around to explaining his main thesis, whatever it is he's trying to prove or disprove." He took another book from the shelf, opened it to the table of contents, closed it almost at once, and put it back where he'd gotten it.

"Do you know his name?"

"Introduced himself as Albert Deighton," Sam said. "The name didn't ring a bell. But the face did. Meek-looking man. Thin lips. Receding hairline. Glasses as thick as the lenses on a telescope. Those glasses make his eyes look like they're popping right out of his head. I *know* I've seen his picture several times in books or magazines, alongside articles he's written." He sighed and turned away from the bookshelves for the first time since Paul came into the room. With one hand he smoothed his white beard. "I can spend all evening up here picking through these books. Right now you want me to take over the counter downstairs so you can escort my daughter to the elegant, incomparable Ultman's Cafe for lunch."

Paul laughed. "Jenny tells me there's no more flu in town. So the worst we can get at Ultman's is food poisoning."

"What about the kids?"

"Mark's spending the afternoon with Bob Thorp's boy.

He's been invited to lunch, and he'll spend it mooning over Emma.''

"Still has a crush on her, does he?"

"He thinks he's in love, but he'd never admit it."

Sam's craggy face was softened by a smile. "And Rya?"

"Emma asked her to come along with Mark. But if you don't mind looking after her, she'd rather stay here with you."

"Mind? Don't be ridiculous."

As he got up from the armchair, Paul said, "Why don't you put her to work after lunch? She could come up here and pore through these books until she found Deighton's name on a table of contents."

"What a dull bit of work for a peppy girl like her!"

"Rya wouldn't be bored," Paul said. "It's right down her alley. She likes working with books—and she'd enjoy doing you a favor."

Sam hesitated, then shrugged and said, "Maybe I'll ask her. When I've read what Deighton's written, I'll know where his interests lie, and I'll have a better idea of what he's up to now. You know me—as curious as the day is long. Once I've got a bee in my bonnet, I've just got to take it out and see whether it's a worker, drone, queen, or maybe even a wasp."

Ultman's Cafe stood on the southwest corner of the town square, shaded by a pair of enormous black oak trees. The restaurant was eighty feet long, an aluminum and glass structure meant to look like an old-fashioned railroad passenger car. It had one narrow window row that ran around three sides; and tacked on the front was an entrance foyer that spoiled the railroad-car effect.

Inside, booths upholstered in blue plastic stood beside the windows. The table at each booth held an ash tray, a cylindrical glass sugar dispenser, salt and pepper shakers, a napkin dispenser, and a selector from the jukebox. An aisle separated the booths from the counter that ran the length of the restaurant.

Ogden Salsbury was in the corner booth at the north end of the cafe. He was drinking a second cup of coffee and watching the other customers.

At 1:50 in the afternoon, most of the lunch-hour rush had

passed. Ultman's was nearly deserted. In a booth near the door, an elderly couple was reading the weekly newspaper, eating roast beef and French fries, and quietly arguing politics. The chief of police, Bob Thorp, was on a stool at the counter, finishing his lunch and joking with the gray-haired waitress named Bess. At the far end of the room, Jenny Edison was in the other corner booth with a good-looking man in his late thirties; Salsbury didn't know him but assumed he worked at the mill or in the logging camp.

Of the five other customers, Jenny was of the greatest interest to Salsbury. A few hours ago, when he talked to Dr. Troutman, he learned that neither Jenny nor her father had complained of the night chills. The fact that a number of children had also escaped them did not disturb him. The effect of the subliminals was, in part, directly proportionate to the subject's language skills and reading ability; and he had expected that some children would be unaffected. But Sam and Jenny were adults, and they should not have gone untouched.

Possibly they hadn't consumed any of the drug. If that was true, then they hadn't drunk any water from the town system, hadn't used it to make ice cubes, and hadn't cooked with it. That was marginally possible, he supposed. Marginally. However, the drug had also been introduced into fourteen products at a food wholesaler's warehouse in Bangor before those products were shipped to Black River, and it was difficult for him to believe that they could have been so fortunate as to have avoided, by chance, *every* contaminated substance.

There was a second possibility. It was conceivable, although highly improbable, that the Edisons had taken the drug but hadn't come into contact with any of the sophisticated subliminal programming that had been designed with such care for the Black River experiment and that had inundated the town through half a dozen forms of print and electronic media for a period of seven days.

Salsbury was nearly certain that neither of these explanations was correct, and that the truth was both complex and technical. Even the most beneficial drugs did not have a benign effect on everyone; any drug could be counted upon to sicken or kill at least a tiny percentage of those people to whom it was administered. Moreover, for virtually every drug, there were some people, another extremely small group, who were either minimally affected or utterly untouched by it, owing to differences in metabolisms, variances in body chemistries, and unknown factors. More likely than not, Jenny and Sam Edison had taken the subliminal primer in water or food but hadn't been altered by it—either not at all or not as they should have been—and subsequently were unimpressed by the subliminals because they hadn't been made ready for them.

Eventually he would have to give the two of them a series of examinations and tests at a fully equipped medical clinic, with the hope that he could find what it was that made them impervious to the drug. But that could wait. During the next three weeks he would be quietly recording and studying the effects that the drug and subliminals produced in the other people of Black River.

Although Salsbury was more interested in Jenny than in any of the other customers, most of the time his attention was focused on the younger of Ultman's two waitresses. She was a lean, lithe brunette with dark eyes and a honey complexion. Perhaps twenty-five years old. A captivating smile. A rich, throaty voice perfect for the bedroom. To Salsbury, her every movement was filled with sexual innuendo and an all but open invitation to violation.

More important, however, the waitress reminded him of Miriam, the wife he had divorced twenty-seven years ago. Like Miriam, she had small, high-set breasts and very beautiful, supple legs. Her throaty voice resembled Miriam's. And she had Miriam's walk: an unstudied grace in every step, an unconscious and sinuous rolling of the hips that took his breath away.

He wanted her.

But he would never take her because she reminded him too much of Miriam, reminded him of the frustrations, angers, and disappointments of that awful five-year marriage. She stirred his lust—but she also stirred his somewhat suppressed, long-nurtured hatred of Miriam and, by extension, of women in general. He knew that, in the act, as he achieved penetration and began to move, her resemblance to Miriam would leave him impotent.

When she brought the check for his lunch, flashing that dazzling smile that had begun to seem smug and superior to him, he said, "I am the key."

He was taking an unwarranted risk. He couldn't defend it

even to himself. Until he was certain that everyone in town, other than the Edisons and a handful of children, was properly programmed, he should restrict the use of the command phrase to telephone conversations, as with Troutman, and to situations wherein he was alone with the subject and free from fear of interruption. Only after three weeks of observation and individual contact could he even begin to assume there was no risk involved; and now, on one level, he was a bit disturbed that he was conducting himself irresponsibly on his first day in town. He didn't particularly mind if absolute power corrupted him absolutely—just so it didn't make him overconfident and careless. On the other hand, so long as they kept their voices low, there was little chance that they would be overheard. The elderly couple in the booth by the door was nearer to Salsbury than anyone else in the cafe, and they were half a room away. Besides, unwarranted risk or not, he couldn't resist taking control of this woman. His emotions had unseated his reason, and he was riding with them.

"I am the lock," she said.

"Keep your voice low."

"Yes, sir."

"What's your name?"

"Alice."

"How old are you?"

"Twenty-six."

"You're lovely," he said.

She said nothing."

"Smile for me, Alice."

She smiled. She didn't look the least bit dazed. Even her big, dark eyes held no hint of a trance. Yet she was unhesitatingly obedient.

He said, "You've got a nice body."

"Thank you."

"Do you like sex?"

"Yeah."

"Do you like it very much?"

"Yeah. I like it."

"When you're in bed with a man, is there anything you won't let him do to you?"

"Yeah. Greek."

"You won't let him take you in the ass?"

She blushed and said, "Yeah. I don't like that."

"If I wanted you, I could have you."

She stared at him.

"Couldn't I?"

"Yeah."

"If I wanted you, I could have you right now, right here, on top of this table."

"Yeah."

"If I wanted to take you Greek-style, I could."

She resisted the idea but finally said, "Is that what you want?"

"If I did want it, I could have it. You'd let me."

"Yeah."

It was his turn to smile. He glanced around the cafe. No one was looking at them; no one had heard. "Are you married, Alice?"

"No. Divorced."

"Why did you get a divorce?"

"He couldn't hold a job."

"Your husband couldn't?"

"Yeah, him."

"Was he good in bed?"

"Not very."

She was even more like Miriam than he had thought.

After all these years he could still remember what Miriam had said to him the day she left. *You're not just bad in bed, Ogden. You're terrible. And you've no inclination to learn. But you know, I could live with that if there were compensations. If you had money and could buy me things, maybe I could live with your fumbling sex. When I said I'd marry you, I thought you were going to make lots of money. Jesus Christ, you were at the top of your class at Harvard! When you completed your doctorate, everyone wanted to hire you. If you had any ambition whatsoever, you'd have already gotten your hands on a decent piece of money. You know what, Ogden? I think you're as inept and unimaginative in your research as you are in bed. You're never going to get anywhere, but I am. I'm getting out.* What a bitch she had been. Just thinking about her, he began to tremble and perspire.

Alice was still smiling at him.

"Stop smiling," he said softly. "I don't like it."

She did as she was told.

"What am I, Alice?"

"You're the key."

"And what are you?"

"The lock."

"Now that I've opened you, you'll do whatever I tell you to do. Isn't that true?"

"Yeah."

He took three one-dollar bills from his wallet and put them on top of the lunch check. "I'm going to test you, Alice. I'm going to see just how obedient you are."

She waited docilely.

"When you leave this table," he said, "you'll take the check and money to the cash register. You'll ring up the sale and take your tip from whatever's left of the three dollars. Is that clear?"

"Yeah."

"Then you will go to the kitchen. Is there anyone back there?"

"No. Randy went to the bank."

"Randy Ultman?"

"Yeah."

"That's good," Salsbury said. "Now, when you go to the kitchen, you'll pick up a meat fork, a cook's fork. One of those big, two-pronged forks. Is there one of those in the kitchen?"

"Yeah. Several."

"You'll pick one of them up and stab yourself with it, run it all the way through your left hand."

She didn't even blink.

"Is that understood, Alice?"

"Yeah. I understand."

"When you turn away from this table, you'll forget everything we've said to each other. Understood?"

"Yeah."

"When you run the fork through your hand, you'll think it was an accident. A freak accident. Won't you, Alice?"

"Sure. An accident."

"Go away, then."

She turned and walked to the half-door at the end of the lunch counter, her smooth hips rolling provocatively.

When she reached the cash register and began to ring up the sale, Salsbury slid out of the booth and started toward the door.

She dropped her tip into a pocket of her uniform, closed the cash register drawer, and went into the kitchen.

At the entrance Salsbury stopped and put a quarter in the newspaper vending machine.

Bob Thorp laughed loudly at some joke, and the waitress named Bess giggled like a young girl.

Salsbury took a copy of the *Black River Bulletin* from the wire rack, folded it, put it under his arm, and opened the door to the foyer. He stepped across the sill and began to pull the door shut behind him, thinking all the while: *Come on, you bitch, come on!* His heart was pounding, and he felt slightly dizzy.

Alice began to scream.

Grinning, Salsbury closed the front door, pushed through the outer door, went down the steps, and walked east on Main Street, as if he were unaware of the uproar in the cafe.

The day was bright and warm. The sky was cloudless.

He had never been happier.

Paul shouldered past Bob Thorp and stepped into the kitchen.

The young waitress was standing at a counter that lay between two upright food freezers. Her left hand was palm down on a wooden cutting board. With her right hand she gripped an eighteen-inch-long meat fork. The two wickedly sharp prongs appeared to have been driven all the way through her left hand and into the wood beneath. Blood spotted her light blue uniform, glistened on the cutting board, and dripped from the edge of the Formica-topped counter. She was screaming and gasping for breath between the screams and shaking and trying to wrench the fork loose.

Turning back to Bob Thorp, who stood transfixed in the doorway, Paul said, "Get Doc Troutman."

Thorp didn't have to be told again. He hurried away.

Taking hold of the woman's right hand, Paul said, "Let go of the fork. I want you to let go of the fork. You're doing more harm than good."

She raised her head and seemed to look straight through him. Her face was chalky beneath her dark complexion; she was obviously in shock. She couldn't stop screaming—an ululating wail more animal than human—and she probably didn't even know that he had spoken to her.

He had to pry her fingers from the handle of the fork.

At his side Jenny said, "Oh, my God!"

"Hold her for me," he said. "Don't let her grab the fork."

Jenny gripped the woman's right wrist. She said, "I think I'm going to be sick."

Paul wouldn't have blamed her if she had been just that. In the tiny restaurant kitchen, with the ceiling only a few inches above their heads, the screams were deafening. The sight of that slender hand with the fork embedded in it was horrifying, the stuff of nightmares. The air was thick with the stale odors of baked ham, roast beef, fried onions, grease—and the fresh, metallic tang of blood. It was enough to nauseate anyone. But he said, "You won't be sick. You're a tough lady."

She bit her lower lip and nodded.

Quickly, as if he had been prepared and waiting for exactly this emergency, Paul took a dishcloth from the towel rack and tore it into two strips. He threw one of these aside. With the other length of cloth and a long wooden tasting spoon, he fashioned a tourniquet for the waitress's left arm. He twisted the wooden spoon with his right hand and covered the handle of the meat fork with his left. To Jenny he said, "Come around here and take the tourniquet."

As soon as her right hand was free, the waitress tried to get to the handle of the fork. She clawed at Paul's fist.

Jenny took hold of the spoon.

Pressing down on the waitress's wounded hand, Paul jerked up on the fork, which was sunk into the wood perhaps half an inch past her flesh, and pulled the tines from her in one sudden, clean movement. He dropped the fork and slipped an arm around her waist to keep her from falling. Her knees had begun to buckle; he had thought they might.

As he stretched the woman out on the floor, Jenny said, "She must be in awful pain."

Those words seemed to shatter the waitress's terror. She stopped screaming and began to cry.

"I don't see how she did it," Paul said as he tended to her. "She put that fork through her hand with incredible force. She was pinned to the board."

Weeping, trembling, the waitress said, "Accident." She gasped and groaned and shook her head. "Terrible . . . accident."

6.

Fourteen Months Earlier:
Thursday, June 10, 1976

NAKED, THE DEAD MAN lay on his back in the center of the slightly tilted autopsy table, framed by blood gutters on all sides.

"Who was he?" Klinger asked.

Salsbury said, "He worked for Leonard."

The room in which the three men stood was illuminated only in the center by two hooded lamps above the autopsy table. Three walls were lined with computer housings, consoles, and monitor boards; and the tiny systems bulbs and glowing scopes made ghostly patches of green, blue, yellow, and pale red light in the surrounding shadows. Nine TV display screens—cathoderay tubes—were set high on three walls, and four other screens were suspended from the ceiling; and all of them emitted a thin bluish-green light.

In that eerie glow the corpse looked less like a real body than like a prop in a horror film.

Somber, almost reverent, Dawson said, "His name was Brian Kingman. He was on my personal staff."

"For very long?" Klinger asked.

"Five years."

The dead man had been in his late twenties and in good condition. Now, circulation having ceased seven hours ago, lividity had set in; the blood had settled into his calves, the backs of his thighs, his buttocks, and his lower back, and in these places the flesh was purple and a bit distended. His face was white and deeply lined. His hands were at his sides, his palms up, the fingers curled.

"Was he married?" Klinger asked.

Dawson shook his head: no.

"Family?"

"Grandparents dead. No brother or sisters. His mother died when he was born, and his father was killed in an auto accident last year."

"Aunts and uncles?"

"None close."

"Girlfriends?"

"None that he was serious about or that were serious about him," Dawson said. "That's why we chose him. If he disappears, there's no one to waste a lot of time and energy looking for him."

Klinger considered that for a few seconds. Then he said, "You expected the experiment to kill him?"

"We thought there was a chance of it," Ogden said.

Smiling grimly, Klinger said, "You were right."

Something about the general's tone angered Salsbury. "You knew the stakes when you came in with Leonard and me."

"Of course I did," Klinger said.

"Then don't act as if Kingman's death is entirely my fault. The blame belongs to all of us."

Frowning, the general said, "Ogden, you misunderstand me. I don't believe that you and Leonard and I are to blame for anything. This man was a machine that broke down. Nothing more. We can always get another machine. You're too sensitive, Ogden."

"Poor boy," Dawson said, regarding the corpse sadly. "He would have done anything for me."

"He did," the general said. He stared thoughtfully at the dead man. "Leonard, you've got seven servants in this house. Did any of them know Kingman was here?"

"That's highly unlikely. We brought him in secretly."

For thirteen months, this wing of the Greenwich house had been sealed off from the other twenty rooms. It had been provided with a new private entrance, and all of the locks had been changed. The servants were told that experiments, none of them dangerous, were being conducted for a subsidiary of Futurex, and that the security precautions were needed to protect the operation's files and discoveries from industrial espionage.

"Is the household staff still curious about what goes on here?" Klinger asked.

"No," Dawson said. "So far as they can see, nothing's happened in the past year. The sealed wing has lost its mystery."

"Then I think we can bury Kingman on the estate without too much risk." He faced Salsbury. "What happened? How did he die?"

Salsbury sat on a high, white stool at the head of the autopsy table, hooked his heels around one of its rungs, and spoke to them across the corpse. "We brought Kingman here for the first time in early February. He thought he was helping us with some sociological research that had important business applications for Futurex. During forty hours of interviews with him, I learned everything I wanted to know about the man's likes, dislikes, prejudices, personality quirks, desires, and basic thought processes. Later, at the end of February, I went through the transcripts of those interviews and selected five test points, five of Kingman's attitudes and/or opinions that I would try to reverse with a series of subliminals."

He had chosen three simple test points and two complex ones. Kingman craved chocolate candy, chocolate cake, chocolate in every form; and Salsbury wanted to make him ill at the first taste of chocolate. He couldn't and wouldn't eat broccoli; but Salsbury wanted to make him like it. Kingman had an ingrained fear of dogs; an attempt to transform that fear into affection would constitute the third of the simple test points. The remaining two indices presented Salsbury with a far greater chance of failure, for to deal with them he would have to design subliminal commands that bored especially deeply into Kingman's psyche. First of all, Kingman was an atheist, a fact he had hidden successfully from Dawson for five years. Secondly, he was extremely prejudiced against blacks. Making him over into a God-loving, prayer-saying champion of the Negro would be far more difficult than twisting his taste for chocolate into a loathing of it.

By the second week of April, Salsbury completed the subliminal program.

Kingman was brought back to the Greenwich house on the fifteenth of that month—ostensibly to participate in additional sociological research for Futurex. Although he wasn't aware of it, he was fed the subliminal primer, the drug, on April 15. Salsbury put him under close medical observation and ran tests on him for three days, but he could find no indications of a temporary toxic state, permanent tissue damage, a change in blood chemistry, noticeable psychological damage, or any other deleterious side-effects attributable to the drug.

At the end of those three days, on April 19, still in excellent health, Kingman took part in what he thought was an experiment in visual perception. He was shown two feature-length motion pictures in one afternoon, and at the conclusion of each film he was required to answer a hundred questions that dealt with what he had just seen. His answers were unimportant, and they were filed only because Salsbury habitually filed every scrap of paper in his laboratory. The experiment actually had only one purpose: while Kingman was watching the films, he was also unwittingly absorbing three hours of subliminal programming that was meant to change five of his attitudes.

The events of the following day, April 20, proved the effectiveness of Salsbury's drug and subliminal programs. At breakfast, Kingman tried to eat a chocolate doughnut, dropped it after one bite, quickly excused himself from the table, went to the nearest bathroom, and threw up. At lunch he ate four portions of broccoli in butter sauce with his pork chops. That afternoon, when Dawson took him on a tour of the estate, Kingman spent fifteen minutes playing with several of the guard dogs in the kennel. After dinner, when Ogden and Dawson began to discuss the continuing efforts to integrate the public schools in the North, Kingman came on like a life-long liberal, an ardent advocate of equal rights. And finally, unaware of the two videotape cameras that monitored his bedroom in the sealed wing, he had said his prayers before going to sleep.

Standing now beside the corpse, smiling beatifically, Dawson said to Klinger, "You should have seen it, Ernst! It was terribly inspiring. Ogden took an atheist, a soul condemned to burn in Hell, and converted him into a faithful disciple of Jesus. And all on *one* day!"

Salsbury was uneasy. He shifted on the stool. Ignoring Dawson, staring at the middle of the general's forehead, he said, "Kingman left the estate on April twenty-first. I set to work immediately to design the ultimate series of subliminals, the one we three have discussed a hundred times, the program that would give me total and permanent control of the subject's mind through the use of a code phrase. I finished it on the fifth of June. We brought Kingman back here on the eighth, two days ago."

"He wasn't suspicious?" Klinger asked. "Or upset about all of this travel he was asked to do?"

"To the contrary," Dawson said. "He was pleased that I was using him for such a special project, even if he didn't fully understand what it was. He saw it as a sign of my faith in him. And he thought that, if he made himself available for Ogden's work, he would be promoted much sooner than he might have been otherwise. His behavior wasn't peculiar. I've seen it in every ambitious young executive and management trainee I've ever known."

Tired of standing, the general went to the nearest computer console, swiveled the command chair away from the keyboard, and sat down. He was almost entirely in the shadows. Green light from a display screen washed across his right shoulder and that side of his brutal face. He looked like a troll. "Okay. You finished the program on the fifth. Kingman came up here again on the eighth. You fed him the primer—"

"No," Salsbury said. "Once the drug has been administered to a subject, there's no need to give him a booster dose, not even years later. When Kingman arrived, I began at once with the subliminal program. I ran two films for him during the evening. That night, the night before last, he had a very bad dream. He woke up, sweating, chilled, shaking, dazed, and nauseated. He had trouble getting his breath. He vomited beside the bed."

"Fever?" Klinger asked.

"No."

"Do you think he had a delayed reaction to the drug—a month and a half delayed?"

"Maybe," Salsbury said. But he obviously didn't think that was the case. He got off the stool, went to his desk in a dark corner of the room, and came back with a computer print-out. "This is a record of Kingman's sleep patterns between one o'clock and three o'clock this morning. That's the crucial period." He handed it to Dawson. "Yesterday, I showed Kingman two more films. That completed the program. Last night—he died in bed."

The general joined Dawson and Salsbury in the oval of light at the autopsy table and began to read the two-yard-long sheet of computer paper.

```
PARTIAL RECAPITULATION

MEDICAL MONITORING PROGRAM:

BK/OB REP 14

RECORDED: 6/10/76

THIS PRINT: 6/10/76

PRINT
↓

HOURS   MIN   SEC   READING

0100    00    00    EEG--STAGE 3 SLEEP

0100    01    00    EEG--STAGE 3 SLEEP

0100    02    00    EEG--STAGE 4 SLEEP

0100    03    00    EEG--STAGE 4 SLEEP

0100    04    00    EEG--STAGE 4 SLEEP
```

Klinger said, "You had Kingman hooked up to a lot of machines while he slept?"

"Nearly every night he was here, right from the beginning," Salsbury said. "The first few times there really wasn't any reason for it. But by the time it *was* necessary for me to keep a close watch on him, he was accustomed to the machines and had learned to sleep tangled up with all those wires."

Indicating the print-out, the general said, "I'm not quite sure what I'm reading here."

"Likewise," Dawson said.

Salsbury suppressed a smile. Months ago he had decided

that his best defense against these two sharks was his highly specialized education. He never missed an opportunity to display it for them—and to impress them with the fact that, if they should dispose of him, neither of them could carry on his research and development or deal with an unexpected scientific crisis after the research and development was finished.

Pointing to the first several lines of the print-out, he said, "The fourth stage of sleep is the deepest. It tends to occur early in the night. Kingman went to bed at midnight and fell asleep at twenty minutes of one. As you can see here, he achieved the fourth level twenty-two minutes later."

"What's the importance of that?" Dawson asked.

"The fourth level is more like a coma than any other stage of sleep," Salsbury said. "The electroencephalogram shows irregular large waves of just a few cycles per second. There is no bodily movement on the part of the sleeper. It's in stage four, with the outer mind virtually comatose and with all sensory input shut down tight, that the inner mind becomes the only truly operative part of the mind. Remember, unlike the conscious mind, it never sleeps. But because there isn't any sensory input, the subconscious can't do anything during stage four sleep except play with itself. Now, Kingman's subconscious had something unique to play with."

The general said, "The key-lock program you implanted in him yesterday and the day before."

"That's right," Salsbury said. "And look here, farther down the print-out."

```
0100    08    00    EEG--STAGE 4 SLEEP

0100    09    00    EEG--STAGE 4 SLEEP

0100    10    00    EEG--STAGE 1 SLEEP/REM

0100    11    00    EEG--STAGE 1 SLEEP/REM
```

"All night long," Salsbury said, "we rise and fall and rise and fall through the stages of sleep. Almost without exception, we descend into sleep in steps and ascend from it in steps as well, spending some time at each level along the way. In this case, however, Kingman soared straight up from deep sleep to light sleep—as if a noise in the bedroom had startled him."

"Was there a noise?" Dawson asked.

"No."

"What's this REM?" Klinger asked.

Salsbury said, "That means rapid eye movement is taking place under the eyelids—which is a highly reliable indication that Kingman was dreaming in stage one."

"Dreaming?" Dawson asked. "About what?"

"There's no way of telling."

The general scratched the shadow of a beard that shaded his blunt chin even when he was freshly shaved. "But you think that the dream was caused by his subconscious playing around with the key-lock implant."

"Yes."

"And that the dream might have been about the sub-liminals."

"Yes. I can't come up with an explanation that makes more sense. Something about the key-lock program so shocked his subconscious that he was propelled straight up into a dream."

"A nightmare?"

"At this point, just a dream. But over the next two hours his sleep patterns became increasingly unusual, erratic."

```
0100    12    00    EEG--STAGE 1 SLEEP/REM

0100    13    00    EEG--ALPHA WAVES

0100    14    00    EEG--ALPHA WAVES
```

"The alpha waves mean Kingman was awake here for two minutes," Salsbury said. "Not wide awake. His eyes were probably still closed. He was hovering on the edge of the first level of sleep."

"The dream woke him," Klinger said.

"Probably."

```
0100    15    00    EEG--STAGE 1 SLEEP/REM

0100    16    00    EEG--STAGE 1 SLEEP

0100    17    00    EEG--STAGE 1 SLEEP

0100    18    00    EEG--STAGE 2 SLEEP

0100    19    00    EEG--STAGE 2 SLEEP

0100    20    00    EEG--STAGE 3 SLEEP

0100    21    00    EEG--STAGE 3 SLEEP

0100    22    00    EEG--STAGE 3 SLEEP
```

0100	23	00	EEG--STAGE 3 SLEEP
0100	24	00	EEG--STAGE 4 SLEEP
0100	25	00	EEG--STAGE 4 SLEEP
0100	26	00	EEG--STAGE 4 SLEEP
0100	27	00	EEG--STAGE 4 SLEEP
0100	28	00	EEG--STAGE 4 SLEEP
0100	29	00	EEG--STAGE 4 SLEEP
0100	30	00	EEG--STAGE 1 SLEEP/REM

"The first time he entered deep sleep," Salsbury said, "he stayed there for eight minutes. This time it lasted only six minutes. That's the start of an interesting pattern."

0100	31	00	EEG--STAGE 1 SLEEP/REM
0100	32	00	EEG--STAGE 1 SLEEP/REM
0100	33	00	EEG--STAGE 1 SLEEP/REM
0100	34	00	EEG--ALPHA WAVES
0100	35	00	EEG--STAGE 1 SLEEP/REM
0100	36	00	EEG--STAGE 1 SLEEP/REM
0100	37	00	EEG--STAGE 2 SLEEP
0100	38	00	EEG--STAGE 2 SLEEP
0100	39	00	EEG--STAGE 2 SLEEP
0100	40	00	EEG--STAGE 3 SLEEP
0100	41	00	EEG--STAGE 3 SLEEP
0100	42	00	EEG--STAGE 3 SLEEP
0100	43	00	EEG--STAGE 3 SLEEP
0100	44	00	EEG--STAGE 3 SLEEP
0100	45	00	EEG--STAGE 3 SLEEP
0100	46	00	EEG--STAGE 3 SLEEP
0100	47	00	EEG--STAGE 3 SLEEP
0100	48	00	EEG--STAGE 4 SLEEP
0100	49	00	EEG--STAGE 4 SLEEP
0100	50	00	EEG--STAGE 4 SLEEP
0100	51	00	EEG--STAGE 1 SLEEP/REM

"He was only in deep sleep three minutes that time," Klinger said. "The cycle is accelerating, at least on the down side."

Dawson said, "But why? Ernst apparently understands, but I'm not sure I do."

"Something's happening in his subconscious mind during deep sleep," Salsbury said. "Something so unsettling that it causes him to leap up into stage one sleep and dream. That subconscious experience, whatever it may be, is getting ever more intense—or, if it isn't getting more intense, then his ability to withstand it is dwindling. Perhaps both. On each occasion, he's able to tolerate it for a shorter period of time than he did before."

"You mean he's in pain in stage four?" Dawson asked.

"Pain is a condition of the flesh," Salsbury said. "It's not the right word for this situation."

"What is the right word."

"Anxiety, perhaps. Or fear."

```
0100    52    00    EEG--STAGE 1 SLEEP/REM
0100    53    00    EEG--STAGE 1 SLEEP/REM
0100    54    00    EEG--STAGE 1 SLEEP/REM
0100    55    00    EEG--ALPHA WAVES
0100    56    00    EEG--ALPHA WAVES
0100    57    00    EEG--STAGE 1 SLEEP/REM
```

"One minute that time," Klinger said.

"By now he's extremely agitated," Salsbury said, speaking of the dead man as if he were still alive. "The pattern becomes increasingly unusual and erratic. At two twenty he gets back to the third level. Look what happens to him after that:"

```
0200    20    00    EEG--STAGE 3 SLEEP
0200    21    00    EEG--STAGE 3 SLEEP
0200    22    00    EEG--STAGE 3 SLEEP
0200    23    00    EEG--STAGE 3 SLEEP
0200    24    00    EEG--STAGE 3 SLEEP
0200    25    00    EEG--STAGE 1 SLEEP/REM
0100    58    00    EEG--STAGE 1 SLEEP/REM
0100    59    00    EEG--STAGE 2 SLEEP/REM
```

```
0200    00    00    EEG--STAGE 2 SLEEP
0200    01    00    EEG--STAGE 2 SLEEP
0200    02    00    EEG--STAGE 2 SLEEP
0200    03    00    EEG--STAGE 3 SLEEP
0200    04    00    EEG--STAGE 3 SLEEP
0200    05    00    EEG--STAGE 3 SLEEP
0200    06    00    EEG--STAGE 3 SLEEP
0200    07    00    EEG--STAGE 4 SLEEP
0200    08    00    EEG--STAGE 1 SLEEP/REM
```

Klinger was as fascinated by the print-out of Brian Kingman's disintegration as he possibly could have been by the sight of the real event. "He didn't even reach the fourth level that time before he popped up to stage one again."

"He's having an acute subconscious anxiety attack," Salsbury said.

Dawson said, "Is there such a thing?"

"There is now. His mind is wildly turbulent at this point—yet in such a way that it doesn't wake him up altogether. And it gets worse:"

```
0200    26    00    EEG--STAGE 1 SLEEP/REM
0200    27    00    EEG--STAGE 1 SLEEP/REM
0200    28    00    EEG--ALPHA WAVES
0200    29    00    EEG--STAGE 1 SLEEP/REM
0200    30    00    EEG--ALPHA WAVES
0200    31    00    EEG--STAGE 1 SLEEP/REM
0200    32    00    EEG--STAGE 1 SLEEP/REM
0200    33    00    EEG--STAGE 2 SLEEP
0200    34    00    EEG--STAGE 2 SLEEP
0200    35    00    EEG--STAGE 2 SLEEP
0200    36    00    EEG--STAGE 3 SLEEP
0200    37    00    EEG--ALPHA WAVES
```

"He was frightened awake at two thirty-seven, wasn't he?" Dawson asked.

Salsbury said, "That's right. Not wide awake. But beyond the first level of sleep, into alpha wave territory. You're learning to read it now."

0200	38	00	EEG--STAGE 1 SLEEP/REM
0200	39	00	EEG--STAGE 1 SLEEP/REM
0200	40	00	EEG--STAGE 1 SLEEP/REM
0200	41	00	EEG--ALPHA WAVES
0200	42	00	EEG--STAGE 1 SLEEP/REM
0200	43	00	EEG--ALPHA WAVES
0200	44	00	EEG--STAGE 1 SLEEP/REM
0200	45	00	EEG--STAGE 1 SLEEP/REM
0200	46	00	EEG--STAGE 2 SLEEP
0200	47	00	EEG--STAGE 2 SLEEP
0200	48	00	EEG--STAGE 1 SLEEP/REM
0200	49	00	EEG--ALPHA WAVES
0200	50	00	EEG--STAGE 1 SLEEP/REM
0200	51	00	EEG--STAGE 1 SLEEP/REM
0200	52	00	EEG--ALPHA WAVES
0200	53	00	EEG--STAGE 1 SLEEP/REM
0200	54	00	EEG--STAGE 1 SLEEP/REM
0200	55	00	EEG--ALPHA WAVES
0200	56	00	EEG--STAGE 1 SLEEP/REM
0200	57	00	EEG--ALPHA WAVES
0200	58	00	EEG--ALPHA WAVES
0200	59	00	EEG--ALPHA WAVES
0300	00	00	EEG--ALPHA WAVES
0300	01	00	EEG--ALPHA WAVES
0300	02	00	EEG--NO READING
0300	03	00	EEG--NO READING
0300	04	00	EEG--NO READING
0300	05	00	EEG--NO READING

LIFE SIGNS NEGATIVE

LIFE SIGNS NEGATIVE

LIFE SIGNS NEGATIVE

PATIENT DECEASED

↓

```
END PRINT

END PROGRAM

::STOP::
```

Dawson let out his breath somewhat explosively; as if he had been holding it for the past minute. "He was a good man. May he rest in peace."

"There at the end," the general said, "there were five consecutive alpha wave readings. Does that mean he was fully awake for five minutes before he died?"

"Fully awake," Salsbury said. "But not rational."

"I thought you said he died in his sleep."

"No. I said he died in bed."

"What happened in those five minutes?"

"I'll show you," Salsbury said. He went to the nearest computer console and briefly used the keyboard.

All but two of the overhead scanners went dark. One of these was an ordinary television screen controlled by the computer on a closed-circuit arrangement. The other was a cathode-ray readout tube.

Getting up from the keyboard, Salsbury said, "The screen on the right will run a videotape of the last six minutes of Kingman's life. The screen on the left will provide a synchronized read-out of some of his vital life signs, updating them every thirty seconds."

Dawson and Klinger moved closer.

The right-hand screen flickered. A sharply focused black-and-white picture appeared on it: Brian Kingman lying atop his covers, on his back, twelve data-gathering patches cemented to his head and torso, wires trailing from the patches to two machines at the side of the bed. A sphygmomanometer was attached to his right arm and wired directly to the smaller of the machines. Kingman glistened with perspiration. He was trembling. Every few seconds one of his arms would jerk up defensively, or one of his legs would kick out at the air. In spite of this movement, his eyes were closed, and he was asleep.

"He's in stage one now," Salsbury said.

"Dreaming," Dawson said.

"Obviously."

At the top of the left-hand screen there was a digital clock that broke down the time count into hours, minutes, seconds, and tenths of seconds. On the soft green background below the clock, white computer-generated characters reported on four of Kingman's most important life signs.

BK/OB REP 14, ONGOING, AS FOLLOWS:

TEST	NORMAL FOR THIS SUBJECT	VALUE
TEMPERATURE	98.6	98.6
RESPIRATION	18 PER MIN	22 PER MIN
PULSE	70 PER MIN	90 PER MIN
BLOOD PRESSURE		
SYSTOLIC	100-120	110
DIASTOLIC	60-70	70

"He's still asleep," Salsbury said. "But his respiration and pulse have picked up approximately twenty-five percent. He appears to be having a bad dream. His thrashing about gets worse in just a moment. He's ready to come out of it now. Ready to wake up. Watch closely. There!"

On the black-and-white screen, Kingman suddenly drew up his knees, kicked out with both feet, drew up his knees again, and kept them drawn up, almost to his chest. He gripped his head with both hands, rolled his eyes, opened his mouth.

"He's screaming now," Salsbury said. "I'm sorry there's no audio."

"What's he screaming at?" Dawson asked. "He's awake now. The nightmare's over."

"Wait," Salsbury said.

"His respiration and pulse are soaring," Klinger said.

Kingman screamed soundlessly.

0200 58 00

"Look how his chest is heaving," Dawson said. "Good God, his lungs will burst!"

Writhing continuously but a degree less violently than he had been a moment ago, Kingman began to chew on his lower lip. In seconds his chin was covered with blood.

"An epileptic seizure?" the general asked.

Salsbury said, "No."

At 2:59, the left-hand screen began a new line print from the top of the tube:

TEST	NORMAL FOR THIS SUBJECT	VALUE
TEMPERATURE	98.6	98.8
RESPIRATION	18 PER MIN	48 PER MIN
PULSE	70 PER MIN	190 PER MIN
BLOOD PRESSURE		
SYSTOLIC	CANCEL CANCEL CANCEL CANCEL CANCEL CANCEL	

CANCEL CANCEL CANCEL

On the black-and-white screen, Kingman convulsed and was almost perfectly still. His feet twitched, and his right hand opened and closed, opened and closed; but otherwise he was motionless. Even his eyes had stopped rolling; they were squeezed tightly shut.

The read-out screen went blank, then an instant later flashed an emergency message.

        0200   59   12

        MASSIVE MYOCARDIAL INFARCTION

        MASSIVE MYOCARDIAL INFARCTION

"Heart attack," Salsbury said.
Kingman's left arm was bent in a V across his chest and seemed to be paralyzed. His left hand was fisted and unmoving against his neck.

        0300   00   00

        PULSE IRREGULAR

        RESPIRATION IRREGULAR

Kingman's eyes were open now. He was staring at the ceiling.
"He's screaming again," Klinger said.
"Trying to scream," Salsbury said. "I doubt if he could manage more than a croak in his present state."

        0300   01   00

        PULSE ERRATIC

        RESPIRATION ERRATIC

        EEG WAVES DETERIORATING TO DELTA

Kingman's feet stopped kicking.
His right hand stopped opening and closing.

He stopped trying to scream.

"It's over," Salsbury said.

Simultaneously, the two screens went blank.

Brian Kingman had died again.

"But what killed him?" Dawson's handsome face was the color of dusting powder. "The drug?"

"Not the drug," Salsbury said. "Fear."

Klinger returned to the autopsy table to have a look at the body. "Fear. I thought that's what you were going to say."

"Sudden, powerful fear *can* kill," Salsbury said. "And in this case, that's where all the evidence points. Of course, I'll do a thorough autopsy. But I don't believe I'll find any physiological cause for the heart attack."

Squeezing Salsbury's shoulder, Dawson said, "Do you mean Brian realized, in his sleep, that we were on the verge of taking control of him? And that he was so terrified of being controlled that the thought killed him?"

"Something like that."

"Then even if the drug works—the subliminals don't."

"Oh, they'll work," Salsbury said. "I've just got to refine the program."

"Refine?"

"I'll put it in lay terms as best I can. You see, to implant the key-lock subliminals, I've got to—to bore a hole through the id and the ego. Apparently, the first program was too crude. It didn't just bore a hole. It shattered the id and ego altogether, or very nearly did. I've got to be more subtle the next time, preface the commands with some careful persuasion." He pushed a wheeled instrument cart to the side of the autopsy table.

Not wholly satisfied with Salsbury's explanation, Dawson said, "But what if you don't refine it quite enough? What if the next test subject dies? It's conceivable that one member of my personal staff might walk off his job, vanish without a trace. But two? Or three? Impossible!"

Salsbury opened a drawer in the cart. He took out a thick white linen towel and spread it across the top of the car. "We won't use anyone from your staff for the second test."

"Where else are we going to get a test subject?"

Salsbury took surgical instruments, one at a time, from the drawer and lined them up on the linen. "I think the time has come to put together that corporation in Liechtenstein. Hire three mercenaries, give them sets of forged papers, and bring them here from Europe under their new names.''

"To this house?" Dawson asked.

"That's right. We won't need the walled estate in Germany or France for some time yet. We'll give the drug to all three of them the first day they're here. The second day, I'll start the new key-lock program with one of them. If it works with him, if it doesn't kill him, then I'll use it on the other two. Eventually, we'll be running the field test in this country. When the time comes for that, we'll be happy to have two or three well-trained submissive men so close at hand."

Scowling, Dawson said, "Hiring lawyers in Vaduz, establishing the corporation, buying the forged papers, hiring the mercenaries, bringing them here . . . these are expenditures I didn't want to make until we were certain the drug and subliminals will work as you say."

"They will."

"We aren't yet *certain*."

Holding a scalpel to the light, studying the silhouette of its razored edge, Salsbury said, "I'm sure the money won't come out of your pocket, Leonard. You'll find some way to squeeze it from the corporation."

"It's not as easy as all that, I assure you. Futurex isn't a private game park, you know. It's a public corporation. I can't raid the treasury at will."

"You're supposed to be a billionaire," Salsbury said. "In the great tradition of Onassis, Getty, Hughes . . . Futurex isn't the only thing you've got your hand in. Somewhere, you found more than two million dollars to set up this lab. And every month you manage to come up with the eighty thousand dollars needed to maintain it. By comparison, this new expense is a trifle."

"I agree," the general said.

"It's not your money that's going down a rat hole," Dawson said irritably.

"If you think the project's a rat hole," Salsbury said, "then we should call it off right now."

Dawson started to pace, stopped after a few steps, put his hands in his trouser pockets, and took them right out again. "It's these men that bother me."

"What men?"

"These mercenaries."

"What about them?"

"They're nothing but killers."

"Of course."

"*Professional* killers. They earn their living by—by murdering people."

"I've never had much of anything good to say about free-lancers," Klinger said. "But that's a simplification, Leonard."

"It's essentially true."

Impatiently, Salsbury said, "So what if it is?"

"Well, I don't like the idea of having them in my home," Dawson said. His tone was almost prissy.

You hypocritical ass, Salsbury thought. He didn't have the nerve to say it. His confidence had increased over the past year—but not enough to enable him to speak so frankly to Dawson.

Klinger said, "Leonard, how in the hell do you think we'd fare with the police and the courts if they found out how Kingman died? Would they just pat us on the head and send us away with a scolding? Do you think that just because we didn't strangle or shoot or stab him, they'd hesitate to call us killers? Do you think we'd get off scot-free because, although we're killers, we don't earn our living that way?"

For an instant Dawson's black eyes, like onyx mirrors, caught the cold fluorescent light and gleamed unnaturally. Then he turned his head a fraction of an inch, and the effect was lost. However, something of the same frigid, alien quality remained in his voice. "I never touched Brian. I never laid a finger on him. I never said an unkind word to him."

Neither Salsbury nor Klinger responded.

"I didn't want him to die."

They waited.

Dawson wiped one hand across his face. "Very well. I'll move ahead in Liechtenstein. I'll get those three mercenaries for you."

"How soon?" Salsbury asked.

"If I'm to maintain secrecy every step of the way—three months. Maybe four."

Salsbury nodded and continued laying out surgical instruments for the autopsy.

7.

Monday, August 22, 1977

AT NINE O'CLOCK Monday morning, Jenny came to visit the Annendale camp, and she brought with her a sturdy, yard-high canary cage.

Mark laughed when he saw her carrying it out of the woods. "What's *that* for?"

"A guest should always bring a gift," she said.

"What will we do with it?"

She put it in the boy's hands as Paul kissed her on the cheek.

Mark grinned at her through the slender, gilded bars.

"You said you wanted to bring your squirrel to town this coming Friday. Well, you can't let him loose in the car. This will be his travel cage."

"He won't like being penned up."

"Not at first. But he'll get used to it."

"He'll have to get used to it sooner or later if he's going to be your pet," Paul said.

Rya nudged her brother and said, "For God's sake, Mark, aren't you going to say thank you? Jenny probably looked all over town for that."

The boy blushed. "Oh, sure. Thanks. Thanks a lot, Jenny."

"Rya, you'll notice there's a small brown bag in the bottom of the cage. That's for you."

The girl tore open the bag and smiled when she saw the three paperback books. "Some of my favorite authors. And I don't have any of these! Thanks, Jenny."

Most eleven-year-old girls liked to read nurse novels, romances, perhaps Barbara Cartland or Mary Roberts Rinehart. But Jenny would have made a serious mistake if she had brought anything of that sort for Rya. Instead: one Louis L'Amour western, one collection of horror stories, and one adventure novel by Alistair MacLean. Rya wasn't a classic tomboy—but she sure as hell wasn't like most other eleven-year-old girls, either.

Both of these children were special. That was why, although she had no particular affection for children in general, she had fallen for them so quickly. She loved them every bit as much as she loved Paul.

Oh, yeah? she thought, catching herself in the admission. You're just brimming with love for Paul, aren't you?

Enough of that.

Love, is it? Then why don't you accept his proposal?

Enough.

Why won't you marry him?

Well, because—

She forced herself to stop arguing with herself. People who indulged in extended interior dialogues, she thought, were candidates for schizophrenia.

For a while the four of them fed the squirrel, which Mark had named Buster, and watched its antics. The boy regaled them with his plans for training the animal. He intended to teach Buster to roll over and play dead, to heel when told, to beg for his supper, and to fetch a stick. No one had the heart to tell him how unlikely it was that a squirrel could ever be made to do any of those things. Jenny wanted to laugh and grab him and hug him—but she only nodded and agreed with him whenever he asked for her opinion.

Later they played a game of tag and several games of badminton.

At eleven o'clock Rya said, "I've got an announcement to make. Mark and I planned lunch. We're going to do all of the cooking ourselves. And we really have some special dishes to make. Don't we, Mark?"

"Yeah, we sure do. My favorite is—"

"Mark!" Rya said quickly. "It's a *surprise.*"

"Yeah," he said, as if he hadn't almost given away everything. "That's right. It's a surprise."

Tucking her long black hair behind her ears, Rya turned to her father and said, "Why don't you and Jenny take a nice long walk up the mountain? There are lots and lots of easy deer trails. You should work up an appetite."

"I've already worked up one by playing badminton," Paul said.

Rya made a face. "I don't want you to see what we're cooking."

"Okay. We'll sit over there with our backs to you."

Rya shook her head: no. She was adamant. "You'll still smell it cooking. There won't be any surprise."

"The wind isn't blowing that way," Paul said. "Cooking odors won't carry far."

Anxiously twisting her badminton racket in her hands, Rya glanced at Jenny.

What a lot of schemes and calculations are whirling around behind those innocent blue eyes of yours, Jenny thought. She was beginning to understand what the girl wanted.

With characteristic bluntness, Mark said, "You got to go for a walk with Jenny, Dad. We know the two of you want to be alone."

"Mark, for God's sake!" Rya was aghast.

"Well," the boy said defensively, "that's why we're making lunch, isn't it? To give them a chance to be alone?"

Jenny laughed.

"I'll be damned," Paul said.

Rya said, "I think I'll cook squirrel for lunch."

A look of horror passed across Mark's face. "That's a terrible, rotten thing to say!"

"I didn't mean it."

"It's still rotten."

"I apologize."

Looking at her out of the corner of his eye, as if he were trying to assess her sincerity, Mark finally said, "Well, okay."

Taking Paul's hand, Jenny said, "If we don't go for a walk, your daughter's going to be very upset. And when your daughter is very upset, she's a dangerous girl."

Grinning, Rya said, "That's true. I'm a terror."

"Jenny and I are going for a walk," Paul said. He leaned toward Rya. "But tonight I'll tell you the shocking story of the hideous fate that befell a conniving child."

"Oh, good!" Rya said. "I like bedtime stories. Lunch will be served at one o'clock." She turned away and, as if she sensed Paul swinging his badminton racket at her backside, jumped to the left and ran into the tent.

The stream gushed noisily around a boulder, surged between banks lined with scrub birch and laurel, descended several rocky shelves, and formed a wide, deep pool at the end of the hollow before racing on to spill down the next step of the mountain. There were fish in the pool: darker shapes gliding in dark water. The surrounding clearing was sheltered by full-sized birches and one gargantuan oak with exposed and twisted roots, like tentacles, thrusting into the leaf mulch and black earth. The ground between the base of the oak and the pool was covered with moss so thick that it made a comfortable mattress for lovers.

Half an hour above the camp and the meadow where they had played badminton, they stopped beside the pool to rest. She stretched out on her back, her hands behind her head. He lay beside her.

She didn't know quite how it had happened, but the conversation had eventually given way to a gentle exchange of kisses. Caresses. Murmurs. He held her to him, his hands on her buttocks, his face in her hair, and licked lightly at her earlobe.

Suddenly she became the bolder of the two. She rubbed one hand across the crotch of his jeans, felt him swelling beneath the denim.

"I want that," she said.

"I want you."

"Then we can both have what we want."

When they were naked, he began to kiss her breasts. He licked her stiffening nipples.

"I want you *now*," she said. "Quickly. We can take longer the second time."

They responded to each other with a powerful, unique, and utterly unexpected sensitivity that neither of them had ever quite achieved before. The pleasure was more than intense. It was very nearly excruciating for her, and she could see that it was much the same for him. Perhaps this was because they had wanted each other so fiercely but had not been together for so long, since March. If absence makes the heart grow fonder, she thought, does it also make the genitals grow randier? Or perhaps this electrifying pleasure was a response to the setting, to the wild land's sounds and odors and textures. Whatever the reason, he needed no lubrication to penetrate her. He slid deep with one fluid thrust and rocked in and out of her, down and down, filling her, tight within her, moving her. She was transfixed by the sight of his arms: the muscles bulged, each well defined, as he supported himself over her. She reached for his buttocks, hard as stone, and pulled him farther into her with each galvanizing stroke. Although she rapidly came into her climax, she coasted down from it so slowly that she wondered if there would be an end to it. Abruptly, when the sensations in her had subsided, he grew still, pinned by the power of his own orgasm. He softly said her name.

Shrinking within her, he kissed her breasts and lips and forehead. Then he rolled off her, onto his side.

She moved against him, belly to belly, and put her lips against the throbbing artery in his neck.

He held her, and she held him. The act that they had just completed seemed to bind them; the memory of joy was an invisible umbilical.

For a few minutes she was not at all aware of the world beyond his shadow. She couldn't hear anything except the beat of her own heart and the heavy drawing of breath from both of them. In time the voices of the mountains filtered back to her: leaves rustling overhead, the stream splashing down the slope into the pool, birds calling to one another in the trees. Likewise, at first she couldn't feel anything but the slight ache in her chest and Paul's warm semen trickling out of her. Gradually, however, she realized that the day was hot and humid, and that their embrace had become less romantic than sticky.

Reluctantly, she disentangled herself from him and rolled onto her back. A sheen of perspiration filmed her breasts and stomach.

She said, "Incredible."

"Incredible."

Neither of them was ready to say more than that.

The breeze had almost dried them when he finally raised up on one elbow and looked down at her. "You know something?"

"What's that?"

"I've never known another woman who was able to enjoy herself as thoroughly as you do."

"Sex, you mean?"

"Sex, I mean."

"Annie enjoyed it."

"Sure. We had a fine marriage. But she didn't enjoy it quite like you do. You put everything you've got into it. You're not aware of anything but your body and mine when we make love. You're consumed by it."

"I can't help it if I'm horny."

"You're more than horny."

"Oversexed, then."

"It's not just sex," he said.

"You're not going to tell me that you like my mind too."

"That's precisely what I'm going to tell you. You enjoy everything. I've seen you savor a glass of water like some people do good wine." He drew a finger down the line between her breasts. "You've got a lust for life."

"Me and Van Gogh."

"I'm serious."

She thought about it. "A friend at college used to say the same thing."

"You see?"

"If it's true," she said, "the credit belongs to my father."

"Oh?"

"He gave me such a happy childhood."

"Your mother died when you were a child."

She nodded. "But she went in her sleep. A cerebral hemorrhage. One day she was there—gone the next. I never saw her in pain, and that makes a difference to a child."

"You grieved. I'm sure you did."

"For a while. But my father worked hard to bring me out of it. He was full of jokes and games and stories and presents, twenty-four hours a day, seven days a week. He worked just like you did to make your kids forget Annie's death."

"If I could have been as successful at that as Sam evidently was with you—"

"Maybe he was too successful," she said.

"How could that be?"

Sighing, she said, "Sometimes I think he should have spent less time making my childhood happy and more time preparing me for the real world."

"Oh, I don't know about that. Happiness is a rare commodity in this life. Don't knock it. Grab every minute of it that's offered to you, and don't look back."

She shook her head, unconvinced. "I was too naïve. A regular Pollyanna. Right up through my wedding day."

"A bad marriage can happen to anybody, wise or innocent."

"Certainly. But the wise aren't shattered by it."

His hand moved in lazy circles on her belly.

She liked the way he touched her. Already, she wanted him again.

He said, "If you can analyze yourself this way, you can overcome your hangups. You can forget the past."

"Oh, I can forget him all right. My husband. No trouble, given time. And not much time at that."

"Well then?"

"I'm not innocent anymore. God knows, I'm not. But naïve? I'm not sure a person can become a cynic overnight. Or even a realist."

"We'd be perfect together," he said, touching her breasts. "I'm certain of it."

"At times I'm certain of it too. And that's what I distrust about it—the certainty."

"Marry me," he said.

"How did we get around to this again?"

"I asked you to marry me."

"I don't want to be set up for another fall."

"I'm not setting you up."

"Not intentionally."

"You can't live without taking risks."

"I can try."

"It'll be a lonely life."

She made a face at him. "Let's not spoil the day."

"It's not spoiled for me."

"Well, it will be for me soon, if we don't change the subject."

"What could we talk about that's more important than this?"

She grinned. "You seem fascinated with my tits. Want to talk about those?"

"Jenny, be serious."

"I am being serious. I think my tits are fascinating. I could spend hours talking about them."

"You're impossible."

"Okay, okay. If you don't want to talk about my tits, we won't talk about them, lovely as they are. Instead—we'll talk about your prick."

"Jenny—"

"I'd like to taste it."

As she spoke she soft center of him swelled and grew hard.

"Defeated by biology," she said.

"You're a minx."

She laughed and started to sit up.

He pushed her back.

"I want to taste it," she said.

"Later."

"Now."

"I want to get you off first."

"And do you always get your way?"

"I will this time. I'm bigger than you."

"Male chauvinist."

"If you say so." He kissed her nipples, shoulders, hands, her navel and thighs. He rubbed his nose gently back and forth in the crinkled hair at the base of her belly.

A shiver passed through her. She said, "You're right. A woman should have her pleasure first."

He lifted his head and smiled at her. He had a charming, almost boyish smile. His eyes were so clear, so blue, and so warm that she felt as if she were being absorbed by them.

What a delightful man you are, she thought as the voices of the mountain faded away and her heartbeat replaced them. So beautiful, so desirable, so tender for a man. So very tender.

The house was on Union Road, one block from the town square. A white frame bungalow. Nicely kept. Windows trimmed in green with matching shutters. Railed front porch with bench swing and glider and bright green floor. Lattice-work festooned with ivy at one end of the porch, a wall of lilac bushes at the other end. Brick walkway with borders of marigolds on each side. A white ceramic birdbath ringed with petunias. According to the sign that hung on a decorative lamppost at the end of the walk, the house belonged to "The Macklins."

At one o'clock that afternoon, Salsbury climbed the three steps to the porch. He was carrying a clipboard with a dozen sheets of paper fixed to it. He rang the bell.

Bees hummed in the lilac leaves.

The woman who opened the door surprised him. Perhaps because of the flowers that had been planted everywhere and because of the pristine condition of the property that seemed the work of a singularly fussy person, he had expected the Macklins to be an elderly couple. A skinny pair who liked to putter in their gardens, who had no grandchildren to spend their time with, who would stare suspiciously at him over the rims of their bifocals. However, the woman who answered the bell was in her middle twenties, a slender blonde with the kind of face that looked good in magazine advertisements for cosmetics. She was tall, five eight or nine, not delicate but feminine, as leggy as a chorus girl. She was wearing dark blue shorts and a blue-and-white polka-dot halter top. Even through the screen door, he could see that her body was well proportioned, firm, resilient, better than any he had ever touched.

As usual, confronted with a woman like one of those who had peopled his fantasies all of his adult life, he was unsettled. He stared at her and licked his lips and couldn't think of a damned thing to say.

"Can I help you?"

He cleared his throat. "My name's—Albert Deighton. I've been in town since last Friday. I don't know if you heard . . . I'm doing some research. Sociological research. I've been talking to people—"

"I know," she said. "You were next door at the Solo-man's yesterday afternoon."

"That's right." Although the sun was hot and the air heavy, he hadn't perspired during any of the first three interviews of the day; but now he felt beads of sweat spring up on his forehead. "I'd like to talk with you and Mr. Macklin, if you can spare me the time. Half an hour ought to be enough. There are about a hundred questions—"

"I'm sorry," she said. "My husband isn't home. He works up at the mill on the day shift. He won't be home till five thirty."

He looked at his clipboard for something to do. "I can always catch him some other time. If I could interview you and the children now, get that out of the way—"

"Oh, we've only been married a year. We haven't any kids."

"Newlyweds."

"Just about." She smiled. She had dimples.

He felt as if he were being dragged along in a dangerous current, swept inexorably toward a decision that could destroy him. "Is there anyone else living here? A relative?"

"Just Richie and me."

"Richie's your husband?"

"That's right."

Last Friday, in Ultman's Cafe, he had risked exposing the entire project by using the code phrase to play with that waitress who looked like Miriam. He had gotten away with it, but he knew he was a fool to allow his emotions to overwhelm him like that. As penance for his behavior, he was far more cautious on Saturday and Sunday than he needed to be. He used the code phrase two dozen times, interviewing the subjects in detail, searching for weak spots in their obedient mode; but he never approached one of them if there was the slimmest chance of discovery. Some of the women had been attractive, and he could have used them any way he wanted. But he had restrained himself. Having tasted total dominance when he opened Alice, that bitch waitress, with the code, he was anxious to make one of them undress and get down on the floor before him. Damned anxious. And this one, standing there in shorts and halter, seemed to radiate heat that evaporated his will power and his caution. He wanted to believe that, unlike the episode at the café, this situation contained no threat; and wanting to believe was the first step toward convincing himself.

"I am the key."

"I am the lock."

Relieved, he wiped his brow. "Are you alone?"

"Yes."

He began to tremble, not with fear but with excitement.

"Are you expecting anyone?"

"No. No one."

"Is anyone expecting you? Were you planning to go visiting?"

"No."

"Let me in."

She pushed open the screen door.

He stepped past her into the air-conditioned foyer. There was an oval mirror and accessory table on the right, a small painting of a storm-tossed sailing ship on his left. "Close the door. And lock it."

She did as she was told.

A short corridor, containing two more paintings of sailing ships, led from the foyer to the kitchen.

On the left the living room opened to the hall through an archway. It was neatly furnished. An oriental carpet. Two crushed velvet sofas and a slate-topped coffee table arranged to form a conversation corner. Matching crushed-velvet drapes at the three windows. A magazine rack. A gun case. Two Stiffel lamps. To harmonize with the carpet, the paintings were of Western sailing ships docked in Chinese harbors.

"Draw the drapes," he said.

She went from window to window, then came back to the center of the room. She stood with her hands at her sides, staring at him, a half-smile on her face.

She was waiting. Waiting for orders. His orders. She was his puppet, his slave.

For more than a minute he stood in the archway, unable to move, unable to decide what he should do next. Immobilized by fear, anticipation, and the grip of lust that made his groin ache almost unpleasantly, he was nevertheless sweating as if he had just run the mile. She was *his*. Entirely his: her mouth, breasts, ass, legs, cunt, every inch and fold of her. Better than that, there was no need for him to worry about whether or not he pleased her. The only consideration was his own pleasure. If he told her that she loved it, she would love it. No complaints afterward. No recriminations. Just the act— and then to hell with her. Here, ready for the first time to *use* a woman exactly as he wanted, he found the reality more exhilarating than the dreams he'd had so many years to elaborate upon.

She regarded him quizzically. "Is that all?"

"No." His voice was hoarse.

"What do you want?"

He went to the nearest lamp, switched it on, and sat down on one of the sofas. "You stand where you are," he said. "Answer my questions and do what I say."

"All right."

"What's your name?"

"Brenda."

"How old are you, Brenda?"

"Twenty-six."

He took his handkerchief from his hip pocket, wiped his face. He looked at the paintings of sailing ships. "Your husband likes the sea?"

"No."

"Then he likes *paintings* of the sea."

"No. He doesn't care for them."

He had only been talking to pass time while he decided how he wanted to proceed with her. Now, her unexpected answer confused him. "Then why the hell do you have all these paintings?"

"I was born and raised in Cape Cod. I love the sea."

"But he doesn't care for it. Why does he let you hang these damned things everywhere?"

"He knows I like them," she said.

He wiped his face again, put the handkerchief away. "He knows if he took them off the wall, you'd freeze him out of bed. Wouldn't you, Brenda?"

"Of course not."

"You know would, you little bitch. You're a pretty little piece. He'd do anything to keep you happy. Any man would. Men have been running to do your bidding since you were old enough to fuck. You snap your fingers, and they dance. Don't they?"

Puzzled, she shook her head. "Dance? No."

He laughed bitterly. "A game of semantics. You know I didn't really mean 'dance.' You're like all the others. You're a bitch, Brenda."

She squinted. Frowned.

"I say you're a bitch. Am I right?"

Her frown vanished. "Yes."

"I'm always right. Isn't that true?"

"Yes. You're always right."

"What am I?"

"You're the key."

"What are you?"

"I'm the lock."

He was feeling better by the minute. Not so tense as he had been. Not so jittery. Calm. In control. As he'd never been. He pushed his glasses up on his nose. "You'd like me to strip you naked and screw you. Wouldn't you like that, Brenda?"

She hesitated.

"You'd like it," he said.

"I'd like it."

"You'd *love* it."

"I'd love it."

"Take off your halter."

Reaching behind her back, she slipped the knot, and the polka-dot cloth fell to her feet. The flesh beneath was white, in stark and erotic contrast to her dark tan. Her breasts were neither large nor small, but exquisitely curved, upthrust. A few freckles. Pink nipples not much darker than her untanned skin. She kicked the halter out of her way.

"Touch them," he said.

"My breasts?"

"Squeeze them. Pull on the nipples." He watched, found her movements too mechanical, and said, "You're horny, Brenda. You want to be fucked. You can't wait to have me. You need it. You want it. You want it more than you've ever wanted it in your life. You're almost sick with wanting it."

As she continued to caress herself, her nipples swelled and turned a darker shade of pink. She was breathing heavily.

He giggled. He couldn't suppress it. He felt terrific. So terrific. "Take off your shorts."

She did.

"And your panties. You're a real blonde, I see. Now, put one hand between those pretty legs. Finger yourself. That's it. That's good. That's a good girl."

Standing, her feet wide apart, masturbating, she was a stunning sight. She threw back her head, golden hair trailing like a banner, mouth open, face slack. She was gasping for breath. Shivering. Twitching. Moaning. With her free hand, she was still caressing her breasts.

The power. Good God, the power he had over them now, would always have over them, from this day forward! He could come into their homes, into their most sacred and private places, and once inside do whatever he wished with them. And not just with the women. Men too. If he ordered it of them, the men would mewl and crawl to him on their hands and knees. They would beg him to screw their wives. They'd give him their daughters, their girl children. They wouldn't deny him any experience, however extravagant or outrageous. He would demand every thrill, and he would enjoy each of them. But on the whole, he would be a benign ruler, a benevolent dictator, more like a father than a jailer. No jackboots in their faces. He laughed at that last thought. Ten years ago, when he was still conducting lecture tours and writing about the future of behavior modification and mind control, he was subjected to extensive ridicule and vehement condemnation from some members of the academic community. In lecture halls, all but forcibly detained at the end of his speeches, he had listened to countless self-righteous bores droning through homilies about invasion of privacy and the sanctity of the human mind. They quoted hundreds of great thinkers, epigrams by the score—some of which he remembered to this day. There was one about the future of mankind amounting to little more than a jackboot in the face. Well, that was crap. Jackboots, and the cruel authoritarian state they symbolized, were only a means of keeping the masses in line. Now, with his drug and the key-lock program, jackboots had become obsolete. No one would have a jackboot pushed in his face. Of course, for selected women, he had something else to push in their faces. Massaging himself through his trousers, he laughed. The power. The sweet, sweet power.

"Brenda."

Shuddering, gasping, her knees bending slightly, she climaxed as her index finger worked industriously between her legs.

"Brenda."

At last she looked up at him. She was beginning to perspire. Her hair was dark and damp at the brow.

He said, "Go to that sofa. Kneel on it with your back to me, and brace your arms against the pillows."

When she was in position, her white butt thrust up at him, she looked over her shoulder. "Hurry. Please."

Laughing, he shoved the coffee table out of the way, sent it sliding off the carpet, across the hardwood floor and into the magazine rack. He stood behind her, dropped his trousers and his yellow-striped shorts. He was ready, the veins about to burst, hard as iron, bigger than he'd ever been, big as a stallion's gun, a horse cock. And red. So red it looked as if it had been smeared with blood. He ran one hand over her buttocks, over the golden hairs on her back, along her side, under to the swinging breast, pinched the nipple, smoothed her flank, pinched her ass, slipped his fingers between her thighs, to her pubes. She was wet, dripping, far more ready than he was. He could even smell her. Giggling, he said, "You're a bitch in more ways than one. A regular little bitch dog. A little animal. Aren't you, Brenda?"

"Yes."

"Say you're a little animal."

"I am. I'm a little animal."

The power.

"What do you want, Brenda?"

"I want you to screw me."

"Do you?"

"Yes."

"How bad do you want it?"

"Real bad."

Sweet, sweet power.

"What do you want?"

"You *know!*"

"Do I?"

"I already *said!*"

"Say it again."

"You're humiliating me."

"I haven't even begun."

"Oh, God."

"Listen to me, Brenda."

"What?"

"Your cunt's getting hotter."

She groaned softly. Shuddered.

"Feel it, Brenda?"

"Yes."

"Hotter and hotter."

"I don't— I can't—"

"You can't stand it?"

"So hot. Almost hurts."

He smiled. "Now what do you want?"

"I want you to screw me."

See, Miriam? I am somebody.

"What are you, Brenda?"

"I am the lock."

"What else are you?"

"A bitch."

"I can't hear it often enough."

"A bitch."

"In heat?"

"Yes, yes. *Please!*"

Poised to enter her, dizzy with excitement, demoniac, electrified by the power he held, Salsbury had no illusions that his orgasm, deep within the silken regions of this woman, was the most important aspect of the rape. The spasmed outpouring of a tablespoon or two of semen was only the punctuation at the end of the sentence, at the conclusion of his declaration of independence. During the past half hour, he had proved himself, had freed himself from the dozens of bitches who had messed in his life all the way back to and including his mother, especially his mother, that goddess of bitches, that empress of ball-breakers. After her came the girls who were frigid and the girls who laughed at him and the girls who whined about his poor technique and the girls who rejected him with unconcealed distaste and Miriam and the contemptible whores to whom he had been forced to resort in later years. Brenda Macklin was only a metaphor, written into his life by chance. If it hadn't been her, it would have been someone else this afternoon or tomorrow or the day after tomorrow. She was the voodoo doll, the totem with which he would exorcise some of those bitches from his past. Each inch of prick he jammed into her was a blow to the Brendas of years gone by. Each stroke—the more brutal it was the better—was an announcement of his triumph. He would pound her. Bruise her. Use her until she was raw. Hurt her. With every blade of pain he sent through her, he would be cutting each of those hated women. By mounting this lean blond animal, by battering relentlessly into her, tearing her apart, he would be proving his superiority to all of them.

He seized her hips and leaned close. But as the tip of his shaft touched her vagina, even before the head of it slipped into her, he ejaculated uncontrollably. His legs gave way. Crying out, he fell on her.

She collapsed against the pillows.

Panic took him. Memories of past failures. The sour looks they gave him afterwards. The contempt with which they treated him. The shame of it. He held Brenda down, weighed her down. Desperately, he said, "You're coming, girl. You're climaxing. Do you hear me? Do you understand? I'm telling you. You're coming."

She made a noise, muffled by pillows.

"Feel it?"

"Mmmmm."

"Do you feel it?"

Raising her head she said, "God, yes!"

"You've never had it better."

"Not ever. Never." She was gasping.

"Feel it?"

"Feel it."

"Is it hot?"

"So hot. *Oh!*"

"Coasting now. You're coming down."

She stopped squirming under him.

"Drifting down. It's almost over."

"So good . . ." Softly.

"You little animal."

With that the tension drained out of her.

The doorbell rang.

"What the hell?"

She didn't react.

Pushing away from her, he swayed to his feet, tried to take a step with his trousers around his ankles and almost fell. He grabbed his shorts, jerked them up, then his trousers. "You said you weren't expecting anyone."

"Wasn't."

"Then who's that?"

She rolled onto her back. She looked sated.

"Who's that?" he asked again.

"Don't know."

"For God's sake, get dressed."

She rose dreamily from the couch.

"*Quickly*, damn you!"

Obediently, she scuttled after her clothes.

At one of the front windows, he parted the drapes a fraction of an inch, just enough to see the porch. A woman was standing at the door, unaware that she was under observation. In sandals, white shorts, and a scoop-necked orange sweater, she was even better-looking than Brenda Macklin.

Brenda said, "I'm dressed."

The doorbell rang again.

Letting go of the drapery, Salsbury said, "It's a woman. You better answer it. But get rid of her. Whatever you do, don't let her inside."

"What should I say?"

"If it's someone you've never seen before, you don't have to say anything."

"Otherwise?"

"Tell her you've got a headache. A terrible migraine headache. Now *go*."

She went out of the room.

When he heard her open the door in the foyer, he parted the velvet again in time to see a smile touch the face of the woman in the orange sweater. She said something, and Brenda replied, and the smile was replaced by a look of concern. Filtered through the walls and windows, their voices were hardly more than whispers. He couldn't follow the conversation, but it seemed to go on forever.

Maybe you should have let her come inside, he thought. Use the code phrase on her. Then screw them both.

But what if you let her come in and then discover she's got a weak spot in her program?

Not much chance of that.

Or what if she's from out of town? A relative from Bexford, perhaps. Then what?

Then she'd have to be killed.

And how would you dispose of the body?

Under his breath he said, "Come on, Brenda, you bitch. Get rid of her."

Finally, the stranger turned away from the door. Salsbury had a brief glimpse of green eyes, ripe lips, a superb profile, extremely deep cleavage in the scoop-necked sweater. When she had her back to him and was going down the steps, he saw that her legs weren't just sexy, as Brenda's were, but sexy *and* elegant, even without nylons. Long, taut, smooth, scissoring legs, feminine muscles bunching and twisting and stretching and compacting and rippling sinuously with each step. An animal. A healthy animal. His animal. Like all of them now: his. At the end of the Macklin property, she turned left into the searing afternoon sun, distorted by waves of heat rising from the concrete sidewalk, soon out of sight.

Brenda came back into the living room.

When she started to sit down, he said, "Stand. The middle of the room."

She did that, her hands at her sides.

Returning to the sofa, he said, "What did you tell her?"

"That I had a migraine headache."

"She believed you?"

"I guess so."

"Did you know her?"

"Yes."

"Who was she?"

"My sister-in-law."

"She lives in Black River?"

"Has most all her life."

"Quite a looker."

"She was in the Miss USA contest."

"Oh? When was that?"

"Twelve, thirteen years ago."

"Still looks twenty-two."

"She's thirty-five."

"She win?"

"Came in third."

"Big disappointment, I'll bet."

"For Black River. She didn't mind."

"She didn't? Why not?"

"Nothing bothers her."

"Is that so?"

"She's that way. Always happy."

"What's her name?"

"Emma."

"Last name?"

"Thorp."

"Thorp? She married?"

"Yes."

He frowned. "To that cop?"

"He's the chief of police."

"Bob Thorp."

"That's right."

"What's she doing with him?"

She was baffled.

She blinked at him.

Cute little animal.

He swore he could still smell her.

She said, "What do you mean?"

"What I said. What's she doing with him?"

"Well . . . they're married."

"A woman like her with a big, dumb cop."

"He's not dumb," she said.

"Looks dumb to me." He thought about it for a moment, and then he smiled. "Your maiden name's Brenda Thorp."

"Yes."

"Bob Thorp's your brother."

"My oldest brother."

"Poor Bob." He leaned back in the sofa and folded his arms on his chest and laughed. "First I get to his kid sister—then I get to his wife."

She smiled uncertainly. Nervously.

"I'll have to be careful, won't I?"

"Careful?" she said.

"Bob may be dumb, but he's big as a bull."

"He isn't dumb," she insisted.

"In high school I dated a girl named Sophia."

She was silent. Confused.

"Sophia Brookman. God, I wanted her."

"Loved her?"

"Love's a lie. A myth. It's bullshit. I just wanted to screw her. But she dropped me after a few dates and started going with this other guy, Joey Duncan. You know what Joey Duncan did after high school?"

"How would I know?"

"He went to junior college."

"So did I."

"Took criminology for a year."

"I majored in history."

"He flunked out."

"Not me."

"Ended up with the home town police."

"Just like my brother."

"I went to Harvard."

"Did you really?"

"I was always a better dresser than Joey was. Besides that, he was as dull as a post. I was much wittier than he was. Joey didn't read anything but the jokes in *Reader's Digest*. I read *The New Yorker* every week."

"I don't like either one."

"In spite of all that, Sophia preferred him. But you know what?"

"What?"

"It was in *The New Yorker* that I first saw something about subliminal perception. Back in the fifties. An article, editorial, maybe a little snippet at the bottom of a column. I forget exactly what it was. But that's what got me started. Something in *The New Yorker*."

Brenda sighed. Fidgeted.

"Tired of standing?"

"A little."

"Are you bored?"

"Kind of."

"Bitch."

She looked at the floor.

"Get your clothes off."

The lovely power. He was filled with it, brimming with it—but it had changed. At first it had seemed to him like a steady, exhilarating current. Part of the time it was still like that, a soft humming inside of him, perhaps imagined but nevertheless electrifying, a river of power on which he sailed in complete command. But occasionally now, for short periods, it felt not like a constant flow but like a continuous and endless series of short, sharp bursts. The power like a submachine gun: *tat-tat-tat-tat-tat-tat-tat* . . . The rhythm of it affected him. His mind spun. Thoughts advanced, no thought finished, leaping from one thing to another: Joey Duncan, Harvard, key-lock, Miriam, his mother, dark-eyed Sophia, breasts, sex, Emma Thorp, bitches, Dawson, Brenda, his growing erection, his mother, Klinger, Brenda, cunt, the power, jackboots, Emma's legs—

"What now?"

She was naked.

He said, "Come here."

Little animal.

"Get down."

"On the floor?"

"On your knees."

She got down.

"Beautiful animal."

"You like me?"

"You'll do until."

"Until what?"

"Until I get your sister-in-law."

"Emma?"

"I'll make him watch."

"Who?"

"That dumb cop."

"He isn't dumb."

"Lovely ass. You're horny, Brenda."

"I'm getting hot. Like before."

"Of course you are. Hotter and hotter."

"I'm shaking."

"You want me more than you did before."

"Do it to me."

"Hotter and hotter."

"I'm—embarrassed."

"No. You aren't."

"Oh, God."

"Feel good?"

"So good."

"You don't look at all like Miriam."

"Who's Miriam?"

"The old bastard should see me now."

"Who? Miriam?"

"He'd be outraged. Quote the Bible."

"Who would?"

"Dawson. Probably can't even get it up."

"I'm scared," she said suddenly.

"Of what?"

"I don't know."

"Stop being scared. You aren't scared."

"Okay."

"Are you scared?"

She smiled. "No. You going to screw me?"

"Batter the hell out of you. Hot, aren't you?"

"Yes. Burning up. Do it. Now."

"Klinger and his damned chorus girls."

"Klinger?"

"Probably queer anyway."

"Are you going to do it?"

"Tear you up. Big as a horse."

"Yes. I want it. I'm hot."

"I think maybe Miriam was queer."
Tat-tat-tat-tat-tat-tat-tat-tat . . .

At five o'clock Monday afternoon, Buddy Pellineri, just
out of bed with seven hours to pass before he had to report to
work at the mill, went to Edison's store to see if any new
magazines had been put on the racks. His favorites were the
ones that had a lot of pictures in them: *People, Travel, Nevada, Arizona Highways, Vermont Life*, a few of the photography journals. He found two issues that he didn't have and
took them to the counter to pay for them.

Jenny was at the cash register. She was wearing a white
blouse with yellow flowers on it. Her long black hair looked
freshly washed, thick and shiny. "You look so pretty, Miss
Jenny."

"Why, thank you, Buddy."

He blushed and wished he had said nothing.

She said, "Is the world treating you right?"

"No complaints."

"I'm glad to hear it."

"How much I owe you?"

"Do you have two dollars?"

He thrust a hand into his pocket, came out with some
change and rumpled bills. "Sure. Here."

"You get three quarters in change," she said.

"I thought they cost more."

"Now, you know you get a discount here."

"I'll pay. Don't want special treatment."

"You're a close friend of the family," she said, shaking a
finger at him. "We give discounts to all close friends of the
family. Sam would be angry if you didn't accept that. You
put those quarters in your pocket."

"Well . . . thanks."

"You're welcome, Buddy."

"Is Sam here?"

She pointed to the curtained doorway. "Upstairs. He's getting dinner."

"I ought to tell him."

"Tell him what?" she asked.

"About this thing I saw."

"Can't you tell me?"

"Well . . . Better him."

"You may go up and see him, if you like."

The invitation frightened him. He was never comfortable in other people's houses. "You have cats up there?"

"Cats? No. No pets at all."

He knew she wouldn't lie to him—but then, cats turned up in the most unexpected places. Two weeks after his mother died, he was asked to visit the parsonage. Reverend Potter and Mrs. Potter had taken him straight to the parlor where she had served homemade cakes and cookies. He sat on the divan, knees together, hands in his lap. Mrs. Potter made hot chocolate. Reverend Potter poured for everyone. The two of them sat opposite Buddy in a pair of wing-backed chairs. For a while everything was so nice. He ate the gingerbread and the little cookies with red and green sugar on them and he drank the cocoa and smiled a lot and talked a little—and then a big white furry cat leaped over his shoulder, onto his lap, claws digging in for an instant, from his lap to the floor. He didn't even know they had a cat. Was that fair? Not to tell him? It had crept onto the window sill behind the divan. How long had it been there? All the while he ate? Paralyzed with fear, unable to speak, wanting to scream, he spilled his chocolate on the carpet and wet himself. Peed in his pants right on the preacher's brocade divan. What a stain. It was awful. An awful day. He never went back there again, and he stopped going to church as well, even if he might go to hell for that.

"Buddy?"

She startled him. "What?"

"Do you want to go upstairs and see Sam?"

Picking up his magazines, he said, "No. No. I'll tell him some time. Some other time. Not now." He started toward the door.

"Buddy?"

He glanced back.

"Is something wrong?" she asked.

"No." He forced a laugh. "No. Nothing. World's treating me okay." He hurried out of the store.

On the other side of Main Street, back in his two-room apartment, he went to the bathroom and peed, opened a bottle of Coca-Cola, and sat down at the kitchen table to look at his magazines. First thing, he paged through both of them, searching for articles about cats and pictures of cats and advertisements for cat food. He found two pages in each magazine that offended him, and he tore them out at once, regardless of what was on the backs of them. Methodically, he ripped each page into hundreds of tiny pieces and threw the resultant heap of confetti into the wastebasket. Only then was he prepared to relax and look at the pictures.

Halfway through the first magazine, he came across an article about a team of skin divers who were, it seemed to him, trying to uncover an ancient treasure ship. He couldn't read more than two words out of five, but he studied the pictures with great interest—and suddenly was reminded of what he had seen in the woods that night. Near the mill. When he was taking a pee. At a quarter of five in the morning, on the day he'd so carefully marked on his calendar. Skin divers. Coming down from the reservoir. Carrying flashlights. And guns. It was such a silly thing, he couldn't forget it. Such a funny . . . such a *scary* thing. They didn't *belong* where he had seen them. *They* hadn't been hunting for treasure, not at night, not up in the reservoir.

What *had* they been doing?

He'd thought about that for ever so long, but he simply couldn't figure it out. He wanted to ask someone to explain it, but he knew they'd laugh at him.

Last week, however, he realized that there was someone in Black River who would listen to him, who would believe him and wouldn't laugh no matter how silly the story was. Sam. Sam always had time for him, even before his mother died. Sam never made fun of him or talked down to him or hurt his feelings. Furthermore, so far as Buddy was concerned, Sam Edison was easily the smartest person in town. He knew just about everything; or Buddy thought he did. If there was anyone who could explain to him what he had seen, it was Sam.

On the other hand, he didn't want to look like a fool in Sam's eyes. He was determined to give himself every chance to work out the answer first. That was why he had delayed going to Sam since he had remembered him last Wednesday.

A while ago in the store, he finally was ready to let Sam take over his thinking for him. But Sam was upstairs, in rooms that were unfamiliar to Buddy, and that raised the question of cats.

Now he had more time to puzzle it out on his own. If Sam was in the store the next time Buddy went there, he would tell him the story. But not for a few days yet. He sat in the patterned late-afternoon sunlight that came through the curtain, drank Coca-Cola, and wondered.

8.

Eight Months Earlier:
Saturday, December 18, 1976

IN THE COMPUTER CENTER of the sealed wing of the Greenwich house, seven days before Christmas, the monitor boards and systems bulbs and cathode-ray tubes and glowing scopes, although they were mostly red and green, had not reminded Salsbury of the holiday.

When he entered the room, his first time there in months, Klinger looked around at the lights and said, "Very Christmasy."

Strangely enough, it *was* rather Christmasy.

However, because he hadn't perceived something which had registered with the general in mere seconds, Salsbury felt uneasy. For almost two years now, day and night, he had been telling himself that he must be quicker, sharper, more cunning, and more forward-thinking than either of his partners—if he was to keep his partners from eventually putting a bullet in his head and burying him at the southern end of the estate beside Brian Kingman. Which was surely what they had in mind for him. And for each other. Either that or slavery through the key-lock program. Therefore, it was quite disturbing to him that Klinger—hairy, flat-faced gorilla that he was—should make, of all things, an aesthetic observation before Salsbury himself had made it.

The only way he could deal with his own uneasiness was to put the general off his stride as quickly as possible. "You can't smoke in here. Put that out at once."

Rolling the cheroot from the center of his thick lips to one side, Klinger said, "Oh, surely—"

"The delicate machinery," Salsbury said sharply, gesturing at the Christmasy lights.

Klinger took the slender cigar from his mouth and appeared to be about to drop it on the floor.

"The waste can."

When he had disposed of the cheroot, the general said, "Sorry."

Salsbury said, "That's all right. You're not familiar with a place like this, with computers and all of that. You couldn't be expected to know."

And he thought: Score one for me.

"Where's Leonard?" Klinger asked.

"He won't be here."

"For such an important test?"

"He wishes it weren't necessary."

"Pontius Pilate."

"What?"

Looking at the ceiling as if he could see through it, Klinger said, "Up there washing his hands."

Salsbury wasn't about to take part in any conversation meant to dissect or analyze Dawson. He had taken every measure to protect himself from any attempt on Dawson's part to plant bugs in his work area. He didn't believe it was possible for anyone to spy on him while he was in here. But he couldn't be positively, absolutely certain of that. Under the circumstances, he felt that paranoia was a rational vantage point from which to view the world.

"What all have you got to show me?" Klinger asked.

"For a start, I thought you'd want to see a few print-outs from the key-lock program."

"I'm curious," the general admitted.

Picking up a sheet of computer paper that was folded like an accordion into dozens of eighteen-inch-long sections, Salsbury said, "All three of our new employees—"

"The mercenaries?"

"Yes. All three of them were given the drug and then shown a series of films, ostensibly as evening entertainment: *The Exorcist, Jaws,* and *Black Sunday,* on successive nights. These were, of course, very special copies of the films. Processed right here on the estate. I did the work personally. Printed each of them over a different stage of the subliminal program."

"Why those three movies in particular?"

"I could have used any I wanted," Salsbury said. "I just chose them at random from Leonard's film library. The movie is simply the package, not the content. It merely establishes a reason for the subjects to stare at the screen for a couple of hours while the subliminal program is running below their recognition threshold." He handed the print-out to Klinger. "This is a second-by-second verbal translation of the images appearing on the screen in the rheostatic film, which begins simultaneously with the movie. Wherever the computer prints 'This Legend' it means that the *visual* subliminals have been interrupted by a block-letter message on the rheostatic film, a direct command to the viewer."

```
SUBJECT CODED--KEY LOCK

REVISED PROGRAM/STAGE ONE

STORAGE MATERIAL

PROGRAM STORED: 8/6/76

THIS PRINT: 12/18/76

PRINT

↓
```

SECONDS	SUBLIMINAL CONTENT
0001	NO CONTENT
0002	NO CONTENT
0003	VISUAL--WOMAN'S BREASTS
0004	VISUAL--WOMAN'S BREASTS
0005	VISUAL--WOMAN'S BREASTS
0006	VISUAL--WOMAN'S BREASTS
0007	VISUAL--WOMAN'S BREASTS

```
0008        THIS LEGEND--YOU WATCH
0009        THIS LEGEND--YOU WATCH
0010        THIS LEGEND--YOU WATCH
0011        THIS LEGEND--YOU WATCH
0012        THIS LEGEND--YOU WATCH THIS FILM
0013        THIS LEGEND--YOU WATCH THIS FILM
0014        THIS LEGEND--YOU WATCH THIS FILM
0015        VISUAL--DETUMESCENT PENIS
0016        VISUAL--DETUMESCENT PENIS
0017        VISUAL--DETUMESCENT PENIS
0018        VISUAL--PENIS IN WOMAN'S HAND
0019        VISUAL--WOMAN STROKING PENIS
0020        VISUAL--WOMAN STROKING PENIS
0021        VISUAL--WOMAN STROKING PENIS
0022        VISUAL--WOMAN STROKING PENIS
0023        THIS LEGEND--YOU WATCH THIS FILM
```

"The first sixty seconds do nothing but insure that the subject will play close attention to the rest of the movie," Salsbury said. "Beginning with the second minute and continuing throughout the movie, he is very carefully, very gradually primed for stage two of the program and for eventual, total submission to the key-lock behavior mode."

"Carefully and slowly—because of what happened to Brian Kingman?" the general asked.

"Because of what happened to Brian Kingman."

```
0061        VISUAL--WOMAN FONDLING TESTICLES
0062        VISUAL--WOMAN FONDLING TESTICLES
0063        VISUAL--WOMAN STROKING PENIS
0064        VISUAL--WOMAN STROKING PENIS
0065        VISUAL--WOMAN STROKING PENIS
0066        THIS LEGEND--OBEDIENCE TO THE KEY=SATISFACTION
0067        THIS LEGEND--OBEDIENCE TO THE KEY=SATISFACTION
0068        THIS LEGEND--OBEDIENCE TO THE KEY=SATISFACTION
0069        VISUAL--ERECT PENIS
```

0070	VISUAL--ERECT PENIS
0071	VISUAL--ERECT PENIS
0072	THIS LEGEND--OBEDIENCE TO THE KEY=SATISFACTION
0073	THIS LEGEND--OBEDIENCE TO THE KEY=SATISFACTION
0074	VISUAL--WOMAN SMILING AT ERECT PENIS
0075	VISUAL--WOMAN SMILING AT ERECT PENIS
0076	VISUAL--WOMAN SMILING AT ERECT PENIS
0077	THIS LEGEND--OBEDIENCE TO THE KEY=SATISFACTION
0078	THIS LEGEND--OBEDIENCE TO THE KEY=SATISFACTION
0079	VISUAL--DOG STYLE INTERCOURSE
0080	VISUAL--DOG STYLE INTERCOURSE
0081	VISUAL--DOG STYLE INTERCOURSE
0082	THIS LEGEND--OBEDIENCE TO THE KEY=SATISFACTION
0083	THIS LEGEND--OBEDIENCE TO THE KEY=SATISFACTION
0084	VISUAL--MALE DOMINANT INTERCOURSE
0085	VISUAL--MALE DOMINANT INTERCOURSE
0086	VISUAL--MALE DOMINANT INTERCOURSE
0087	THIS LEGEND--OBEDIENCE TO THE KEY=SATISFACTION
0088	THIS LEGEND--OBEDIENCE TO THE KEY=SATISFACTION
0089	VISUAL--WOMAN'S FACE EXPRESSING ECSTASY
0090	VISUAL--WOMAN'S FACE EXPRESSING ECSTASY
0091	VISUAL--WOMAN'S FACE EXPRESSING ECSTASY
0092	THIS LEGEND--OBEDIENCE TO THE KEY=SATISFACTION
0093	THIS LEGEND--OBEDIENCE TO THE KEY=SATISFACTION
0094	VISUAL--EJACULATION ON WOMAN'S PUBIC HAIR
0095	THIS LEGEND--OBEDIENCE TO THE KEY=SATISFACTION
0096	VISUAL--EJACULATION ON WOMAN'S PUBIC HAIR
0097	THIS LEGEND--OBEDIENCE TO THE KEY=SATISFACTION
0098	VISUAL--WOMAN'S FACE EXPRESSING ECSTASY
0099	THIS LEGEND--OBEDIENCE TO THE KEY=SATISFACTION
0100	VISUAL--EJACULATION ON WOMAN'S PUBIC HAIR

Klinger said, ''The penis doesn't become erect until the viewer is told that obedience to the key equals satisfaction.''

"That's right. And you'll notice that both the man's and woman's orgasms are represented. This program would be effective with either sex."

"Was all this taken from some porno movie?"

"It was shot especially for me by a professional pornographic film maker in New York City," Salsbury said, pushing his glasses up on his nose and wiping his damp forehead. "He was instructed to use only the most attractive performers. He shot everything at regular light intensity, but I used a special process to print below the recognition threshold. Then I intercut the sex footage with the block-letter messages." He unfolded some of the print-out. "This first sequence lasts another forty seconds. Then there is a two-second pause, and another message is presented in the same fashion."

0143	VISUAL--WOMAN FINGERING CLITORIS
0144	VISUAL--WOMAN FINGERING CLITORIS
0145	VISUAL--MAN STROKING DETUMESCENT PENIS
0146	VISUAL--MAN STROKING DETUMESCENT PENIS
0147	VISUAL--MAN STROKING DETUMESCENT PENIS
0148	THIS LEGEND--SUBMISSION TO THE KEY= FREEDOM FROM FAILURE
0149	THIS LEGEND--SUBMISSION TO THE KEY= FREEDOM FROM FAILURE
0150	THIS LEGEND--SUBMISSION TO THE KEY= FREEDOM FROM FAILURE
0151	VISUAL--WOMAN SMILING AT ERECT PENIS
0152	VISUAL--WOMAN SMILING AT ERECT PENIS
0153	VISUAL--WOMAN SMILING AT ERECT PENIS
0154	THIS LEGEND--SUBMISSION TO THE KEY= FREEDOM FROM FAILURE
0155	THIS LEGEND--SUBMISSION TO THE KEY= FREEDOM FROM FAILURE
0156	VISUAL--WOMAN DOMINANT INTERCOURSE
0157	VISUAL--WOMAN DOMINANT INTERCOURSE
0158	VISUAL--WOMAN DOMINANT INTERCOURSE

0159	THIS LEGEND--SUBMISSION TO THE KEY-
	FREEDOM FROM FAILURE
0160	THIS LEGEND--SUBMISSION TO THE KEY-
	FREEDOM FROM FAILURE
0161	VISUAL--DOG STYLE INTERCOURSE
0162	VISUAL--DOG STYLE INTERCOURSE
0163	VISUAL--DOG STYLE INTERCOURSE
0164	THIS LEGEND--SUBMISSION TO THE KEY-
	FREEDOM FROM FAILURE
0165	THIS LEGEND--SUBMISSION TO THE KEY-
	FREEDOM FROM FAILURE
0166	VISUAL--WOMAN'S FACE EXPRESSING ECSTASY
0167	VISUAL--WOMAN'S FACE EXPRESSING ECSTASY
0168	VISUAL--WOMAN'S FACE EXPRESSING ECSTASY
0169	THIS LEGEND--SUBMISSION TO THE KEY-
	FREEDOM FROM FAILURE
0170	THIS LEGEND--SUBMISSION TO THE KEY-
	FREEDOM FROM FAILURE
0171	VISUAL--EJACULATION ON WOMAN'S BUTTOCKS
0172	THIS LEGEND--SUBMISSION TO THE KEY-
	FREEDOM FROM FAILURE
0173	VISUAL--EJACULATION ON WOMAN'S BUTTOCKS
0174	THIS LEGEND--SUBMISSION TO THE KEY-
	FREEDOM FROM FAILURE
0175	VISUAL--WOMAN'S FACE EXPRESSING ECSTASY

''I see the pattern,'' Klinger said. ''How many of these 'legends' were there?''

They were standing at one of the computer consoles. Salsbury leaned over and used the keyboard.

One of the screens mounted on the wall began a line-print:

```
KEY/LOCK STAGE ONE BLOCK-LETTER MESSAGES, IN ORDER OF

APPEARANCE, AS FOLLOWS:

  01  OBEDIENCE TO THE KEY-SATISFACTION

  02  SUBMISSION TO THE KEY-FREEDOM FROM FAILURE
```

```
03  SUBMISSION TO THE KEY-FREEDOM FROM FEAR

04  SUBMISSION TO THE KEY-FREEDOM FROM GUILT

05  SUBMISSION TO THE KEY-FREEDOM FROM WORRY

06  SUBMISSION TO THE KEY-FREEDOM FROM MORAL CODES

07  SUBMISSION TO THE KEY-FREEDOM FROM RESPONSIBILITY

08  SUBMISSION TO THE KEY-FREEDOM FROM DEPRESSION

09  SUBMISSION TO THE KEY-FREEDOM FROM TENSION

10  SUBMISSION TO THE KEY-CONTENTMENT

11  SUBMISSION TO THE KEY-HAPPINESS

12  SUBMISSION TO THE KEY-YOUR GREATEST DESIRE
```

Salsbury touched a tab on the console.

The screen went blank.

"The series was repeated three times through the film."

"The same thing the second night?" Klinger asked.

"No." He picked up another folded print-out from the seat of the console chair and exchanged it for the stage one analysis. "The first minute is spent securing the subjects' undivided attention, as it was in the first film. The difference between stage one and stage two becomes evident starting with the second minute."

```
0061    VISUAL--WOMAN WEEPING

0062    VISUAL--WOMAN WEEPING

0063    VISUAL--WOMAN WEEPING

0064    VISUAL--MAN WEEPING

0065    VISUAL--MAN WEEPING

0066    THIS LEGEND--REFUSAL TO OBEY THE KEY-PAIN

0067    THIS LEGEND--REFUSAL TO OBEY THE KEY-PAIN

0068    VISUAL--WOMAN, COVERED WITH BLOOD, SCREAMING

0069    VISUAL--WOMAN, COVERED WITH BLOOD, SCREAMING

0070    THIS LEGEND--REFUSAL TO OBEY THE KEY-PAIN

0071    THIS LEGEND--REFUSAL TO OBEY THE KEY-PAIN

0072    VISUAL--MAN, COVERED WITH BLOOD, SCREAMING

0073    VISUAL--MAN, COVERED WITH BLOOD, SCREAMING

0074    THIS LEGEND--REFUSAL TO OBEY THE KEY-PAIN

0075    THIS LEGEND--REFUSAL TO OBEY THE KEY-PAIN
```

0076	VISUAL--WOMAN, COVERED WITH BLOOD, SCREAMING
0077	VISUAL--MAN, COVERED WITH BLOOD, SCREAMING
0078	THIS LEGEND--REFUSAL TO OBEY THE KEY=PAIN
0079	THIS LEGEND--PAIN, PAIN, PAIN, PAIN
0080	NO CONTENT
0081	NO CONTENT
0082	VISUAL--WOMAN SMILING AT ERECT PENIS

"The second stage of the program alternates between negative reinforcement and positive reinforcement," Salsbury said. "The next twenty-five seconds are devoted to a sex reinforcement sequence much like those you saw on the first print-out. Skip ahead just a bit."

0110	VISUAL--WOLF'S FACE, SNARLING
0111	VISUAL--WOLF'S FACE, SNARLING
0112	VISUAL--SCORPION STINGING A MOUSE
0113	VISUAL--SCORPION STINGING A MOUSE
0114	VISUAL--COFFIN
0115	VISUAL--COFFIN
0116	VISUAL--COFFIN
0117	THIS LEGEND--REFUSAL TO OBEY THE KEY=DEATH
0118	THIS LEGEND--REFUSAL TO OBEY THE KEY=DEATH
0119	VISUAL--HUMAN SKULL
0120	VISUAL--HUMAN SKULL
0121	VISUAL--ROTTING CORPSE
0122	THIS LEGEND--REFUSAL TO OBEY THE KEY=DEATH
0123	VISUAL--ROTTING CORPSE
0124	THIS LEGEND--REFUSAL TO OBEY THE KEY=DEATH

Looking up from the print-out, Klinger said, "Do you mean that death is as effective as sex in subliminal persuasion?"

"Nearly so, yes. In advertising, subliminals can be used to establish the same sort of motivational equation with death as with sex. According to Wilson Bryan Key, who wrote a book about the nature of subceptive manipulation a few years back, the first use of death images might have come in a Calvert Whiskey ad that appeared in a number of magazines in 1971. Since then hundreds of death symbols have become standard tools of the major ad agencies."

Putting down the second print-out, the general said, "What about the third stage? What was hidden in the film you showed them on the third night?"

Salsbury had another length of computer paper. "In the beginning, this one just reinforces and strengthens the messages and effects of the first two films. It's broken down into tenths of seconds in some places because by this time the subjects are primed for faster input, rapid-fire commands. Like the others, it really begins with the second minute."

```
0060  00     VISUAL--WOMAN'S FACE EXPRESSING ECSTASY
0061  00     THIS LEGEND--OBEDIENCE TO THE KEY=SATISFACTION
0061  05     VISUAL--PENIS EJACULATING
0062  00     VISUAL--WOMAN'S FACE EXPRESSING ECSTASY
0062  05     THIS LEGEND--OBEDIENCE TO THE KEY=SATISFACTION
0063  00     VISUAL--WOMAN WEEPING
0063  03     VISUAL--MAN WEEPING
0063  06     VISUAL--WOLF'S FACE, SNARLING
0063  09     VISUAL--SCORPION STINGING A MOUSE
0064  02     VISUAL--COFFIN
0064  05     THIS LEGEND--REFUSAL TO OBEY THE KEY=DEATH
0065  00     VISUAL--WOMAN KISSING PENIS
0065  05     VISUAL--PENIS SLIDING BETWEEN WOMAN'S BREASTS
0065  08     VISUAL--PENIS ENTERING VAGINA
0066  00     THIS LEGEND--SUBMISSION TO THE KEY=
                          FREEDOM FROM FAILURE
0066  05     VISUAL--SEVERED, BLOODY HUMAN ARM
0066  08     VISUAL--ROTTING CORPSE
```

Farther on, both the tempo and the emotional impact of the images increased drastically:

```
0800  00     VISUAL--HUMAN HEAD WITH GUNSHOT WOUND
0800  02     VISUAL--DEAD VIETNAMESE BABY
```

0800	04	VISUAL--MAGGOTS IN PIECE OF BEEF
0800	06	VISUAL--RAT'S FACE, SNARLING
0800	07	VISUAL--WOLF'S FACE, SNARLING
0800	08	VISUAL--COFFIN
0800	09	VISUAL--MAGGOTS IN PIECE OF BEEF
0801	00	THIS LEGEND--REFUSAL TO OBEY THE KEY—DEATH
0801	02	VISUAL--ERECT PENIS
0801	04	VISUAL--WOMAN'S FACE EXPRESSING ECSTASY
0801	06	VISUAL--TONGUE ON CLITORIS
0801	08	VISUAL--WOMAN KISSING PENIS
0801	09	VISUAL--PENIS IN VAGINA
0802	00	VISUAL--EJACULATION ON WOMAN'S PUBIC HAIR
0802	01	THIS LEGEND--SUBMISSION TO THE KEY—
		YOUR GREATEST DESIRE

Much farther on, faster and faster:

2400	00	VISUAL--DEAD BABY'S FACE, CLOSE-UP
2400	01	VISUAL--MAGGOTS IN HORSE MANURE
2400	02	THIS LEGEND--REFUSE THE KEY: DEATH
2400	03	VISUAL--MAN FINGERING CLITORIS
2400	04	VISUAL--WOMAN LICKING PENIS
2400	05	THIS LEGEND--SUBMIT TO THE KEY: HAPPINESS
2400	06	VISUAL--STEAMING ENTRAILS OF COW
2400	07	THIS LEGEND--REFUSAL: PAIN
2400	08	THIS LEGEND--REFUSAL: DEATH
2400	09	VISUAL--EJACULATION INTO WOMAN'S MOUTH
2401	00	VISUAL--WOMAN'S FACE EXPRESSING ECSTASY
2401	01	THIS LEGEND--SUBMISSION: HAPPINESS
2401	02	THIS LEGEND--SUBMISSION: BLISS

Eventually, there was less time given to the motivating images and more to the direct commands:

3600	00	VISUAL--MAGGOTS IN PIECE OF BEEF
3600	01	THIS LEGEND--REFUSAL: DEATH

3600	02	VISUAL--DEAD CAT
3600	03	THIS LEGEND--OBEY THE KEY
3600	04	THIS LEGEND--OBEY, OBEY, OBEY
3600	05	VISUAL--WOMAN LICKING PENIS
3600	06	THIS LEGEND--SUBMISSION: LIFE
3600	07	THIS LEGEND--OBEY THE KEY
3600	08	VISUAL--EJACULATION ON WOMAN'S THIGH
3600	09	THIS LEGEND--OBEY THE KEY
3600	10	THIS LEGEND--LIFE, LIFE, LIFE

"That pace is maintained straight through to the end of the film," Salsbury said. "During the last fifteen minutes, while all of this sex and death input continues, the concept of the key-lock code phrases is also introduced and implanted permanently in the viewer's deep subconscious mind."

"That's all there is to it?"

"Thanks to the drug that primes them for the subliminals—yes, that's all there is to it."

"And they don't realize they've seen any of it."

"If they did know, the program would have no effect on them. It has to speak solely to the subconscious in order to pass the natural reasoning ability of the conscious mind."

Klinger pulled the command chair away from the console and sat down. His left hand was curled in his lap. It was so matted with black hair that it reminded Salsbury of a sewer rat. The general petted it with his other hand while he considered the print-outs he had just seen. At last he said, "Our three mercenaries. When did they complete the third stage of the program?"

"Thirty days ago. I've been observing them and testing their submissiveness for the past few weeks."

"Any of them react at all as Kingman did?"

"They all had bad dreams," Salsbury said. "Probably about what they had seen on the rheostatic screen. None of them could recall. Furthermore, they all had severe night chills and mild nausea. But they lived."

"Encountered any other problems?"

"None."

"No weak spots in the program? No moments when they refused to obey you?"

"None at all, so far. In a few minutes, after we've put

them to the ultimate test, we'll know whether or not we have absolute control of them. If not, I'll start over. If we do—champagne.''

Klinger sighed. ''I suppose this is something we have to know. I suppose this last test is entirely necessary.''

''Entirely.''

''I don't like it.''

''Weren't you an officer in Vietnam?''

''What's *that* got to do with *this?*''

''You've sent men to die before.''

Grimacing, Klinger said, ''But always with honor. Always with honor. And there's sure as hell no honor in what's going to happen here.''

Honor, Salsbury thought acidly. You're as big an idiot as Leonard. There isn't any heaven, and there's no such thing as honor. All that counts is getting what you want. You know that and I know that and even Leonard, when he's humbled over his fruit cup at a White House prayer breakfast with Billy Graham and the President, knows that—but I'm the only one of us who will admit it to himself.

Getting to his feet, Klinger said, ''Okay. Let's finish this. Where are they?''

''In the next room. Waiting.''

''They know what they're going to do?''

''No.'' Salsbury went to his desk, thumbed a button on the intercom, and spoke into the wire grid. ''Rossner, Holbrook, and Picard. Come in now. We're ready for you.''

A few seconds later the door opened, and three men filed inside.

''Go to the center of the room,'' Salsbury said.

They did as he directed.

''You've already opened them with the code phrase?'' Klinger asked.

''Before you came.''

The first of them, in spite of the fact that he was in his late thirties or early forties, looked like a dangerous street-corner punk. Slim but hard and wiry. Five feet ten. Dark complexion. Dark brown hair combed straight back and graying at the temples. A way of standing with his feet apart and most of his weight on his toes so that he was always prepared to move and move quickly. His face was pinched, his eyes a bit too close together, his lips thin and a grayish-pink above a pointed chin.

"This is Rossner," Salsbury told Klinger. "Glenn Rossner. American. He's been a free-lance soldier for sixteen years."

"Hello," Rossner said.

"None of you is to speak unless spoken to," Salsbury said. "Is that understood?"

Three voices: "Yes."

The second man was approximately the same age as the first; otherwise, he could not have been less like Rossner. Six feet two. Husky. Fair complexion. Reddish-blond hair cropped close to his head. A broad face. Heavy jowls. His stern expression had been held for so many years that it seemed graven in his flesh. He looked like the sort of father who made arbitrary rules, used corporal punishment with a child at least twice a week, talked tough, acted bullheaded, and turned sons like Glenn Rossner into street-corner punks.

Salsbury said, "This is Peter Holbrook. He's British. He's been a mercenary for twenty years, ever since he was twenty-two."

The last man was no older than thirty, and he was the only one of the three who could be called handsome. Six feet. Lean and muscular. Thick brown hair. A broad brow. Peculiar green-gray eyes with long lashes that any woman would have been proud to have for her own. Very rectangular features and an especially strong jawline and chin. He somewhat resembled the young Rex Harrison.

"Michel Picard," Salsbury said. "French. Speaks fluent English. He's been a mercenary for four years."

"Which will it be?" Klinger asked.

"Picard, I think."

"Let's get on with it, then."

Salsbury turned to Rossner and said, "Glenn, there's a folded canvas dropcloth on my desk. Bring it here."

Rossner went to the desk, came back with the cloth.

"Peter, you help him unfold it on the floor."

A minute later the nine-foot-square canvas sheet was spread out in the middle of the room.

"Michel, stand in the middle of the cloth."

The Frenchman obeyed.

"Michel, what am I?"

"You are the key."

"And what are you?"

"I am the lock."

"You will do what I tell you to do."

"Yes. Of course," Picard said.

"Relax, Michel. You are very relaxed."

"Yes. I feel fine."

"You are very happy."

Picard smiled.

"You will remain happy, regardless of what happens to you in the next few minutes. Is that understood?"

"Yes."

"You will not attempt to stop Peter and Glenn from carrying out the orders I give them, regardless of what those orders are. Is that understood?"

"Yes."

Taking a three-foot length of heavy nylon cord from a pocket of his white laboratory smock, Salsbury said, "Peter, take this. Slip it about Michel's neck as if you were going to strangle him—but proceed no further than that."

Holbrook stepped behind the Frenchman and looped the cord around his throat.

"Michel, are you relaxed?"

"Oh, yes. Quite relaxed."

"Your hands are at your sides now. You will keep them at your sides until I tell you to move them."

Still smiling, Picard said, "All right."

"You will smile as long as you are able to smile."

"Yes."

"And even when you are no longer able to smile, you'll know this is for the best."

Picard smiled.

"Glenn, you will observe. You will not become involved in the little drama these two are about to act out."

"I won't become involved," Rossner said.

"Peter, you will do what I tell you."

The big man nodded.

"Without hesitation."

"Without hesitation."

"Strangle Michel."

If the Frenchman's smile slipped, it was only by the slightest fraction.

Then Holbrook jerked on both ends of the cord.

Picard's mouth flew open. He seemed to be trying to scream, but he had no voice. He began to gag.

Although Holbrook was wearing a long-sleeved shirt, Salsbury could see the muscles bunching and straining in his thick arms.

Each desperate breath that Picard drew produced a thin, rattling wheeze. His eyes bulged. His face was flushed.

"Pull tighter," Salsbury told Holbrook.

The Englishman obliged. A fierce grin, not of humor but of effort, seemed to transform his face into a death's head.

Picard fell against Holbrook.

Holbrook stepped back.

Picard went to his knees.

His hands were still at his sides. He was making no effort to save himself.

"Jesus jump to hell," Klinger said, amazed, numbed, unable to speak above a whisper.

Shuddering, convulsing, Picard lost control of his bladder and bowels.

Salsbury was pleased that he had thought to provide the canvas dropcloth.

Seconds later Holbrook stepped away from Picard, his task completed. The garrote had made deep, angry red impressions in the palms of his hands.

Salsbury took another length of cord from another pocket in his smock and gave it to Rossner. "Do you know what that is, Glenn?"

"Yes." He had watched impassively as Holbrook murdered the Frenchman.

"Glenn, I want you to give the cord to Peter."

Without even pausing to think about it, Rossner placed the second garrote in the Englishman's hands.

"Now turn your back to Peter."

Rossner turned.

"Are you relaxed, Glenn?"

"No."

"Relax. Be calm. Don't worry about anything at all. That's an order."

The lines in Rossner's face softened.

"How do you feel, Glenn?"

"Relaxed."

"Good. You won't try to keep Peter from obeying the orders I give him, regardless of what those orders are."

"I won't interfere," Rossner said.

Salsbury turned to the Englishman. "Loop that cord around Glenn's neck as you did with Michel."

With an expert flip and twist of the garrote, Holbrook was in position. He waited for orders.

"Glenn," Salsbury said, "are you tense?"

"No. I'm relaxed."

"That's fine. Just fine. You will continue to be relaxed. Now, I'm going to tell Peter to kill you—and you are going to permit him to do that. Is that clear?"

"Yes. I understand." His placid expression didn't waver.

"Don't you want to live?"

"Yes. Yes, I want to live."

"Then why are you willing to die?"

"I—I—" He looked confused.

"You are willing to die because refusal to obey the key means pain and death anyway. Isn't that right, Glenn?"

"That's right."

Salsbury watched the two men closely for signs of panic. There were none. Nor even any of stress.

The stench from Michel Picard's fouled body was nearly overpowering and getting worse.

Rossner surely knew what was about to happen to him. He had seen Michel die, had been told he would die in the same way. Yet he stood ummoving, apparently unafraid.

He was willing to commit what amounted to suicide rather than disobey the key. In fact disobedience was literally inconceivable to him.

"*Total* control," the general said. "Yet they don't look or behave like zombies."

"Because they aren't. There's nothing supernatural involved. Just the ultimate in behavior modification techniques." Salsbury was elated. "Peter, give me the cord. Thank you. You have both done well. Exceptionally well. Now, I want you to wrap Michel's body in the canvas and move it to the next room. Wait there until I have additional orders for you."

As if they were a pair of ordinary laborers talking about how to move a load of bricks from here to there, Rossner and Holbrook quickly discussed the job at hand. When they had decided on the best way to roll and carry the corpse, they set to work.

"Congratulations," Klinger said. He was perspiring. Cool, dry, steady-eyed Ernst Klinger was sweating like a pig.

What do you think of the computer lights now? Salsbury

wondered. Do they look as Christmasy as they did ten minutes ago?

The computer room smelled of lemons. Salsbury had used an aerosol spray to get rid of the odor of feces and urine.

He took a bottle of whiskey from his desk drawer and poured himself a shot to celebrate.

Klinger had a double shot to steady his nerves. When he had tossed it back he said, "And now what?"

"The field test."

"You've mentioned that before. But why? Why can't we go ahead with the Middle East plan as Leonard outlined it in Tahoe, nearly two years ago? We know the drug works, don't we? And we know the subliminals work."

"I achieved the desired results with Holbrook, Rossner, and poor Picard," Salsbury said, sipping his whiskey. "But it doesn't necessarily follow that *everyone* will react as they have. I can't possibly have complete confidence in the program until I've treated and observed and tested a few hundred subjects of both sexes and of all ages. Furthermore, our three mercenaries were treated and responded in controlled lab situations. Before we can take the extraordinary risks involved with something like the Middle East plan—where we've got to create a new subliminal series for another culture and in another language—we've simply got to know what the results will be in the field."

Klinger poured himself another shot of whiskey. As he lifted the glass to his lips, a look of fear flitted across his face. It lasted no more than a second or two. Pretending to be thinking about the field test, he stared at the liquor in his glass and then at the bottle on the desk and then at Salsbury's glass.

Laughing, Salsbury said, "Don't worry, Ernst. I wouldn't slip the drug into my own Jack Daniels. Besides, you're not a potential subject. You're my partner."

Klinger nodded. Nevertheless, he put his glass down without tasting the whiskey. "Where would you run a field test like this?"

"Black River, Maine. It's a small town near the Canadian border."

"Why there?"

Salsbury went to the nearest programming console and typed out an order to the computer. As he typed he said,

"Two months ago I drew a list of the basic requirements for the ideal test site."

All of the screens began to present the same information:

```
KEY/LOCK FIELD TEST DATA, AS FOLLOWS:

  1A.  SITE SHOULD BE SMALL TOWN, YET PROVIDE SUFFICIENT

       NUMBER OF SUBJECTS FOR STATISTICAL ACCURACY

  1B.  BLACK RIVER, MAINE--POPULATION 402

       LUMBER CAMP--POPULATION 188

       ADDITIONAL POPULATION WITHIN 5 MILES--NONE
```

"Lumber camp?" Klinger asked.

"It's a company town for Big Union Supply. Nearly everyone in Black River works for Big Union or services the people who do. The company maintains a full-scale camp—barracks, mess hall, recreation facilities, the whole works—near their planned forests for unmarried loggers who don't want to go to the expense of renting a room or an apartment in the village."

```
  2A.  SITE SHOULD BE GEOGRAPHICALLY ISOLATED BY CURRENT

       SOCIAL STANDARDS

  2B.  FIRST NEAREST TOWN TO BLACK RIVER--30 MILES

       SECOND NEAREST TOWN TO BLACK RIVER--62 MILES

       LAND ROUTES TO BLACK RIVER--1 STATE HIGHWAY, 2-LANE

                                --1 RAILROAD LINE, ONLY

                                   INDUSTRIAL TRAFFIC

       RIVER ROUTES TO BLACK RIVER--RIVER NAVIGABLE, NO

                                    REGULAR TRAFFIC

       AIRFIELD FACILITIES AT BLACK RIVER--NONE

  3A.  SITE SHOULD BE WITHIN RECEPTION RANGE OF ONE OR MORE

       TELEVISION STATIONS

  3B.  STATIONS RECEIVED IN BLACK RIVER--1 AMERICAN

                                         1 CANADIAN
```

"There's an interesting bit of additional data that goes with that one," Salsbury said. "The American station is owned by a subsidiary of Futurex. It plays a lot of old movies at night and on weekends. We'll be able to get copies of the station's program schedules well in advance. We can prepare subliminally augmented prints of the movies they're going to show and switch those for the original prints in the station's film library.''

"That's a bit of luck."

"Saves us some time. Otherwise, Futurex would have had to acquire one of the stations, and that could take years."

"But how can you be certain the people in Black River will watch these movies you've doctored?"

"They're going to be inundated with subliminals in a variety of media that will command them to watch. For instance, the Dawson Foundation for Christian Ethics will run dozens of public service commercials on both the Canadian and American stations, two days in advance of the movies. Each of these commercials will harbor very strong subliminal commands directing the people in town and in the lumber camp to tune in at the right time on the right channel. We'll also do direct mail advertising for several of Leonard's companies— as a means of getting even more subceptive messages to them. Everyone in town will receive ads in the mail and some free gifts like soap samples, shampoo samples, and free rolls of photographic film. The advertisements and the samples will be packaged in wrappers rich in subliminal commands to watch a certain television station at a certain hour on a certain day. Even if the subject throws the piece of mail away without opening it, he'll be affected, because the envelopes will also be printed over with subliminal messages. The major magazines and newspapers entering Black River during the period of programming will carry ads full of subceptive commands that direct the people to watch the movies." He was getting a bit breathless in his recital. "A motion picture theater could not ordinarily prosper in a town the size of Black River. But Big Union runs one as a service to the town. During the summer, every day but Sunday, there's a matinee show for children. The prints of the films shown at those matinees will be our prints, with subliminals urging the children to watch the television movies that will contain the keylock program. All radio stations reaching the area will carry special thirty-second spot ads, hundreds of them, with subaudial subliminal directives. These account for only half our methods. By the time all of this washes through the community, everyone will be in front of a television set at the right time."

"What about the people who don't have television sets?" Klinger asked.

"There's not much to do in a place as isolated as Black River," Salsbury said. "The recreation hall in the camp has ten sets. Virtually everyone in town owns a set. Those who don't will be directed, by the first wave of preliminary subliminals, to watch the movies at a friend's house. Or with a relative or neighbor."

For the first time, Klinger looked at Salsbury with respect. "Incredible."

"Thank you."

"What about the drug? How will that be introduced?"

Salsbury finished his whiskey. He felt wonderful. "There are only two sources of food and beverage within the site. The lumber camp men get what they want from the mess hall. In town everyone buys from Edison's General Store. Edison has no competition. He even supplies the town's only diner. Now, both the mess hall and the general store receive their goods from the same food wholesaler in Augusta."

"Ahhh," the general said. He smiled.

"It's a perfect commando operation for Holbrook and Rossner. They can break into the wholesaler's warehouse at night and quickly contaminate several different items set aside for shipment to Black River." He pointed to the cathode-ray tubes where the list of requirements for an ideal site was being reprinted. "Number four."

Klinger looked at the screen to his left.

4A. SITE SHOULD HAVE RESERVOIR THAT SERVES NO LESS THAN
     90 PERCENT OF TOTAL POPULATION

4B. BLACK RIVER RESERVOIR SERVES--100 PERCENT OF TOWN
                                  RESIDENTS
                                  --100 PERCENT OF LUMBER
                                  CAMP RESIDENTS

"Ordinarily, in a backwoods village like this," Salsbury said, "each house would have its own fresh-water well. But the mill needs a reservoir for industrial purposes, so the town benefits."

"How did you choose Black River? Where did you learn all of this stuff?"

Salsbury depressed a tab on the programming keyboard and cleared the screen. "In 1960, Leonard bankrolled a company named Statistical Profiles Incorporated. It does all the marketing research for his other companies—and for companies he doesn't own. It pays for a trunk line to the Census Bureau data banks. We used Statistical Profiles to run a search for the ideal test site. Of course, they didn't know why we were interested in a town that met these particular requirements."

Frowning, the general said, "How many people at Statistical Profiles were involved in the search?"

"Two," Salsbury said. "I know what you're thinking. Don't worry. They're both scheduled to die in accidents well before we begin the field test."

"I suppose we'll send Rossner and Holbrook to contaminate the reservoir."

"Then we get rid of them."

The general raised his bushy eyebrows. "Kill them?"

"Or order them to commit suicide."

"Why not just tell them to forget everything they've done, to wipe it from their minds?"

"That might save them from prosecution if things went badly wrong. But it wouldn't save us. We can't wipe from our minds all memory of what we had them do. If problems develop with the field tests, serious problems that throw our entire operation in the garbage, and if it turns out that Rossner and Holbrook were seen at the reservoir or left any clues behind—well, we don't want the authorities to connect us with Glenn and Peter."

"What problems could arise that would be that serious?"

"Anything. Nothing. I don't know."

After he had thought about it for a while, Klinger said, "Yes, I suppose you're right."

"I know I am."

"Have you set a date yet? For the field test?"

"We should be ready by August," Salsbury said.

9.

Friday, August 26, 1977

TAT-TAT-TAT-TAT-TAT-TAT . . . Since his experience with
Brenda Macklin on Monday, Salsbury had been able to resist
temptation. At any time he could have taken full control of
another good-looking woman, could have raped her and
erased all memory of the act from her mind. He took strength
from the knowledge that the bitches were his for the asking.
Whenever he could honestly conclude that the field test was a
smashing success, and that no danger of discovery existed, he
would screw every one of them that he wanted. The bitches.
Animals. Little animals. Dozens of them. All of them. Because he *knew* the future held an almost endless orgy for him,
he was able to cope, if only temporarily, with his desire. He
went from house to house, using the key-lock code phrase,
interviewing his subjects, observing and testing. Denying
himself. Working hard. Doing his job. So strict with himself . . . He was proud of his willpower.

This morning his willpower shattered. For the past four
nights, his sleep had been disturbed by grotesque dreams that

featured his mother and Miriam and sudden violence and blood—and an eerie, indescribable atmosphere of perverted sex. When he came awake this morning, shouting and flailing at the bedclothes, he thought of Emma Thorp—deep cleavage in an orange sweater—and she seemed to him like an antidote for the poisons that had churned through him while he slept. He had to have her, was going to have her, today, soon, and to hell with self-denial.

The smooth stream of power in him was again transformed into a rhythmic, alternating current, crackling across countless arcs, a hundred million synapses. His thoughts ricocheted with great energy from one subject to another, submachine-gun thoughts: *tat-tat-tat-tat-tat-tat-tat* . . .

At 7:45 he left Pauline Vicker's rooming house and went to the cafe on the square.

The sky was cloudy, the air humid.

At 8:25 he finished breakfast and left the cafe.

At 8:40 he reached the Thorps' place, the last house on Union Road, next to the river.

He rang the doorbell twice.

The chief of police himself answered. He hadn't gone to work yet. Good. Wonderful.

Salsbury said, "I am the key."

"I am the lock."

"Let me in."

Bob Thorp stepped out of his way, let him by, then closed the door after him.

"Is your wife here?"

"Yes."

"Your son?"

"He's here too."

"Anyone else?"

"Just you and me."

"Your son's name?"

"Jeremy."

"Where are they?"

"In the kitchen."

"Take me to them."

Thorp hesitated.

"Take me to them!"

They went along a narrow but brightly papered hallway. The kitchen was modern and stylish. Mediterranean cupboards and fixtures. Coppertone refrigerator *and* upright free-zer. A microwave oven. A television set was suspended from the ceiling in one corner and angled toward the big round table by the window.

Jeremy was at the table, eating eggs and toast, facing the hall.

To the boy's right, Emma sat with one elbow on the table, drinking a glass of orange juice. Her hair was as golden and full as he remembered it. As she turned to ask her husband who had rung the bell, he saw that her lovely face was still soft with sleep—and for some reason that aroused him.

She said, "Bob? Who's this?"

Salsbury said, "I am the key."

Two voices responded.

At 8:55, making the weekly trip into town to lay in a fresh supply of perishables, Paul Annendale braked at the end of the gravel road, looked both ways, then turned left onto Main Street.

From the back seat Mark said, "Don't take me all the way to Sam's place. Let me out at the square."

Looking in the rearview mirror, Paul said, "Where are you going?"

Mark patted the large canary cage that stood on the seat beside him. The squirrel danced about and chattered. "I want to take Buster to see Jeremy."

Swiveling around in her seat and looking back at her brother, Rya said, "Why don't you admit that you don't go over to their house to see Jeremy? We all know you've got a crush on Emma."

"Not so!" Mark said in such a way that he proved absolutely that what she said was true.

"Oh, Mark," she said exasperatingly.

"Well, it's a lie," Mark insisted. "I don't have a crush on Emma. I'm not some sappy kid."

Rya turned around again.

"No fights," Paul said. "We'll leave Mark off at the square with Buster, and there will be no fights."

Salsbury said, "Do you understand that, Bob?"

"I understand."

"You will not speak unless spoken to. And you will not

move from that chair unless I tell you to move.''

"I won't move.''

"But you'll watch.''

"I'll watch.''

"Jeremy?''

"I'll watch too.''

"Watch what?'' Salsbury asked.

"Watch you—screw her.''

Dumb cop. Dumb kid.

He stood by the sink, leaned against the counter. "Come here, Emma.''

She got up. Came to him.

"Take off your robe.''

She took it off. She was wearing a yellow bra and yellow panties with three embroidered red flowers at the left hip.

"Take off your bra.''

Her breasts fell free. Heavy. Beautiful.

"Jeremy, did you know your mother looked so nice?''

The boy swallowed hard. "No.''

Thorp's hands were on the table. They had curled into fists.

"Relax, Bob. You're going to enjoy this. You're going to love it. You can't wait for me to have her.''

Thorp's hands opened. He leaned back in his chair.

Touching her breasts, staring into her shimmering green eyes, Salsbury had a delightful idea. Marvelous. Exciting. He said, "Emma, I think this would be more enjoyable if you resisted me a bit. Not seriously, you understand. Not physically. Just keep asking me not to hurt you. And cry.''

She stared at him.

"Could you cry for me, Emma?''

"I'm so scared.''

"Good! Excellent! I didn't tell *you* to relax, did I? You should be scared. Damned scared. And obedient. Are you frightened enough to cry, Emma?''

She shivered.

"You're very firm.''

She said nothing.''

"Cry for me.''

"Bob . . .''

"He can't help you.''

He squeezed her breasts.

"My son . . .''

"He's watching. It's all right if he watches. Didn't he suck these when he was a baby?"

Tears formed at the corners of her eyes.

"Fine," he said. "Oh, that's sweet."

Mark could only carry the squirrel and the cage for fifteen or twenty steps at a time. Then he had to put it down and shake his arms to get the pain out of them.

"Cup your breasts with your hands."

She did as she was told.

She wept.

"Pull on the nipples."

"Don't make me do this."

"Come on, little animal."

At first, upset by all the jerking and shaking and swinging of his cage, Buster ran in tight little circles and squealed like an injured rabbit.

"You sound like a rabbit," Mark told him during one of the rest stops.

Buster squealed, unconcerned with his image.

"You should be ashamed of yourself. You're not a dumb bunny. You're a *squirrel*."

In front of Edison's store, as he was closing the car door, Paul saw something gleam on the back seat. "What's that?"

Rya was still in the car, undoing her safety belt. "What's what?"

"On the back seat. It's the key to Buster's cage."

Rya squirmed into the back seat. "I'd better take it to him."

"He won't need it," Paul said. "Just don't lose it."

"No," she said. "I'd better take it to him. He'll want to let Buster out so he can show off for Emma."

"Who are you—Cupid?"

She grinned at him.

"Unzip my trousers."

"I don't want to."

"Do it!"

She did.

"Enjoying yourself, Bob?"

"Yes."

He laughed. "Dumb cop."

By the time he reached the edge of the Thorp property, Mark had found a better way to grip the cage. The new method didn't strain his arms so much, and he didn't have to stop every few yards to rest.

Buster had become *so* upset by the erratic movement of his pen that he had stopped squealing. He was gripping the bars with all four feet, hanging on the side of the cage, very still and quiet, frozen as if he were in the woods and had just seen a predator creeping through the brush.

"They'll be eating breakfast," Mark said. "We'll go around to the back door."

"Squeeze it."

She did.

"Hot?"

"Yes."

"Little animal."

"Don't hurt me."

"Is it hard?"

"Yes." Crying.

"Bend over."

Sobbing, shaking, begging him not to hurt her, she did as she had been told. Her face glistened with tears. She was almost hysterical. So beautiful . . .

Mark was passing the kitchen window when he heard the woman crying. He stopped and listened closely to the broken words, the pitiful pleas that were punctuated by long sobs. He knew at once that it was Emma.

The window was only two feet away, and it seemed to beckon him. He couldn't resist. He went to it.

The curtains were drawn shut, but there was a narrow gap between them. He pressed his face to the windowpane.

10.

Sixteen Days Earlier:
Wednesday, August 10, 1977

AT THREE O'CLOCK in the morning, Salsbury joined Dawson
in the first-floor study of the Greenwich house.

"Have they begun already?"

"Ten minutes ago," Dawson said.

"What's coming in?"

"Exactly what we'd hoped for."

Four men sat on straight-backed chairs around a massive
walnut desk, one at each side of it. They were all household
servants: the butler, the chauffeur, the cook, and the gar-
dener. Three months ago the entire staff of the house had
been given the drug and treated to the subliminal program;
and there was no longer any need to hide the project from
them. On occasion, as now, they made very useful tools.
There were four telephones on the desk, each connected to an
infinity transmitter. The men were referring to lists of Black
River telephone numbers, dialing, listening for a few seconds
or a minute, hanging up and dialing again.

The infinity transmitters—purchased in Brussels for $2,500 each—allowed them to eavesdrop on most of the bedrooms of Black River in perfect anonymity. With an IF hooked to a telephone, they could dial any number they wished, long distance or local, without going through an operator and without leaving a record of the call in the telephone company's computer. An electric tone oscillator deactivated the bell on the phone being called—and simultaneously opened that receiver's microphone. The people at the other end of the line heard no ringing and were not aware that they were being monitored. These four servants were able, therefore, to hear anything said in the room where the distant telephone was placed.

Salsbury went around the desk, leaned down and listened at each earpiece.

". . . nightmare. So vivid. I can't remember what it was, but it scared the hell out of me. Look how I'm shaking."

". . . so cold. You too? What the devil?"

". . . feel like I'm going to throw up."

". . . all right? Maybe we should call Doc Troutman."

And around again:

". . . something we ate?"

". . . flu. But at this time of year?"

". . . first thing in the morning. God, if I don't stop shaking, I'll rattle myself to pieces!"

". . . running with sweat but cold."

Dawson tapped Salsbury on the shoulder. "Are you going to stay here and watch over them?"

"I might as well."

"Then I'll go the chapel for a while."

He was wearing pajamas, a dark blue silk robe, and soft leather slippers. At this hour, with rain falling outside, it didn't seem likely that even a religious fanatic of Dawson's bent would get dressed and go out to church.

Salsbury said, "You've got a chapel in the house?"

"I have a chapel in each of my residences," Dawson said proudly. "I wouldn't build a house without one. It's a way of thanking Him for all that He's done for me. After all, it's because of Him that I have the houses in the first place." Dawson went to the door, paused, looked back, and said, "I'll thank Him for our success and pray for more of the same."

"Say one for me," Salsbury said with sarcasm he knew would escape the man.

Frowning, Dawson said, "I don't believe in that."

"In what?"

"I can't pray for your soul. And I can only pray for your success so far as it supports my own. I don't believe one man should pray for another. The salvation of your soul is your own concern—and the most vital of your life. The notion that you can buy indulgences or have someone else—a priest, anyone else—pray for you . . . Well, that strikes me as Roman Catholic. I'm not Roman Catholic."

Salsbury said, "Neither am I."

"I'm glad to hear it," Leonard said. He smiled warmly, one Pope-hater to another, and went out.

A maniac, Salsbury thought. What am I doing in partnership with that maniac?

Disturbed by his own question, he went around the desk again, listening to the voices of the people in Black River. Gradually he forgot about Dawson and regained his confidence. It *was* going to work out as planned. He *knew* it. He was *sure* of it. What could possibly go wrong?

11.

Friday, August 26, 1977

RYA FLUNG THE CAGE KEY high into the air and a few feet ahead of her. She ran forward as if she were playing center field, and she caught the golden "ball." Then she flipped it up and ran after it again.

At the corner of Main Street and Union Road, she tossed the key once more—and missed. She heard the metal edge ring as it struck the sidewalk behind her, but when she turned she couldn't see the trinket anywhere.

Emma Thorp bent over and braced her arms on the kitchen table. She accidentally knocked aside an empty coffee cup. It fell off the table and shattered on the tile floor.

Kicking the fragments out of his way, Salsbury stepped in behind her and with both hands stroked the graceful curve of her back.

Bob watched, smiling primly.

Jeremy watched, amazed.

Tat-tat-tat-tat-tat: the power, Miriam, his mother, the whores, Dawson, Klinger, women, vengeance . . . Ricocheting thoughts.

She looked over her shoulder at him.

"I've always wanted one of you like this." He giggled. He could not suppress it. He felt good. "Scared of me. Of *me!*"

Her face was pale and streaked with tears. Her eyes were wide.

"Lovely," he said.

"I don't want you touching me."

"Miriam used to say that. But with Miriam it was an order. She never begged." He touched her.

She was covered with gooseflesh.

"Don't stop crying," he said. "I like you crying."

She wept, not quietly but uncontrollably and unashamedly, as if she were a child—as if she were in agony.

As he prepared to enter her, he heard someone shout just beyond the window. Startled, he said, "Who—"

The kitchen door crashed open. A boy, no older than Jeremy Thorp, came inside, shouting at the top of his voice and windmilling his thin arms.

At the edge of the Thorp property, Rya tossed the key and missed it again.

Two errors out of forty catches isn't so bad, she thought. In fact that's major league talent. Rya Annendale of the Boston Red Sox! Didn't sound bad. Not bad at all. Rya Annendale of the Pittsburgh Pirates! That was even better.

This time she saw where the key fell in the grass. She went straight to it and picked it up.

When the door flew open and the boy charged in like a dangerous animal breaking free of its cage, Salsbury stepped away from the woman and pulled up his trousers.

"You let go of her!"

The boy collided with him.

"Get *out* of here! Now! *Out!*"

Under attack, Salsbury staggered backwards. He was strong enough to handle the boy, but he was suffering from surprise and confusion; and he had lost his balance. When he backed into the refrigerator, still trying to button the waistband of his slacks, the boy pummeling him, he realized that it was ridiculous for him, of all people, to retreat. "I am the key."

The boy hit him. Called him names.

Desperate, Salsbury fought back, seized him by the wrists and struggled with him. "I am the key!"

"Mr. Thorp! Jeremy! Help me!"

"Stay right where you are," Salsbury told them.

They didn't move.

He swung the boy around, reversing their positions, and slammed him against the refrigerator. Bottles and cans and jars rattled loudly on the shelves.

Very young children would not have been affected by the subliminal program that had been played for Black River. Below the age of eight, children were not sufficiently aware of death and sex to respond to the motivational equations that the subceptive films established in older individuals. Furthermore, although the vocabulary had been made as simple as possible since the Holbrook-Rossner-Picard indoctrination, a child had to have at least a third-grade reading ability to be properly impressed by the block-letter messages that established the key-lock code phrases. But this boy was older than eight, and he should respond.

Through clenched teeth Salsbury said, *"I'm the key, damn you!"*

Halfway across the lawn, atop the grape arbor, a robin bounced along the interlocking vines, stopped after every second or third hop, cocked its head, and peered between the leaves. Rya paused to watch him for a moment.

Panic.

He had to guard against panic.

But he had made a fatal mistake, and he might have the power taken away from him.

No. It was a serious mistake. Granted. Very serious. But not fatal. He must not panic. Keep cool.

"Who are you?" he asked.

The boy squirmed, tried to free himself.

"Where are you from?" Salsbury demanded, gripping him so tightly that he gasped.

The boy kicked him in the shin. Hard.

For an instant Salsbury's whole world was reduced to a bright bolt of pain that shot from his ankle to his thigh, coruscated in his bones. Howling, wincing, he almost fell.

Wrenching loose, the boy ran toward the sink, away from the table, intent on getting around Salsbury.

Salsbury stumbled after him, cursing. He grabbed at the boy's shirt, hooked it with his fingers, lost hold of it in the same second, tripped and fell.

If the little bastard gets away . . .

"Bob!" Panic. "Stop him." Hysteria. "Kill him. For God's sake, *kill him!*"

The canary cage was on the lawn by the kitchen window.

Rya heard Buster chattering—and then she heard someone shouting in the house.

Tat-tat-tat-tat . . .

Salsbury got up.

Sick. Scared.

The naked woman wept.

Crazily, he thought of the refrain from the rhyme that went with a child's game that he had once played: *all fall down . . . all fall down . . . all fall down . . .*

Thorp blocked the door.

The boy tried to dodge him.

"Kill him."

Thorp caught the intruder and drove him backwards, knocked him against the electric range with devastating force, clutched him by the throat, and pounded his head into the stainless steel brightwork that ringed the four burners. A frying pan fell to the floor with a *clang!* As if he were a machine, an automaton, Thorp hammered the boy's head against the metal edge until he felt the skull give way. When blood sprayed across the wall behind the range and streamed from the boy's nostrils, the big man let go, stepped back as the body crumpled at his feet.

Jeremy was crying.

"Stop that," Salsbury said sharply.

The boy stopped, reluctantly.

On his way to the bloodied child, Salsbury saw a girl in the open door. She was staring at the blood, and she seemed mesmerized by the sight. He started toward her.

She looked up, dazed.

"I am the key."

She turned and fled.

Salsbury ran to the door—but when he got there, she was already gone around the corner of the house, out of sight.

Part Two

TERROR

1.

Friday, August 26, 1977

9:45 A.M.

RYA SAT IN THE FRONT SEAT of the station wagon between
Paul and Jenny, silent and unmoving, gripped by what appeared to be fear and by anger as well. Her hands were curled
into solid little fists in her lap. Beneath her summer tan she
was ashen. Fine beads of perspiration were strung along her
hairline. She pressed her lips together like the halves of a
vise, partly to keep them from trembling, partly as a sign of
her extreme anger, frustration, and determination to prove
herself right.

   Although she had never lied to him about anything serious,
Paul couldn't believe the story she had told them minutes
ago. She had seen *something* odd at the Thorp house. He was
fairly certain of that. However, she had surely misinterpreted
what she had seen. When she burst in upon Sam, Jenny, and
him at the store, her tears and horror had been genuine; of
that there was absolutely no doubt. But Mark dead? Un-
thinkable. Beaten to death by Bob Thorp, the chief of police?
Ridiculous. If she wasn't lying—well, then she was at least
terribly confused.

"It's t-t-true, Daddy. It's true! I swear to God it's true. They . . . they k-k-killed him. They did. Mr. Thorp did. The other man t-told Mr. Thorp to k-kill, and he did. He kept b-b-banging Mark's head . . . his head . . . banging it against the stove. It was awful. B-banging it . . . over and over again . . . and all the blood . . . Oh, God, Daddy, it's crazy but it's true!"

It *was* crazy.

And it *couldn't* be true.

Yet when she first came into the store—breathing hard, half-choking and half-crying, babbling as if she were in a fever, so unlike herself—he felt an icy hand on the back of his neck. As she told her improbable story, the glacial fingers lingered. And they were still there.

He turned the corner onto Union Road. The police chief's house was a quarter of a mile away, the last on the street, near the river. The garage, large enough for two cars and topped by a workman's loft, lay fifty yards beyond the house. He pulled into the driveway and parked the station wagon in front of the garage.

"Where's the canary cage?" he asked.

Rya said, "It was over there. Near the window. They've moved it."

"Looks calm. Peaceful. Doesn't seem like a murder took place half an hour ago."

"Inside," Rya said sharply. "They killed him inside."

Jenny took hold of the girl's hand and squeezed it. "Rya—"

"*Inside.*" Her face was set; she was resolute.

"Let's have a look," Paul said.

They got out of the car and crossed the freshly mown lawn to the back of the house.

Emma had evidently heard them drive up; for by the time they reached the kitchen stoop, she had the door open and was waiting for them. She wore a royal blue floor-length corduroy housecoat with a high neckline, round collar, and light blue corduroy belt at the waist. Her long hair was combed back and tucked behind her ears, held in place by a few bobby pins. She was smiling, pleased to see them.

"Hi," Paul said awkwardly. He was suddenly at a loss for words. If even a tiny fraction of Rya's tale were true, Emma would not be this serene. He began to feel foolish for having placed any faith whatsoever in such a bizarre story. He couldn't imagine how he would ever tell Emma about it.

"Hi there," she said cheerily. "Hello, Rya. Jenny, how is your father?"

"Fine, thanks," Jenny said. She sounded quite as bewildered as Paul felt.

"Well," Emma said, "I'm still in my robe. The breakfast dishes haven't been washed. The kitchen's a greasy mess. But if you don't mind sitting down in a disaster zone, you're welcome to visit."

Paul hesitated.

"Something wrong?" Emma asked.

"Is Bob home?"

"He's at work."

"When did he leave?"

"Same as every day. A few minutes before nine."

"He's at the police station?"

"Or cruising around in the patrol car." Emma no longer needed to ask if something was wrong; she knew. "Why?"

Why indeed? Paul thought. Rather than explain, he said, "Is Mark here?"

"He was," Emma said. "He and Jeremy went over to the basketball court behind the Union Theater."

"When was that?"

"Half an hour ago."

It seemed to him that she *had* to be telling the truth, for her statement could be verified or disproved so easily. If her husband had killed Mark, what could he hope to gain by such a flimsy lie? Besides, he didn't think she was the sort of woman who could take part in the cover-up of a murder—certainly not with such apparent equanimity, not without showing a great deal of stress and guilt.

Paul looked down at Rya.

Her face was still a mask of stubbornness—and even more pale and drawn than it had been in the car. "What about Buster?" she asked Emma. Her voice was sharp and too loud. "Did they take Buster over to the court so he could play basketball with them?"

Understandably bewildered by the girl's uncharacteristic nastiness and her intense reaction to such a simple statement, Emma said, "The squirrel? Oh, they left him with me. Do you want the squirrel?" She stepped back, out of the doorway. "Come in."

For a moment, recalling the tale of mindless violence that Rya had related just thirty minutes ago, Paul wondered if Bob Thorp was in the kitchen, waiting for him . . .

But that was absurd. Emma was not aware that supposedly a boy had been slain in her kitchen this morning; he would have wagered nearly any sum on that. And in the light of Emma's innocence, Rya's story seemed altogether a fantasy—and not really a very good one, at that.

He went inside.

The canary cage stood in one corner, next to the flip-top waste can. Buster sat on his hind feet and busily nibbled an apple. His tail flicked straight up, and he went stiff as a wooden squirrel when he became aware of the guests. He assessed Paul and Rya and Jenny as if he had never seen them before, decided there was no danger, and returned to his breakfast.

"Mark told me he likes apples," Emma said.

"He does."

The kitchen held no evidence that a violent and deadly struggle had taken place there. The dishes on the table were spotted with dried egg yolk, butter, and crumbs of toast. The clock-radio produced soft instrumental music, an orchestrated version of a pop tune. The new issue of the weekly newspaper, distributed that morning, was folded in half and propped against two empty juice glasses and the sugar bowl. A cup of steaming coffee stood beside the paper. If she had watched her husband murder a child, could Emma have sat down to read less than an hour after the killing? Improbable. Impossible. There was no blood on the wall behind the electric range, no blood on the range itself, and no blood, not even one thin smear, on the tile floor.

"Did you come to get Buster?" Emma asked. She was clearly perplexed by their behavior.

"No," Paul said. "But we'll take him off your hands. Actually, I'm ashamed to tell you why we *did* come."

"They cleaned it up," Rya said.

"I don't want to hear—"

"They cleaned up the blood," she said excitedly.

Paul pointed one finger at her. "You have caused quite enough trouble for one day, young lady. You keep quiet. I'll talk to you later."

Ignoring his warning, she said, "They cleaned up the blood and hid his body."

"Body?" Emma looked confused. "What body?"

"It's a misunderstanding, a hoax, or—" Paul began.

Rya interrupted him. To Emma she said, "Mr. Thorp killed Mark. You know he did. Don't lie! You stood at that chair and watched him beat Mark to death. You were naked and—"

"Rya!" Paul said sharply.

"It's true!"

"I told you to be quiet."

"She was naked and—"

In eleven years he had never been required to deal out any punishment more severe than a twenty-four-hour suspension of some of her privileges. But now, angry, he started toward her.

Rya pushed past Jenny, threw open the kitchen door, and ran.

Shocked by her defiance, angry and yet worried about her, Paul went after her. When he set foot on the stoop, she was already out of sight. She couldn't have had time to run to the garage or to the station wagon; therefore, she must have slipped around the corner of the house, either left or right. He decided she would most likely head for Union Road, and he went that way. When he reached the sidewalk he saw her and called to her.

She was nearly a block away, on the far side of the street, still running. If she heard him, she didn't respond; she disappeared between two houses.

He crossed the street and followed her. But when he reached the rear lawns of those houses, she wasn't there.

"Rya!"

She didn't answer him. She might have been too far away to hear—but he suspected that she was hiding nearby.

"Rya, I just want to talk to you!"

Nothing. Silence.

Already his anger had largely given way to concern for her. What in the name of God had possessed the girl? Why had she concocted such a grisly story? And how had she managed to tell it with such passion? He hadn't really believed any of it, not from the start—yet he'd been so impressed by her sincerity that he'd come to the Thorp house to see for himself. She wasn't a liar by nature. She wasn't *that* good an actress. At least not in his experience. And when her story was shown to be a lie, why had she defended it so ardently?

How had she defended it so ardently, knowing it was a lie? Did she believe, perhaps, that it *wasn't* a fabrication? Did she think that she actually *had* seen her brother killed? But if that was the case, she was—mentally disturbed. Rya? Mentally disturbed? Rya was tough. Rya knew how to cope. Rya was a rock. Even an hour ago he would have staked his life on her soundness of mind. Was there any psychological disorder that could strike a child so suddenly, without warning, without any symptoms beforehand?

Deeply worried, he went back across the street to apologize to Emma Thorp.

2.

JEREMY THORP STOOD, almost as if at attention before a military court, in the center of the kitchen.

"Do you understand what I've said?" Salsbury asked.

"Yeah."

"You know what to do?"

"Yeah. I know."

"Any questions?"

"Just one."

"What is it?"

"What do I do if they don't show up?"

"They'll show up," Salsbury said.

"But what if they don't?"

"You have a watch, don't you?"

The boy held up one thin wrist.

"You wait twenty minutes for them. If they don't show up in that time, come straight back here. Is that understood?"

"Yeah. Twenty minutes."

"Get moving."

The boy started toward the door.

"Don't leave that way. They'll see you. Go out the front."

Jeremy went down the narrow hall to the door.

Salsbury followed, watched until the boy was out of sight behind the neighboring house, closed the door, locked it, and went back to the kitchen.

Not bad, he thought. You're holding up well, Ogden. H. Leonard himself couldn't have coped any faster than you've done. Clever as hell. You are certainly clever. With your mind and the advantage of the power, the key-lock code phrases, you'll weather this crisis. If Miriam could see you now . . . What would old Miriam say now? You aren't anything like Miriam said you were. You're a tough customer. Jesus, what a tough customer. You make sound decisions under pressure, and you stick with them. Smart. Damned smart. *But oh, my God, what a razor edge you're walking!*

Standing next to the rear window, he pushed the curtain aside a fraction of an inch, until he could see the garage. Annendale slid the squirrel's cage into the cargo bed of the station wagon, closed the tailgate, and put up the electric window. Jenny Edison got in the car. Annendale and Emma talked for perhaps a minute. Then he got behind the wheel and reversed out of the driveway. When Emma waved good-by to them and started back toward the house, Salsbury let the curtain fall into place.

She came into the kitchen, saw him, and was startled. She looked as if she was ready to scream. "What are you doing here? Who are you?"

"I am the key."

"I am the lock."

"Relax."

She did.

"Sit down."

She sat.

He stood in front of her, loomed over her. "What were you and Annendale talking about out there?"

"He kept apologizing for his daughter's behavior."

Salsbury laughed.

Because her memories of this morning's events had been selectively edited, she didn't see the humor in the situation. "Why would Rya accuse Bob of murder? What a terrible thing. Does she think she's being funny? What a gruesome joke!"

* * *

The entrance foyer of St. Margaret Mary's Roman Catholic Church was quiet and nearly lightless. The entire interior was done in dark pine—pegged pine floors, dark pine walls, open-beam ceilings, an intricately carved twelve-foot-high crucifix—as befitted the major house of worship in a lumber mill town. A five-watt bulb burned above the holy water font twelve feet away. At the far end of the auditorium, votive candles flickered in ruby-colored glass cups, and soft lights shone at the base of the altar. However, little of this ghostly illumination filtered through the open archway into the foyer.

Cloaked in these shadows and in the holy silence, Jeremy Thorp leaned against one of the two heavy, brass-fitted front doors of the church. He opened it only two or three inches and held it in place with his hip. Beyond lay a set of brick steps, the sidewalk, a pair of birch trees, and then the western end of Main Street. The Union Theater was directly across the street; he had an adequate view of it in spite of the birches.

Jeremy looked at his watch in the blade of light that sliced through the narrow crack between the doors. 10:20.

As they approached the traffic light at the town square, Paul switched on the righthand turn signal.

Jenny said, "The store's to the left."

"I know."

"Where are we going?"

"To the basketball court behind the theater."

"To check up on Emma?"

"No. I'm sure she's telling the truth."

"Why, then?"

"I want to ask Mark exactly what *did* happen this morning," he said, tapping his fingers on the steering wheel as he waited impatiently for the light to change.

"Emma told us what happened. Nothing."

He said, "Emma's eyes were red and puffy, as if she'd been crying. Maybe she and Bob had an argument while Mark was there. Rya might have come to the door at the height of the shouting. She might have misunderstood what was happening; she panicked and ran."

"Emma would have told us."

"She might have been too embarrassed."

As the traffic light turned green, Jenny said, "Panic? That sure doesn't sound like Rya."

"I know. But is it more in character for her to fabricate extravagant lies?"

She nodded. "You're right. As unlikely as it is, it's *more* likely that she was confused and that she panicked."

"We'll ask Mark."

According to Jeremy Thorp's wrist watch it was 10:22 when Paul Annendale drove his station wagon up Main Street and into the alleyway beside the theater. As soon as the car was out of sight, the boy left the church. He went down the front steps, stood at the curb, and waited for the station wagon to reappear.

During the last hour the sky had come closer to the earth. From horizon to horizon, a solid mass of lowering gray-black clouds rolled eastward, driven by a strong high-altitude wind. Some of that wind had begun to sweep the streets of Black River, just enough of it to turn the leaves on the trees—a sign, according to folklore, of oncoming rain.

No rain, please, Jeremy thought. We don't want any damn rain. At least not before tonight. This summer a dozen kids had organized a series of bicycle races to be held every Friday. Last week he had placed second in the main event, the cross-town dash. But I'll be first this week, he thought. I've been in training. Heavy training. Not wasting my time like those other kids. I'm sure to be the first this week—if it doesn't rain.

He glanced at his watch again. 10:26.

A few seconds later, when he saw the station wagon coming back down the alley, Jeremy started walking east along Main Street at a brisk pace.

As the car nosed out of the alley, just as Paul was about to turn right onto Main Street, Jenny said, "There's Jeremy."

Paul tapped the brakes. "Where?"

"Across the street."

"Mark's not with him." He blew the horn, put down his window, and motioned for the boy to come to him.

After he had looked both ways, Jeremy crossed the street. "Hi, Mr. Annendale, Hi, Jenny."

Paul said, "Your mother told me you and Mark were playing basketball behind the theater."

"We started to. But it wasn't much fun, so we went up to Gordon's Woods."

"Where's that?"

They were in the final block of Main Street; but the road continued to the west. It rose with the land, rounded a bluff, and went on until it reached the mill and after that the logging camp.

Jeremy pointed to the forest atop the bluff. "That's Gordon's Woods."

"Why would you want to go up there?" Paul asked.

"We've got a treehouse in Gordon's Woods." The boy read Paul's expression accurately, and he quickly said, "Oh, don't worry, Mr. Annendale. It's not a rickety old place. It's completely safe. Some of our fathers built it for all the kids in town."

"He's right," Jenny said. "It's safe. Sam was one of the fathers who built it." She smiled. "Even though his daughter is a bit too old for treehouses."

Jeremy grinned. He wore braces. Those and the freckles that peppered his face disarmed Paul. The boy clearly didn't have the guile, the dark personality, or the experience to take part in a murder conspiracy.

Paul felt somewhat relieved. When he hadn't found Jeremy and Mark at the basketball court, that icy hand had settled once more, if briefly, on the back of his neck. He said, "Is Mark up at the treehouse now?"

"Yeah."

"Why aren't you there?"

"Me and Mark and a couple of other kids want to play Monopoly. So I'm going home to get my set."

"Jeremy . . ." How could he possibly find out what he wanted to know? "Did anything—happen in your kitchen this morning?"

The boy blinked, a bit perplexed by the question. "We had breakfast."

Feeling more foolish than ever, Paul said, "Well . . . You better get your Monopoly set. The other kids are waiting."

Jeremy said good-by to Jenny and Paul and to Buster, turned, looked both ways, and crossed the street.

Paul watched him until he turned the corner at the square.

"Now what?" Jenny said.

"Rya probably ran to Sam for sympathy and protection." He sighed. "She's had time to calm down. Maybe she realizes that she panicked. We'll see what her story is now.''

"If she didn't run to Sam?"

"Then there's no use looking for her all over town. If she wants to hide from us, she can with little trouble. Sooner or later she'll come to the store.''

Sitting at the kitchen table, across from his mother, Jeremy recounted the conversation he'd had with Paul Annendale a few minutes ago.

When the boy finished, Salsbury said, "And he believed it?''

Jeremy frowned. "Believed what?''

"He believed that Mark was at the treehouse?''

"Well, sure. Isn't he?''

Okay. Okay, okay, Salsbury thought. This isn't the end of the crisis. You've bought some time to think. An hour or two. Maybe three hours. Eventually Annendale will go looking for his son. Two or three hours. You've no time to waste. Be decisive. You've been wonderfully decisive so far. What you've got to do is be decisive and get this straightened out before you have to tell Dawson about it.

Earlier, within twenty minutes of the boy's death, he had edited the Thorp family's memories, had erased all remembrance of the killing from their minds. That editing took no longer than two or three minutes—but it was only the first stage of a plan to conceal his involvement in the murder. If the situation were any less desperate, if a capital offense hadn't been committed, if the entire key-lock program didn't hang in the balance, he could have left the Thorps with blank spots in their memories, and he would have felt perfectly safe in spite of that. But the circumstances were such that he knew he should not merely wipe out the truth but that he should also replace it with a detailed set of false memories, recollections of routine events which might have happened that morning but which in reality did not.

He decided to begin with the woman. To the boy he said, "Go into the living room and sit on the couch. Don't move from there until I call for you. Understood?''

"Yeah." Jeremy left the room.

Salsbury thought for a minute about how to proceed.

Emma watched him, waited.

Finally he said, "Emma, what time is it?''

She looked at the clock-radio. "Twenty minutes of eleven."

"No," he said softly. "That's wrong. It's twenty minutes of nine. Twenty minutes of nine this morning."

"It is?"

"Look at the clock, Emma."

"Twenty of nine," she said.

"Where are you, Emma?"

"In my kitchen."

"Who else is here?"

"Just you."

"No." He sat in Jeremy's chair. "You can't see me. You can't see me at all. Can you, Emma?"

"No. I can't see you."

"You *can* hear me. But you know what? Whenever our little conversation is over, you won't remember we've had it. Every event that I describe to you in the next couple of minutes will become a part of your memories. You won't remember that you were *told* these things. You will think that you actually experienced them. Is that clear, Emma?"

"Yes." Her eyes glazed. Her facial muscles went slack.

"All right. What time is it?"

"Twenty minutes of nine."

"Where are you?"

"In my kitchen."

"Who else is here?"

"No one."

"Bob and Jeremy are here."

"Bob and Jeremy are here," she said.

"Bob's in that chair."

She smiled at Bob.

"Jeremy's sitting there. The three of you are eating breakfast."

"Yes. Breakfast."

"Fried eggs. Toast. Orange juice."

"Fried eggs. Toast. Orange juice."

"Pick up that glass, Emma."

She lifted the empty glass in front of her.

"Drink, Emma."

She stared doubtfully at the tumbler.

"It's filled to the top with cold, sweet orange juice. Do you see it?"

"Yes."

"Doesn't it look good?"

"Yes."

"Drink some of it, Emma."

She drank from the empty glass.

He laughed aloud. The power . . . It was going to work. He could make her remember whatever he wished. "How does it taste?"

She licked her lips. "Delicious."

Lovely animal, he thought, suddenly giddy. Lovely, lovely little animal.

3.

IN BUDDY'S NIGHTMARE two men were filling the town's reservoir with cats. In the deepest shadows of the night, just before sunrise, they were standing at the edge of the pool, opening cages and pitching the animals into the water. The felines squalled about this assault on their dignity and comfort. Soon the reservoir was teeming with cats: alley cats, Siamese cats, Angora cats, Persian cats, black cats and gray cats and white cats and yellow cats, striped cats, spotted cats, old cats and kittens. Below the reservoir in Black River, Buddy innocently turned on the cold water tap in his kitchen—and cats, dozens upon dozens of fiercely angry cats, began to spill into the sink, full-sized cats that had somehow, miraculously, passed through the plumbing, through narrow-gauge pipe and rat traps and elbow joints and filter screens. Screeching, wailing, hissing, biting, scratching cats fell over one another and clawed the porcelain and scrambled inexorably out of the sink as new streams of cats poured in behind them. Cats on the counter. Cats on the breadbox. Cats in the dish rack. They leapt to the floor and clambered atop the cupboards. One of them jumped on Buddy's back as he turned to run. He tore it loose and threw it against the wall. The other cats were outraged by this cruelty. They swarmed after Buddy, all of them spitting and snarling. He reached the bedroom/living room inches ahead of them, slammed and locked the door. They threw themselves against the far side of the barrier and yammered incessantly, but they weren't strong enough to force their way through it. Relieved that he had escaped them, Buddy turned—and saw ten-yard-square cages full of cats, scores of green eyes studying him intensely, and behind the cages two men wearing shoulder holsters, holding pistols, and dressed in black rubber scuba suits.

He woke up, sat up, and screamed. He flailed at the mattress, wrestled with the sheets, and pounded his fists into the pillows for a few seconds until, gradually, he realized that none of these things was a cat.

"Dream," he mumbled.

Because Buddy slept in the mornings and early afternoons, the drapes were heavy, and there was virtually no light in the room. He quickly switched on the bedside lamp.

No cats.

No men in scuba suits.

Although he knew that he had been dreaming, although he'd had this same dream on each of the last three days, Buddy got out of bed, stepped into a pair of slippers that were as large as most men's boots, and lumbered into the kitchen to check the water faucets. There were no cats streaming out of them, and that was a good thing to know.

However, he was badly shaken. He was no less affected by the dream for having endured it on two other occasions. All week his sleep had been disturbed by dreams of one sort or another; and he never was able to fall back to sleep once brought awake by a vivid nightmare.

The wall clock showed 12:13. He came home from the mill at half past eight and went to bed at half past nine, five days a week, as if he were a clockwork mechanism. Which meant that he had gotten barely three hours of sleep.

He went to the kitchen table, sat down, and opened the travel magazine that he had bought at the general store last Monday. He studied the photographs of divers in scuba suits.

Why? he thought. Divers. Seamen. Guns. At the reservoir.

Why? So late. Late at night. Dark, Divers. Why? Figure it. Come on. Figure it. Can't. Can. Can't. Can. Can't. Divers. In woods. Night. So crazy. Can't figure it.

He decided to shower, get dressed, and walk across the street to Edison's General Store. It was time he asked Sam to figure it for him.

At 12:05 Rya watched a man in thick glasses, gray trousers, and a dark blue shirt enter Pauline Vicker's rooming house. He was the man who had ordered Bob Thorp to kill Mark.

At 12:10 she went to St. Margaret Mary's and hid in one of the confessionals at the right rear corner of the nave. Last week she had heard Emma mention the Friday lunch and card club that met all afternoon in the church basement. Through a chink in the crimson velveteen confessional curtains, she could look across the back of the nave to the steps that led down to the recreation room. Women in bright summer dresses and pantsuits, many of them carrying umbrellas, arrived singly and in pairs for the next fifteen minutes—and Emma Thorp came through the foyer arch promptly at twelve thirty. Rya recognized her even in the dim light. As soon as Emma disappeared down the stairs, Rya left the confessional.

For a moment she was transfixed by the sight of the crucifix at the far end of the chamber. The wooden Christ seemed to be staring over all the pews, directly at her.

You could have saved my mother, she thought. You could have saved Mark. Why did you put killers on earth?

Of course the crucifix had no answer.

God helps those who help themselves, she thought. Okay. I'm going to help myself. I'm going to make them pay for what they did to Mark. I'm going to get proof of it. You wait and see if I don't. You wait and see.

She was beginning to tremble again, and she felt tears at the corners of her eyes. She took a minute to calm herself, then walked out of the nave.

In the foyer she discovered that one of the main doors was open, and that the lowest of its four hinges had been removed. A toolbox stood on the foyer floor, and a variety of tools were spread out around it. The workman apparently had gone to get some piece of material that he had forgotten on his first trip.

She turned and looked through the archway at the twelve-foot-high crucifix.

The wooden eyes still seemed to be staring at her, a terribly sad expression in them.

Quickly, worried that the workman might return at any moment, she bent down, peered into the toolbox, and plucked a heavy wrench from it. She slipped the wrench into a pocket of her windbreaker and left the church.

At 12:35 she strolled past the municipal building which was at the northeast corner of the square. The police chief's office was toward the rear of the first floor, and it had two large windows. The venetian blinds were raised. As she passed she saw Bob Thorp sitting at his desk, facing the windows; he was eating a sandwich and reading a magazine.

At 12:40 she stood in front of Ultman's Cafe and watched as a dozen kids cycled north on Union Road toward the macadamed alley where some of the Friday races were held. Jeremy Thorp was one of the cyclists.

At 12:45, at the southern end of Union Road, Rya crossed the street, walked under the grapevine arbor, and went around to the back of the Thorp place. The lawn ended in brush and trees, no parallel streets and no buildings in that direction. There was no house to her left—just the lawn and the garage and the river. To her right the nearest dwelling was set closer to Union Road than was the Thorp house; therefore, she was not in anyone's line of sight.

A polished copper knocker gleamed in the center of the door. To one side of that, near the knob, were three decorative windows, each six inches wide and nine inches long.

She knocked loudly.

No one answered.

When she tried the door she found that it was locked. She had expected as much.

She took the stolen wrench from her windbreaker, gripped it tightly in one hand, and used it to smash the middle pane in the vertical row of three. The blow made considerably more noise than she had anticipated—although not sufficient noise to discourage her. When she had broken every shard of glass out of the frame, she pocketed the wrench, reached through the window, and felt for the latch. She began to despair of ever locating the mechanism—and then her fingers touched cool metal. She fumbled with the lock for almost a minute,

finally released it, withdrew her arm from the window, and
shoved open the door.

Standing on the stoop, staring warily into the shadow-hung
kitchen, she thought: What if one of them comes back home
and finds me in there?

Go ahead, she urged herself. You better go inside before
you lose your courage.

I'm scared. They killed Mark.

You ran away this morning. Are you going to run away
again? Are you going to run away from everything that scares
you, from now until the day you die?

She walked into the kitchen.

Glass crunched underfoot.

When she reached the electric range where the murder had
taken place, she stood quite still, poised to flee, and listened
closely for movement. The refrigerator and the upright freezer
rumbled softly, steadily. The clock-radio hummed. A loose
window rattled as a gust of wind rushed along the side of the
house. In the living room a grandfather clock, running a few
minutes late, solemnly chimed the third quarter of the hour;
the note reverberated long after the pipe had been struck. The
house was filled with noises; but none of them had a human
source; she was alone.

Having broken the law, having violated the sanctity of another person's home, with the first and most dangerous step
already taken, she couldn't decide what to do next. Well . . .
Search the house. Of course. Search it from top to bottom.
Look for the body. But where to begin?

At last, when she realized that her indecision was an out-
growth of the fear which she was determined to overcome,
when she realized that she was desperately afraid of finding
Mark's corpse even though she had come here to do precisely
that, she began the search in the kitchen. There were only a
few places in that room where the body of a nine-year-old
boy might possibly be concealed. She looked in the pantry, in
the refrigerator, and then in the freezer, but she uncovered
nothing out of the ordinary.

When she opened the cabinet beneath the sink, however,
she saw a bucket full of bloody rags. Not rags, really. Dish
towels. They had used the towels to clean up, had thrown
them in the bucket—and then apparently had forgotten to destroy the evidence. She picked up one of the cloths. It was

wet, cold, and heavy with blood. She dropped it and gazed at her stained hand.

"Oh, Mark," she said sadly, a bit breathlessly. A pain rose from deep inside of her, filled her chest. "Little Mark . . . You never ever hurt anyone. Not anyone. What they did to you. What an awful thing they did to you. *Why?*"

She stood up. Her knees felt weak.

Find the body, she thought.

No, she told herself.

You came here to find the body.

I've changed my mind. Find the body? No. No, that's just . . . too much. Much too much. Finding him . . . Mark . . . with his skull cracked open . . . and his eyes rolled back in his head . . . and dried blood all over his face . . . Too much. Even strong girls can't deal with everything in life. Even strong girls have their limits, don't they? This is mine. My limit. I can't go looking . . . all through the house . . . just can't . . .

Beginning to cry, beginning to shake, she picked up the bucket and left the house.

At 12:45 Salsbury carried his briefcase down from his room and went to the parlor.

Pauline Vicker was sitting in the largest of the three arm-chairs. She was a heavyset woman in her early sixties. Fluffy gray hair. Ruddy complexion. Double chin. Merry eyes and a nearly constant smile. She had the archetypal grandmother's face, the model for grandmothers' faces in storybooks and movies. Her bare feet were propped up on a hassock. She was eating candies and watching a television soap opera.

From the doorway he said, "Mrs. Vicker."

She glanced up, chewing a caramel. She had some trouble swallowing. Then: "Good afternoon, Mr. Deighton. If you've a complaint about your room or anything—do you think perhaps it could wait just a bit, a few minutes—not longer than that mind you—just until this show ends? It's one of my favorite shows and—"

"I am the key," he said impatiently.

"Oh," she said, disappointed that she wasn't going to be able to finish watching the program. "I am the lock."

"Get up, Mrs. Vicker."

She struggled out of the chair.

Fat old cow, he thought.

"What do you need?" she asked pleasantly.

"I'll need this room for a while," he said, walking to the desk which held her private telephone. "Don't disturb me."

"Am I to leave?"

"Yes. Now."

She looked wistfully at the round maple table beside her armchair. "May I take my box of candy?"

"Yes, yes. Just get the hell out of here."

Pleased, she snatched up the candy. "I'm as good as gone. As good as gone, Mr. Deighton. You take your time here. I won't let anyone disturb you."

"Mrs. Vicker."

"Yes?"

"Go to the kitchen."

"All right."

"Eat your chocolates if you want."

"I will."

"Listen to your radio, and wait in the kitchen until I come to see you."

"Yes, sir."

"Is that completely clear?"

"Certainly. Certainly. I'll do just what you say. See if I don't. I'll go straight out to the kitchen and eat my chocolates and listen—"

"And close the door as you leave," he said sharply. "Leave now, Mrs. Vicker."

She shut the parlor door behind her.

At the desk Salsbury opened his briefcase. He took from it a set of screwdrivers and one of the infinity transmitters—a small black box with several wires trailing from it—that Dawson had purchased in Brussels.

Smart, he thought. Clever. Clever of me to bring the IF. Didn't know why I was packing it at the time. A hunch. Just a hunch. And it's paid off now. Clever. I'm on top of the situation. Right up there on top, in control. Full control.

Having carefully considered his options, algebraic even when he was so recently returned from the edge of panic, he had decided that it was time to hear what Paul Annendale was saying to the Edisons. There were a dozen miniature glass swans lined up across the top of the desk, each slightly different in size and shape and color from the one that preceded it. He brushed these figurines to the floor; they bounced on the carpet and clinked against one another. His mother had collected hand-blown figurines, although not swans. She favored glass dogs. By the hundreds. He crushed one of the swans under his heel and imagined that it was a glass dog. Curiously satisfied by this gesture, he connected the infinity transmitter to the telephone and dialed the number of the general store. Across the street no telephone rang at the Edison's place. Nevertheless, every receiver in the store, as well as in the family's living quarters above the store, opened to Salsbury's ear.

What he heard in the first couple of minutes broke down the paper-thin wall of composure that he had managed to rebuild since the murder. Buddy Pellineri, in his own half-literate fashion, was telling Sam and Jenny and Paul about the two men who had come down from the reservoir on the morning of August sixth.

Rossner and Holbrook had been seen!

However, that was neither the only nor the worst piece of bad news. Before Buddy had reached the end of his story, before Edison and the others had finished questioning him, Annendale's daughter arrived with the bucket full of bloody rags. The damned bucket! In his haste to clean up the kitchen and hide the corpse, he had shoved the bucket under the sink and then had completely forgotten about it. The boy's body wasn't all that well hidden—but at least it wasn't in the room where the murder had occurred. The damned bloody rags. *He had left evidence at the scene of the crime, virtually out in plain sight where any fool could have found it!*

He could no longer afford to spend hours formulating his response to the events of the morning. If he was to contain the crisis and save the project, he would have to think faster and move faster than he had ever done before.

He stepped on another glass swan and snapped it to pieces.

4.

A PEAL OF THUNDER rumbled across the valley, and the wind seemed to gain considerable force in the wake of the noise.

Torn between a desire to believe Emma Thorp and a growing conviction that Rya was telling the truth, Paul Annendale climbed the steps to the stoop at the back of the Thorp house.

Putting a hand on his shoulder, pressing with fingers like talons, Sam said, "Wait."

Paul turned. The wind mussed his hair, blew it into his eyes. "Wait for what?"

"This is breaking and entering."

"The door's open."

"That doesn't change anything," Sam said, letting go of him. "Besides, it's open because Rya broke it open."

Aware that Sam was trying to reason with him for his own good but nonetheless impatient, Paul said, "What in the hell am I supposed to do, Sam? Call the cops? Or maybe pull some strings, use my connections, put a call through to the chief of police, and have him investigate himself?"

"We could call the state police."

"No."

"The body might not even be here."

"If they could avoid it, they wouldn't move a corpse in broad daylight."

"Maybe there is no corpse, not here, not anywhere."

"I hope to God you're right."

"Come on, Paul. Let's call the state police."

"You said they'd need as much as two hours to get here. If the body still *is* in this house—well, it most likely won't be here two hours from now."

"But this is all so improbable! Why on earth would Bob want to murder Mark?"

"You heard what Rya said. That sociologist ordered him to kill. That Albert Deighton."

"She didn't know it was Deighton," Sam said.

"Sam, *you're* the one who recognized him from her description."

"Okay. Granted. But why would Emma go to a church luncheon and card game just after watching her husband kill a defenseless child? *How* could she? And how could a boy like Jeremy witness a brutal murder and then lie to you so smoothly?"

"They're your neighbors. You tell me."

"That's just the point," Sam insisted. "They're *my* neighbors. They have been all their lives. Nearly all their lives. I know them well. As well as I know anyone. And I'm telling you, Paul, they simply aren't capable of this sort of thing."

Paul put one hand to his belly. His stomach spasmed with cramps. The memory of what he had seen in that bucket—the thickening blood and the strands of hair that were the same color as Mark's hair—had affected him physically as well as emotionally. Or perhaps the emotional impact had been so devastating, so overwhelming that a sharp physical revulsion could not help but follow. "You've known these people under ordinary circumstances, during ordinary times. But I swear, Sam, there's something extraordinary happening in this town. First Rya's story. Mark's disappearance. The bloody rags. And on top of that, Buddy comes around with this story of strange men at the reservoir in the dead of night—just a few days before the whole town suffered from a curious, unexplained epidemic—''

Sam blinked in surprise. ''You think the chills are connected with *this*, with—''

A deafening crack of thunder interrupted him.

As the sky grew quiet, Sam said, ''Buddy's not a very reliable witness.''

''You believed him, didn't you?''

''I believe he saw something strange, yes. Whether or not it was precisely what Buddy *thinks* it was—''

''Oh, I know he didn't see skin divers. Skin divers don't wear hip boots. What he saw—I think maybe he saw two men with empty chemical dispersion tanks.''

''Someone contaminated the reservoir?'' Sam asked incredulously.

''Looks that way to me.''

''Who? The government?''

''Maybe. Or maybe terrorists. Or even a private company.''

''But why?''

''To see if the contaminate did what it was supposed to do.''

Sam said, ''Contaminated the reservoir . . . with what?'' He frowned. ''Something that turns sane men into psychopaths who will kill when told to?''

Paul began to shake.

''We haven't found him yet,'' Sam said quickly. ''Don't lose hope. We haven't found him dead.''

''Sam . . . Oh God, Sam, I think we will. I really think we will.'' He was close to tears, but he knew that, for the time being, they were a luxury that he couldn't allow himself to have. He cleared his throat. ''And I'll bet this sociologist, Deighton, is involved with the men Buddy saw. He's not here to study Black River. He knows what was put in the reservoir, and he's in town only to see what effect that substance has on the people here.''

''Why didn't Jenny and I get the night chills?''

Paul shrugged. ''I don't know. And I've no idea what Mark walked into this morning. What did he see that made it necessary for him to be killed?''

They stared at each other, horrified by the idea that the

townspeople were unwitting guinea pigs in some bizarre experiment. Both of them wanted to laugh off the entire notion, dismiss it with a joke or two; but neither of them could even smile.

"If any of this is true," Sam said worriedly, "there's even more reason to call in the state police right now."

Paul said, "We'll find the body first. *Then* we'll call the state police. I'm going to find my son before he winds up in an unmarked grave way to hell and gone in the mountatins."

Gradually, Sam's face became as white as his hair. "Don't talk about him as if you know he's dead. You don't *know* that he's dead, dammit!"

Paul took a deep breath. His chest ached. "Sam, I should have believed Rya this morning. She's no liar. Those bloody dish towels . . . Look, I've got to talk about him as if he's dead. I've got to *think* of him that way. If I convince myself that he's still alive and *then* I find his body—it'll hurt too much. It'll destroy me. Do you understand?"

"Yes."

"You don't have to come in with me."

"I can't let you go alone," Sam said.

"Yes, you can. I'll be fine."

"I *won't* let you go alone."

"All right. Let's get this over with."

"He's a good boy," Sam said quietly. "He's always been such a good boy. I love him like my own."

Paul nodded, turned, and went into the dark house.

The telephone company maintained a narrow, two-story brick building on West Main Street, half a block from the square. It was a two-minute walk from Pauline Vicker's rooming house.

The front office on the first floor—where complaints could be lodged and bills paid—was small and neat. It contained eight gray filing cabinets, a cash register, an electronic calculator, a photostatic copier, a typewriter, a long pine worktable, and two straight-backed chairs in one corner, a large metal desk with a sturdy swivel chair, a Sierra Club calendar, several telephones, stacks of company pamphlets, a radio, and the United States flag in a stainless steel stand. There was no dust on the furniture, no dirt on the tile floor; and every pile of typing paper, forms, and envelopes was properly squared off and neatly stacked.

The only person in the office was as businesslike as the room. She was a thin but not unattractive woman in her middle or late forties. Her short-cropped chestnut hair had no more than a dozen strands of gray in it. Her skin was smooth and milky. Although her features were very angular, they were balanced by a generous, sensuous mouth that saved her looks but seemed to have been borrowed from another face. She wore a smart and efficient green pantsuit with a white cotton blouse. Her glasses were on a chain so that when she took them off they hung ready at her breast.

When Salsbury entered the office, she stepped up to the counter, smiled professionally, and said, "Does it still look like rain out there?"

Closing the mullioned-window door, Salsbury said, "Yes. Yes, it does."

"What can I do for you?"

"I am the lock."

"I am the key."

He went to the counter.

She toyed with the glasses at her breast.

He said, "What's your name?"

"Joan Markham."

"Are you a secretary?"

"I'm the assistant manager."

"How many people are working here?"

"Right now?"

"Right now," he said.

"Six, including me."

"Name them for me, one by one."

"Well, there's Mr. Pulchaski."

"Who's he?"

"The manager."

"Where is he now?"

"In his office. The front room upstairs."

"Who else, Joan?"

"Leona Ives. Mr. Pulchaski's secretary."

"Is she upstairs too?"

"Yes."

"That leaves three."

"Those are operators."

"Switchboard operators?"

"Yes. Mary Ultman, Betty Zimmerman, and Louise Pulchaski."

"Mr. Pulchaski's wife?"

"His daughter," Joan said.

"Where do the operators work?"

She pointed to a door at the back of the room. "That leads to the downstairs hall. The switchboards are in the next room, at the back of the building."

"When do these operators go off duty?"

"At five o'clock."

"And three more come on the new shift?"

"No. Just two. There isn't that much business at night."

"The new shift works until—one in the morning?"

"That's right."

"And two more operators come on duty until nine o'clock in the morning?"

"No. There's just one during the graveyard watch."

She put on her glasses, took them off again a second later.

"Are you nervous, Joan?"

"Yes. Terribly."

"Don't be nervous. Relax. Be calm."

Some of the stiffness went out of her slender neck and shoulders. She smiled.

"Tomorrow is Saturday," he said. "Will there be three operators on duty during the daylight shift?"

"No. On weekends there're never more than two."

"Joan, I see you've got a notebook and pen next to your typewriter. I want you to prepare for me a list of all the operators who are scheduled to work tonight and during the first two shifts tomorrow. I want their names and their home telephone numbers. Understood?"

"Oh, yes."

She went to her desk.

Salsbury crossed to the front door. He studied West Main Street through the six-inch-square panes of glass.

Presaging a summer storm, the wind whipped the trees mercilessly, as if trying to drive them to shelter.

There was no one in sight on either side of the street.

Salsbury looked at his watch. 1:15.

"Hurry up, you stupid bitch."

She looked up. "What?"

"I called you a stupid bitch. Forget that. Just finish the list. Quickly now."

She busied herself with pen and notebook.

Bitches, he thought. Rotten bitches. All of them. Every last one of them. Always fouling up. Nothing but bitches.

An empty lumber truck went past on Main Street, heading toward the mill.

"Here it is," she said.

He returned to the customer service counter, took the notebook page from her hand, and glanced at it. Seven names. Seven telephone numbers. He folded the paper and put it in his shirt pocket. "Now, what about repairmen? Don't you have linemen or repairmen on duty all the time?"

"We have a crew of four men," she said. "There are two on the day shift and two on the evening shift. There's no one regularly scheduled for night shift or for the weekends, but every one of the crew's on call in case of emergencies."

"And there are two men on duty now?"

"Yes."

"Where are they?"

"Working on a problem at the mill."

"When will they be back?"

"By three. Maybe three thirty."

"When they come in, you send them over to Bob Thorp's office." He had already decided to make the police chief's office his headquarters for the duration of the crisis. "Understood, Joan?"

"Yes."

"Write down for me the names and home telephone numbers of the other two repairmen."

She needed half a minute for that assignment.

"Now listen closely, Joan."

Resting her arms on the counter, she leaned toward him. She seemed almost eager to hear what he had to tell her.

"Within the next few minutes, the wind will blow down the lines between here and Bexford. It won't be possible for anyone in Black River or up at the mill to make or receive a long-distance call."

"Oh," she said wearily. "Well, that sure is going to ruin *my* day. It sure is."

"Complaints, you mean?"

"Each one nastier than the one before it."

"If people complain, tell them that linemen from Bexford are working on the break. But there was a great deal of damage. The repairs will take hours. The job might not be done until tomorrow afternoon. Is that clear?"

"They won't like it."

"But is that clear?"

"It's clear."

"All right." He sighed. "In a moment I'm going to go back to talk with the girls at the switchboard. Then upstairs to see your boss and his secretary. When I leave this room, you'll forget everything we've said. You'll remember me as a lineman from Bexford. I was just a lineman from Bexford who stopped in to tell you that my crew was already on the job. Understood?"

"Yes."

"Go back to work."

She returned to her desk.

He walked behind the counter. He left the room by the hall door and went to talk to the switchboard operators.

Paul felt like a burglar.

You're not here to steal anything, he told himself. Just your son's body. If there is a body. And that belongs to you.

Nevertheless, as he poked through the house, undeterred by the Thorps' right to privacy, he felt like a thief.

By 1:45 he and Sam had searched upstairs and down, through the bedrooms and baths and closets, through the living room and den and dining room and kitchen. There was no corpse.

In the kitchen Paul opened the cellar door and switched on the light. "Down here. We should have looked down there first. It's the most likely place."

"Even if Rya's story is true," Sam said, "this isn't easy for me. This prying around. These people are old friends."

"It isn't my style either."

"I feel like such a shit."

"It's almost finished."

They descended the stairs.

The first basement room was a well-used work center. The nearer end contained two stainless-steel sinks, an electric washer-dryer, a pair of wicker clothes baskets, a table large enough for folding freshly laundered towels, and shelves on which stood bottles of bleach, bottles of spot removers, and boxes of detergents. At the other end of the room there was a workbench equipped with vises and all of the other tools that Bob Thorp needed to tie flies. He was an enthusiastic and dedicated fly fisherman who enjoyed creating his own "bait"; but he also sold between two and three hundred pieces of his handiwork every year, more than enough to make his hobby a very profitable one.

Sam peered into the shadow cavity beneath the stairs and then searched the cupboards beside the washer-dryer.

No corpse. No blood. Nothing.

Paul's stomach burned and gurgled as if he had swallowed a glassful of acid.

He looked in the cabinets above and below the workbench, flinching each time he opened a door.

Nothing.

The second basement room, less than half the size of the first, was used entirely for food storage. Two walls were covered with floor-to-ceiling shelves; and these were lined with store-bought as well as home-canned fruits and vegetables. A large, chest-style freezer stood against the far wall.

"In there or nowhere," Sam said.

Paul went to the freezer.

He lifted the lid.

Sam stepped in beside him.

Frigid air rushed over them. Streams of ghostly vapor snaked into the room and were dissipated by the warmer air.

The freezer contained two or three dozen plastic-wrapped and labeled packages of meat. These bundles weren't stacked for optimum use of the space—and to Paul at least, that looked rather odd. Furthermore, they hadn't been arranged according to size or weight or similarity of contents. They were merely dumped together every which way. They appeared to have been thrown into the freezer in great haste.

Paul took a five-pound beef roast from the chest and dropped it on the floor. Then a ten-pound package of bacon. Another five-pound beef roast. Another roast. More bacon. A twenty-pound box of pork chops . . .

The dead boy had been placed in the bottom of the freezer, his arms on his chest and his knees drawn up; and the packages of meat had been used to conceal him. His nostrils were caked with blood. An icy, ruby crust of blood sealed his lips and masked his chin. He stared up at them with milky, frozen eyes that were as opaque as heavy cataracts.

"Oh . . . no. No. Oh, Jesus," Sam murmured. He swung away from the freezer and ran. In the other room he turned on a faucet; the water splashed loudly.

Paul heard him gagging and puking violently into one of the stainless-steel sinks.

Strangely, he was now in full control of his emotions. When he saw his dead son, his intense anger and despair and grief were at once transformed into a deep compassion, into a tenderness that was beyond description.

"Mark," he said softly. "It's okay. Okay now. I'm here. I'm here with you now. You aren't alone anymore."

He took the remaining packages of meat from the freezer, one at a time, slowly excavating the grave.

As Paul removed the last bundle from atop the body, Sam came to the doorway. "Paul? I'll . . . go upstairs. Use the phone. Call . . . the state police."

Paul stared into the freezer.

"Did you hear me?"

"Yes. I heard you."

"Should I call the state police now?"

"Yes. It's time."

"How are you feeling?"

"I'm all right, Sam."

"Will you be okay here—alone?"

"Sure. Fine."

"Are you certain?"

"Sure."

Sam hesitated, finally turned away. He took the steps two at a time, thunderously.

Paul touched the boy's cheek.

It was cold and hard.

Somehow he found the strength to pull the body, stiff as it was, out of the freezer. He balanced his son on the edge of the chest, got both arms under him and lifted him. He swung around and put the boy on the floor, in the center of the room.

He blew on his hands to warm them.

Sam came back, still as pale as the belly of a fish. He looked at Mark. His face twisted with pain, but he didn't cry. He kept control of himself. "There seems to be some trouble with the telephones."

"What sort of trouble?"

"Well, the lines have been blown down between here and Bexford."

Frowning, Paul said, "Blown down? It doesn't seem windy enough for that."

"Not here it isn't. But it probably is much windier farther on toward Bexford. In these mountains you can have a pocket of relative calm right next to a fierce storm."

"The lines to Bexford . . ." Paul brushed strands of stiff, frozen, blood-crusted hair from his son's white forehead. "What does that mean to us?"

"You can ring up anyone you want in town or up at the mill. But you can't place a long-distance call."

"Who told you?"

"The operator. Mandy Ultman."

"Does she have any idea when they'll get it fixed?"

"Evidently, there's been a lot of damage," Sam said. "She tells me a crew of linemen from Bexford are already working. But they'll need several hours to put things right."

"How many hours?"

"Well, they're not even sure they can patch it up any time before tomorrow morning."

Paul remained at his son's side, kneeling on the concrete floor, and he thought about what Sam had said.

"One of us should drive into Bexford and call the state police from there."

"Okay," Paul said.

"You want me to do it?"

"If you want. Or I will. It doesn't matter. But first we have to move Mark to your place."

"Move him?"

"Of course."

"But isn't that against the law?" He cleared his throat. "I mean, the scene of the crime and all that."

"I can't leave him here, Sam."

"But if Bob Thorp did this, you want him to pay for it. Don't you? If you move—move the body, what proof do you have that you actually found it here?"

Surprised by the steadiness of his own voice, Paul said, "The police forensic specialists will be able to find traces of Mark's hair and blood in the freezer."

"But—"

"I can't leave him here!"

Sam nodded. "All right."

"I just can't, Sam."

"Okay. We'll get him to the car."

"Thank you."

"We'll take him to my place."

"Thank you."

"How will we carry him?"

"You—take his feet."

Sam touched the boy. "So cold."

"Be careful with him, Sam."

Sam nodded as they lifted the body.

"Be gentle with him, please."

"Okay."

"Please."

"I will," Sam said. "I will."

5.

2:00 P.M.

THUNDER CANNONADED, and rain shattered against the windows of the police chief's office.

Two men, employees of other governmental departments that shared the municipal building, stood with their backs to the windows, trying to look stern, authoritarian, and eminently reliable. Bob Thorp had provided them with bright yellow hooded rain slickers with POLICE stenciled across their shoulders and chests. Both men were in their middle or late thirties, yet they expressed an almost childish delight at the opportunity to wear these raincoats: adults playing cops and robbers.

"Can you use a gun?" Salsbury asked them.

They both said that they could.

Salsbury turned to Bob Thorp. "Give them guns."

"Revolvers?" the police chief asked.

"Do you have shotguns?"

"Yes."

"I believe those would be better than revolvers," Salsbury said. "Don't you agree?"

"For this operation?" Thorp said. "Yes. Much better."

"Then give them shotguns."

A brilliant explosion of lightning flashed against the windows. The effect was stroboscopic: everyone and every object in the room seemed to jump rapidly back and forth for an instant, although in reality nothing moved.

Overhead the fluorescent lights flickered.

Thorp went to the metal firearms cabinet behind his desk, unlocked it, and fetched two shotguns.

"Do you know how to use these?" Salsbury asked the men in the yellow raincoats.

One of them nodded.

The other said, "Not much to it. These babies pack a hell of a lot of punch. You pretty much just have to point in the general direction of the target and pull the trigger." He gripped the gun with both hands, admired it, smiled at it.

"Good enough," Salsbury said. "The two of you will go out to the parking lot behind this building, get in the spare patrol car, and drive to the east end of town. Understand me so far?"

"To the east end," one of them said.

"A hundred yards short of the turn at the mouth of the valley, you'll park the cruiser across the highway and block both lanes as best you can."

"A roadblock," one of them said, obviously pleased with the way the game was developing.

"Exactly," Salsbury said. "If anyone wants to enter Black River—logging trucks, local citizens, maybe visitors from out of town, anyone at all—you'll let them in. However, you'll send them here, straight to this office. You'll tell them that a state of emergency has been declared in Black River and that they absolutely must, without exception, check in with the chief of police before they go on about their business."

"What kind of emergency?"

"You don't need to know."

One of them frowned.

The other said, "Everyone we stop will want to know."

"If they ask, tell them that the chief will explain it."

Both men nodded.

Thorp distributed a dozen shotgun shells to each of them.

"If anyone tries to *leave* Black River," Salsbury said,

"you'll also direct them to the chief, and you'll give them the same story about a state of emergency. Understood?"

"Yes."

"Yes."

"Every time you send someone to see Bob, whether they were coming into town or trying to get out of it, you'll radio this office. That way, if they don't show up within a few minutes, we'll know that we've got some renegades on our hands. Understood?"

They both said, "Yes."

Salsbury took his handkerchief from his hip pocket and blotted the perspiration from his face. "If anyone leaving town tries to run your roadblock, stop them. If you can't stop them any other way, use the guns."

"Shoot to kill?"

"Shoot to kill," Salsbury said. "But only if there's no other way to stop them."

One of the men tried to look like John Wayne receiving orders at the Alamo, shook his head, solemnly, and said, "Don't worry. You can count on us."

"Any questions?"

"How long will we be in charge of this roadblock?"

"Another team of men will relieve you in six hours," Salsbury said. "At eight o'clock this evening." He jammed his handkerchief back into his pocket. "One other thing. When you leave this room, you will forget that you ever met me. You'll forget that I was here. You'll remember everything I've said to you prior to what I'm saying to you now, every precious exchange of this conversation we've just had—but you'll think that Bob Thorp gave you your instructions. Is that perfectly clear?"

"Yes."

"Perfectly."

"Then get moving."

The two men went out of the room, forgetting him the moment they set foot in the corridor.

A fiercely white pulse of lightning washed over the town, and a crack of thunder followed, rattling the windows.

"Close those blinds," Salsbury said irritably.

Thorp did as he was told.

Salsbury sat down behind the desk.

When he had drawn the Venetian blinds, Bob Thorp returned to the desk and stood in front of it.

Salsbury looked up at him and said, "Bob, I want to seal this burg up tight. Real tight." He made a fist with his right hand by way of example. "I want to make damned sure that no one can get out of town. Is there anything else that I should block in addition to the highway?"

Scratching his beetled brow, Thorp said, "You need two more men at the east end of the valley. One to watch the river. He should be armed with a rifle so he can pick off anyone in a boat if he has to do that. The other man should be stationed in the trees between the river and the highway. Give him a shotgun and tell him to stop anyone who tries to sneak out through the woods."

"The man at the river—he'd have to be an expert with a rifle, wouldn't he?" Salsbury asked.

"You wouldn't need a master rifleman. But he would have to be a fairly good shot."

"Okay. We'll use one of your deputies for that. They're all good with a rifle, aren't they?"

"Oh, sure."

"Good enough for this?"

"No doubt about it."

"Anything else?"

Thorp thought about the situation for almost a minute. Finally he said, "There's a series of old logging roads that lead up to the mountains and eventually hook up with a second series of roads that come from the lumber operations around Bexford. A lot of that route has been abandoned. None of it's paved. A few sections may be graveled if they haven't been washed out this summer, but mostly it's just dirt. Narrow. Full of weeds. But I guess if a man was determined enough, he could drive out that way."

"Then we'll block it," Salsbury said, getting up from the chair. He paced nervously to the windows and back to the desk. "This town is mine. *Mine.* And it'll stay that way. I'm going to keep my hands on every man, woman, and child here until I've solved this problem."

The situation had gotten incredibly far out of hand. He would have to call Dawson. Sooner or later. Probably sooner. Couldn't be avoided. But before he placed that call, he wanted to be certain that he had done everything that he could possibly do without Leonard's help, without Klinger's help.

Show them he was decisive. Clever. A good man to have around. His efficiency might impress the general. And that Christ-kissing bastard. Impress them enough to compensate for his having caused the crisis in the first place. That was very important. Very important. Right now the trick was to survive his partners' wrath.

2:30 P.M.

The air in Sam's library was stale and humid.

Rain drummed on the outside window, and hundreds of tiny beads of dew formed on the inside.

Still numb with the discovery of his son's body, Paul sat in one of the easy chairs, his hands on the arms of the chair and his fingertips pressed like claws into the upholstery.

Sam stood by one of the bookcases, pulling volumes of collected psychology essays from the stacks and leafing through them.

On the wide window ledge, an antique mantel clock ticked hollowly, monotonously.

Jenny came into the room from the hall, letting the door stand open behind her. She knelt on the floor beside Paul's chair and put her hand over his.

"How's Rya?" he asked.

Before they had gone to the Thorp house to search for the body, Sam had given the girl a sedative.

"Sleeping soundly," Jenny said. "She'll be out for at least two more hours."

"Here!" Sam said excitedly.

They looked up, startled.

He came to them, holding up a book of essays. "His picture. The one who calls himself Deighton."

Paul stood up to have a better look at it.

"No wonder Rya and I couldn't find any of his articles," Sam said. "We were looking through tables of contents for something written by Albert Deighton. But that's not his name. His real name's Ogden Salsbury."

"I've seen him," Paul said. "He was in Ultman's Cafe the day that waitress drove the meat fork through her hand. In fact she waited on him."

Rising to her feet, Jenny said, "You think that was connected with the rest of this, with the story Buddy Pellineri told us—with what they did to Mark?'' Her voice faltered slightly on those last few words, and her eyes grew shiny. But she bit her lip and held back the tears.

''Yes,'' Paul said, wondering again at his own inability to weep. He ached. God, he was *full* of pain! But the tears would not come. ''It must be connected. Somehow.'' To Sam he said, ''Salsbury wrote this article?''

''According to the introductory blurb, it was the last piece he ever published—more than twelve years ago.''

''But he's not dead.''

''Unfortunately.''

''Then why the last?''

''Seems he was quite a controversial figure. Praised and damned but mostly damned. And he got tired of the controversy. He dropped out of his lecture tours and gave up his writing so that he'd have more time to dedicate to his research.''

''What's the article about?''

Sam read the title. '' 'Total Behavioral Modification through Subliminal Perception.' '' And the subtitle: '' 'Mind Control from the Inside Out.' ''

''What does all of that mean?''

''Do you want me to read it aloud?''

Paul looked at his watch.

''It wouldn't hurt if we knew the enemy before we went into Bexford to see the state police,'' Jenny said.

''She's right,'' Sam said.

Paul nodded. ''Go ahead. Read it.''

2:40 P.M.

Friday afternoon H. Leonard Dawson was in the study of his Greenwich, Connecticut house, reading a long letter on lavender paper from his wife. Julia was one-third of the way through a three-week trip to the Holy Land, and day by day she was discovering that it was less and less like she had imagined and hoped it would be. The best hotels were all owned by Arabs and Jews, she said; therefore, she felt unclean every time she went to bed. There were plenty of rooms in the inns, she said, but she would almost have preferred to sleep in the stables. That morning (as she wrote the letter) her chauffeur had driven her to Golgotha, that most sweetly sacred of places; and she had read to herself from the Bible as the car wended its way to that shrine of both sorrow and everlasting joy. But even Golgotha had been spoiled for her. Upon arriving there, she found that the holy hill was literally *swarming* with sweaty Southern Negro Baptists. Southern *Negro* Baptists, of all people. Furthermore . . .

The white telephone rang. Its soft, throaty *burrrr-burrrr-burrrr* was instantly recognizable.

The white phone was the most private line in the house. Only Ogden and Ernst knew the number.

He put down the letter, waited until the telephone had rung a second time, picked up the receiver. "Hello?"

"I recognize your voice," Salsbury said guardedly. "Do you find mine familiar?"

"Of course. Are you using your scrambler?"

"Oh, yes," Salsbury said.

"Then there's no need to talk in riddles and be mysterious. Even if the line is tapped, which it isn't, they can't make sense of what we're saying."

"With the situation what it is at my end," Salsbury said, "I think we should take the precaution of riddle and mystery and not trust solely in the scrambler."

"What *is* the situation at your end?"

"We've got serious trouble here."

"At the test site?"

"At the test site."

"Trouble of what sort?"

"There's been one fatality."

"Will it pass for natural causes?"

"Not in a million years."

"Can you handle it yourself?"

"No. There are going to be more."

"Fatalities?" Dawson asked.

"We've got people here who are unaffected."

"Unaffected by the program?"

"That's right."

"Why should that lead to fatalities?"

"My cover is blown."

"How did that happen?"

Salsbury hesitated.

"You'd better tell me the truth," Dawson said sharply. "For all our sakes. You'd better tell me the truth."

"I was with a woman."

"You fool."

"It was a mistake," Salsbury admitted.

"It was idiotic. We'll discuss it later. One of these unaffected people came upon you while you were with the woman."

"That's right."

"If your cover is blown it can be repaired. Undramatically."

"I'm afraid not. I ordered the killer to do what he did."

Despite the riddle form of the conversation, the events in Black River were becoming all too clear to Dawson. "I see." He thought for a moment. "How many are unaffected?"

"Besides a couple of dozen babies and very young children, at least four more. Maybe five."

"That's not so many."

"There's another problem. You know the two men we sent up here at the beginning of the month?"

"To the reservoir."

"They were seen."

Dawson was silent.

"If you don't want to come," Salsbury said, "that's okay. But I have to have some help. Send our partner and—"

"We'll both arrive tonight by helicopter," Dawson said. "Can you hold it yourself until nine or ten o'clock?"

"I think so."

"You had better."

Dawson hung up.

Oh Lord, he thought. You sent him to me as an instrument of Your will. Now Satan's gotten to him. Help me to set all of this aright. I only want to serve You.

He telephoned his pilot and ordered him to fuel the helicopter and have it at the landing pad behind the Greenwich house within the hour.

He dialed three numbers before he located Klinger. "There's some trouble up north."

"Serious?"

"Extremely serious. Can you be here in an hour?"

"Only if I drive like a maniac. Better make it an hour and a quarter."

"Get moving."

Dawson hung up again.

Oh Lord, he thought, both of these men are infidels. I know that. But You sent them to me for Your own purposes, didn't You? Don't punish me for doing Your will, Lord.

He opened the lower right-hand drawer of the desk and took out a folder thick with papers.

The label on it said:

HARRISON-BODREI DETECTIVE AGENCY
SUBJECT: OGDEN SALSBURY

Thanks to the Harrison-Bodrei Agency, he understood his partners almost better than they understood themselves. For the past fifteen years he had kept a constantly updated file on Ernst Klinger. The Salsbury dossier was comparatively new, begun only in January 1975; but it traced his life all the way back through his childhood, and it was undeniably complete. Having read it ten or twelve times, from cover to cover, Dawson felt that he should have anticipated the current crisis.

Ogden was neither stark-raving mad nor perfectly sound of mind. He was a pathological woman-hater. Yet periodically he indulged in lascivious sprees of whoring, using as many as seven or eight prostitutes during a single weekend. Occasionally, there was trouble.

To Dawson's way of thinking, two of the reports in the file were more important, told more about Ogden, than all of the others combined. He withdrew the first of them from the folder and read it yet again.

A week past his eleventh birthday, Ogden was taken from his mother and made a ward of the court. Katherine Salsbury (widowed) and her lover, Howard Parker, were later convicted of child abuse, child molestation, and corrupting the morals of a minor. Mrs. Salsbury was sentenced to seven to ten years in the New Jersey Correctional Institution for Women. Upon her conviction, Ogden was transferred to the home of a neighbor, Mrs. Carrie Barger (now Peterson), where he became one of several foster children. This interview was conducted with Mrs. Carrie Peterson (now sixty-nine years old) in her home in Teaneck, New Jersey, on the morning of Wednesday, January 22, 1975. The sub-

*ject was obviously intoxicated even at that early hour and
sipped at a glass of "just plain orange juice" throughout
the interview. The subject was not aware that she was being
recorded.*

Dawson had marked the sections of the report that most
interested him. He skipped ahead to the third page.

AGENT: Living next door to Mrs. Salsbury, you must
have witnessed a great many of those beatings.

MRS. PETERSON: Oh, yes. Oh, I should say. From the
time that Ogden was old enough to walk, he was a target for
her. That woman! The least little thing he did—*whup!* she
beat him black and blue.

AGENT: Spanked him?

MRS. PETERSON: No, no. She hardly ever spanked. Had
she *only* spanked! That wouldn't have been so horrid. But
that woman! She started out hitting him with her open
hands. On the head and all about his sweet little face. As he
got older she'd sometimes use her fists. She was a big
woman, you know. She'd use her fists. And she'd pinch.
Pinch his little arms . . . I cried many the time. He'd come
over to play with my foster children, and he'd be a mess.
His little arms would be spotted with bruises. Just spotted
all over with bruises.

AGENT: Was she an alcoholic?

MRS. PETERSON: She drank. Some. But she wasn't ad-
dicted to gin or anything. She was just mean. Naturally
mean. And I don't think she was too smart. Sometimes,
very dim-witted people, when they get frustrated, they take
it out on children. I've seen it before. Too often. Suffer the
little children. Oh, they suffer so much, I tell you.

AGENT: She had a great many lovers?

MRS. PETERSON: Dozens. She was a vile woman. Very
common-looking men. Always very common-looking.
Dirty. Crude laborers. Her *men* drank a lot. Sometimes
they'd stay with her as much as a year. More often it was a
week or two, a month.

AGENT: This Howard Parker—

MRS. PETERSON: Him!

AGENT: How long was he with Mrs. Salsbury?

MRS. PETERSON: Nearly six months, I think, before the
crime. What a horrible man. Horrible!

AGENT: Did you know what was happening in the Salsbury house when Parker was there?

MRS. PETERSON: Of course not! I'd have called the police at once! Of course the night of the crime—Ogden came to me. And then I did call the police.

AGENT: Do you mind talking about the crime?

MRS. PETERSON: It still upsets me. To think of it. What a horrible man! And that woman. To do that to a child.

AGENT: Parker was—bisexual?

MRS. PETERSON: He was what?

AGENT: He customarily had relations with both sexes. Is that right?

MRS. PETERSON: He raped a little boy! It's . . . I don't know. I just don't know. Why did God make some people so wicked? I love children. Have all my life. Love them more than anything. I can't understand a man like that Parker.

AGENT: Does it embarrass you to talk about the crime?

MRS. PETERSON: A little bit.

AGENT: If you can bear with me . . . It's really important that you answer a few more questions.

MRS. PETERSON: If it's for Ogden's sake, like you said, I surely can. For Ogden's sake. Although he never comes back to see me. You know that? After I took him in and raised him from the age of eleven. He just never comes back.

AGENT: The court records of that time were not properly explicit. Either that or the judge had some of the testimony altered to protect the boy's reputation. I am not certain whether Mr. Parker subjected the boy to—you'll excuse me, but it has to be said—to oral or anal intercourse.

MRS. PETERSON: That horrible man!

AGENT: Do you know which it was?

MRS. PETERSON: Both.

AGENT: I see.

MRS. PETERSON: With the mother watching. His mother watched! Can you imagine such a thing? Such a rotten thing? To do that to a defenseless child . . . What monsters they were!

AGENT: I didn't mean to make you cry.

MRS. PETERSON: I'm not crying. Just a tear or two. It's so sad. Don't you think? So terribly sad. Suffer the little children.

AGENT: There's no need to continue with—

MRS. PETERSON: Oh, but you said this was for Ogden's sake, that you needed to ask all of this for Ogden's sake. He was one of my children. Foster children. But I felt like they were my own. I loved them dearly. Loved all of them. Little dears, every one. So if it's for Ogden's sake . . . Well . . . For months, without anyone at all knowing, with poor little Ogden too afraid to tell anyone, that terrible Howard Parker . . . was using the boy . . . using . . . his mouth. And the mother watching! She was a vicious woman. And sick. Very sick.

AGENT: And the night of the crime—

MRS. PETERSON: Parker used the boy . . . he used . . . the boy's rectum. Hurt him terribly. You can't know the pain that boy suffered.

AGENT: Ogden came to you that night.

MRS. PETERSON: I lived right next door to them. He came to me. Shaking like a leaf. Scared out of his wits. The poor, poor baby . . . Crying his heart out, he was. That awful Parker had beat him up. His lips were cracked. One eye was puffed and black. At first I thought that was all that was wrong with him. But I soon discovered . . . the other. We rushed him to the hospital. He needed eleven stitches. Eleven!

AGENT: Eleven—rectal stitches?

MRS. PETERSON: That's right. He was in such pain. And he was bleeding. He had to stay in the hospital for nearly a week.

AGENT: And eventually you became his foster mother.

MRS. PETERSON: Yes. And never sorry for it. He was a fine boy. A dear boy. Very bright too. At school they said he was a genius. He won all of those scholarships and went up to Harvard. You'd think he'd come to see me, wouldn't you? After all I did for him? But no. He never comes. He never comes around. And now the social workers won't let me have any more children. Not since my second husband died. They say there have to be two parents in a foster home. And besides they say that I'm too old. Well, that's craziness. I love children, and that's all that should count. I love each and every one of them. Haven't I dedicated my life to foster children? I'm not too old for them. And when I think of all the suffering children, I could just cry.

The last half of that report was a transcription of a long and rambling conversation with the man to whom Mrs. Peterson had been married at the time that she took the eleven-year-old Ogden Salsbury into her home.

This interview was conducted with Mr. Allen J. Barger (now

*eighty-three years old) in the Evins-Maebry Nursing Home
in Huntington, Long Island, on the afternoon of Friday,
January 24, 1975. The subject is supported at the home by
the three children from his second marriage. The subject,
who suffers from senility, was alternately lucid and in-
coherent. The subject was not aware that he was being recorded.*

Dawson leafed ahead to the passage he had marked.

AGENT: Do you remember any of the foster children that
you took in while you were married to Carrie?

MR. BARGER: She took them in. Not me.

AGENT: Do you remember any of them?

MR. BARGER: Oh, Christ.

AGENT: What's the matter?

MR. BARGER: I try not to remember them.

AGENT: You didn't enjoy them like she did?

MR. BARGER: All those dirty little faces when I came
home from work. She tried to say we needed the extra
money, the few dollars the government gave us for keeping
the kids. It *was* the Depression. But she drank up the
money.

AGENT: She was an alcoholic?

MR. BARGER: Not when I married her. But she was sure
on her way to being one.

AGENT: Do you remember a child named—

MR. BARGER: My trouble was I didn't marry her for her
mind.

AGENT: Excuse me?

MR. BARGER: I married my second wife for her mind,
and that worked out swell. But when I got hitched to Carrie . . . Well, I was forty years old and still single and sick
to death of going to whores. Carrie came along, twenty-six
and fresh as a peach, so much younger than me but interested in me, and I let my balls do my thinking for me.
Married her for her body with no thought as to what was in
her head. That was a big mistake.

AGENT: I'm sure it was. Well . . . Now, could you tell
me if you can remember a child named—

MR. BARGER: She had magnificent jugs.

AGENT: I beg your pardon?

MR. BARGER: Jugs. Boobs. Carrie had a magnificent set.

AGENT: Oh. Yes. Uh . . .

MR. BARGER: She was pretty good in bed too. When you

could get her away from those goddamned kids. Those kids! I don't know why I ever agreed to take the first one in. After that we never had less than four and usually six or seven. She had always wanted a big family. But she wasn't able to have children of her own. I guess maybe that made her want them even more. But she didn't really want to be a mother. It was just a dream, a sort of sentimental thing with her.

AGENT: What do you mean?

MR. BARGER: Oh, she liked the *idea* of having children more than she liked really having them.

AGENT: I see.

MR. BARGER: She couldn't discipline them worth a damn. They walked right over her. And I wasn't about to take over that chore. No, sir! I worked hard, long hours in those days. When I came home I didn't want to do anything but relax. I didn't spend my time chasing after a pack of brats. So long as they left me alone, they could do what they wanted. They knew that, and they never bothered me. Hell, they weren't *my* kids.

AGENT: Do you remember one of them named Ogden Salsbury?

MR. BARGER: No.

AGENT: His mother lived next door to you. She had a lot of lovers. One of them, a man named Parker, raped the boy. Homosexual rape.

MR. BARGER: Come to think of it, I do remember him. Ogden. Yeah. He came to the house at a bad time.

AGENT: A bad time? How's that?

MR. BARGER: It was all girls then.

AGENT: All girls?

MR. BARGER: Carrie was on a kick. She wouldn't take in any but little girls. Maybe she thought she could control them better than she could a bunch of boys. So this Ogden and I were the only men in the house for about two or three years.

AGENT: And that was bad for him?

MR. BARGER: The older girls knew what had happened to him. They used to tease him something fierce. He couldn't take it. He'd blow up every time. Start yelling and screaming at them. Of course that was what they wanted, so they just teased him some more. When this Ogden used to let the girls get his goat, I'd take him aside and talk to him—almost father to son. I used to tell him not to pay them any mind. I used to tell him that they were just women and that women were good for only two things. Fucking and cooking. That was my attitude before I met my second wife. Anyway, I think I must have been a great help to that boy. A great help . . . Do you know they won't let you fuck in this nursing home?

The other report that Dawson found especially interesting was an interview with Laird Richardson, a first-level clerk in the Pentagon's Bureau of Security Clearance Investigations. A Harrison-Bodrei agent had offered Richardson five hundred dollars to pull Salsbury's army security file, study it, and report its contents.

Again, Dawson had bracketed the most relevant passages with a red pen.

RICHARDSON: Whatever research he's doing must be damned important. They've spent a lot of money covering for the sonofabitch over the past ten years. And the Pentagon just doesn't do that unless it expects to be repaid in spades some day.

AGENT: Covering for him? How?

RICHARDSON: He liked to mark up prostitutes.

AGENT: Mark them up?

RICHARDSON: Mostly with his fists.

AGENT: How often does this happen?

RICHARDSON: Once or twice a year.

AGENT: How often does he see prostitutes?

RICHARDSON: He goes whoring the first weekend of every other month. Regular as you please. Like he's a robot or something. You could set your watch by his need. Usually, he goes into Manhattan, makes the rounds of the leisure and health spas, phones a couple of call girls and has them up to his hotel room. Now and then one of them comes along with the kind of look that sets him off, and he beats the shit out of her.

AGENT: What look is that?

RICHARDSON: Usually blond, but not always. Usually pale, but not always. But she *is* always small. Five one or five two. A hundred pounds. And delicate. Very delicate features.

AGENT: Why would a girl like that set him off?

RICHARDSON: The Pentagon tried to force him into psychoanalysis. He went to one session and refused to go the second time. He *did* tell the psychiatrist that these frenzies of his were generated by more than the girls' appearance. They have to be delicate—but not just in a physical sense. They have to seem emotionally vulnerable to him before he gets the urge to pound them senseless.

AGENT: In other words if he thinks the woman is his equal or his superior, she's safe. But if he feels that he can dominate her—

RICHARDSON: Then she'd better have her Blue Cross paid in full.

AGENT: He hasn't killed any of these women, has he?

RICHARDSON: Not yet. But he's come close a couple of times.

AGENT: You said someone in the Pentagon covers up for him.

RICHARDSON: Usually someone from our bureau.

AGENT: How?

RICHARDSON: By paying the girl's hospital bills and giving her a lump sum. The size of the pay-off depends on the extent of her injuries.

AGENT: Is he considered a high security risk?

RICHARDSON: Oh, no. If he was a closet queen and we found out about it, he'd be classified as a fairly bad risk. But his hangups and vices aren't secret. They're out in the open. No one can blackmail him, threaten him with the loss of his job because we already know all of his dirty little secrets. In fact, whenever he marks up a girl, he has a special number to call, a relay point right in my department. Someone is at his hotel room within an hour to clean up after him.

AGENT: Nice people you work for.

RICHARDSON: Aren't they? But I'm surprised that even they put up with this sonofabitch Salsbury. He's a sick man. He's a real can of worms all by himself. They should stick him away in a cell somewhere and just forget all about him.

AGENT: Do you know about his childhood?

RICHARDSON: About his mother and the man who raped him? It's in the file.

AGENT: It helps to explain why he—

RICHARDSON: You know what? Even though I can see where his craziness comes from, even though I can see that it isn't entirely his fault that he is what he is, I can't dredge up any compassion for him. When I think about all of those girls who ended up in hospitals with their jaws broken and their eyes swollen shut . . . Listen, did any of those girls feel less pain because Salsbury's evil isn't entirely his own doing? I'm an old-style liberal when it comes to most things. But this liberal line about compassion for the criminal—that's ninety percent horseshit. You can only spout that kind of garbage if you and your own family have been lucky enough to avoid animals like Salsbury. If it was up to me, I'd put him on trial for all those beatings. Then I'd send him away to a cell somewhere, hundreds of miles from the nearest woman.

Dawson sighed.

He put the reports in the folder and returned the folder to the lower right-hand desk drawer.

O Lord, he thought prayerfully, give me the power to undo what damage he's done in Black River. If this mistake can be remedied, if the field test can be completed properly, then I will be able to feed the drug to both Ernst and Ogden. I'll be able to program them. I've been making preparations. You know that. I'll be able to program them and convert them to Your holy fellowship. And not just them. The world. There will be no more souls for Satan. Heaven on earth. That's what it'll be, Lord. True heaven on earth, all in the shining light of Your love.

2:55 P.M.

Sam read the last line of Salsbury's article, closed the book, and said, *"Jesus!"*

"At least now we have some idea of what's happening in Black River," Paul said.

"All of that crazy stuff about breaking down the ego, primer drugs, code phrases, achieving total control, bringing contentment to the masses through behavioral modification, the benefits of a subliminally directed society . . ." Somewhat dazed by Salsbury's rhetoric, Jenny shook her head as if that would help her to think more clearly. "He sounds like a lunatic. He's certifiable."

"He's a Nazi," Sam said, "in spirit if not in name. That's a very special breed of lunatic. A very deadly breed. And there are literally thousands of people like him, hundreds of thousands who would agree with every word he said about the benefits of a 'subliminally directed society.'"

Thunder exploded with such violence that it sounded as if the bowl of the sky had cracked in two. A fierce gust of wind slammed against the house. The tempo of the rain on the roof and windows picked up to double time.

"Whatever he is," Paul said, "he's done exactly what he said could be done. He's made this insane scheme work. By God, that *has* to be what's happening here. It explains everything since the epidemic of night chills and nausea."

"I still don't understand why Dad and I weren't afflicted," Jenny said. "Salsbury mentions in the article that the subliminal program would not affect illiterates and children who haven't yet come to terms, however crude, with sex and death. But neither Dad nor I fit into one of those categories."

"I think I can answer that," Paul said.

Sam said, "So can I. One thing they teach budding pharmacologists is that no drug affects everyone the same way. On some people, for instance, penicillin has little or no effect. Some people don't respond well at all to sulfa drugs. I suspect that, for whatever reasons of genes and metabolisms and body chemistries, we're among the tiny percentage of those who aren't touched by Salsbury's drug."

"And thank God for that," Jenny said. She hugged herself and shivered.

"There ought to be more adults unaffected," Paul said. "It's summertime. People take vacations. Wasn't anyone out of town during the week when the reservoir was contaminated and the subliminal messages broadcast?"

"When the heavy snows come," Sam said, "logging operations have to stop. So in the warm months everyone connected with the mill works his butt off to make sure there will be a stockpile of logs to keep the saws going all winter. No one at the mill takes a vacation in the summer. And everyone in town who serves the mill takes his time off in the winter too."

Paul felt as if he were on a turntable, whirling around and around. His mind spun with the implications of the article that Sam had read. "Mark and Rya and I weren't affected because we got to town after the contaminant had passed out of the reservoir—and because we didn't watch whatever television programs or commercials contained the subliminal messages.

But virtually everyone else in Black River is now under Salsbury's control.''

They stared at one another.

The storm moaned at the window.

Finally Sam said, ''We enjoy the benefits and luxuries provided by modern science—all the while forgetting that the technological revolution, just like the industrial revolution before it, has its dark side.'' For several long seconds, with the mantel clock ticking behind him, he studied the cover of the book in his hand. ''The more complex a society becomes, the more dependent each part of it becomes on every other part of it, the easier it is for one man, one lunatic or true believer, to destroy it all on a whim. One man working alone can assassinate a chief of state and precipitate major changes in his country's foreign and domestic policies. They tell us that one man with a degree in biology and a lot of determination can culture more than enough plague bacillus to destroy the world. One man working alone can even build a nuclear bomb. All he needs is a college degree in physics. And the ability to get his hands on a few pounds of plutonium. Which isn't so damned hard to do either. He can build a bomb inside a suitcase and wipe out New York City because . . . Well, hell, why not because he was mugged there, or because he once got a traffic ticket in Manhattan and he doesn't think he deserved it.''

''But Salsbury can't be working alone,'' Jenny said.

''I agree with you.''

''The resources needed to perfect and implement the program that he described in his article . . . Why, they would be enormous.''

''A private industry might be able to finance it,'' Paul said. ''A company as large as AT&T.''

''No,'' Sam said. ''Too many executives and research people would have to know about it. There would be a leak. It would never get this far without a leak to the press and a major scandal.''

''A single wealthy man could provide what Salsbury needed,'' Jenny said. ''Someone as rich as Onassis was. Or Hughes.''

Tugging gently on his beard, Sam said, ''It's possible, I suppose. But we're all avoiding the most logical explanation.''

"That Salsbury is working for the United States government," Paul said worriedly.

"Exactly," Sam said. "And if he *is* working for the government or the CIA or any branch of the military—then we're finished. Not just the three of us and Rya, but the whole damned country."

Paul went to the window, wiped away some of the dew, and stared at wind-lashed trees and billowing gray sheets of rain. "Do you think that what's happening here is happening all over the country?"

"No," Sam said. "If there were a general takeover in progress, Salsbury wouldn't be in a backwoods mill town. He'd be at a command post in Washington. Or somewhere else, anywhere else."

"Then it's a test. A field test."

"Probably."

"And that's maybe a good sign," Sam said. "The government would run a field test where it already had tight security. Most likely on an army or air force base. Not here."

Lightning blasted through the thunderheads; and for an instant the patterns of rain on the window seemed to form faces: Annie's face, Mark's face . . .

Suddenly Paul thought that his wife and son, although they had met quite different deaths, had been killed by the same force. Technology. Science. Annie had gone into the hospital for a simple appendectomy. It hadn't even been an emergency operation. The anesthesiologist had given her a brand-new-on-the-market-revolutionary-you-couldn't-ask-for-better anesthetic, something that wasn't as messy as ether, something that was easier to use (easier for the anesthesiologist) than pentothal. But after the operation she didn't regain consciousness as she should have done. She slipped, instead, into a coma. She'd had an allergic reaction to the brand-new-on-the-market-revolutionary-you-couldn't-ask-for-better anesthetic; and it had destroyed a large part of her liver. Fortunately, the doctors told him, the liver was the one organ of the body that could regenerate itself. If they kept her in the intensive care unit, supporting her life processes with machines, the liver would repair itself day by day, until eventually she would be well again. She was in intensive care for five weeks, at which time the doctors fed all of the data from the life-support machines into a Medico computer, and the computer told them that she was well enough to be moved out of intensive care and into a private room. Eleven weeks later, the same computer said she was well enough to go home. She was listless and apathetic—but she agreed that the computer must be right. Two weeks after she came home, she had a relapse and died within forty-eight hours. Sometimes he thought that if he had only been a medical doctor instead of a veterinarian, he might have saved her. But that was pointless masochism. What he *could* have done was demand that her original surgery be performed with ether or pentothal, something known to be safe, something that had stood the test of decades. He could have told them to stuff their computer up their collective ass. But he hadn't done that either. He had trusted in their technology simply because it *was* technology, because it was all *new*. Americans were brought up to respect what was new and progressive—and more often than they wanted to admit, they died for their faith in what was bright and shiny.

After Annie died he became suspicious of technology, of every new wonder that science gave to mankind. He read Paul Ehrlich and other back-to-the-land reformers. Gradually he came to see that the yearly camping trips to Black River could be the beginning of a serious program to free his children from the city, from the ever-growing dangers of the science and technology that the cities represented. The yearly trips became an education for lives they would live in harmony with nature.

But the back-to-the-land advocates were possessed by an impossible dream. He saw that now, saw it as clearly as he had ever seen anything in his life. They were trying to run away from technology—but it moved much faster than they did. There was no land to get back to anymore. The city, its science and technology, the effects of its life-style, had tendrils snaking out into even the most remote mountains and forests.

Furthermore, you ignored the advancements of science at your own peril. His ignorance about anesthetics and the reliability of the Medico computer had cost Annie her life. His ignorance of subliminal advertising and the research being done in that field had, if you wanted to stretch a point, cost Mark his life. The only way to survive in the 1970s and in the decades to follow was to plunge into the fast-moving, super-technical society, swim with it, learn from it and about it, learn all that you could, and be its equal in any confrontation.

He turned away from the window. "We can't go to Bexford and call the state police. If our own government *is* behind Salsbury, if our own leaders want to enslave us, we'll never win. It's hopeless. But if it *isn't* behind him, if it doesn't know what he's achieved, then we don't dare let it know. Because the moment the military finds out—it'll appropriate Salsbury's discoveries; and there are some factions of the military that wouldn't be opposed to using subliminal programming against us."

Looking around at the books about Nazism, totalitarianism, and mob psychology, thinking ruefully of what he'd learned about some men's lust for power, Sam said, "You're right. Besides, I've been thinking about the problems with the long-distance phone service."

Paul knew what he meant. "Salsbury's taken over the telephone exchange."

"And if he's done that," Sam said, "he's taken other precautions too. He's probably blockaded the roads and every other route out of town. We couldn't go to Bexford and tell the state police even if we still wanted to."

"We're trapped," Jenny said quietly.

"For the time being," Paul said, "that really doesn't matter. We've already decided there's no place to run anyway. But if he's not working for the government, if he's backed by a corporation or a single wealthy man, maybe we've got a chance to stop him here in Black River."

"Stop him . . ." Sam stared thoughtfully at the floor. "Do you realize what you're saying? We'd have to get our hands on him, interrogate him—and then kill him. Death is the only thing that will stop a man like that. We'd also have to find out from him who he's associated with—and kill anyone else who might understand how the drug was made and how the subliminal program was constructed." He looked up from the floor. "That could mean two murders, three, four, or a dozen."

"None of us is a killer," Jenny said.

"Every man's a potential killer," Paul said. "When it comes to matters of survival, any man is capable of anything. And this is sure as hell a matter of survival."

"I killed men in the war," Sam said.

"So did I," Paul said. "A different war than yours. But the same act."

"That was different," Jenny said.

"Was it?"

"That was *war*," she said.

"This is war too," Paul said.

She stared at Paul's hands, as if imagining them with a knife or a gun or clamped around a man's throat.

Sensing her thoughts, he raised his hands and studied them for a moment. On occasion, washing his hands before dinner or after treating a sick animal, he would flash back to the war, back to Southeast Asia. He would hear the guns and see the blood again in his memory. In these almost psychic moments, he was both amazed and dismayed that the same hands were accustomed to mundane *and* horrible acts, that they could heal or injure, make love or kill, and look no different after the task was done. Codified morality, he thought, was indeed a blessing but also a curse of civilization. A blessing because it permitted men to live in harmony most of the time. A curse because—when the laws of nature and especially of human nature made it necessary for a man to wound or kill another man in order to save himself and his family—it spawned remorse and guilt even if the violence was unwanted and unavoidable.

Besides, he reminded himself, these are the 1970s. This is the age of science and technology when a man often is required to act with the implacable and unemotional savagery of the machine. For better or worse, in these times gentility is becoming less and less a sign of the civilized man and is, in fact, very nearly an obsolescent quality. You see gentility, most often, in those who are least likely to survive wave after wave of future shock.

Lowering his hands he said, "In the classic paranoid vein, it's us against them. Except that this isn't a delusion or an illusion; it's *real*."

Jenny seemed to accept the need for murder as quickly as he had accepted the fact that he might be called upon to commit it. By this point in her life, she had experienced, as had all but the most gentle people, at least the flickering of a homicidal urge in a moment of despair or great frustration. She hadn't accepted it as the solution to whatever problem had inspired it. But she was not incapable of conceiving of a situation in which homicide *was* the most reasonable response to a threat. In spite of the overprotected, sheltered upbringing of which she'd spoken last Monday, she could adapt to even the most unpleasant truths. Perhaps, Paul thought, the ordeal with her first husband had made her stronger, tougher, and more resilient than she realized.

She said, "Even if we could bring ourselves to kill in order to stop this thing . . . Well, it's still too much. To stop Salsbury, we need to know more about him. And how do we learn anything? He's got hundreds of bodyguards. Or if he wants, he can turn everyone in town into killers and send them after us. Do we just sit here, pass the time, wait for him to stop around for a chat?"

Returning the hardbound volume of essays to the shelf from which he'd taken it, Sam said, "Wait a minute . . . Suppose . . ." He faced them. He was excited. All three of them were tense, twisted as tight as watch springs. But now a glimmer of *pleasurable* excitement was in his Santa Claus-like features. "When Salsbury saw Rya standing in the kitchen doorway at the Thorp house, what do you imagine he did, very first thing?"

"Grabbed for her," Jenny said.

"Wrong."

Bitterly, Paul said, "Ordered Bob to kill her."

"Not that either. Remember, he would expect her to be another one of his—zombies."

Sucking in her breath, Jenny said, "He would use the code phrase on her, the system he talks about in the article. He'd try to open her up and take control of her before she ran away. So . . . Rya must have heard the code phrase!"

"And if she can recall it," Sam said, *"we'll* have control of everyone in Black River, the same as Salsbury. He won't be able to send them after us. He won't have hundreds of bodyguards to hide behind. It won't be us against them. It'll be us against *him.*"

6.

DR. WALTER TROUTMAN entered the police chief's office. He was carrying his black leather satchel in his right hand and a chocolate candy bar with almonds in his left. He appeared to be delighted with the world and with himself. "You wanted to see me, Bob?"

Before Thorp could answer, Salsbury stepped away from the windows and said, "I am the key."

"I am the lock."

"Buddy Pellineri is waiting in the room across the hall," Salsbury said. "You know him, don't you?"

"Buddy?" Troutman asked, wrinkling his fleshy face. "Well, of course I know him."

"I've told him that we're afraid he's picked up a very bad germ and that you're going to give him a vaccination so he won't get sick. As you know, he's not especially bright. He believed me. He's waiting for you."

"Vaccination?" Troutman said, perplexed.

"That's what I told him to keep him here. Instead, you'll

231

inject an air bubble into his bloodstream.''

Troutman was shocked. ''That would cause an embolism.''

''I know.''

''It would kill him!''

Salsbury smiled and nodded. ''It had better. That's the whole idea, doctor.''

Looking at Bob Thorp, who was seated behind the desk, then back at Salsbury, Troutman said miserably, ''But I can't do a thing like that. I can't possibly.''

''Who am I, doctor?''

''You're—the key.''

''Very good. And who are you?''

''I'm the lock.''

''All right. You will go across the hall to the room where Buddy is waiting. You'll chat with him, be very pleasant, give him no cause to be suspicious. You'll tell him that you're going to give him a vaccination, and you'll inject an air bubble into his bloodstream. You won't mind killing him. You won't hesitate. As soon as he is dead, you'll leave the room—and you will remember only that you gave him a shot of penicillin. You won't remember killing him when you leave that room. You will come back here, look in the door, and say to Bob, 'He'll be better in the morning.' Then you'll go back to your house, having forgotten entirely about these instructions. Is that clear?''

''Yes.''

''Go do it.''

Troutman left the room.

Ten minutes ago Salsbury had decided to eliminate Buddy Pellineri. Although the man had experienced the night chills and nausea, and although he had been partially brainwashed by the subceptive program, he was not a good subject. He could not be fully and easily controlled. When told to erase from his memory the men he had seen coming down from the reservoir on the morning of August sixth, he might forget them forever—or only for a few hours. Or not at all. Had he been a genius, the drug and the subliminals would have transformed him into the ideal slave. Ironically, however, his ignorance condemned him.

It was a pity that Buddy had to die. In his own way he was a likable brute.

But I've got the power, Salsbury thought. And I'm going

to keep it. I'm going to eliminate as many people as have to be eliminated for me to keep the power. I'll show them. All of them. Dawson, good old Miriam, the bitches, the holier-than-thou college professors with their snotty questions and self-righteous denunciations of my work, the whores, my mother, the bitches . . . *Tat-tat-tat-tat* . . . No one is going to take this away from me. No one. Not ever. Never.

3:20 P.M.

Rya sat up in bed, yawning and smacking her lips. She looked from Jenny to Sam to Paul—but she didn't seem to know for certain who they were.

"Do you remember what he said?" Paul asked again. "The man with the thick glasses. Do you remember?"

Squinting at him, scratching her head, she said, "Who . . . am this?"

"She's still dopey," Jenny said, "and will be for a while yet."

Studying the girl from the foot of the bed, Sam said, "Salsbury knows he's got to deal with us. As soon as he's decided *how,* he'll come here. We don't have time to wait for the sedative to wear off. We've got to help her come out of it." He looked at Jenny. "You give her a cold shower. A long one. I'll make some fresh coffee."

"Don't like coffee," Rya said sullenly.

"You like tea, don't you?"

"S'okay." She yawned.

Sam hurried downstairs to make a pot of tea.

Jenny hustled Rya out of bed and into the bathroom at the end of the hallway.

Left alone, Paul went to the living room to sit with Mark's body until Rya was ready to be questioned.

When you decide to meet that big, bright, shiny chrome-edged American world on its own terms, he thought, things start to move. Faster and faster and faster.

3:26 P.M.

Dr. Troutman leaned in the open doorway and said, "He'll be better in the morning."

"That's fine," Bob Thorp said. "You go along home now."

Popping the last piece of chocolate-almond bar into his mouth, the doctor said, "Take care." He walked away.

To Thorp, Salsbury said, "Get some help. Move the body into one of the cells. Stretch him out on the bunk so that he looks like he's sleeping."

4:16 P.M.

Rain gurgled noisily down the leader beside the kitchen window.

The room smelled of lemons.

Steam rose from the spout of the teapot and from the china cup.

Rya wiped away her tears, blinked in sudden recollection, and said, "Oh. Oh, yes . . . 'I am the key.'"

4:45 P.M.

The downpour dwindled abruptly to a drizzle. Soon the rain stopped altogether.

Salsbury raised one of the Venetian blinds and looked out at North Union Road. The gutters were overflowing. A miniature lake had formed down toward the square where a drainage grating was clogged with leaves and grass. The trees dripped like melting candles.

He was glad to see it end. He had begun to worry about the turbulent flying conditions that Dawson's helicopter pilot would have to face.

One way or another, Dawson *had* to get to Black River tonight. Salsbury didn't actually need help to deal with the situation; but he did need to be able to share the blame if the field test went even further awry.

Neither of his current options was without risk. He could send Bob Thorp and a couple of deputies to the general store to arrest the Edisons and the Annendales. Of course there might be trouble, violence, even a shoot-out. Every additional corpse or missing person that had to be explained to the authorities outside of Black River increased the chance of discovery. On the other hand, if he had to maintain the road-block through tomorrow, keep control of the town, and perpetuate the state of siege, his chances of coming out on top of this would be less promising than they were now.

What in the devil was happening at Edison's place? They had found the boy's body. He knew that. He had assigned several guards to cover the store. Why hadn't they come here to see Bob Thorp? Why hadn't they tried to leave town? Why hadn't they, in short, acted like anyone else would have done? Surely, even with Buddy's story to build from, they couldn't have reconstructed the truth behind the events of the past few weeks. They couldn't know who he really was. They probably didn't know about subliminal advertising in general—and certainly not about his research in specific. He suddenly wished that he had brought his briefcase with the infinity transmitter from Pauline Vicker's rooming house.

"Everything looks so crisp and fresh after a summer rain, doesn't it?" Bob Thorp asked.

"I'm glad it's over," Salsbury said.

"It isn't. Not by a long shot."

Salsbury turned from the windows. "What?"

Smiling, as amiable as Salsbury had ordered him to be, Bob Thorp said, "These summer storms start and stop half a dozen times before they're finished. That's because they bounce back and forth, back and forth between the mountains until they finally find a way out."

Thinking of Dawson's helicopter, Salsbury said, "Since when are you a meteorologist?"

"Well, I've lived here all my life, except for my hitch in the service. I've seen hundreds of storms like this one, and they—"

"*I said it's over!* The storm is over. Finished. Done with. Do you understand?"

Frowning, Thorp said, "The storm is over."

"I want it to be over," Salsbury said. "So it is. It's over if I say it is. Isn't it?"

"Of course."

"All right."

"It's over."

"Dumb cop."

Thorp said nothing.

"Aren't you a dumb cop?"

"I'm not dumb."

"I say you are. You're dumb. Stupid. Stupid as an ox. Aren't you, Bob?"

"Yes."

"Say it."

"What?"

"That you're as stupid as an ox."

"I'm as stupid as an ox."

Returning to the window, Salsbury stared angrily at the lowering cobalt clouds.

Eventually he said, "Bob, I want you to go to Pauline Vicker's house."

Thorp stood up at once.

"I've got a room on the second floor, the first door on the right at the head of the stairs. You'll find a leather briefcase beside the bed. Fetch it for me."

4:55 P.M.

The four of them went through the crowded stockroom and onto the rear porch of the general store.

Immediately, twenty yards away on the wet emerald-green lawn, a man moved out of the niche formed by two angled rows of lilac bushes. He was a tall, hawk-faced man in horn-rimmed glasses. He was wearing a dark raincoat and holding a double-barreled shotgun.

"Do you know him?" Paul asked.

"Harry Thurston," Jenny said. "He's a foreman up at the mill. Lives next door."

With one hand Rya clutched Paul's shirt. Her self-confidence and her faith in people had been seriously eroded by what she had seen Bob Thorp do to her brother. Watching the man with the shotgun, trembling, her voice pitched slightly higher than it normally was, she said, "Is he . . . going to shoot us?"

Paul placed one hand on her shoulder, squeezed gently, reassuringly. "Nobody's going to be shot."

As he spoke he ardently wished that he could believe what he was telling her.

Fortunately, Sam Edison sold a line of firearms in addition to groceries, dry goods, drugs, notions and sundries; therefore, they weren't defenseless. Jenny had a .22 rifle. Sam and Paul were both carrying Smith & Wesson .357 Combat Magnum revolvers loaded with .38 Special cartridges which would produce only half the fierce kick of Magnum ammunition. However, they didn't want to use the guns, for they were trying to leave the house secretly; they kept the guns at their sides, barrels aimed at the porch floor.

"I'll handle this," Sam said. He went across the porch to the wooden steps and started down.

"Hold it right there," said the man with the shotgun. He came ten yards closer. He pointed the weapon at Sam's chest, kept his finger on the trigger, and watched all of them with unconcealed anxiety and distrust.

Paul glanced at Jenny.

She was biting her lower lip. She looked as if she wanted to swing up her rifle and level it at Harry Thurston's head.

That might set off a meaningless but disastrous exchange of gunfire.

He had a mental image of the shotgun booming. Booming again . . . Flame blossoming from the muzzles . . .

"Calm," he said quietly.

Jenny nodded.

At the bottom of the steps, still twenty-five feet from the man with the shotgun, Sam held out a hand in greeting. When Thurston ignored it, Sam said, "Harry?"

Thurston's shotgun didn't waver. Neither did his expression. But he said, "Hello, Sam."

"What are you doing here, Harry?"

"You know," Thurston said.

"I'm afraid I don't."

"Guarding you," Thurston said.

"From what?"

"From escaping."

"You're here to keep us from escaping from our own house?" Sam grimaced. "Why would we want to escape from our own house? Harry, you aren't talking sense."

Thurston frowned. "I'm guarding you," he said stubbornly.

"For whom?"

"The police. I've been deputized."

"Deputized? By whom?"

"Bob Thorp."

"When?"

"An hour . . . hour and a half."

"Why does Bob want you to keep us in the house?"

"You know why," Thurston said again.

"I've already told you that I *don't* know."

"You've done something."

"What have we done?"

"Something wrong. Illegal."

"You know us better than that."

Thurston said nothing.

"Don't you, Harry?"

Silence.

"What have we done?" Sam insisted.

"I don't know."

"Bob didn't tell you?"

"I'm just an emergency deputy."

The shotgun looks nonetheless deadly for that, Paul thought.

"You don't know what we're supposed to have done?" Sam asked. "But you're willing to shoot us if we try to leave?"

"Those are my orders."

"How long have you known me?"

"Twenty years anyway."

"And Jenny?"

"A long time."

"You're willing to kill old friends just because someone tells you to?" Sam asked. He was probing, trying to discover the breadth and depth of Salsbury's control.

Thurston couldn't answer that question. His eyes flicked from one to the other of them, and he shuffled his feet in the wet grass. He was exceedingly nervous, confused, and exasperated—but he was determined to do what the chief of police had asked of him.

Unable to take his eyes off the finger that was curled tightly around the shotgun trigger, unable to look at Sam when he spoke to him, Paul said, "We better get on with this. I think maybe you've pushed him far enough."

"I think so too," Sam said tensely. And then to Thurston: "I am the key."

"I am the lock."

"Lower the gun, Harry."

Thurston obeyed.

"Thank God," Jenny said.

"Come here, Harry."

Thurston went to Sam.

"I'll be damned," Jenny said.

A perfect zombie, Paul thought. A regular little tin soldier . . . A chill passed along his spine.

Sam said, "Harry, who *really* told you to come over here and keep a watch on us?"

"Bob Thorp."

"Tell me the truth."

"It was Bob Thorp," Thurston said, perplexed.

"It wasn't a man named Salsbury?"

"Salsbury? No."

"Haven't you met Salsbury?"

"No. Who are you talking about?"

"Maybe he called himself Albert Deighton."

"Who did?" Thurston asked.

"Salsbury."

"I don't know anyone named Deighton."

Jenny, Rya, and Paul came down the rain-slick steps and joined the two men.

"Salsbury's obviously working through Bob Thorp," Jenny said, "one way or another."

"What are you people talking about?" Thurston asked.

Sam said, "Harry, I am the key."

"I am the lock."

Taking a moment to study Thurston and to decide upon his approach, Sam finally said, "Harry, we are going for a walk up toward Hattie Lange's house. You won't try to stop us. Is that clear?"

"I won't stop you."

"You won't shoot us."

"No. Of course not."

"You won't call out or make trouble of any kind."

Thurston shook his head: no.

"When we leave here," Sam said, "you'll go back to the lilac bush. You'll forget that we ever came out of the house. Is that clear?"

"Yes."

"I want you to forget that we've had this little talk. When the four of us leave here, I want you to forget every word that's been spoken between us. Can you do that, Harry?"

"Sure. I'll forget that we talked, that I saw any of you just now, all of it, like you said."

For a human robot, for an honest-to-God zombie, Paul thought, he seemed damned relaxed.

"You'll think we're still inside," Sam said.

Thurston stared at the back of the general store.

"You'll guard the place exactly as you were doing a few minutes ago," Sam said.

"Guard it . . . That's what Bob told me to do."

"Then do it," Sam said. "And forget you've seen us."

Obediently, Harry Thurston returned to the man-size niche in the wall of lilac bushes. He stood with his feet apart. He held the shotgun in both hands, parallel to the ground, prepared to raise it and fire within a second if faced with a sudden threat.

"Incredible," Jenny said.

"Looks like a storm trooper," Sam said wearily. "Come on. Let's get out of here."

Jenny followed him.

Paul took hold of Rya's icy hand.

Her face drawn, a haunted look in her eyes, she squeezed his hand and said, "Will it be all right again?"

"Sure. Everything will be fine before much longer," he told her, not certain if that was the truth or another lie.

They went west, across the rear lawns of the neighboring houses, walking fast and hoping they wouldn't be seen.

With every step Paul expected someone to shout at them. And in spite of the manner in which Harry Thurston had behaved, he also expected to hear a shotgun blast close behind him, much too close behind him, inches from his shoulder blades: one sudden apocalyptic roar and then an endless silence.

Halfway down the block they came to the back of St. Lukes, the town's all-denominational church. It was a freshly painted, neatly kept rectangular white frame structure on a brick-faced foundation. There was a five-story-high bell tower at the front of the building, out on the Main Street side.

Sam tried the rear door and found it unlocked. They slipped inside, one at a time.

For two or three minutes they stood in the narrow, musty, windowless foyer, and waited to see if Harry Thurston or anyone else would follow them.

No one did.

"Small blessings," Jenny said.

Sam led them into the chamber behind the altar. That room was even darker than the foyer. They accidentally knocked over a rack full of choir gowns—and stood very still until the echo of the crash had faded away, until they were certain that they hadn't revealed themselves.

Holding hands, forming a human chain, they stumbled out of that room and onto the altar platform. Because the storm clouds filtered the day into twilight before it was filtered again by the leaded stained-glass windows, the church proper was only marginally brighter than the room behind it. Nevertheless, there was sufficient light to allow them to break the chain; and they followed Sam along the center aisle, between the two ranks of pews, without having to feel their way as if they were blind people in a strange house.

At the rear of the nave, on the left-hand side, Sam pulled open a door. Beyond lay an enclosed spiral staircase. Sam went first; Jenny went next, then Rya.

Paul stood on the bottom step, staring out at the shadowy church for a minute or two. His revolver was ready in his right hand. When the big room remained silent and deserted, he closed the stairwell door and went up to join the others.

The top of the bell tower was a nine-foot-square platform. The bell—one yard wide at the mouth—was at the center of the platform, of course, suspended from the highest point of the arched ceiling. A chain was welded to the rim of the bell and trailed through a small hole in the floor, down to the base of the tower where the toller could tug on it. The walls were only four feet high, open from there to the ceiling. A white pillar rose at each corner, supporting the peaked, slate-shingled roof. Because the roof overhung the walls by four feet on all sides, the rain hadn't come in through the open spaces; and the belfry platform was dry.

When he reached the head of the stairs, Paul got on his hands and knees. People seldom looked up as they hurried about their business, especially when they were in a familiar place; however, there was no reason to risk being seen. He crawled around the bell to the opposite side of the platform.

Jenny and Rya were sitting on the floor, their back to the half-wall. The .22 rifle lay at Jenny's side. She was talking to the girl in a low voice, telling her a joke or a story, trying to help her ease her tensions and overcome some of her grief. Jenny glanced at Paul, smiled, but kept her attention focused on Rya.

That should be my job, Paul thought. Helping Rya. Reassuring her and comforting her, being with her.

And then he thought, No. For the time being, your job is to prepare yourself to kill at least one man. Maybe two or three. Maybe as many as half a dozen.

Suddenly he wondered how the violence past and the violence yet to come would affect his relationship with his daughter. Knowing he had killed several men, would Rya fear him as she now feared Bob Thorp? Knowing he was capable of the ultimate brutal act, would she ever be at ease with him again? Death had taken his wife and his son. Would alienation take his daughter from him?

Sam was on his knees, peering over the belfry wall.

Deeply disturbed but aware that this wasn't the time to worry about more than a few hours of the future, easing in beside Sam, Paul looked eastward, to his left. He could see Edison's General Store half a block away. Karkov's service station and garage. The houses in the last section of town. The baseball diamond on the meadow near the river. At the end of the valley, near the bend in the highway, a police car was angled across both lanes.

"Roadblock."

Sam said, "I've seen it."

"Salsbury does have us penned up."

"And right now he's probably wondering why the hell we haven't tried to call the cops or leave Black River."

To Paul's right was the main part of town. The square. Ultman's Cafe with its pair of enormous black oak trees. The municipal building. Beyond the square, more lovely houses: brick houses and stone houses and white gingerbread Gothic houses and trim little bungalows. A couple of shops with striped awnings out in front. The telephone company office. St. Margaret Mary's. The cemetery. The Union Theater with its old-fashioned marquee. And then the road to the mill. The entire panorama, so recently scrubbed by the storm, looked crisp and bright and quaint—and too innocent to contain the evil that he knew it harbored.

"You still think Salsbury's holed up in the municipal building?" Paul asked.

"Where else?"

"I guess so."

"The chief's office is the logical command center."

Paul looked at his watch. "A quarter past five."

"We'll wait here until dark," Sam said. "Nine o'clock or thereabouts. Then we'll sneak across the street, get past his guards with the code phrase, and reach him before he's seen us coming."

"It sounds so easy."

"It will be," Sam said.

Lightning flashed like a fuse and thunder exploded and rain like shrapnel clattered on the tower roof and on the streets below.

5:20 P.M.

Smiling as he had been told to smile, his arms folded across his broad chest, Bob Thorp leaned casually against the window sill and watched Salsbury, who was working at Bob's desk.

The infinity transmitter was connected to the office telephone. The line was open to Sam Edison's place—or at least the number had been dialed, and the line *should* have been open.

Salsbury hunched over the chief's desk, the receiver gripped so tightly in his right hand that his knuckles appeared to be about to slice through the pale skin that sheathed them. He listened closely for some sound, some insignificant tiny little sound of human origin, from the general store or from the living quarters on the two floors above the store.

Nothing.

"Come on," he said impatiently.

Silence.

Cursing the infinity transmitter, telling himself that the damned thing hadn't worked, that it was a piece of crappy Belgian-made hardware and so what could you expect, he hung up. He checked to see if the wires were attached to the proper terminals, then dialed the Edisons' number again.

The line opened: hissing, a soft roar not unlike the echo of your own circulation when you held a seashell to your ear.

In the background at the Edison's place, a clock ticked rather noisily, hollowly.

He looked at his watch. 5:24.

Nothing. Silence.

5:26.

He hung up, dialed again.

He heard the ticking clock.

5:28.

5:29.

5:30.

No one spoke over there. No one cried or laughed or sighed or coughed or yawned or *moved*.

5:32.

5:33.

Salsbury pressed the receiver to his ear as hard as he could, concentrated, strained with his whole body and attention to hear Edison or Annendale or one of the others.

5:34.

5:35.

They were over there. Dammit, they *were!*

5:36.

He slammed the receiver into its cradle.

The bastards know I'm listening to them, he thought. They're trying to be quiet, trying to worry me. That's it. That has to be it.

He picked up the telephone and dialed the Edisons' number.

A ticking clock. Nothing else.

5:39.

5:40.

"Bastards!"

He hung up the phone with a *bang!*

Suddenly he was drenched with perspiration.

Clammy and uncomfortable, he got to his feet. But he was frozen by rage; he couldn't move.

He said to Thorp, "Even if they did get out of the store some way, somehow, they can't have left town. That's absolutely impossible. None of them's a magician. They can't have done it. I've got it all sewed up. Haven't I?''

Thorp smiled at him. He was still operating under the previous orders Salsbury had given him.

"Answer me, damn you!"

Thorp's smile vanished.

Salsbury was livid and greasy with sweat. "Haven't I got this fucking town sewed up tight?"

"Oh, yes," Thorp said obediently.

"No one can get out of this crummy burg unless I let them out of it. Isn't that right?"

"Yes. You've got it sewn up."

Salsbury was shaking. Dizzy. "Even if they slipped out of the store, I can find them. I can find them any damned time I want to. Can't I?"

"Yes."

"I can tear this goddamned town apart, rip it wide open and find those sonsofbitches."

"Any time you want."

"They can't escape."

"No."

Abruptly sitting down, almost as if he had collapsed, Salsbury said, "But that doesn't matter. They *haven't* left the store. They can't have left it. It's guarded. Closely guarded. It's a damned prison. So they're still in the place. Being quiet as mice. They know I'm listening. They're trying to trick me. That's what it is. A trick. That's precisely what it is."

He dialed the Edisons' number.

He heard the familiar ticking of the clock in one of the rooms where there was a receiver.

5:44.

5:45.

He hung up.

Dialed again.

Ticking . . .

5:46.

5:47.

He hung up.

Grinning at the chief of police, he said, "Do you realize what they want me to do?"

Thorp shook his head: no.

"They want me to panic. They want me to order you to make a house-to-house search for them." He giggled. "I could do that. I could make everyone in town cooperate in a house-to-house search. But that would take hours. And then I'd have to erase the memory of it from everyone's mind. Four hundred minds. That would take a couple of hours more. They want me to waste my time. Precious time. They want me to panic and waste hours and maybe give them a chance to slip by me in the confusion. Isn't that what they want?''

"Yes."

Salsbury giggled. "Well, I'm not playing their game. I'm going to wait for Dawson and Klinger. I'm not going to panic. Not me. I am in control of the situation—and I'll stay that way."

Thunder boomed over the valley and reverberated in the two office windows.

He dialed the general store.

5:50.

5:51.

He giggled and hung up.

Then he had a startling thought: if the Edisons and the Annendales knew he was listening to them, that meant they knew the entire story, the truth, knew who he was, really was, and what he was doing here in Black River . . . And that was impossible.

He dialed again.

5:52.

Nothing. Silence.

He put down the receiver and turned to Thorp. "Well, I guess it doesn't matter if they *do* know. They can't get away. I've got them where I want them. I have the power . . ." He stared at the infinity transmitter for a while, then looked back at Thorp. "What do you think Miriam will do when she finds out about the power I've got?"

"Who's Miriam?"

"You know Miriam."

"I don't know her."

"She's my ex-wife."

"Oh."

"A rotten bitch."

Thorp said nothing.

"Frigid as a popsicle."

"I'm sorry."

"I know what she'll do," Salsbury said. "She'll come crawling to me. Old Miriam. Crawling to me, Bob. On her hands and knees. She will. Won't she?"

"Yes," Thorp said.

The power . . .

"You know what I'll do?"

Thorp said, "No."

"You know what the hell I'll do when that rotten bitch comes on her hands and knees, crawling on her hands and knees to me?"

"No."

"Kick her in the face."

"That's assault," Thorp said.

"Same for Dawson. Kick him in the face."

"That's assault. You'll wind up in jail."

"I'll get Dawson," Salsbury said solemnly. Then he giggled. "I'll get that sanctimonious old bastard."

Thorp frowned.

"Think I could find a pair of jackboots, Bob?"

"A pair of what?"

"Maybe there *are* a few people, just a few people, not many mind you, that I'd want jackboots for."

Tat-tat-tat-tat-tat-tat . . .

6:30 P.M.

"Hello?"

"Mrs. Wolinski?"

"Yes."

"I am the key."

"I am the lock."

"Is your husband there?"

"He's upstairs right now."

"Is he alone upstairs?"

"Alone? Yes."

"Are you alone downstairs?"

"Yes."

"Do you know Sam Edison?"

"Oh, sure."

"Is he at your house now?"

"Sam? No."

"Is Jenny Edison at your house?"

"No. Why should she be?"

"Haven't you seen either of the Edisons today?"

"No. Look here, I—"

"Mrs. Wolinski, when you hang up your telephone, you'll forget every word of this conversation. You'll only remember that someone called and tried to sell you life insurance. Someone from Bexford. Is that understood?"

"Yes."

"Hang up, Mrs. Wolinski."

6:45 P.M.

"St. Margaret Mary's."

"Is this the rectory?"

"Yes, it is."

"Father O'Hara?"

"Speaking."

"I am the key."

"I am the lock."

"Are you alone, father?"

"Yes."

"What about your housekeeper?"

"She's gone home for the day."

"Do you know Sam and Jenny Edison?"

"Certainly. Fine people."

"Is either of them with you now?"

"Here at the rectory? No."

"In the church perhaps?"

"No. Why do you ask?"

"Have you seen either of the Edisons today?"

"No. I—"

"Do you know Paul Annendale?"

"I don't believe so. If there's some sort of emergency—"

"Shut up, O'Hara. When you hang up your telephone, you'll forget every word of this conversation. You'll only remember that someone dialed a wrong number. Is that understood?"

"Yes."

"Hang up, O'Hara."

7:00 P.M.

". . . either of the Edisons today?"

"I saw Sam. Down at the store."

"When was that, Mrs. Jamison?"

"This morning. Around nine."

"You haven't seen him since?"

"No."

"Mrs. Jamison, I don't want you to go away from the phone. You stand right there. But give the receiver to your husband."

"Hello?"

"Mr. Jamison?"

"Yes?"

"I am the key."

"I am the lock."

7:30 P.M.

". . . don't want you to go away from the phone, Mrs. Potter. You stand right there. But give the receiver to Reverend Potter."

"All right. Just a minute . . ."

"Hello?"

"Reverend Potter?"

"This is he."

"I am the key."

"I am the lock."

"Do you know Sam and Jenny Edison?"

"Yes. Very well, in fact."

"Have you seen either of them today?"

"No."

"Are you absolutely sure of that?"

"Oh, yes. Absolutely."

"Have you talked to either of them today?"

"No. I—"

"Do you know Paul Annendale or his daughter?"

"Yes. Every year they—"

"Have you seen or talked to them today?"

"No. I've spent the day—"

"What the fuck's happening, Potter?"

"I beg your pardon?"

"Where in the hell *are* they?"

"I don't like foul language or—"

"I've called fifty people in the past hour and a half. Nobody's seen them. Nobody's heard from them. Nobody knows anything. Well, they've got to be in this town. I'm *damn* sure of that! They can't get out . . . Christ. You know what I think, Potter? I think they're still in the general store."

"If—"

"Being quiet as mice. Trying to fool me. They want me to come looking for them. They want me to send Bob Thorp after them. They probably have guns in there. Well, they *can't* fool me. They're not going to start a shooting match and leave me with a dozen bodies to account for. I'll wait them out. I'll get them, Potter. And you know what I'll do when I get my hands on them? The Edisons will have to be studied, of course. I'll have to find out why they didn't respond to the drug and the subliminals. But I *know* why the Annendales didn't respond. They weren't here for the program. So when I get them, I can dispose of them right away. Right away. I'll have Bob Thorp blow their fucking heads off. The sonsofbitches. That's exactly what I'll do."

7.

AT DUSK, when the thunderstorm temporarily abated for the fourth time that day, a streamlined executive helicopter, painted bright yellow and black like a hornet, already gleaming with green and red running lights, fluttered into the east end of the Black River valley. It was flying low, no higher than sixty feet above the ground. It followed Main Street toward the town square, chopping up the humid air. A flat echo of the stuttering blades rebounded from the wet pavement below.

In the bell tower of the all-denominational church, also sixty feet above the ground—but safely hidden in the deep shadows that were cast by the overhanging belfry roof—Rya, Jenny, Paul, and Sam watched the aircraft as it approached. In the penumbral, purple-gray twilight the helicopter seemed dangerously close to them; but no one in it was looking their way. However, the waning daylight was still bright enough to allow them to see into the flight deck and into the cozy passenger cabin behind it.

"Two men besides the pilot," Sam said.

At the square the helicopter hovered for a moment, then swept across the municipal building and settled into the parking lot ten yards from the spare police car.

As the evening quietude returned in the aircraft's wake, Jenny said, "Do you think those men are connected with Salsbury?"

"No doubt about it," Sam said.

"Government?"

Paul said, "No."

"I agree," Sam said almost happily. "Even the President's chopper is military-style on the outside—although probably not on the inside. The government doesn't use sleek little executive machines like that yellow and black job."

"Which doesn't rule out the government's having a part in this," Paul said.

"Oh, certainly not. It doesn't rule out anything," Sam said. "But it's a good sign."

"What now?" Rya asked.

"Now we watch and wait," Paul said, his eyes fixed on the white-brick municipal building. "Just watch and wait."

The damp air still held an unpleasant tang of the helicopter's exhaust fumes.

Up in the mountains, thunder rumbled menacingly. Lightning arced between two of the higher peaks as if they were terminals in Frankenstein's laboratory.

To Paul time seemed almost at a standstill. Each minute ticked on and on and on. Each second was like a tiny bubble of air rising slowly through the bottle of glucose on the intravenous-feeding rack that he had watched for hour after leaden hour at Annie's hospital bedside.

Finally, at 9:20 two cars came down Main Street from the municipal building: the second police cruiser and a one-year-old Ford LTD. The four headlamps sliced open the crescent darkness. Half a block beyond the church, they parked at the curb in front of the general store.

Bob Thorp and two men with handguns climbed out of the squad car. For a moment they stood in the splash of amber-white light from the LTD; then they went up the porch steps and disappeared beneath the veranda roof.

Three men got out of the second car. They left the engine running and the doors open. They didn't follow Thorp; they remained at the LTD. Because they were standing behind the headlights, they were for the most part in darkness. Paul couldn't tell if they were armed or not. But he knew for certain who they were: Salsbury and the two passengers from the helicopter.

"Do you want to go down there and take them now?" Paul asked Sam. "While they have their backs to us?"

"Too risky. We don't know if they've got guns. They might hear us coming. And even if we did catch them by surprise, one of them would get away, sure as hell. Let's wait a bit."

At 9:35 one of Bob Thorp's "deputies" came down the porch steps and joined the three men at the second car. They talked, possibly argued, for a few seconds. The deputy remained at the LTD while Salsbury and his associates mounted the steps to the general store.

9:50 P.M.

Turning away from the bookshelves in Sam Edison's study, Dawson said, "All right then. Now we understand how they might have pieced it together. Ogden, do they know the code phrases?"

Shocked by the question, Salsbury said, "Of course not! How in the hell could they know?"

"The little girl might have heard you use them with Thorp or with her brother."

"No," he said. "Impossible. She didn't step into that doorway until long after I gave up trying to get control of her brother—and long, *long* after I'd already assumed control of Thorp."

"Did you try to use the phrase on her?"

Did I? Salsbury wondered. I remember seeing her there, taking a step toward her, being unable to catch her. But did I use the code phrase?

He rejected that notion because if he accepted it he would have to accept defeat, complete destruction." No," he told Dawson. "I didn't have time to use the phrase. I saw her. She turned and ran. I ran after her, but she was too fast."

"You're absolutely certain?"

"Absolutely."

Regarding Salsbury with unvarnished disgust, the general said, "You should have foreseen this development with Edison. You should have known about this library, this hobby of his."

"How in the hell could I foresee any of it?" Salsbury asked. His face was flushed. His myopic eyes seemed to bulge even more than usual behind his thick glasses.

"If you had done your duty—"

"Duty," Salsbury said scornfully. Half of his anger was generated by his fear; but it was important that neither Dawson nor Klinger see that. "This isn't the stinking military, Ernst. This isn't the army. I'm not one of your oh-so-humble enlisted men."

Klinger turned away from him, went to the window, and said, "Maybe we'd all be better off if you were."

Willing the general to look at him, aware that he was at a disadvantage so long as Klinger felt safe enough to turn his back, Salsbury said, "Christ! No matter how careful I'd been—"

"That's enough," Dawson said. He spoke softly but with such command that Salsbury stopped talking and the general looked away from the window. "We haven't time for arguments and accusations. We've got to find those four people."

"They can't have gotten out of town through the east end of the valley," Salsbury said. "I *know* I've got that sealed tight."

"You thought you had this house sealed up tight too," Klinger said. "But they slipped past you."

"Let's not judge too harshly, Ernst," Dawson said. He smiled in a fatherly, Christian fashion and nodded at Salsbury. But there was only hatred and loathing in his black eyes. "I agree with Ogden. His precautions at the east end are certainly adequate. Although we might consider tripling the number of men along the river and in the woods now that night has fallen. And I believe Ogden's also covered the logging roads well enough."

"Then there are two possibilities," Klinger said, deciding to play the military strategist. "One—they might still be in town, hiding somewhere, waiting for a chance to get past the roadblock or the men guarding the river. Or two—maybe they're going to walk out through the mountains. We know from Thorp that the Annendales are experienced campers and hikers."

Bob Thorp was standing by the door, as if he were an honor guard. He said, "That's true."

"I don't see it," Salsbury said. "I mean, they have an eleven-year-old girl with them. She'll slow them down. They'll need *days* to reach help that way."

"That little girl has spent a big part of the last seven summers in these forests," the general said. "She might not be as much of a drag on them as you think. Besides, if we don't locate them, they'll do the same damage whether they reach help tonight or not until the middle of next week."

Dawson thought about that. Then: "If they're trying to walk out through the mountains, sixty miles round-about to Bexford, how far do you think they've gotten by now?"

"Three, maybe three and a half miles," Klinger said.

"No farther than that?"

"I doubt it," Klinger said. "They'd have to be damned careful leaving town if they didn't want to be seen. They'd move slowly, a few yards at a time for the first mile. In the forest they'd need a while to really hit their stride. And even if the little girl *is* at home in the woods, she'd slow them down a bit."

"Three and a half miles," Dawson said thoughtfully. "Wouldn't that put them somewhere between the Big Union mill and the planned forests?"

"That's about right."

Dawson closed his eyes and seemed to mutter a few words of silent prayer; his lips moved slightly. Then his eyes snapped open, as if sprung by a holy revelation, and he said, "The first thing we'll do is organize a search in the mountains."

"That's absurd," Salsbury said, although he was aware that Dawson probably thought of his plan as a divine inspiration, the very handiwork of God. "It would be like—well, like hunting for a needle in a haystack."

His voice as cold as the dead boy in the next room, Dawson said, "We have nearly two hundred men at the logging camp, all of them familiar with these mountains. We'll mobilize them. Arm them with axes and rifles and shotguns. Give them flaslights and Coleman lanterns. We'll put them in trucks and jeeps and send them a mile or so beyond the logging camp. They can form a search line and walk back. Forty feet between the men. That way, the line will be a mile and a half from one end to the other—yet each man will have only a small area of ground to cover. The Edisons and the Annendales won't be able to get by them."

"It'll work," Klinger said admiringly.

"But what if they aren't up there in the mountains?" Salsbury said. "What if they're right here in town?"

"Then we've nothing to worry about," Dawson said. "They can't get to you because you're surrounded by Bob Thorp and his deputies. They can't get out of town because every exit is blocked. All they can do is wait." He smiled wolfishly. "If we don't find them in the mountains by three or four o'clock in the morning, we'll begin a house-to-house search here in town. One way or another, I want this whole affair wrapped up by noon tomorrow."

"That's asking a lot," the general said.

"I don't care," Dawson said. "It isn't asking too much. I want the four of them dead by noon. I want to restructure the memories of everyone in this town to cover our trail completely. By noon."

"Dead?" Salsbury said, confused. He pushed his glasses up on his nose. "But I need to study the Edisons. You can kill the Annendales if you want. But I've got to know why the Edisons weren't affected. I've got—"

"Forget that," Dawson said brusquely. "If we attempted to capture them and take them back to the laboratory at Greenwich, there's a good chance they'd escape along the way. We can't risk that. They know too much. Much too much."

"But we'll have so damned many corpses!" Salsbury said. "For God's sake, there's already the boy. And Buddy Pellineri. Four more . . . And if they fight back, we may have as many as a dozen to bury. How are we going to account for so many?"

Obviously pleased with himself, Dawson said, "We'll put the lot of them in the Union Theater. Then we'll stage a tragic fire. We've got Dr. Troutman to issue death certificates. And we can use the key-lock program to keep the relatives from requesting autopsies."

"Excellent," Klinger said, grinning, lightly clapping his hands.

Sycophant to the court of King Leonard the First, Salsbury thought sourly.

"Really excellent, Leonard," Klinger said.

"Thank you, Ernst."

"Christ on a crutch," Salsbury said weakly.

Dawson gave him a nasty look. He was displeased with such strong profanity. "For every sin that we commit, the Lord will have His awful retribution one day. There's no escaping that."

Salsbury said nothing.

"There *is* a hell."

Looking at Klinger, finding no support nor even a wink of sympathy, Salsbury managed to keep quiet. There was something in Dawson's voice—like a well-honed knife hidden in the soft folds of a priest's gown—something hard and sharp that frightened him.

Dawson glanced at his watch and said, "Time to be moving, gentlemen. Let's get this over with."

10:12 P.M.

The helicopter rose from the parking lot behind the municipal building. It swung gracefully over the town square where several people stood watching it, and then it clattered westward toward the mountain, into the darkness.

In a moment it was gone.

Sam turned away from the street and slumped with his back to the belfry wall. "On their way to the mill?"

"Looks like it," Paul said. "But why?"

"Good question. I would have asked the same thing myself if you hadn't."

"Another thing," Paul said. "What if they've figured out how we escaped? What if they realize we know the code phrase?"

"That's not very likely."

"But if it's the case?"

"I wish I knew," Sam said worriedly. He sighed. "But remember that even under the worst circumstances, it's just us against them. If they realize how much we know, we lose the advantage of surprise. But *they've* lost the advantage of an army of programmed bodyguards. So it balances out."

Jenny said, "Do you think both of Salsbury's friends are aboard the helicopter?"

Sam held his revolver before him. He was unable to see

more than the outline of it in the darkness. Nevertheless, studying it with dread fascination, he said, "Well now, that's another thing I sure wish I knew."

Paul's hands were shaking. His own Smith & Wesson felt as if it weighed a hundred pounds. He said, "I guess we go after Salsbury now."

"It's past time we did."

Jenny touched her father's hand, the one that held the gun. "But what if one of those men *did* stay with Salsbury?"

"Then it's two against two," Sam said. "And we sure as hell can handle that."

"If I went along," she said, "it would be three against two, and that would have to improve the odds."

"Rya needs you," Sam said. He hugged her, kissed her on the cheek. "We'll be okay, Jen. I know we will. You just watch after Rya while we're gone."

"And if you don't come back?"

"We will."

"If you don't," she insisted.

"Then—you're on your own," Sam said, his voice almost breaking. If there were tears in the corners of his eyes, the darkness hid them. "There's nothing more I can do for you."

"Look," Paul said, "even if Salsbury does know how much we've learned, he doesn't know where we are. But we know exactly where *he* is. So we still have some advantage."

Rya clung to Paul. She didn't want to let him go. She spoke in a quiet but fierce voice, and she virtually demanded that he not leave her in the tower.

He stroked her dark hair, held her tight, spoke softly to her, calmed and reassured her as best he could.

And at 10:20 he followed Sam down the tower stairs.

8.

PHIL KARKOV, the proprietor of Black River's only service station and garage, and his girl friend, Lolah Tayback, tried to leave town a few minutes past ten o'clock. As programmed, the deputies who manned the roadblock sent them to the municipal building to have a talk with Bob Thorp.

The mechanic was soft-spoken, courteous, and obviously liked to think of himself as a model citizen. He was a tall, broad-shouldered, red-haired man in his middle thirties. His good looks were marred only by a bulbous and somewhat misshapen nose that appeared to have been broken in more than one fight. He was an amicable man with a ready smile; and he was most anxious to help the chief of police in any way that he could.

After he opened the two of them with the code phrase and spent a minute interrogating them, Salsbury was satisfied that Karkov and Lolah Tayback were fully, properly programmed. They hadn't been trying to escape. They hadn't seen anything out of the ordinary in town today. They had only been going to a bar in Bexford for beer and sandwiches.

He sent the mechanic home and told him to stay there for the rest of the night.

The woman was another matter altogether.

"Child-woman" was a better word for her, he thought. Her silvery-blond hair hung to her narrow shoulders and framed a face of childlike beauty: crystalline green eyes, a perfectly clear and milky complexion with a light, cinnamonlike dusting of freckles across her cheekbones, an upturned pixie nose, dimples, a blade-straight jawline and round little chin . . . Every feature was delicate and somehow bespoke naïveté. She stood perhaps five feet two and weighed no more than one hundred pounds. She seemed fragile. Yet in her red-and-white-striped T-shirt (sans bra) and blue jean shorts, she presented a strikingly desirable, quite womanly figure. Her breasts were small, high set, accentuated by an extremely thin waistline, the nipples delectably silhouetted through the thin material of the T-shirt. Her legs were sleek, supple, shapely. As he stood in front of her, looking her up and down, she regarded him shyly. She was unable to meet his eyes. She fidgeted. If appearance could count for anything, she ought to have been one of the most malleable, vulnerable women he had ever met.

However, even if she were a fighter, a real hellcat, she was now vulnerable. As vulnerable as he wished her to be. Because he had the power . . .

"Lolah?"

"Yes."

"How old are you?"

"Twenty-six."

"Are you engaged to Phil Karkov?"

"No." Softly.

"Going steady with him?"

"More or less."

"Are you sleeping with him?"

She blushed. Fidgeted.

Lovely little animal . . .

Screw you, Dawson.

You too, Ernst.

He giggled.

"Are you sleeping with him, Lolah?"

Almost inaudibly: "Do I have to say?"

"You must tell me the truth."

"Yes," she whispered.

"You're sleeping with him?"

"Yes."

"How often?"

"Oh . . . Every week."

"Speak up."

"Every week."

"Little minx."

"Are you going to hurt me?"

He laughed. "Once a week? Twice?"

"Twice," she said. "Sometimes three . . ."

Salsbury turned to Bob Thorp. "Get the hell out of here. Go down to the end of the hall and wait with the guard there until I call you."

"Sure." Thorp closed the door as he left.

"Lolah?"

"Yes?"

"What does Phil do to you?"

"What do you mean?"

"In bed."

She stared at her sandaled feet.

The power filled him, pulsed within him, leaped across tens of thousands of terminals in his flesh: sparked, flashed, crackled. He was exhilarated. *This* was what the key-lock program was all about: this power, this mastery, this unlimited command of other people's souls. No one could ever touch him again. No one could ever use him. *He* was the user now. Always would be. From here on out. Now and forever, amen. Amen, Dawson. Did you hear that? Amen. Thank you, God, for sending along this cute little piece of ass, amen. He was happy again for the first time since this morning, since he had touched Thorp's wife.

"I'll bet Phil does *everything* to you," he said.

She said nothing. Shuffled her feet.

"Doesn't he? Doesn't he do everything to you, Lolah? Admit it. Say it. I want to hear you say it."

"He does—everything."

He put his hand under her chin, lifted her head.

She gazed at him. Timid, frightened.

"I'm going to do everything to you," he said.

"Don't hurt me."

"Lovely, lovely little bitch," he said. He was excited as he had never been in his life. Breathing hard. Yet everything so clear. So in control. Firmly in control. Her absolute master. Everyone's absolute master. That was Howard Parker's phrase, flashing back to him across the decades, much as a bizarre hallucination erupting in an acidhead's mind years after his last tab of LSD: *absolute master.* "That's exactly what I'm going to do to you," he told Lolah Tayback. "I'm going to hurt you, just like I hurt the others. Make you pay. Make you bleed. I'm your absolute master. You're going to take everything I dish out to you. Everything. Maybe even like it. Learn to like it. Maybe . . ."

His hands curled into fists at his sides.

The pilot flew the helicopter in a wide circle around the logging camp, searching for the best place to set down between the scattered lights from the buildings.

In the passenger cabin, Dawson broke an extended silence. "Ogden has to be eliminated."

Klinger had no difficulty accepting that judgment. "Of course. He's untrustworthy."

"Unstable."

"But if we eliminate him," the general said, "can we continue with the plan?"

"Everything that Ogden has learned is in the Greenwich computer," Dawson said. "The research was beyond us. But we can use the finished product well enough."

"Hasn't he encoded his data?"

"Naturally. But the day after the computer was installed, long before Ogden began to use it, I had my people program it to decode and print out any data that I requested—regardless of how the request was phrased, regardless of passwords or number keys or other security devices that he might use to limit my access to the information."

The helicopter hovered, descended.

"When do we deal with him?"

"*You* deal with him," Dawson said.

"Me—or do I program someone to do it?"

"Do it yourself. He can deprogram anyone else." Dawson smiled. "You do have a handgun with you?"

"Oh, yes."

"In the small of your back?"

"Strapped to my right ankle."

"Marvelous."

"Back to the original question," Klinger said. "When do I eliminate him?"

"Tonight. Within the hour, if possible."

"Why not back in Greenwich?"

"I don't want to bury him on the estate. That's taking too great a chance."

"What *will* we do with the body?"

"Bury it here. In the woods."

The helicopter touched ground.

The pilot shut off the engines.

Overhead, the rotors coughed and slowed down. A welcome silence gradually replaced the racket they had made.

Klinger said, "You intend for him to just—disappear off the face of the earth?"

"That's correct."

"His vacation ends on the fifth of next month. That's when he's due back at the Brockert Institute. He's a punctual man. The morning of the fifth, when he doesn't show up, there's going to be some commotion. They'll come looking for him."

"They won't come looking in Black River. There's nothing at all to connect Ogden with this place. He's supposed to be vacationing in Miami."

"There's going to be a very quiet and very big manhunt," Klinger said. "Pentagon security people, the FBI . . ."

Unbuckling his seat belt, Dawson said, "And there's nothing to connect him with you or with me. Eventually they'll decide that he went over to the other side, defected."

"Maybe."

"Definitely."

Dawson opened his door.

"Do I take the chopper back to town?" Klinger asked.

"No. He might hear you coming and suspect what you're there for. Take a car or a jeep from here. And you'd better walk the last few hundred yards."

"All right."

"And Ernst?"

"Yes?"

In the amber cabin light, Dawson's five-hundred-dollars-apiece capped teeth gleamed in a broad and dangerous smile. There seemed to be light *behind* his eyes. His nostrils were flared: a wolf on the trail of a blood scent. "Ernst, don't worry so much."

"Can't help but."

"We're destined to survive this night, to win this battle and all of those battles that will come after it," Dawson said with solemn conviction.

"I wish I could be as confident of that as you are."

"But you *should* be. We're blessed, my friend. This entire enterprise is blessed, you see. Don't you ever forget that, Ernst." He smiled again.

"I won't forget," Klinger said.

But he was reassured more by the weight of the revolver at his ankle than by Dawson's words.

Straining to hear any sound other than their own footsteps, Paul and Sam left the church by the rear door and crossed the open fields to the riverbank.

The high grass was heavy with rain. Within twenty yards, Paul's shoes and socks were wet through to his skin. The legs of his jeans were soaked almost to the knees.

Sam located a footpath that traversed the bank of the river at a forty-five-degree angle. Every groove and depression in the earth had been transformed into a puddle. The way was exceedingly muddy and slick. They slipped and slid and waved their arms to keep their balance.

At the bottom of the path, they came onto a two-foot-wide rocky shelf. On the right the river rolled and gurgled, filling the darkness with syrupy sound: a wide ebony strip which, at this hour of the night, looked like crude oil rather than water. On their left the bank of the river rose up eight or nine feet; and in some places the exposed roots of willow trees and oaks and maples overlaid the earthen wall.

Without benefit of a flashlight, Sam led Paul westward, toward the mountains. His snowy hair was a ghostly, luminescent sign for Paul to follow. The older man stumbled occasionally; but he was for the most part sure-footed, and he never cursed when he misstepped. He was surprisingly quiet, as if the skills and talents of an experienced warrior suddenly had come back to him after all these years.

This *is* war, Paul reminded himself. We're on our way to kill a man. The enemy. Several men . . .

The warm, heavy air was redolent with the odor of damp

moss and with the stale fumes of the plants that were decomposing in the muck at the water's edge.

Eventually, Sam found a series of wind- and water-chiseled ledges, steps that took them up from the river again. They came out in an apple orchard on the slopes at the extreme west end of town.

Thunder roared down from the peaks, disturbing the birds in the apple trees.

They went north. They were taking the safest—and also the most roundabout—route to the back of the municipal building. Soon they came to a waist-high white picket fence that marked the end of the orchard and the verge of Main Street, where it became known to the locals as the mill road.

After he had looked both ways and had carefully studied the land to which he was running, when he was certain that there was no one to see him, Sam slipped over the fence. He was as agile as a young man. He sprinted silently across the lane and quickly disappeared into a dense stand of scrub pines, scraggly birches, and brush on the other side.

Paul tucked his revolver into his belt, put both hands on the fence, looked up and down the street as Sam had done—but was suddenly arrested by a severe spell of uncontrollable shivering. His stomach twisted, and he was short of breath.

He tried to tell himself that the shakes were caused by his wet feet, but he knew that wasn't true. The night was warm. His feet were wet but not cold.

He was shivering for only one reason: because he was going to kill a man.

Or be killed . . .

That was a possibility.

He felt sick.

Dizzy.

He followed Sam.

10:30 P.M.

Lolah Tayback stood before him, naked.

"I'm the absolute master," he said.

"Yes, sir."

"Look at me, Lolah."

She stared at the floor.

"Lolah?"

"Let me go." Soft voice. Tears.

"What's the matter?"

"I'm scared."

"Don't you like me?"

She didn't respond.

"Do you like me, Lolah?"

"Yes, sir."

"Tell the truth, Lolah."

"I . . . don't . . . like you."

He slapped her face.

She fell against the desk.

"Bitch."

"Don't hurt me."

"Animal."

"Don't hurt me. Please."

"I'll kill you."

"Don't—"

He struck her with his fist.

Then he struck her again.

Twin arc lamps on ribbed aluminum poles bracketed the parking lot behind the municipal building. In the stark blue-white light the needles of nearby pine trees resembled feathers. The lamps made the wet macadam shine like molten tar and transformed the puddles into broken mirrors. It glinted coldly on the windshields of several automobiles, including the town ambulance and the spare police cruiser.

When Sam opened the rear door of the building and Paul stepped into the first-floor corridor, two men looked up in surprise. Bob Thorp reached for the revolver in the holster at his hip. The other man, a uniformed deputy, raised his shotgun.

"I am the key," Paul said quickly.

They both said, "I am the lock."

"Speak softly."

They nodded.

"Bob, leave your gun in the holster."

"All right."

"And you. Put down that shotgun."

The deputy obeyed.

Opening these men, using them, pushing buttons deep

within their minds, Paul felt neither triumph nor the exhilaration of command. Instead, aware that their lives and sanity and dignity were in his hands, he had an almost overpowering sense of solemn responsibility; and for a moment he was paralyzed by it.

Sam opened the first door on the right, switched on the overhead fluorescent lights, and ushered everyone into a file room.

10:36 P.M.

Tat-tat-tat-tat-tat-tat . . .

Salsbury's knuckles were skinned. His hands were covered with thin gloves of blood: his blood and hers.

He took a Smith & Wesson .38 Police Special from the firearms cabinet behind Thorp's desk. He located a box of shells on the top shelf and loaded the handgun.

He returned to Lolah Tayback.

She was on the floor in the center of the room, lying on her side with her knees drawn up. Both of her eyes were bruised and swollen. Her lower lip was split. Her septum was broken, and blood trickled from her delicate nostrils. Although she was barely conscious, she groaned miserably when she saw him.

"Poor Lolah," he said mock sympathetically.

Through the thin slits of her swollen eyelids, she watched him apprehensively.

He held the gun to her face.

She closed her eyes.

With the barrel of the .38, he drew circles around her breasts and prodded her nipples.

She shuddered.

He liked that.

The file room was a cold, impersonal place. The fluorescent strip lighting, institutional-green walls, yellowed Venetian blinds, rank on rank of gray metal cabinets, and brown tile floor made it a perfect place for an interrogation.

Sam said, "Bob, is there anyone in your office right now?"

"Yes. A couple of people."

"Who?"

"Lolah Tayback—and him."

"Who is 'him'?"

"I . . . don't know."

"You don't know his name?"

"Gee, I guess not."

"Is it Salsbury?"

Thorp shrugged.

"Is he a somewhat chubby man?"

"About forty pounds too heavy," Thorp said.

"And he wears very thick glasses?"

"Yeah. That's him."

"And he's alone with Lolah?"

"Like I said."

"You're certain of that?"

"Sure."

Paul said, "And his friends?"

"What friends?" Thorp asked.

"In the helicopter."

"They aren't here"

"Neither of them?"

"Neither of them."

"Where are they?"

"I don't know."

"Aren't they at the mill?"

"I don't know."

"Will they be back?"

"I don't know that either."

"Who are they?"

"I'm sorry. I don't know."

Sam said, "That's it, then."

"We go after him?" Paul asked.

"Right now.

"I'll hit the door first."

"I'm older," Sam said. "I've got less to lose."

"I'm younger—and faster," Paul said.

"Speed won't matter. He won't be expecting us."

"And maybe he will," Paul said.

Reluctantly, Sam said, "All right. You first. But I'll be damned close behind."

Salsbury forced her to lie on her back. He parted her legs with one hand and put the cool steel barrel of the .38 between her silken thighs. He shivered and licked his lips. With his left hand he slid his glasses up on his nose. "Do you want it?" he asked eagerly. "Do you want it? Well, I'm going to give it to you. All of it. Every last inch of it. Do you hear me, you little bitch? Little animal. Bust you wide open. Wide open. Going to truly and really give it to you . . ."

Paul hesitated outside of the closed door to the police chief's office. When he heard Salsbury talking inside and knew that the man was unaware of their presence in the building, he threw open the door and went inside fast, crouching, the big .357 Magnum shoved out in front of him.

At first he couldn't believe what he saw, didn't *want* to believe what he saw. There was a badly beaten, naked young woman lying on the floor, spread-eagled, conscious but dazed. And Salsbury: face flushed, sweat-filmed, spotted with blood, eyes wild, savage-looking. He was kneeling over the woman, and he seemed like a troll, an evil and disgusting bug-eyed troll. He was pressing a revolver between her pale thighs in a vile, grotesque imitation of the sex act. Paul was so mesmerized by the scene, so riveted by revulsion and outrage, that for a few seconds he forgot altogether that he was in terrible danger.

Salsbury took advantage of Paul's and Sam's inability to act. He stood up as if he had had an electric shock, pointed his revolver, and fired at Paul's head.

The shot was a bit too high, an inch or two, no more than that. The bullet slammed into the wall beside the door. Chips of plaster rained down on Paul's shoulders.

Still crouching, he pulled off two quick shots of his own. The first was wide of the mark; it smashed through the Venetian blinds and shattered one of the windows. The second struck Salsbury in the left shoulder, approximately four inches above the nipple. It caused him to drop his gun, almost lifted him off his feet, pitched him backward as if he were a sack full of rags.

He was thrown to the floor by the impact of the bullet, and he slumped against the wall beneath the windows. He clutched his left shoulder with his right hand, but for all the pressure he applied, blood still streamed between his fingers. Pain pulsed rhythmically within him, deep within him exactly as the power had once done: *tat-tat-tat-tat-tat-tat* . . .

A man came toward him. Blue-eyed. Curly-haired.

He couldn't see very well. His vision was blurred. But the sight of those bright blue eyes was sufficient to catapult him back in time, back to the memory of another pair of blue eyes, and he said, "Parker."

The blue-eyed man said, "Who's Parker?"

"Don't tease me," Salsbury said. "Please don't tease me."

"I'm not teasing."

"Don't touch me."

"Who's Parker?"

"Please don't touch me, Parker."

"Me? That's not my name."

Salsbury began to cry.

The blue-eyed man took him by the chin and forced his head up. "Look at me, damn you. Look at me closely."

"You hurt me bad, Parker."

"I. Am. Not. Parker."

For a moment the blazing pain subsided. Salsbury said, "Not Parker?"

"My name's Annendale."

The pain blossomed again, but the past receded to its proper place. He blinked and said, "Oh. Oh, yes. Annendale."

"I'm going to ask you a lot of questions."

"I'm in terrible *pain*," Salsbury said. "You shot me. You hurt me. That isn't right."

"You're going to answer my questions."

"No," Salsbury said adamantly. "None of them."

"All of them. You'll answer all of them, or I'll blow your damned head off," the blue-eyed man said.

"Okay. Do it. Blow my head off. That's better than losing all of it. That's better than losing the power."

"Who were those men in the helicopter?"

"None of your business."

"Were they government men?"

"Go away."

"You're going to die sooner or later, Salsbury."

"Oh, is that so? Like hell I am."

"You are. So save yourself some pain."

Salsbury said nothing.

"Were they government men?"

"Fuck off."

The blue-eyed man reversed the revolver in his right hand, and he used the butt to rap hard on Salsbury's right hand. The blow seemed to send jagged shards of glass through his skinned knuckles. But that was the least of the pain. The shock was transmitted through his hand, to and into the tender, bloody wound in his shoulder.

He gasped. He bent over and almost vomited.

"Do you see what I mean?"

"Bastard."

"Were they government men?"

"I . . . told you . . . to . . . fuck off."

Klinger parked the car on West Main Street, two blocks from the town square.

He slid out from behind the wheel, closed the door—and heard gunfire. Three shots. One right after the other. Inside, muffled by walls. Not far away. Toward town. The municipal building? He stood very still and listened for at least a minute, but there was nothing more.

He took the snub-nosed .32 Webley from the ankle holster and flicked off the safety.

He hurried in to the alleyway beside the Union Theater, taking a safe if circuitous route to the back door of the municipal building.

9.

IN THE AMBULANCE Lolah Tayback lay on a cot, strapped
down at chest and thighs. A crisp white sheet was drawn up
to her neck. Her head had been elevated with two pillows to
prevent her from choking on her own blood during the trip to
the hospital in Bexford. Although her breathing was regular,
it was labored; and she moaned softly as she exhaled.

Behind the ambulance, at the open bay doors, Sam stood
with Anson Crowell, Thorp's night deputy. "All right. Let's
go through it one more time. What happened to her?"

"She was attacked by a rapist," the deputy said, as Sam
had programmed him to say.

"Where did it happen?"

"In her apartment."

"Who found her?"

"I did."

"Who called the police?"

"Her neighbors."

"Why?"

272

"They heard screaming."

"Did you catch her assailant?"

"I'm afraid not."

"Do you know who he is?"

"No. But we're working on it."

"Have any leads?"

"A couple."

"What are they?"

"I'd prefer not to say at this time."

"Why not?"

"I might prejudice the case."

"By talking to other policemen?"

"We're real careful in Black River."

"That's being too careful, isn't it?"

"No offense. That's just how we operate."

"Do you have a description of the man?"

The deputy recited a list of physical characteristics that Sam had made up off the top of his head. The fictitious assailant did not remotely resemble the real one, Ogden Salsbury.

"What if the state police or the Bexford police offer assistance in the case?"

"I tell them thanks but no thanks," the deputy said. "We'll handle it ourselves. We prefer it that way. Besides, I don't have the authority to allow them to come in on it. That would be up to the chief."

"Good enough," Sam said. "Get in."

The deputy clambered into the passenger bay of the ambulance and sat on the padded bench beside Lolah Tayback's cot.

"You'll be stopping at the end of Main Street to pick up her boyfriend," Sam said. He had already talked to Phil Karkov on the telephone, had primed him to play the role of the anxiety-stricken lover at the hospital—just as he had primed Lolah to play a bewildered rape victim who had been attacked in her apartment. "Phil will be staying at the hospital with her, but you'll come back as soon as you've learned she's going to be okay."

"I understand," Crowell said.

Sam closed the doors. He went around to the driver's window to reinforce the story that he had planted in the mind of the night duty volunteer fireman who was behind the wheel.

* * *

At first it seemed that there was no way to break through Salsbury's iron resolve, no way to open him up and make him talk. He was in great pain—shaking, sweating, dizzy—but he refused to make things easier for himself. He sat in Thorp's office chair with an air of authority that simply did not make sense under the circumstances. He leaned back and gripped his shoulder wound and kept his eyes shut. Most of the time he ignored Paul's questions. Occasionally he responded with a string of profanities and sex words that sounded as if they had been arranged to convey the minimum of meaning.

Furthermore, Paul wasn't a born inquisitor. He supposed that if he knew the proper way to torture Salsbury, if he knew how he could cause the man mind-shattering pain without actually destroying him—and if he had the stomach for it—he could get the truth in short order. When Salsbury's stubbornness became particularly infuriating, Paul used the butt of his revolver to jar the man's shoulder wound. That left Salsbury gasping. But it wasn't enough to make him talk. And Paul was incapable of any more effective cruelties.

"Who were the men in the helicopter?"

Salsbury didn't answer.

"Were they government people?"

Silence.

"Is this a government project?"

"Go to hell."

If he knew what most terrified Salsbury, he could use that to crack him. Every man had one or two deeply ingrained fears—some of them quite rational and some utterly irrational—that shaped him. And with a man like this, a man so apparently in the borderlands of sanity, there should be more than the usual number of terrors to play upon. If Salsbury were afraid of heights, he could take the bastard up to the church bell tower and threaten to throw him off if he didn't talk. If Salsbury were severely afflicted with agoraphobia, he could take him to the flattest and biggest open space in town—perhaps to the baseball field—and stake him down in the very center of it. If, like the protagonist in *1984*, he were brought near to madness merely by the *thought* of being placed in a cage with rats—

Suddenly Paul remembered how Salsbury had reacted to him when he had first come into the room. The man had been shocked, damned scared, devastated. But not just because Paul had surprised him. He had been terrified because, for some reason known only to himself, he had thought that Paul was a man named Parker.

What did this Parker do to him? Paul wondered. What could he possibly have done to leave such a deep and indelible scar?

"Salsbury?"

Silence.

"Who were the men in the helicopter?"

"You're a fucking bore."

"Were they government people?"

"A regular broken record."

"You know what I'm going to do to you, Salsbury?"

He didn't deign to answer.

"You know what I'm going to do?" Paul asked again.

"Doesn't matter. Nothing will work."

"I'll do—what Parker did."

Salsbury didn't respond. He didn't open his eyes. However, he grew stiff in the chair, tense, every muscle knotted tight.

"Exactly what Parker did," Paul said.

When Salsbury finally opened his eyes there was a monstrous horror in them, a trapped and haunted look that Paul had never seen anywhere but in the eyes of cornered, panic-stricken wild animals.

This is it, Paul thought. This is the key, the pressure point, the knife with which I'll open him. But how should I react if he calls my bluff?

He was close to getting the truth, so close—but he hadn't the vaguest idea what Parker had done.

"How do you . . . How do you know Parker?" Salsbury asked. His voice was a thin, pathetic whine.

Paul's spirits lifted even further. If Salsbury didn't recall that it was *he* who had first mentioned this Parker, then the use of the name carried a great deal of weight.

"Never mind how I know him," Paul said shortly. "But I do. I know him well. And I know what he did to you."

"I . . . was only . . . eleven. You wouldn't."

"I would. And enjoy it."

"But you aren't the type," Salsbury said desperately. He had been shiny with sweat; now he was dripping with it. "You just aren't the type!"

"What type is that?"

"Queer!" he blurted. "You aren't a damned queer!"

Still bluffing but with more good cards on the table to back his hand, Paul said, ''We don't all look like what we are, you know. Most of us don't advertise it.''

''You were married.''

''Doesn't matter.''

''You had children!''

Paul shrugged.

''You're sniffing around that Edison bitch!''

''Have you ever heard of AC-DC?'' Paul asked. He grinned.

Salsbury closed his eyes.

''Ogden?''

He said nothing.

''Get up, Ogden.''

''Don't touch me.''

''Lean against the desk.''

''I won't get up.''

''Come on. You'll love it.''

''No. I won't.''

''You loved it from Parker.''

''That's not true!''

''You're not the type.''

''I'm not.''

''Admit it.''

He didn't move.

''A talent for Greek.''

Salsbury winced. ''No.''

''Lean on the desk.''

''It hurts . . .''

''Of course. Now get up and lean on the desk and drop your pants. Come on.''

Salsbury shuddered. His face was drawn and ashen.

''If you don't get up, Ogden, I'll have to throw you out of that chair. You can't refuse me. You can't get away from me. You can't fight me off, not when I've got the gun, not when your arm's all torn up like that.''

''Oh, Jesus God,'' Salsbury said miserably.

''You'll love it. You'll love the pain. Parker told me how much you love the pain.''

Salsbury began to cry. He didn't weep gently or quietly, but let go with great, wracking sobs. Tears seemed to spurt from his eyes. He shook and gagged.

"Are you scared, Ogden?"

"S-Scared. Yes."

"You can save yourself."

"From . . . from . . ."

"From being raped."

"H-How?"

"Answer my questions."

"Don't want to."

"Get up then."

"Please . . ."

Ashamed of himself, sick of this violent game but determined to carry on with it, Paul took hold of the front of Salsbury's shirt. He shook him and tried to lift him out of the chair. "When I'm done with you, I'll let Bob Thorp have you. I'll tape your mouth so you can't talk to him, and I'll program him to put it to you." He was incapable of doing that, of course. But Salsbury obviously believed he would. "And not just Thorp. Others. Half a dozen others."

With that, Salsbury's resistance dissolved. "Anything. I'll tell you anything," he said, his voice distorted by the wretched sobbing that he couldn't control. "Anything you want. Just don't touch me. Oh, Jesus. Oh, don't touch me. Don't make me undress. Don't touch. Don't."

Still twisting Salsbury's shirt in his left hand, leaning toward the man, nearly shouting in his face, Paul said, "Who were those men in the helicopter? Unless you want to be used until you're raw, you better tell me who they were."

"Dawson and Klinger."

"There were three."

"I don't know the pilot's name."

"Dawson and Klinger. First names?"

"Leonard Dawson and—"

"The Leonard Dawson?"

"Yes. And Ernst Klinger."

"Is Klinger a government man?"

"He's an army general."

"Is this a military project?"

"No."

"A government project?"

"No," Salsbury said.

Paul knew all of the questions. There was no point in the rapid-fire interrogation at which he had to hesitate.

And there was never a single moment when Salsbury *dared* hesitate.

Ernst Klinger crouched behind a yard-high wall of shrubbery across the alleyway from the municipal parking lot. Stunned, confused, he watched them load the woman into the white Cadillac van with the words BLACK RIVER—EMERGENCY painted in red letters on the side.

At 11:02 the ambulance pulled out of the parking lot, swung into the alley and from there onto North Union Road. It turned right, toward the square.

Its bright red flashers washed the trees and the buildings, and sent crimson snakes of light wriggling along the wet pavement.

The bearded, white-haired man who stood in the parking lot was Sam Edison. Klinger recognized him from a photograph that he had seen in one of the rooms above the general store, little more than an hour ago.

Edison watched the ambulance until it turned east at the square. He was too far away for Klinger to get a shot at him with the Webley. When the ambulance was out of sight, he went inside the municipal building.

Have we lost control of the town? Klinger asked himself. Is it all coming down on our heads: the field test, the plan, the project, the future? Sure as hell looks that way. Sure does. So . . . Is it time to get out of Black River, out of the country with a big bundle of cash and the phony identity Leonard provided?

Don't panic, another part of him thought. Don't be rash. Wait. See what happens. Give it a few minutes.

He looked at his watch. 11:03.

Thunder rumbled in the mountains.

It was going to rain again.

11:04.

He had been hunkered down for so long that his legs ached. He longed to stand up and stretch.

What are you waiting here for? he asked himself. You can't plan your strategy without information. You've got to reconnoiter. They're probably in Thorp's office. Get under those windows. Maybe you can hear what they're up to.

At five minutes past the hour, he hurried across the alley. He dodged from car to car in the parking lot, and then to the thick trunk of a pine tree.

Just like in Korea, he thought almost happily. Or Laos in the late fifties. Just like it must have been for the younger guys in Nam. Commando work in an enemy town. Except this time the enemy town is American.

11:05 P.M.

Sam stood in the doorway and studied Ogden Salsbury, who was still in the spring-backed office chair. To Paul, Sam said, "You're sure he told you everything?"

"Yes."

"And that everything he's told you is true?"

"Yes."

"This is important, Paul."

"He didn't withhold anything," Paul said. "And he didn't lie to me. I'm sure of it."

Stinking of sweat and blood, crying quietly, Salsbury looked from one to the other of them.

Does he understand what we're saying? Paul wondered. Or is he broken, shattered, unable to think clearly, unable to think at all?

Paul felt unclean, sick to his soul. In dealing with Salsbury, he had descended to the man's own level. He told himself that these were after all the 1970s, the very first years of a brave new world, a time when individual survival was difficult and when it counted for more than all else, the age of the machine and of the machine's morality, perhaps the only era in the entire span of history when the ends truly *did* justify the means—but he still felt unclean.

"Then the time has come," Sam said quietly. "One of us has to—do it."

"A man named Parker apparently raped him when he was eleven years old," Paul said. He was speaking to Sam, but he was watching Ogden Salsbury.

"Does that make any difference?" Sam asked.

"It should."

"Does it make any difference that Hitler might have been born of a syphilitic parent? Does it make any difference that he was mad? Does that bring back the six million dead?" Sam was talking softly but with tremendous force. He was trembling. "Does what happened to him when he was eleven justify what he did to Mark? If Salsbury wins, if he takes control of everyone, does it matter what happened to him when he was eleven?"

"There's no other way to stop him?" Paul asked, although he knew the answer.

"We've already discussed that."

"I guess we have."

"I'll do it," Sam said.

"No. If I can't get up the courage here, I won't be any help to you later, with Dawson and Klinger. We may be in a tight spot with one of those. You'll have to know that you can count on me in the clinches."

Salsbury licked his lips. He glanced down at the blood-soaked front of his shirt, then up at Paul. "You aren't going to—kill me. You aren't . . . Are you?"

Paul raised the Smith & Wesson Combat Magnum.

Letting go of his left shoulder, reaching out as if to shake with one bloody hand, Salsbury said, "Wait. I'll make you a partner. Both of you. Partners."

Paul aimed at the center of the man's chest.

"If you're partners, you'll have everything. Everything you could want. All the money you could ever spend. All the money in the world. Think of that!"

Paul thought of Lolah Tayback.

"Partners. That doesn't mean just money. Women. You can have all of the women you want, any women you want, no matter who they are. They'll *crawl* to you. Or men, if that's what you like. You can even have children. Little girls. Nine or ten years old. Little boys. *Anything you want.*"

Paul thought of Mark: a lump of frosted meat jammed into a food freezer.

And he thought of Rya: traumatized perhaps, but with a chance to live a halfway normal life.

He squeezed the trigger.

The .357 Magnum bucked in his hand.

Because of his revolver's impressive kick—which jolted Paul from hand to shoulder in spite of that fact that he was using .38 Special ammunition rather than Magnums—the bullet was high. It tore through Salsbury's throat.

Blood and bits of flesh spattered the metal firearms cabinet.

The roar of the shot was deafening. It bounced back and forth between the walls, echoed inside Paul's skull, reverberated as it would forever in his memory.

He squeezed off another round.

That one took Salsbury in the chest, nearly rocked him and the chair backward onto the floor.

He turned away from the dead man.

"Are you going to be sick?" Sam asked.

"I'm all right." He was numb.

"There's a toilet at the end of the hall, to your left."

"I'm okay, Sam."

"You look—"

"I killed men in the war. Killed men over in Asia. Remember?"

"This is different. I understand that. In the war it's always with rifles or grenades or mortars. It's never from three feet with a handgun."

"I'm fine. Believe me. Just fine." He went to the door, pushed past Sam, stumbled into the corridor as if he had tripped, turned left, ran to the washroom, and threw up.

Scuttling sideways like a hermit crab, the Webley ready in his right hand, Klinger reached the western flank of the municipal building and found that the lawn there was littered with glass. He hadn't made a sound on his run from the shrubbery. Now, pieces of glass snapped and crunched under his shoes, and he cursed silently. One of the windows in the police chief's office was broken, and a few of the slats in the Venetian blind were bent out of shape, providing a convenient peephole for his reconnaissance work.

As he was rising up to have a look inside—cautious as a suspicious mouse sniffing the cheese in the trap—two shots exploded virtually in front of his face. He froze—then realized that he hadn't been seen, that no one was firing at *him*.

Through the twisted slats of the blind, he could see two-thirds of Thorp's starkly furnished and somewhat sterile office: gray-blue walls, a pair of three-drawer filing cabinets, an oak work table, a bulletin board with an aluminum frame, bookshelves, most of a massive metal desk—

And Salsbury.

Dead. Very dead.

Where was Sam Edison? And the other one, Annendale? And the woman, the little girl?

There appeared to be no one in the room except Salsbury. Salsbury's corpse.

Suddenly afraid of losing track of Edison and Annendale, afraid that they might somehow get away or sneak around behind him, afraid of being outmaneuvered, Klinger turned from the windows. He loped to the end of the lawn, then across the parking lot and the alleyway. He hid behind the hedge again, where he commanded a good view of the back door of the municipal building.

When he came out of the washroom, Sam was waiting in the corridor for him.

"Feeling better?"

"Yeah," Paul said.

"It's rough."

"It'll get worse."

"That it will."

"Christ."

"What did you learn from Salsbury? Who were those men in the helicopter?"

Leaning against the wall, Paul said, "His partners. One of them was H. Leonard Dawson."

"I'll be damned."

"The other one is a general. United States Army. His name's Ernst Klinger."

Scowling, Sam said, "Then this is a government project?"

"Surprisingly, no. Just Salsbury, Dawson, and Klinger. A bit of private enterprise." Paul took three minutes to outline what he had learned about the field test and the conspiracy behind it.

Sam's scowl disappeared. He risked a slight smile. "Then we have a chance of stopping it right here, for good."

"Maybe."

"It's just a simple four-part problem," Sam said. He held up one finger. "Kill Dawson." Two fingers. "Kill Ernst Klinger." Three fingers. "Destroy the data in the computer at the house in Greenwich." Four fingers. "Then use the key-lock code to restructure the memories of everyone in town who's seen or heard anything, to cover up every last trace of this field test."

Paul shook his head. "I don't know. It doesn't sound so simple to me."

For the moment at least, positive thinking was the only sort of thinking that interested Sam. "It can be done. First . . . where did Dawson and Klinger go when they left here?"

"To the logging camp."

"Why?"

Quoting Salsbury, he told Sam about Dawson's plan to organize a search in the mountains. "But he and Klinger won't be at the camp now. They intended to fall back to the mill and establish a sort of field headquarters there once the manhunt was underway. There are about eighty or ninety men working on the night and graveyard shifts up there. Dawson wants to post a dozen of them as guards around the mill and pack the rest of them off to join the search beyond the logging camp."

"Any guards he posts are worthless," Sam said. "We'll use the code phrase to get past them. We'll move in on Dawson and Klinger before they know what's happened."

"I suppose it's possible."

"Of course it is."

"But what about the computer in Greenwich?"

"We can deal with that later," Sam said.

"How do we get to it?"

"Didn't you say Dawson's household staff is programmed?"

"According to Salsbury."

"Then we can get to the computer."

"And the cover-up here?"

"We'll manage."

"How?"

"That's the least of our problems."

"You're so goddamned optimistic."

"I've got to be. So do you."

Paul pushed away from the wall. "All right. But Jenny and Rya must have heard the shots. They'll be worried. Before we go to the mill, we should stop back at the church and fill them in, let them know where we all stand."

Sam nodded. "Lead the way."

"What about—Salsbury?"

"Later."

They left by the rear door and started across the parking lot toward the alley.

After a few steps Paul said, "Wait."

Sam stopped, turned back.

"We don't have to sneak around the long way," Paul said. "We're in control of the town now."

"Good point."

They circled around the municipal building and went out to East Main Street.

11:45 P.M.

Klinger stood in the velvety darkness, two-thirds of the way up the bell tower stairs, *listening*. Voices drifted down from above: two men, a woman, a child. Edison. And Jenny Edison. Annendale and his daughter . . .

He now knew what was happening in Black River, what the carnage at Thorp's office signified. He knew the extent of these people's knowledge of the field test and of all the working, planning, and scheming that lay behind the field test— and he was shocked.

Because of what he had heard, he knew that they were motivated to resist, at least in part, for altruistic reasons. He didn't understand that. He could easily have understood them if they had wanted to seize the power of the subliminals for their own. But altruism . . . That had always seemed foolish to him. He had decided a long time ago that men who eschewed power were far more dangerous and deadly than those who pursued it, if only because they were so difficult to fathom, so unpredictable.

However, he also knew that these people could be stopped. The field test wasn't an unmitigated disaster; not yet. They weren't going to win as easily as they thought. They hadn't yet brought him or Dawson to ruin. The project could be saved.

Overhead, they finished discussing their plans. They said good-by to one another and told one another to be careful and wished one another luck and hugged and kissed and said they would pray for one another and said that they really had to get on with it.

In the perfect darkness, without a flashlight or even a match to show them the way, out of sight around two or three bends in the long spiral staircase, Sam Edison and Paul Annendale started down the narrow, creaking steps.

Klinger's own hurried descent was masked by the noise that the two men made above him.

He paused in the whispery, echo-filled nave of the church, where the walls and the altar and the pews were no more than adumbrated by the meager nocturnal storm light that shone through the arched windows. He wasn't certain what he should do next.

Confront them here and now? Shoot them both as they came out of the stairwell?

No. The light was much too poor for gunplay. He couldn't target them with any accuracy. Under these conditions he would never bring down both of them—and perhaps not either of them.

He thought of searching quickly for a light switch. He could flip it on as they entered the nave and open fire on them in the same instant. But if there was a switch nearby, he would never find it in time. And if he did find it in time, he would be every bit as surprised and blinded by the light as they would be.

Even if, by the grace of one of the saints depicted in these stained-glass windows, he *did* somehow kill both of them, then he would have alerted the woman in the tower. She might be armed; she almost certainly was. And if that was the case, the belfry would be virtually impregnable. With any sort of weapon at all—rifle or shotgun or handgun—and a supply of ammunition, she would be able to hold him off indefinitely.

He wished to God that he were properly equipped. He should have at least those few essentials of behind-the-lines combat: a pretty damned good machine pistol, preferably German-made or Belgian, and several fully loaded magazines for it; an automatic rifle with a bandolier of ammo; and a few grenades, three or four. Especially the grenades. After all, this was no ladies' tea party. This was a classic commando operation, a classic clandestine raid, deep in hostile territory.

Behind him, Edison and Annendale were unsettlingly close, on the last twenty steps and coming fast.

He dashed along the side aisle to the fourth or fifth row of pews where he intended to hide between the high-backed seats. He tripped over a kneeler that some thoughtless member of the congregation had forgotten to put up after saying a prayer, and he fell with a loud crash. His heart hammering, he scrambled farther along the row toward the center aisle, then stretched out on the bench of the pew, flat on his back, the Webley at his side.

As they came into the dark church, Paul put one hand on Sam's shoulder.

Sam stopped. "Yeah?" he said softly.

"Sssshhh," Paul said.

They listened to the storm wind and to the distant thunder and to the settling sounds that the building made.

Finally Sam said, "Is something wrong?"

"Yeah. What was that?"

"What was what?"

"That noise."

"I didn't hear anything."

Paul studied the darkness that seemed to pulse around them. He squinted as if that would help him penetrate the inky pools in the corners and the purple-black shadows elsewhere. The atmosphere was Lovecraftian, a dank seed bed of paranoia. He rubbed the back of his neck which was suddenly cold.

"How could you have heard anything with all that racket we were making on the stairs?" Sam asked.

"I heard it. Something . . ."

"Probably the wind."

"No. It was too loud for that. Sharp. It sounded as if—as if someone knocked over a chair."

They waited.

Half a minute. A minute.

Nothing.

"Come on," Sam said. "Let's go."

"Give it another minute."

As Paul spoke a particularly violent gust of wind battered the east side of the church; and one of the ten-foot-high windows fluttered noisily in its frame.

"There you are," Sam said. "You see? That's what you heard. It was just the window."

Relieved, Paul said, "Yeah."

"We've got work to do," Sam said.

They left the church by the front door. They went east on Main Street to Paul's station wagon, which was parked in front of the general store.

As the station wagon reached the mill road and its taillights dwindled to tiny red dots beyond the west end of town, Klinger left the church and ran half a block to the telephone booth beside Ultman's Cafe. He paged through the slim directory until he found the numbers for the Big Union Supply Company: twenty of them, eight at the logging camp and twelve at the mill complex. There wasn't time to try all of them. In what part of the mill would Dawson establish his HQ? Klinger wondered. He thought about it, painfully aware of the precious seconds ticking by. Finally he decided that the main office was the location most consistent with Dawson's personality, and he dialed that number.

After it had rung fifteen times, just as Klinger was about to give up, Dawson answered it warily. "Big Union Supply Company."

"Klinger here."

"Have you finished?"

"He's dead, but I didn't kill him. Edison and Annendale got to him first."

"They're in town?"

"That's right. Or they were. Right now they're coming for you. And for me. They think we're both at the mill." As best he could in less than a minute, the general summed up the situation.

"Why didn't you eliminate them when you had the chance, in the church?" Dawson asked.

"Because I *didn't* have the chance," Klinger said impatiently. "I didn't have time to set it up right. But *you* can set it up just perfectly. They'll probably park half a mile from the mill and walk in to you. They expect to surprise you. But now *you* can surprise *them*."

"Look, why don't you get in a car and come up here right away?" Dawson asked. "Come in behind them. Trap them between us."

"Under the circumstances," Klinger said, "that makes no military sense, Leonard. As a group of four, three of them armed, they'd be too formidable for us. Now that they're split into pairs and puffed up with self-confidence, the advantage is ours."

"But if Edison and Annendale know the key-lock phrases, I can't keep guards posted. I can't use any of these people up here. I'm alone."

"You can handle it."

"Ernst, my training is in business, finance. This is more your line of work."

"And I've got work down here in town."

"I don't eliminate people."

"Oh?"

"Not like this."

"What do you mean?"

"Not personally."

"You brought guns back from the camp?"

"A few of them. I've posted guards."

"With a rifle or shotgun, you can do what's necessary. I know you can. I've seen you shoot skeet both ways."

"You don't understand. It's against my beliefs. My religious beliefs."

"You'll have to set those aside for now," Klinger said. "This is a matter of survival."

"You can't just set aside morality, Ernst, whether or not it's a matter of survival. Anyway, I don't like being here alone. Handling this alone. It's no good."

Trying to think of some way to convince the man that he could and should do what had to be done so that he would get off the phone, the general hit upon an approach that he recognized at once as custom-tailored for Dawson. "Leonard, there's one thing that every soldier learns his first day on the battlefield, when the enemy is firing at him and grenades are exploding around him and it seems like he'll never get through to the next day alive. If he's fighting for the right cause, for the just cause, he learns that he's never alone. God's always with him."

"You're right," Dawson said.

"You do believe ours is a just cause?"

"Of course. I'm doing all of this for Him."

"Then you'll come out just fine."

"You're right," Dawson said. "I shouldn't have hesitated to do what He so obviously wishes me to do. Thank you, Ernst."

"Don't mention it," Klinger said. "You better get moving. They're probably leaving the station wagon about now. You'll have ten minutes at most to prepare for them."

"And you?"

"I'll go back to the church."

"God be with you."

"Good luck."

They both hung up.

10.

Saturday, August 27, 1977

12:10 A.M.

THE WIND RAISED a steady, haunting *whooooo!* in the highest
reaches of the trees. Thunder rumbled frequently, each peal
louder and more unsettling than the one that had come before
it. Above the forest, the sky periodically blazed with lightning; the electric glow pulsed down through the canopy of
interlaced branches and left in its wake a series of stroboscopic images that dazzled the eye.

In the dense underbrush, small animals scampered this way
and that, busily searching for food or water or companionship
or safety. Or perhaps, Paul thought as one of them dashed
across the path and startled him, they were frightened of the
oncoming storm.

Paul and Sam had expected to find armed guards rather
than animals at the edge of the woods that surrounded the
mill, but there were none. Although all of the lights were on
in the main building, the structure seemed—as did the land
around it—deserted.

They circled through the woods. Eventually they came to the employee parking lot and studied the scene from behind a thick clump of laurel.

The helicopter was there, on the macadam, thirty feet away. A man stood beside it in the darkness, smoking a cigarette, watching the lightning and the fast-moving clouds.

Paul whispered: "Dawson or Klinger?"

"I don't think so," Sam said.

"Neither do I."

"Then he's the pilot."

"You see a gun?"

"No. Nothing."

"Move in now?"

"Wait."

"For what?"

"The right moment."

They watched.

A few seconds later the pilot dropped his cigarette and crushed it under the sole of his shoe. He put his hands in his pockets and began to walk aimlessly about, just killing time. At first he came toward the trees, wandered within ten or twelve feet of them, then turned and went back the way he'd come.

"Quickly," Sam said.

Paul stood up. He eased through the laurel and ran after the pilot.

The man heard him and turned. His face was a black mask, but his eyes seemed phosphorescent. "Who—"

"I am the key," Paul said.

"I am the lock."

"Speak softly."

"Yes, sir."

Paul looked beyond the helicopter. He could see the windows—most of them with light behind them—on the second and third floors of the main building at the end of the storage yard. If he could see the windows, anyone who happened to glance out might be able to see him, in turn, despite the darkness. He hustled the pilot closer to the helicopter, where they were pretty much hidden from the main building.

Sam joined them and said, "What's your name?"

"Malcolm Spencer."

"You *are* the pilot?"

"Yes. I am."

"Where's Leonard Dawson?"

"In the mill," Spencer said.

"Which building?"

"The biggest one."

"Which floor? First, second, or third?"

"First floor. There's a sort of public sales area with—"

"And Ernst Klinger," Sam said. "Where's he?"

"He's in Black River," Spencer said.

"That can't be right."

"Sir?"

"You mean he's in *town?*" Paul asked.

"That's right."

Paul and Sam glanced at each other.

"Something wrong?" the pilot asked. He seemed to be concerned about them.

"You're lying," Paul said.

Surprised, Spencer said, "No, sir."

"I am the lock," Paul said.

"I am the key," Spencer said.

"Where's Klinger?"

"He's in Black River."

Paul stared at Sam. "Christ!"

To the pilot, Sam said, "You took Klinger and Dawson to the logging camp, didn't you? And then brought them to the mill?"

"No. Just Mr. Dawson. General Klinger went to town from the camp."

"When?"

"A couple of minutes after we got there," Spencer said. He smiled uncertainly. His teeth seemed even more radiant than his eyes.

"How did he go? Not in the chopper?"

"No, sir. He took a car."

"Why—"

Before he could get out more than one word of the question, Sam screamed and stumbled forward against the helicopter.

In the same instant, the night silence was split open by a single rifle shot.

Instinctively, Paul dropped to the ground and rolled.

A bullet cracked into the pavement where he'd just been, ricocheted into the darkness.

A second bullet smashed the macadam on the other side of him, bracketing him.

He rolled onto his back and sat up. He saw the rifleman at once: down on one knee in a sportsman's pose, thirty feet away at the edge of the woods. On the drive from town, Paul had reloaded the Combat Magnum; now he held it with both hands and squeezed off five quick shots.

All of them missed the mark.

However, the sharp barking of the revolver and the deadly whine of all those bullets skipping across the pavement apparently unnerved the man with the rifle. Instead of trying to finish what he had begun, he stood and ran.

Paul scrambled to his feet, took a few steps after him and fired once more.

Untouched, the rifleman headed away in a big loop that would take him back to the mill complex.

"Sam?"

"Here."

He could barely see Sam—dark clothes against the macadam—and was thankful for the older man's telltale white hair and beard. "You were hit."

"In the leg."

Paul started toward him. "How bad?"

"Flesh wound," Sam said. "That was Dawson. Get after him, for God's sake."

"But if you're hurt—"

"I'll be fine. Malcolm can make a tourniquet. Now get after him, dammit!"

Paul ran. At the end of the parking area he passed the rifle: it was on the ground; Dawson had either dropped it by accident and had been too frightened to stop and retrieve it—or he had discarded it in panic. Still running, Paul fished in his pocket with one hand for the extra bullets he was carrying.

12:15 A.M.

The wooden tower stairs creaked under Klinger's weight. He paused and counted slowly to thirty before going up three more steps and pausing again. If he climbed too fast, the woman and the girl would know that he was coming. And if they were ready and waiting for him—well, he would be committing suicide when he walked onto the belfry platform. He hoped that, by waiting for thirty seconds or as much as a minute between brief advances, he could make them think that the creaking stairs were only settling noises or a product of the wind.

He went up three more steps.

12:16 A.M.

Ahead, Dawson disappeared around a corner of the mill.

When he reached the same corner a moment later, Paul stopped and studied the north work yard: huge stacks of logs that had been piled up to feed the mill during the long winter; several pieces of heavy equipment; a couple of lumber trucks; a conveyor belt running on an inclined ramp from the mill to the maw of a big furnace where sawdust and scrap wood were incinerated . . . There were simply too many places out there in which Dawson could hide and wait for him.

He turned away from the north yard and went to the door in the west wall of the building, back the way he had come, thirty feet from the corner. It wasn't locked.

He stepped into a short, well-lighted corridor. The enormous processing room lay at the end of it: the bull chain leading from the mill pond, up feeding shoots, into the building; then a cross-cut saw, a log deck, the carriage that moved logs into the waiting blades that would make the lumber of them, the giant band saw, edging machine, trimmer saws, dip tank, grading ramp, the green chain, and then the storage racks . . . He remembered all of those terms from a tour that the manager had given Rya and Mark two summers ago. In the processing room the fluorescent strip lights were burning, but none of the machines was working; there were no men tending them. To his right was a washroom, to his left a set of stairs.

Taking the steps two at a time for four flights—the first level was two floors high in order to accommodate the machines in it—he came out in the second-floor hallway. He stopped to think, then went to the fifth office on the left.

The door was locked.

He kicked it twice.

The lock held.

There was glass case bolted to the corridor wall. It contained a fire extinguisher and an ax.

He jammed the revolver in his belt, opened the front of the case, and took out the ax. He used the flat head of it to batter the knob from the office door. When the knob fell off, the cheap latch snapped. He dropped the ax, pushed open the ruined door, and went inside.

The office was dark. He didn't switch on any lights because he didn't want to reveal his position. He closed the door to the hall so that he would not be silhouetted by the pale light that spilled in.

The windows in the north wall of the office opened above the first-floor terrace. He slid one of them up, slipped through it, and stepped onto the tar-papered terrace roof.

The wind buffeted him.

He took the Combat Magnum from his belt.

If Dawson was hiding anywhere in the north yard, this was the best vantage point from which to spot him.

The darkness offered Dawson good protection, for none of the lights was on in the yard.

He could have turned them on, of course. But he didn't know where to find the switches, and he didn't want to waste a lot of time looking for them.

The only thing that moved out there was the clattering conveyor belt that rolled continuously up the inclined ramp to the scrap furnace. It should have been shut down with the rest of the equipment, but it had been overlooked. The belt came out of the building directly beneath him and sloped to a high point twenty feet above the ground. It met the furnace door forty yards away. Because the cone-shaped furnace—thirty feet in diameter at the base, ten feet in diameter at the top; forty feet high—was primed by a gas flame, the fire in it was never out unless the mill foreman ordered it extinguished. Even now, when the belt had no fuel for it, the furnace roared. Judging by the intensity of the flames leaping beyond the open door, however, several hundred pounds of the day's input—conveyed out of the mill before Dawson had halted operations—had yet to be fully consumed.

Otherwise, the yard was quiet, still. The mill pond—with

the giant grappling hook suspended from thick wires over the center of it—lay to the right of the ramp and the furnace. It was dotted with logs that looked a bit like dozing alligators. A narrow channel of water called the slip led from the pond to the terrace. When the mill was in operation, slip men poled logs along the slip to the chutes that were covered by the terrace roof. Once in the chutes, the logs were snared by hooked bull chains and dragged into the processing system. East and north of the pond was the deck, those forty-foot-high walls of gargantuan logs set aside to supply the mill with work during the winter. To the left of the ramp and the furnace, two lumber trucks, a high-lift, and a few other pieces of heavy equipment were parked in a row, backed up against the chain-link fence of a storage yard. Dawson wasn't to be seen in any of that.

Thunder and lightning brought a sudden fall of fat raindrops.

Some sixth sense told Paul that he had heard more than the clap of thunder. Propelled by an icy premonition, he spun around.

Dawson had come out of the window behind him. He was no more than a yard away. He was older than Paul, a decade and a half older, but he was also taller and heavier; and he looked deadly in the rain-lashed night. He had an ax. The goddamned fire ax! In both hands. Raised over his head. He swung it.

Klinger was at the mid-point of the tower when the rain began to fall again. It drummed noisily on the belfry shingles and on the roof of the church, providing excellent cover for his ascent.

He waited until he was absolutely certain that the downpour would last—then he went upward without pausing after every third step. He couldn't even hear the creaking himself. Exhilarated, brimming with confidence now, the Webley clutched in his right hand, he climbed through the last half of the tower in less than a minute and rushed onto the belfry platform.

Paul crouched.
The ax blade whistled over his head.
Startled to hear himself screaming, unable to stop scream-

ing, abruptly aware that the Smith & Wesson was still in his hand, Paul pulled the trigger.

The bullet tore through Dawson's right shoulder.

The ax flew from his hands. It arced out into the darkness and smashed through the windshield of one of the lumber trucks.

With a certain eerie grace, Dawson pirouetted just once and toppled into Paul.

The Combat Magnum tumbled in the path of the ax.

Grappling with each other, clinging to each other, they fell off the terrace roof.

The belfry held very little light in the midst of that primeval storm, but it was bright enough for Klinger to see that the only person there was the Annendale girl.

Impossible.

She was sitting on the platform, her back to the half-wall. And she seemed to be regarding him with dread.

What the hell?

There should have been two of them. The nine-foot-square belfry wasn't large enough for a game of hide-and-seek. What he saw must be true. *But there should have been two of them.*

The night was rocked with thunder, and razor-tined forks of white lightning stabbed the earth. Wind boomed through the open tower.

He stood over the child.

Looking up at him, her voice wavering, she said, "Please . . . please . . . don't . . . shoot me."

"Where is the other one?" Klinger asked. "Where did she go?"

A voice behind him said, "Hey, mister."

They *had* heard him coming up the stairs. They were ready and waiting for him.

But how had they done it?

Sick, trembling, aware that it was too late for him to save himself, he nevertheless turned to meet the danger.

There was no one behind him. The storm conveniently provided another short burst of incandescent light, confirming that he saw what he thought he saw: he and the child were alone on the platform.

"Hey, mister."

He looked up.

A black form, like a monstrous bat, was suspended above him. The woman. Jenny Edison. He could not see her face, but he had no doubt about who she was. She had heard him coming up the stairs when he thought he was being so clever. She had climbed atop the bell and had braced herself in the steel bell supports, against the ceiling, at the highest point of the arch, six feet overhead, like a goddamned bat.

It's twenty-seven years since I was in Korea, he thought. I'm too old for commando raids. Too old . . .

He couldn't see the gun she held, but he knew he was looking into the barrel of it.

Behind him the Annendale girl scrambled out of the line of fire.

It happened so fast, too fast.

"Good riddance, you bastard," the Edison woman said.

He never heard the shot.

Dawson landed on his back in the middle of the inclined ramp. Trapped in the other man's clumsy but effective embrace, Paul fell on top of him, driving the breath from both of them.

After a long shudder, the conveyor belt adjusted to their weight. It swiftly carried them headfirst toward the open mouth of the scrap furnace.

Gasping, limp, Paul managed to raise his head from Dawson's heaving chest. He saw a circle of yellow and orange and red flames flickering satanically thirty yards ahead.

Twenty-five yards . . .

Winded, with a bullet wound in one shoulder, having cracked his head against the ramp when he fell, Dawson was not immediately in a fighting mood. He sucked air, choked on the fiercely heavy rain, and blew water from his nostrils.

The belt clattered and thumped upward.

Twenty yards . . .

Paul tried to roll off that highway of death.

With his good hand Dawson held Paul by the shirt.

Fifteen yards . . .

"Let go . . . you . . . bastard." Paul twisted, squirmed, hadn't the strength to free himself.

Dawson's fingers were like claws.

Ten yards . . .

Tapping his last reserves of energy, the dregs from the barrel, Paul pulled back his fist and punched Dawson in the face.

Dawson let go of him.

Five yards . . .

Whimpering, already feeling the furnace heat, he threw himself to the right, off the ramp.

How far to the ground?

He fell with surprisingly little pain into a bed of weeds and mud beside the mill pond.

When he looked up he saw Dawson—delirious, unaware of the danger until it was too late for him—dropping headfirst into that crackling, spitting, roiling, hellish pit of fire.

If the man screamed, his voice was blotted out by a cymbal-like crash of thunder.

THE ENDING

Saturday, August 27, 1977

5:00 A.M.

THE MESS HALL at the logging camp was a rectangle, eighty feet by forty feet. Sam and Rya sat behind a dining table at one end of the long room. A single-file line of weary lumbermen stretched from their table across the hall and out the door at the far end.

As each man stepped up to the table, Sam used the power of the key-lock program to restructure his memory. When the new recollections were firmly implanted, he excused the man—and Rya struck a name from the Big Union Supply Company's employee list.

Between the thirtieth and the thirty-first subject, Rya said to Sam, "How do you feel?"

"How do *you* feel?"

"I'm not the one who was shot."

"You've been hurt too," he said.

"All I feel is—grown up."

"More than that."

"And sad," she said.

"And sad."

"Because it'll never be the same. Not ever." Her lips trembled. She cleared her throat. "Now, how's your leg?"

"About a yard long," he said.

He pulled on her chin.

She pulled on his beard.

He managed to get a smile from her, and that was better medicine than Doc Troutman's antibiotics.

6:30 A.M.

The storm clouds had begun to break up two hours ago. Dawn brought welcome shafts of autumn sunlight.

In the dense pine forest, half a mile above Black River, three men lowered the remains of Dawson, and the bodies of Salsbury and Klinger into a common grave.

"All right," Jenny told them. "Fill it in."

With each shovelful of dirt that struck the corpses, she felt more alive.

9:30 A.M.

After a refueling stop in Augusta, the hornetlike helicopter put down on the landing pad behind the Greenwich house at nine thirty in the morning.

"Get it gassed up and serviced for a trip back to Black River this evening," Paul said.

"Yes, sir," Malcolm Spencer said.

"Then go home and get some sleep. Be back here by seven o'clock this evening. That should give us both time to rest."

"I can use it," Spencer said.

Paul got out of the helicopter and stretched. He had showered and shaved and changed clothes before leaving Maine, but that had refreshed him only temporarily. He was stiff, sore, and tired deep in his bones.

He went to the rear door of the stone house and knocked.

A servant answered. She was a plump, pleasant-faced woman in her fifties. Her hair was tied back in a bun. Her hands were white with flour. "Yes, sir?"

"I am the key."

"I am the lock."

"Let me in."

She stepped out of his way.

Inside, he said, "Where's the computer?"

"The what, sir?" she asked.

"The computer. Dawson's computer."

"I haven't any idea, sir."

He nodded. "Okay. Forget about me. Go back to whatever you were doing." He looked around the elaborately equipped kitchen. "Doing a bit of baking, I see. Go ahead with it. Forget that I was ever here."

Humming to herself, she returned to the counter beside the oven.

He poked about on his own until he located the computer room. When he found it, he sat before one of the programming consoles and typed out the access code that he had gotten from Salsbury.

The computer responded on all of its read-out screens:

```
PROCEED
```

Pecking at the typewriter keys with one finger, doing precisely what Salsbury had told him to do, he ordered it to:

```
ERASE ALL STORED DATA
```

Five seconds later the read-out screen flickered:

```
ALL STORED DATA ERASED
```

That message disappeared from the tubes, and his second order was displayed for a few seconds:

```
ERASE ALL PROGRAMS
```

It said:
```
REQUEST CONFIRMATION
OF LAST DIRECTIVE
```

So weary that the letters on the keys blurred before him, Paul again typed:

```
ERASE ALL PROGRAMS
```

Those three words shimmered on the green background for perhaps half a minute. Then they blinked several times, vanished.

He typed the words "Black River" and asked for a read-out and a full print-out of associated data.

The computer did nothing.

Next, he typed the words "key-lock" and asked for a read-out and a full print-out of all information in that file.

Nothing.

He requested that the computer run a systems check on itself and display its circuitry on the cathode-ray tubes.

The tubes showed nothing.

He leaned back in the programmer's chair and closed his eyes.

Years ago, when he had been in high school, he had seen a boy lose a finger in woodworking shop. The boy had sliced it off on the band saw, a very even cut between the second and third knuckles. For two or three minutes, while everyone around him babbled in panic, the boy had treated the bloody stump as little more than a curiosity. He had even joked about it. And then, when his composure had infected those who were giving him first aid, he suddenly came to terms with what had happened, suddenly recognized the loss and the pain, began to scream and wail.

In much the same fashion, the meaning of Mark's death exploded in Paul, hit him with the emotional equivalent of a truck plowing through a stone wall. He doubled over in the chair and, for the first time since he'd come across the pathetic body in the freezer, he wept.

6:00 P.M.

When he got out of the car, Sam stood for a while, looking at the general store.

Jenny said, "What's the matter, Dad?"

"Just deciding how much I can get for it."

"For the store? You're selling?"

"I'm selling."

"But . . . it's your life."

"I'm getting out of Black River," he said. "I can't stay here . . . knowing that any time I want . . . I can just open these people with the phrase . . . use them . . .''

"You wouldn't use them," she said, taking him by the arm as Rya took his other arm.

"But knowing that I could . . . That sort of thing can eat at the soul, rot a man up inside . . ." Flanked by them, he went up the porch steps. For the first time in his life, he felt like an old man.

SATURDAY, OCTOBER 1, 1977

The following headline appeared at the bottom of the front page of *The New York Times:*

MRS. DAWSON HIRES INVESTIGATORS;
DISSATISFIED WITH F.B.I.'S WORK

SATURDAY, OCTOBER 8, 1977

Two bellhops showed them to the honeymoon suite.

On the desk in the parlor, there was an arrangement of carnations and roses, compliments of the management. Jenny made him savor the fragrances: first a rose by itself, then a carnation, then a rose and a carnation together.

Later, they made love, taking their time about it, doing what most pleased each other. He seemed to float on her and she on him, he in her and she in him. It was a rich, full experience; and they were sated afterwards.

For a while they were silent, lying on their backs, holding hands, eyes closed.

At last she said, "It was different that time."

"Not bad, though," he said. "At least not for me."

"Oh, no. Not bad. Not for me either."

"What then?"

"Just . . . different. I don't know. Maybe . . . We've gained something—intensity, I think. But we've also lost something. There wasn't any *innocence* to it this time."

"We're not innocent people anymore."

"I guess we aren't," she said.

We're killers, he thought. Children of the 1970s, sons and

daughters of the great machine age, survivalists.

All right, he told himself angrily. Enough. We're killers. But even killers can grab hold of a little happiness. More important, even killers can *give* a little happiness. And isn't that the most anyone can do in this life? Give a little happiness?

He thought of Mark: the faked death certificate, the small grave next to Annie's casket . . .

He turned to Jenny again and took her in his arms and let the world shrink until it was no larger than their two bodies.

REFERENCES

Arnheim, Rudolph. *Art and Visual Perception: A Psychology of the Creative Eye*. (Berkeley and Los Angeles: University of California, 1964).

Berelson, Bernard, and Steiner, Gary A. *Human Behavior: An Inventory of Scientific Findings*. (New York: Harcourt, Brace and World, 1964).

Carpenter, Edmund, and Hayman, Ken. *They Became What They Beheld*. (New York: Outerbridge and Lazard, 1970).

De Bono, Edward. *The Mechanism of the Mind*. (New York: Simon and Schuster, 1969).

Dixon, N. F. *Subliminal Perception: The Nature of the Controversy*. (New York: McGraw-Hill, 1971).

Farr, Robert. *The Electronic Criminals*. (New York: McGraw-Hill, 1975).

Freud, Sigmund. *On Creativity and the Unconscious*. (New York: Harper Bros., 1958).

Jung, C. G. *Psyche and Symbol*. (New York: Doubleday, 1958).

Key, Wilson Bryan. *Subliminal Seduction: Ad Media's Manipulation of a Not So Innocent America.* (Englewood Cliffs, N.J.: Prentice-Hall, 1973).

Morris, Charles. *Language and Communication.* (New York: McGraw-Hill, 1951).

Mussen, P. H., and Rosenzweig, M. R. *Psychology: An Introduction.* (Lexington, Mass.: D. C. Heath and Company, 1974).

Packard, Vance. *The Hidden Persuaders.* (New York: David McKay, 1957).

————. *The Sexual Wilderness.* (New York: David McKay, 1968).

Piaget, Jean. *The Mechanisms of Perception.* (London: Routledge and Kegan Paul, 1969).

Pines, Maya. *The Brain Changers: Scientists and the New Mind Control.* (New York: Harcourt, Brace, Jovanovich, 1973).

Reinert, Jeanne. "Brain Control: Tomorrow's Curse or Blessing?" *Science Digest,* November, 1969.

Storr, Anthony. *Human Aggression.* (New York: Atheneum, 1968).

Swartz, Robert J. *Perceiving, Sensing and Knowing.* (New York: Doubleday, 1965).

Taylor, John. *The Shape of Minds to Come.* (New York: Weybright and Talley, 1971).

Young, John Z. *Doubt and Certainty in Science: A Biologist's Reflections on the Brain.* (New York: Oxford University Press, 1960).